A Woman's Worth

by Bertrand Brown

authorHOUSE®

AuthorHouse™
1663 Liberty Drive, Suite 200
Bloomington, IN 47403
www.authorhouse.com
Phone: 1-800-839-8640

First published by AuthorHouse 10/28/2008

ISBN: 978-1-4389-2234-8 (sc)

Printed in the United States of America
Bloomington, Indiana

This book is printed on acid-free paper.

Contents

Chapter 1

All her life, all she had ever really wanted was the same thing every other Black woman wanted, a good decent hard-working man. There was nothing that she could see that was particularly special at all about wanting someone to share the good times with and maybe, just maybe, someone who occasionally told her that he loved her and meant it.

Hell, did she have to look like a Cosmopolitan cover girl to get a decent man or maybe there just weren't any decent men out there? But if looking like a magazine cover girl is what it took then chances were good that she'd be single for the rest of her natural born life.

As far back as she could remember, she'd never worn anything below a size sixteen and the last time she'd accomplished that feat was at her high school prom and that was with the help of a girdle and a good deal of encouragement in the months prior to the big day from family members who loved her daily and saw her date, Marshall Manning as a pretty good catch.

Her senior prom seemed like only yesterday but Lord knows how times had changed. She'd been in love then. She couldn't be sure if she was deeply in love or just infatuated with the only boy that had ever really given her the time of day. There were no secrets or mysteries then. There were no games, no ulterior motives. The fact of the matter was simple. She loved Marshall and Marshall loved her and that was as much planning, as she needed when it came to her life and what lay down the road for the two of them.

In her eyes the fact that she'd finally had the courage to trust a man enough to be intimate with him was proof enough that she loved him. And despite her misgivings about her size she was quite sure that he loved her as well. At least he said he did. And he said it with no apprehension, and with no reservation. Since nobody else was looking in her direction that was good enough for her. Besides he said it frequently. So frequently, in fact, that each time he told her, it warmed her to her very soul, immersing her in a pool of belonging she had never known outside of her family.

There were times Monica questioned her family's love for her with momma always drinking and carrying on. Daddy, unable to handle momma's drinking was hardly ever there anymore as he sought solace in some woman or another's arms. Still, she knew that in crunch time, they were there for her. But during these unsteady times she could never be certain where she really stood with them. With Marshall she was more than certain. And after the pain of him entering her for the very first time and taking her virginity, she learned to endure the pain. And even though Monica wasn't crazy about the act of lovemaking itself, she welcomed the closeness and the intimacy it brought.

Marshall Manning had been her first and though she didn't know it at the time that probably had as much to do with her loving him the way she did as any other factor.

Neither wanted for much during the years following high school, aside from being in each other's company. Not long after they were married without her even as much as having dated another man. At the time she felt no need to. After all, she had everything she could possibly want in Marshall. If it were up to her to make sure that he was happy and content and satisfied then that she would do. What she didn't know about men, she would learn. They would learn together. That was the beauty of marriage. The companionship, the navigating of unchartered waters together, the exploration and the glory of finally arriving together.

The reality, however, was quite different. And despite her love Monica soon discovered that no one can really, truly, know another person or what goes on beneath the surface and after ten years of marriage, of giving her all to the man she so adored and two children later Marshall Manning had decided not to continue on the course she had seen them taking and as suddenly as he had entered her life decided to abandon ship.

It was hardly the first time she had faced abandonment. In her eyes, her mother had chosen to abandon her years ago for the bottle. And her father also feeling abandoned by momma left for another woman. So, Marshall's decision to fly the coop was hardly a new phenomenon to Monica. In fact, if he had left for another woman she may have had an easier time dealing with the pain and the loss but the fact of the matter was Marshall, like her mother, left for a substance. Only this time it wasn't alcohol but drugs.

Although the symptoms and the results were the same she had a hard time fathoming what it was that made people choose a substance over her. Could it be something in her that was driving them away? She had a hard time comprehending but here it was slapping her square in the face once again with an open palm that caught her flush with the intent of doing irreparable damage when she'd finally considered herself almost immune to pain of any kind. For some reason she believed that she could, after all she'd been through; endure the hurt, and the pain. Yet, here it was rearing its ugly head again and she felt worse now than when she learned about momma's drinking.

She was pretty sure according to the marriage handbook passed along to her by momma and Bridget, that it was her job to stand by her man despite everything, including the abuse. That she knew she was supposed to do. But to inquire about the nature of her man's unhappiness, though well within her realm, she could not bring herself to do. For if she sought the truth of Marshall's unhappiness it might just bring on the verbal barrages that rang with so many ugly truths she'd tried so hard to mask in his love.

There was no doubt that she had her shortcomings. But then who didn't? They were nothing new to her. She'd grown up with them, grown into them, and at twenty-three she'd grown accustomed to them being apart of her.

She'd come to wrap herself in them like a silver badge of courage.

She pinned them on and wore them if not proudly, at least for all to see. There was little else for her to do. She wrapped herself in her flaws the same way her Aunt Kitty did that ol' musty chinchilla wrap.

Monica remembered how she and her cousins used to giggle 'til their sides ached every Sunday morning as they plodded along behind their aunt as she made her way to church during those chilly, Detroit winters.

All wrapped you couldn't tell Aunt Kitty she wasn't looking good with that stole on with the face like a rat and the sharp little toes that stuck out and hung down across her chest.

Monica and her cousins thought that chinchilla wrap was the ugliest piece of fur they'd ever seen but Aunt Kitty loved it and every Sunday she'd wrap it around her neck and let the tail of that old chinchilla hang down and ignore them all.

That was a long time ago. It seemed like forever. But in the years that passed she'd also learned to wrap herself up and hide behind the mask of pretending not to know she was different from those around her, scarred from birth. And somehow, when Marshall came into her life, he made all the petty insecurities fade away.

Never once, even during the worst of times, and there had been some pretty awful times, did he mention her inadequacies. Never once did he point out that she was somehow different, somehow flawed. It did loads for her confidence and after awhile she began to believe that she was as normal as the next person. She'd been happy then even if Marshall wasn't. And if he wasn't happy with the life she'd created for them, Lord knows it wasn't her fault.

In her eyes, she'd done her part. She worked when he didn't, birthed his children, and loved him on the regular; though at times she wondered if he realized she was there, lying beneath him. Those were the times it seemed like he was digging for gold between her legs so deeply and with such force would he drive his shaft down into her. When that wasn't enough and he had taken his frustrations out between her legs she endured the abuse that brought her to her knees when he wanted someone, anyone, but usually her to feel even lower than he did.

Monica hated those times the most but still catered to Marshall's wishes, kneeling down in front of him knowing full-well that the drugs would hinder his coming and have her down on her knees for what would seem like forever. And yet, despite the abuse she would don one of the negligees he liked so much, throw on a pair of those six-inch spiked heels he was always clamoring for when he was sober and sweet, before the drugs had come into play and turned their lives upside down.

When he was particularly distraught and on the verge of being violent she'd throw on his favorites, the clear heels and kneel down, jar of Vaseline to her right, scoop out a sizeable portion and rub his limp penis hoping that she could bring it to attention before he demanded she give it mouth-to-mouth resuscitation to bring it back to life.

She hated those times. It wasn't merely the act that she hated. She would have done so almost willingly at almost any other time. It was the drugs and the way they changed his personality and made the man she'd known most of her life a stranger before her very eyes.

There were the times when he'd hurl the jar of Vaseline across the room. Never mind that the children were both asleep. Then he'd grab her head by her hair like she was some common, two-bit whore, and shove himself in her mouth and scream expletives at her until she had managed to make him erect. By the time she had finished sucking his limp, life-less member to the point of orgasm the inside of her mouth would be raw from the friction and she could hardly swallow. Her jaws would ache when she opened her mouth to eat or to speak and she wondered if this is what it felt like to be abused.

Marshall would usually pass out when she'd completed her 'wifely duties' as he liked to call it. Watching him lie there asleep, the pity she felt for this shell of a man quickly turned to contempt and hatred and the thought of cutting his throat or something else was always in her mind.

Nowadays, he hardly noticed her, hardly cared about how she felt about anything anymore. They seldom made love during that time and if they had sex at all anymore it was usually forced and she was, like it or not, becoming more and more simply the recipient of his frustrations and lately he was always stressed or frustrated about something or another; the drugs only serving to enhance his frustrations.

At other times, he hated to come home but there was nowhere else to go. He hated the fact that he was married and married to Monica's fat ass in particular. In his eyes, she had not grown since their days in high school--accept in dress size. Now here he was burdened with the responsibility of having two children by her and although he loved his children deeply, he hated the burden of having to have to take care of them if it meant coming home each evening and having to face her in her old worn, torn, pink and white housecoat. It was at those times when he caught her off guard that he wondered what in the hell had attracted him to her in the first place.

At these times, she knew she was as much a disappointment to him as he was to her and would assume the position when he told her to bend her ass over. She just hoped he would give her the chance to bend over the couch or the bed instead of pushing her to the floor in his haste and causing her those awfully painful rug burns.

When that happened it was a week or so before she was unable to wear dresses since dresses demanded she wear pantyhose and pantyhose would ultimately stick to the scabs on her knees. She had done this the first time, not knowing and ended up spending a large portion of her night in tears as she tried to peel the stockings from the scabs on her knees. When all else failed she was forced to get in a hot tub of water, pantyhose and all and let the burning water soak the stockings from the scabs. Momma said she could get used to anything but this was one thing she never told momma and one thing she would never ever get used to. Earlier on in their relationship, Marshall hinted regularly about the prospect of them trying anal sex and although at first she'd been vehemently opposed she finally acquiesced after his continually badgering.

After the first time, the pain was so great that she swore that no matter what course their marriage took she would never ever give in to his demands again. It was two days and countless baths before she could resign herself to sit and then quite gingerly—at her desk at work so excruciating was the pain.

Ten years later, she really had to wondered if Marshall had some sugar in his coffee since that was the only position he seemed happy with—well—other than he having his penis in her mouth. But now she recognized the fact that the real reason he seemed to so enjoy this position was not out of enjoyment or sheer pleasure at all but because of the dominance and the pain it caused her and of course because it allowed him to relieve himself without facing her directly.

In the years since they'd expanded their sexual appetites or at least the years since Marshall had decided that he was only content to have her ass up in the air and her face crushed into the pillow or ground against the floor she had gotten to the point where after flinching or screaming at his initial entry—and depending on how many days had passed since his last tryst, she could handle the pounding without so much as a whimper. This seemed to infuriate him even more and so she would scream and holler just to ease the torture but the truth of the matter was that his constant pounding had left her ass, if not numb—totally open, almost receptive, to his invasions.

By this time, most of her high school buddies had gone their separate ways and those that remained she hardly spoke to and would have never dared to confide in. The one time she had, it seemed that all of East Detroit was aware that Monica and Marshall's storybook romance was having anything but a happy ending.

The only people left were family. And daddy never liked Marshall anyway and especially after the day he'd come home early from work and found them in bed together. If he knew what Marshall had been doing to his baby girl he would have killed him on the spot. That left momma and Bridget. And though neither had any success with men she had no one else to turn to or ask for advice. She wondered though, if they really had her best interest at heart.

Both seemed to want her to find some happiness in her life. They seemed to want to see her marriage work out but were they serious? She couldn't be sure but there was one thing she was sure of. She could never tell them of Marshall's sexual abuse and really wasn't sure that it was abuse being that she'd never been with another man and really didn't know what to expect in the bedroom.

In truth, she hadn't seen it as abuse at first and had pretty much taken it all in stride—chalking it up to her wifely duties. And there wasn't anything that Marshall could dish out in bed that she couldn't handle—and a lot of it she had to admit she enjoyed but people were funny and she wasn't sure if their sexual escapades was within the realm of normal sex or not. And for this reason she could not share with the only two people she had to confide in.

By this time, everyone was aware of the fact that Marshall was struggling with a drug problem but then who wasn't these days. Have momma and Bridget tell it, the drugs were fulfilling a void, and only meant there was the absence of Jesus in their lives.

Momma said that everyone needed Jesus and every marriage that had a chance of making it in these troubled times better have Jesus in it. Besides, have momma tell it, every marriage was apt to go through some trials and tribulations, but when it finally came down to it Jesus was the only marriage counselor needed.

Both momma and her sister Bridget both told her to go to Him, Jesus that is, and then go and reach out and talk to Marshall—get to know her man, to find out just what was eating away at him and was making him so unlike the man they had once known. But despite their advice and attempts to help her floundering marriage, she could not bring herself to reach out anymore than she already had. After all, she could only do so much to save their marriage. Marshall had to do something, too.

Despite the family concern, Monica wondered if down deep in the recesses of momma and Bridget's subconscious, they too were glad that her marriage had hit rocky ground since both of theirs had failed. Who was it that made the observation that misery loves company? Only thing was that momma and Bridget didn't realize was that Monica wasn't miserable.

No longer were her lips and jaw sore from trying to soothe a man's dick and his ego at the same time and for the first time in heaven knows how long she could go to work and not slide into her seat but plop right down in it because her ass didn't throb from having been probed on a daily basis.

Monica did feel some remorse when the po po came to take Marshall away for the armed robbery and kidnapping he'd committed during one of his drug binges. But the remorse she felt was primarily for her little ones who hardly understood any more than that there were some strange men in uniforms in the house trying to take their daddy away when he didn't want to go. They would miss him. There was no doubt about that but there had been some days, quite a few, in fact, right before his arrest that he hardly recognized them or even gave them the time of day despite their undying devotion to their father.

When she'd been called to testify against him, she'd done so reluctantly and with trepidation. She still blamed herself in part for her failed marriage but as the days went on she blamed herself less and less and eventually came to the conclusion that she was not alone to blame. Jesus helps those that help themselves, she would remind herself and no matter what she proposed or how she gave in to his sexual fantasies in hopes of appeasing him and being the good wife the truth of the matter was Marshall wasn't willing to help himself.

With Marshall sentenced to twenty-five years, Monica assumed the role of single parent as if she'd been doing it all her life. And eleven months later, a new man entered her life. And she gladly

9

took Jesus Christ into her heart and into her life.

Momma and Bridget seemed elated for her, for the progress that she'd made since Marshall was gone. But what they weren't aware of was that she'd been used to carrying a family. Sure, Marshall had been there, well at least physically but she couldn't remember the last time he'd held a steady job and towards the end of their marriage it had become a well-known fact that with his addiction, Marshall couldn't keep a job.

The thought that she accepted Jesus was all her family needed to know to bring her back into the fold. The fact that all three women were without a spouse hardly mattered to Bridget and momma. According to them, they had a man in their lives. And what better man could a woman have than Jesus. Never would he let them down. He was there for them, giving them the daily support they needed. And like Monica they hardly needed any help financially as they'd all been carrying the ball for this long with men passing through more regularly than Amtrak trains making their way through town just long enough for Jim and Joe and who knows who to get on, catch a quick ride and get off.

No, in their minds they'd resigned themselves to the fact that Jesus would not only do in a pinch but would suffice in filling their every need. Well, those were momma's sentiments. Bridget, on the other hand, accepted men as readily as she accepted Jesus and was not at all opposed to having a man in her life when she the need arose. Still, if none met her rather finicky standards then she would just as well do without. But not Monica. She welcomed Jesus in her life; welcomed his support and his strength even though she missed and *needed* the physical presence of a man. More than anything she felt less than whole, less than a woman without a man by her side. She had to admit that Marshall had a lot to do with that. He was her first love. He'd introduced her to sex and whether it was Marshall or just the fact that she craved sex the fact remained. She needed a man not only in her bed for the closeness, and warmth but also for her sense of self-worth. She needed to feel the stiff erectness of a man's rock hard penis in her coochie on the regular. Yet, despite an insatiable sexual appetite, the male callers were few and far between.

The one or two girlfriends who she still remained friends with her from her high school days had moved away. But on their return home for the holidays they'd always make it a point to call and invite her to frequent the local nightspots.

In the early years, when her girlfriends would call and she was married to Marshall she always thought she was missing out on something but with two kids and a husband she had entirely too much on her plate to be grinding the night away at some local meat market with a pack of wild dogs in heat. Besides, the days of wine and romance were long gone. The men didn't even try to seduce her anymore. Now it seemed like they were just as content to have sex right there on the floor and call it dancing. If she opposed their lewd advances, chances were good that they'd curse you out in front of everybody right there on the floor. My how times had changed.

Yet, despite that when Tracy or Alexis came home for the week around the Christmas holidays she looked forward to their calls and felt somehow compelled to make the club scene with her girls. But no one was looking for a middle-aged mama with two kids and a spreading waistline to latch onto, or push up on in some dark corner when there were so many young hoochie mamas, half her age and half her size, wearing halter tops and g-strings and willing to give it up for a drink and a drive in the Durango.

Still, with the pickings slim and having already dated all the eligible bachelors and a married man co-worker or two at the job she had little choice but to tag along behind her girls when they called.

Fact of the matter was, and as much as Monica hated to entertain such dispelling thoughts, the hard truth remained—greeting her each day in the mirror of the small, brass vanity that stood in the corner of her bedroom as she spread L'Oreal mascara to cover the tiny crows feet that were beginning to take shape at the corners of her eyes. One thing was for sure; the days that forced their way into long months and eventually turned into so many tough, long, drawn-out years with an abusive drug addicted leech for a husband had taken its toll on her physically and mentally. And although she had recuperated with the Lord's help mentally and found some of her old zest for living and for life she knew the years had not been good to her physically. By now the accumulation of men who'd crossed her sacred threshold had erased the pious innocence that had remained even after Marshall's departure.

This was by no means her intention. She intended only to love and as with Marshall she gave her all. All any man had to do was to show some interest, some promise, and promise her that he would call her tomorrow. If he kept his word the chances were good, at least in Monica's eyes that perhaps this was *the* one that was sincere and could be trusted. At least those were her hopes, her dream. Personality meant little. She was old school and back in the day marriages had been arranged. Often times the two parties involved would not even have the chance to meet. And yet, back then the divorce rate was almost nil.

She didn't have to love him. Well, not at first anyway. She could do as people used to do and learn to love him over time. All she needed was a good man—a man willing to cherish her, the way her father had coveted her mother. And she would not disappoint. Not at this stage in her life and after all she'd been through with Marshall and the rest of these shiftless, whorish, no-good men she'd had the opportunity to meet since Marshall 's departure.

She could work around a man's shortcomings—whatever they might be. After all, everyone had his or her shortcomings. And no one had more than Marshall and she'd learned to work around his. But that was then and this was now. She'd had trouble getting dates even then and she'd been younger and slimmer and well— truth be told—there just weren't a whole lot of good men out there and if she narrowed her quest to good Black men in her mental and physical condition and then decided to discriminate and narrow it down to her Mr. Right—with the Denzel looks along with a Ving Rhames sort of cockiness and Ja Rule's voice she'd find herself right where she was when Marshall left—home alone—with Orville Redenbacher catering her dinner or in front of the TV with the kids until their bedtime and then off to cross the threshold that was her exquisitely decorated bedroom with the canopied bed—content to occupy herself with her two newest play toys from the Feminine Fetish mail order catalog that came complete with two "D" batteries for extended life and pleasure.

This had sufficed in the past. In fact, when Marshall first left it was more than enough and she really had no desire to have a man around. She welcomed her newfound freedom, the sudden surge of independence she'd never really known. But then she had to. But as time went on and despite her faith and her taking the Lord Jesus Christ into her life a craving emerged. And no matter what she did the craving remained and not just for sex but for something else as well. She couldn't put her finger on exactly what it was that she needed but felt more and more out of sorts as the weeks and months passed.

She needed more than just the one-night stands now, more than just a roll in the hay. At forty-two she needed a man to not only enter her life for the sake of being there but to define her, to give credibility assuring her that she was a woman—a beautiful sensitive full-figured woman with more to love and hug and caress than any anorexic looking fourteen year old model gracing the cover of Cosmopolitan or Essence. Yes, even Essence was buying into the myth that thin was in. Well, at least since they'd been taken over by Time Warner or whoever the hell had them now.

No, she could hardly fit the mold. It wasn't in her genes. Her daddy stood a little over six feet and her momma was as short and wide as her father was tall and thin. Of course, she could have been tall and thin like her father and then she would probably have to beat the men away and change her number on the weekly. But it had been a union between her mother and her father and she was the result—tall—yes—but hardly thin—she stood close to six feet and was closer to Oprah before than after. And as rich as Oprah was, everyone knew that her before look had to be the driving force keeping Stedman at bay.

There was Monique, the comedian—wanna be actress—whose body type resembled hers more than a little bit. Her claim to fame was that she was big and beautiful with her full-figured, sexy self. She was on top right now but it wasn't 'cause she was big and beautiful or wore expensive designer made suits or had people around her who knew how to take every curve and bulge and accentuate her robust attributes until she was lookin' downright sexy doing the MTV or BET Awards. It was because she was loud and had the ability to laugh at herself, and her infinite waistline.

And no matter how Just My Size tried to reshape the image of larger women being sexy there was in the heart of America a deep, ingrained sense that full-figured women were anything but sexy no matter how what they did to reshape the image.

Meanwhile, while some marketing rep up on Fifth Avenue decided to makeover the full-figured woman to sell girdles and knee-highs; spas and workout centers like Curves and Gold's Gyms were springing up all over East Detroit dispelling the Fifth Avenue myth. No, America, like R. Kelly, was more interested in the very young and the petite.

And this fact, more than any other, tormented Monica. She knew what men wanted. She knew because she had been a full-figured woman all her life—well at least since she was thirteen and those tiny marbles which had adorned the front of her chest as a little girl became massive protrusions and then a major intrusion into her life by the time she was thirteen.

It graved her deeply but it by no means dispelled men from coming on to her. In fact, the sudden change in her physical appearance had just the opposite effect among her classmates or so it seemed at the time. Behind closed doors, teenage boys called incessantly, conversating easily, about anything and everything under the sun but mostly concerning their chances on bedding her down. At least when she was in high school they'd called. She wasn't insulted by their forays into the prospects of having sex with her but was, on the contrary, quite infatuated by their interest in her regardless of the subject and she shared the news with all of her girls who it just so happened were receiving the same propositions.

That was, after all, what young boys did in their quest for manhood. They were no different than Marco Polo seeking a new route to the East in search of gold and spices and other riches. They were explorers seeking something new and different and undiscovered in the name of Spain and England and Africa and above all their conquering spirits. They were young boys whose hormones were riding as high as the surf on a Hawaiian Beach at high tide constantly trying to relieve themselves into something hot and moist with the moniker of females stamped on it.

For most of them, the time had arrived in their young, chaotic, rebellious lives when Monica and those like her made a nice substitute, a necessary substitute for a Playboy magazine, a calloused hand and a jar of petroleum jelly.

When the rumor emerged from one overheated, little wannabe thug in her senior class that she went to her homecoming dance with that she gave good head the phone rang off the hook for two weeks until she got wind of it and approached him in the library at East Detroit High and gave him more than a piece of her mind, letting him know in no uncertain terms that she wasn't that type of girl and didn't appreciate him saying such things about her and sullying her reputation. Then as part of the final coup de tat she gave him a fat lip causing the phone calls to quiet down to normal once again. She missed the attention and the phone calls but thought 'what price fame'. Then, when it seemed that her life had reached an all-time low, Marshall had entered the picture.

Marshall was different from the rest of the boys. Not a particularly good athlete or scholar, he appeared quiet and shy, almost unnoticeable. Well, at least in school that's the way he appeared, anyway. And it wasn't 'til damn near the end of her senior year that she even knew that he had been in one or more of her classes and admired her secretly on the down low since third grade. Later, she was to find out that he had also bestowed a thorough ass whoopin' on the young man who propagated the rumor the same day Monica fattened the boys' already big lips.

It had been different after the marriage to Marshall though. There were no more rumors or whispers about her being larger than life or her administering the best oral sex west of the Pecos. Grown men were, or they appeared to be, far too sophisticated for that kind of thing. Now, at forty-two, she was full-figured and voluptuous or so she liked to think when she viewed herself. And Lord knows she could dress. She had a flair for color and design that made even the young girls take notice but she remained not voluptuous or sexy or endearing but fat in the eyes of most men and most men didn't, or wouldn't, or better yet couldn't take home a fat girl to momma.

Of course, that didn't mean they wouldn't sleep with her. It just meant that they couldn't be seen in public or take her home to see momma. By no means could she ever carry the label of being their woman. But that hardly meant that she couldn't entertain him at work or in class when she finally decided at forty that it was time for her to go back to school and get her Bachelor's Degree.

Those that she did come into contact with, loved her buoyancy, her light heartedness, her cheerfulness and sense of humor and almost every man she encountered and came to conversate with for any length of time invariably asked her out, with the hopes of cornering her and sharing some time, if for no other reason than so as not to have to share her with anyone else.

Most of them were married but because they were friends first—at least that was their pretense--that made it right ethically or at least that was the lie she told herself at the time of their asking. Still, Monica made sure they knew that she was aware that they were married with the hopes that her awareness would dispel any unwanted sexual advances from them later on in the evening. If they really weren't sincere about their proposal to share a quiet drink as friends and co-workers often do they could bail now. That way it would save them both the embarrassment of them making unwanted advances and being turned down as the liquor flowed and the evening wore on.

Setting the rules beforehand kept them from having their egos shattered by the dismissal from this full-figured woman who they wouldn't haven't given a second glance to if they had seen her walking down a Detroit street nude in winter.

Funny thing though, but more often than not they would still entertain the idea of going somewhere, anywhere with her just to be alone. And more often than not, they would take her to some out of the way restaurant and bar; pumping as many drinks as possible into her with the hopes that the alcohol would tear down her inhibitions to the point that she would beg them to take her to the nearest hotel before the night was over   so sure were they that a woman of her size and magnitude would almost have to be honored to be in their presence.

Monica would laugh at their tactics. The male ego was certainly something she'd conclude as round after round of expensive liquor was ordered for her consumption. Little did they know that Monica Manning could hold her liquor as well as anyone.

Monica remembered frequenting her mother's bar at the age of twelve or thirteen. She'd been curious to know what momma got out of drinking. Whatever it was; momma was always happier when she'd had a drink or two. Monica, following her mother's example would sit around and sip until the bottle had a sizeable portion missing. Then, when it got to the point where the bottle was half-empty she'd refill the bottle with water giving it the appearance that there was nothing missing. And it wasn't until momma had a party celebratin' somethin' or another—and momma was always having a party celebratin' somethin' or another—that anyone noticed that the liquor had been watered down.

By the time she was seventeen or eighteen most of her friends were made up of the guys on the football and basketball teams at school and she'd gotten to the point where she could hold her own with the best of them when it came to drinking. And by the time she reached forty-two, the thought of some man thinking he was going to get her drunk and take advantage of her was downright ludicrous.

Yet, on more than one occasion she'd played the role if she was attracted to them—let them think she was intoxicated and then allow them to get their hopes up before turning them down and watching their egos crash and burn. At other times, she'd have to take their drunken asses home and catch a cab home herself. And once a rather handsome co-worker had talked so much shit before passing out in the parking lot that she had to literally carry him to the hotel where she promptly gave him two Viagra which he thought were aspirin and when the Viagra took effect she promptly rode him in every possible position she could think of without his ever knowing it and left him worn, torn and in a drunken stupor.

All too often she'd return to work to glares and stares from some of those she'd rejected making her feel quite uncomfortable and wondering why she even bothered entertaining these fools when only the night before they'd been the best of friends until the conversation turned to sex and the idea of friendships being consummated with casual sex somehow always brought the evening to a close.

She'd heard all the lines and all the stories by this. They were the usual stories of men being married; being devoted husbands and fathers but somehow needing more than what the wife was bringing to the table.

There were the stories of spouses who failed to grow after twenty years of marriage. And how they'd forgotten to work at the marriage to keep it fresh and new and vibrant and… And the truth was, she somehow believed every story they told her.

More often than not she could attest to the fact that these men were not fabricating. Despite the fact that they were out with her, trying to procure sex with her at any cost they still grappled the night through with the idea of their own infidelity and spent the other half of the night explaining why they were forced to be in this situation in the first place.

Funny thing though, was the fact that she knew that in many instances they weren't lying in their accusations and their wives were as guilty as they were for their indiscretions. Yes, she understood and she empathized with them in their search for happiness.

How many times had she seen women, friends of hers, sistas in the church, sitting home all day with not a care in the world while their man was out there slavin' in some dead–end job with no future while all wifey did was curl up on the couch and watch Charmed and ol' reruns of Living Single until a half an hour before hubby dragged his way in the door, dog tired, greeted by his so-called woman, his lover, his spouse in an old faded terry-cloth robe and slippers. Sure, she might be a good mother. Hell, he wasn't trying to take that away from her. She might even be a fairly good cook to boot but after twenty some odd years of marriage and a television that only promoted the beautiful people ol' girl needed to come with more than just being a good mother and a decent cook. Hell, a man could make babies with any woman and if he just took the money she spent on her hair and nails every week he could eat out everyday and not be limited to McDonald's or Wendy's for his sustenance.

Most of the men she dated complained about their women, their wives and their girlfriends. And they all had the same complaints. They were genuine in most respects and were more often than not a far cry from the only other males she'd known back in high school. The only thing they were concerned with was getting her to perform fellatio or to masturbate inside of her.

The men she encountered now, though few and far between had a fine-tuned approach that hummed with the precise tuning of a well-oiled engine. The truth and desperation that gave foundation to their quest for some 'strange', for the punanny, for some uncomplicated sex arose from the same foundation, from the same roots as her classmates in high school.

The only difference was in the technique they used. With a wife at home who had fallen into a rut without her even knowing it, it

19

wasn't hard for a man to become disinterested and disenchanted. The same woman that had appealed to them so many years ago failed to realize that her marriage and her man were both and at the same time an on-going project that required her to stay on top of the situation.

Monica remembered sittin' down with her best friend Alexis at Starbuck's only a month or so before and having a similar conversation. Alexis having just come out of a wicked divorce where no stone was left unturned was hardly over her divorce although the marriage had been over long before the judge made his decree in her husband's favor.

"You know Monica; I can't blame James one bit for wanting out of the marriage. After all I left it years before he even considered a divorce."

"So you're conceding?" Monica asked eyeing Alexis closely, wearily for any signs of hedging. Never one to concede anything it didn't seem right that Alexis was surrendering now after raking James over the coals for the better part of two years, contesting his every allegation and charging him with everything from infidelity to mental cruelty.

"Hell, yeah I'm conceding. But I had to let James know that I thought he was worth fighting for. To tell you the truth, Monica, I think the divorce was the best thing that's happened to our marriage in the last ten years. You know once Chris went away to college neither of us really felt the need to be forced to live in the same house.

But the real truth of the matter is that we were married so long ago that we actually forgot that we were married. We didn't know each other, we took each other for granted and lost the focal point of our relationship. It happens a lot you know. All too often a woman gets so caught up in childbirth and child rearing and the kids in general that she forgets why or how she ended up having children. That's probably what happened to you and Marshall."

Monica interrupted before Alexis continued with hopes that she could steer the conversation away from her marriage to Ma[...] wasn't one of her favorite topics. Marshall was Marshall. [...] was responsible for Marshall's stupidity but Marshall.

But her error in judgment—her error in not being able to see the flaws in Marshall's character only gave credibility to the fact that she was a poor judge of character. A poor judge indeed who chose to ignore the man's obvious inadequacies for the possibility of gaining a foothold in her own quest for happiness. And these inadequacies had cost her dearly and kept her on her knees groveling, begging for the love of a human being who couldn't even love himself enough to maintain his own freedom for the sake of his children, if not himself.

Marshall was, if nothing else, a reflection of herself, of her own character flaws, of her low self-esteem which allowed her to be abused by him sexually and psychologically because if nothing else he was a man and if there was one thing that bothered her, ate at her and would eventually devour her if she let it, it was the fact that she could not keep a man.

No, she didn't want to talk about Marshall and her quick interruption let Alexis know that this line of questioning would not be admitted.

"Okay, so maybe Marshall's a bad example," Alexis continued, aware that Monica really didn't want to discuss Marshall or their marriage in any detail.

"All I'm saying is that when a man commits to marrying a woman that's a huge step for someone of his species. Men are not like us Monica. Men don't need women. Once they're weaned from their mother's apron strings they are independent beings. They're cold, calloused, logical entities that plot, scheme, and need only one thing out of life and that one thing is to conquer.

They have an inherent need that's almost instinctual to dominate and control everyone and everything they come into contact with. We just happen to be one of the things that they entertain along the way to fulfilling their goals. That's all we are to them--entertainment. It

21

takes a good woman, a smart woman, to recognize these features in men. And it takes a woman, a strong woman to not only recognize this but to act upon them. Wouldn't you agree?" She asked Monica as she sipped the espresso before her.

"Don't know that I would necessarily agree. I haven't really given that much thought to a man being a completely separate species. That's a new one on me. Is that like an alien or something out of a sci-fi movie or something?" Monica said smiling not attempting to dissuade her friends' theory but commenting just enough to let her know that she still had her ear.

Alexis was a psychology instructor at the local university and was one of the more astute women in Monica's small circle of friends. They'd been best friends and confidantes since grade school. But unlike the woman sitting before her, Alexis was tiny, a size six and the apple of every man's eye she came into contact with. She had long ago grown tired of men and the game.

And her marriage to James LeBrandt came as a shock to everyone since it was a well-known fact that she had the utmost contempt for the opposite sex. Besides James was the quiet unobtrusive type, content to sit home and baby sit—a cold beer in one hand, the remote in the other while his baby girl drooled down the front of his beige khaki shirt that read James LeBrandt, mechanic.

During their twenty-year marriage, Alexis, always the earth shaker had prodded James to return to school though he was quite happy just being a father and an auto mechanic at J.C.Penny's. His love for his wife forced him to go back to school despite his obvious objections and at the time of their divorce James LeBrandt was teaching auto mechanics at Detroit Central Community College while still managing to keep an iron in the fire working as a part-time mechanic at Penny's on the weekends. Despite their marriage Alexis never stopped clubbing despite what appeared to be her utter distaste for men.

Monica and no one else could understand Alexis's penchant for the club scene and yet at forty-two she experienced the same meteoric success she had when they were high schoolers. Men flocked to her.

Monica wondered for a time if her best friend, the very logical Alexis LeBrandt might simply be amassing research material for her doctorate thesis but that thought was quickly dispelled when Alexis said, "Hell no girl. I wouldn't waste my time researching something so banal. I just like to watch men grovel, baby—just enjoy breaking them down to the very last compound. That's all. That's it in the nutshell. And I'll tell you what. The reason I have so much success with men is that I have a man's mentality at heart. You see a man— in a world of mediocrity—a thinking man is a driven man. His very essence, his very existence arises out of the fact that the world is his oyster, his play toy and he comes out of the womb thinking and believing that he is supposed to, by divine right, taste the fruits of this world. Not just one or two fruits but all the fruits. *He really believes he is supposed to taste each and every one.* His goal is to nibble, then bite, then immerse himself in their succulent flavors, and move on. He receives nourishment and wisdom at each tree, from each fruit. He devours the fruit and then moves on to seek other varieties until alas he realizes that there are so many delicious varieties of fruits, so many different flavors that he would be less than a fool to limit himself to one.

But a woman is not made up that way and it's not because she is any different than a man. It's simply the fact that a man being the dominant of the two simply sets the rules and the standards. He's done it for so long that it's become an accepted part of our culture. Do you follow me?

Monica grinned.

"Preach preacher! Preach!" Monica shouted, laughing at the same time.

"Let me give you an example honey. Just look at how you were raised Monica. From the time you were knee-high to a grasshopper your momma gave you everything that she could afford to give you. She did the same for your brother, Augustus, I'm sure. But while

23

she was giving you Barbie dolls and Gus, G.I.Joe's she was also giving Gus trucks and cars and Lego's so he could build things. She gave him sports equipment, remote controlled cars, airplanes, and chemistry sets. You name it, he got it, I'm sure.

One thing's for sure; Hattie Mae never neglected her son. And in her mind she didn't neglect you either. But she did. Consciously or unconsciously she did. You see Lego's gave little Gus the idea that he could be a builder, a contractor maybe even an architect or an engineer. Remote controlled planes instilled in him the idea that he could be an aviator if he so chose to be. All these things were within the realm of possibility for little Gus. But when it came to you everything centered on that one Barbie. You could accessorize Barbie with cars and wigs and nail polish and strollers and bottles and pampers. But everything centered on that Barbie, a baby doll because inevitably that was your role in life, to be a mother, a caretaker, and a support system for the man as he went out into the world to pursue his dreams. You were a second-class citizen the minute you left your mother's womb. You were not encouraged to think or to develop your talents because then you'd be an intelligent, productive entity on your own and perhaps even a threat to your man.

That's just the way our society was set up. Hell, I've accepted it. That's why I enjoy going out and rubbing noses and asses with the movers and shakers. Know what I'm sayin'? I ain't never been what you'd consider traditional. Guess I got a few too many male hormones in me although you could never tell by my tight, little round ass, now can you?" Alexis laughed.

"There's somethin' wrong with you, Alexis," Monica laughed.

"It's hard to argue with you though. But I don't see how you do it. I mean I don't see the purpose of going out on the regular to have men pawing all over you knowing full well that their only objective is to get you to the nearest hotel so they can see firsthand what's up under that tight little dress and once they see you know that all they wanna do is part your thighs and shove that shit up in you."

Alexis picked up the tiny cup, took a swig of the cold espresso and looked at Monica as if she hadn't said anything.

"Did I tell you that I just bought another piece of rental property off of Alamance Church Road? It's not much—a little brick, three-bedroom starter home. Cost me eighty grand. Nice little piece of property. It should bring me about four or five hundred a month. No money down. A broker friend of mine hipped me to it and with the other two rental properties I didn't have to put a dime down. Collateral honey. I ain't put a dime down. A cute little house. It needs some minor repairs since the last tenants decided to make a fire in the fireplace without opening the flue. It's got some smoke damage but Henry L. who owns The Cellar Restaurant downtown turned me on to a maintenance company who are as cheap as they come. Soon as the house is ready and I get it rented out, I'm outta here. Gonna see my broker and scrape off some of the dividends from my Wachovia stock which just split and spend Christmas and New Years down in the Caribbean. I've got a friend down in St. Lucia who's got some land for sale. Thinkin' about putting up some condos that I can turn into time-sharing lots."

Monica interrupted.

"I know you're doin' it girl. Livin' large and all, but I thought you were givin' me your theory on the male species. How the hell you gonna flip the script on me just like that? You know you're my only source on men."

"I sure hope not. If I am you're in more trouble than I thought, honey." Alexis laughed. "Here I am being sued for divorce under every possible statute that I could write the handbook on how to fail in marriage and *I'm* your yardstick on men?" Alexis laughed again. "I truly hope you're not serious, sweetie. Shit, I wouldn't have married James in the first place if I had the knowledge you think I had. Sweetheart, James and I are like Tom and Jerry, like oil and water. And believe you me I knew that when I lured him into marrying me. But I was trippin' at the time.

But it is what it is. I had my reasons for marrying James when

25

ut things change. I've changed. I want more than I did
day and certainly more than I did at that point in my life. In
the beginning, I dedicated myself to my children and my husband.
But that was then. My kids are grown now and I must admit that I
like the job that we did as parents and I respect him for being a good
father in spite of his shortcomings and mine as well. But together
we did a fine job or so I'd like to think but that stage of my life is
over and it's time to move on.

I'm like every goddamn businessman I bump heads with. I want
to suck the juice from the very marrow of life, baby. Every last
fuckin' drop.

I can't be content to just sit back in my easy chair and say—well
hey—the kids are grown and now I can relax. I ain't got time for
that. Too much shit out there I haven't seen or done yet. And you
know me Monica; I'm inquisitive by my very nature. But hell,
when you think about it none of us have really have that luxury.
We can be here today and gone tomorrow. Know what I'm sayin'?
Ain't none of us guaranteed tomorrow.

I realized that shit when my momma passed away so abruptly
and out of the clear blue. I was out there bullshittin', and carryin'
on kind of aimlessly and then boom, she just up and died with no
warning and no goodbyes or nothing. And that's when I had to stop
and ask myself some hard questions that I wasn't really ready to
face. But I did and I ain't gonna lie, it took a while for me to come to
grips with who I was and what I was doing out here. But I didn't see
any choice and so I answered those questions even though I didn't
like most of the answers I came up with and you know what else I
found out? I found out I really didn't like myself, or the course my
life was taking. So I decided it was time for a change.

I got up the next day and promised myself that I was gonna make
a change in my life and those who cared to come along for the ride
were welcome to but the time for complacency was long gone.

When those Jehovah Witness people used to come around on
Saturday mornings and my daddy used to answer the door and they

started talking religion and about becoming a Witness and everything he used to tell them without being disrespectful that he was glad they'd found their religion but please don't try to force your God on me. Everyone finds their own religion in their own time. Well, that may be all well and good but I can't wait for someone to find religion or reason for living.

You see, now is my time and I just decided that it's high time I got my house in order and then do what dumbass, Martin Lawrence of all people suggested when he was coming back from whatever addiction he was denying. I am gonna do just what Martin suggested. I am going to take this thing called life and 'ride it 'til the mothafuckin wheels fall off'. That's basically my whole philosophy on life. Just ride it 'til the wheels fall off.

But anyway, the point that I was trying to make as far as men were concerned was that they are, simply because of how our society is set up the cogs that make the wheels turn. You probably thought I was ego trippin' when I told you about the rental property, the stock options, and the vacation down in St Lucia's but I didn't tell you that because I was ego-trippin' or on my own tip. I told you that because it wasn't me who caused those seismic movements in what had been an otherwise dull and tedious life. I told you because I just happened to be in the presence of men who met to make moves over martinis and Mudslides. That's all.

I talked, you know, conversated, investigated, researched and was bright enough and inquisitive enough, I suppose, that they eventually looked at me as one of the fellas and took me into their confidence enough to share with me the intimacies of what it takes to climb out of the muck and the mire, the hellhole that had become my life with James.

That's what I was trying to tell you, honey. I just got tired of the bullshit nine to five, shit. Got tired of living in a city that had nothing to offer, tired of soccer games and sucking dick, tired of backyard barbeques and ballgames and all that other shit that comes with being married to a man with no aspirations other than to watch ball and my Black butt bounce around the bedroom in a brassiere and bath robe while all I got to watch was his beer belly grow while he watched ballgames. Or maybe he just got tired of my shit. I don't know. But what I do know is that I'm forty-two years young and sometimes I feel it and sometimes I don't but I know that if this is the way I've spent half my life this is sure as hell not the way I intend to spend the second half. Do you feel me, girl? You may not necessarily agree, but can you feel me?"

Monica understood. Alexis had always been an overachiever. Ever since high school when she'd cried a river of tears because she hadn't been chosen valedictorian when everyone else, including Monica was thankful just to have graduated she'd been driven.

Everyone knew that Alexis was destined for great things. One thing that they did not know was that she'd made a vow to herself on that final day of high school that she would never be denied or fall short on anything she desired again. And in the decades that passed since then there was nothing that Alexis LeBrandt laid her sights on that she didn't eventually attain.

"I understand what you're saying. I don't necessarily agree with what you're saying but I hear you. We're just two very different people, Alexis, that's all. Always have been. I think we want the same things out of life. I just think we go about acquiring them differently.

I'm happy raising children, being there as a support system for my man, making sure that he leaves home happy and making sure that no matter what kind of day he has out there slavin' for the man, he gets the all the creature comforts I can afford to give him when he gets home from a long hard day. Even if the roles were reversed, and I was out there working and he was a strong enough individual that he could be at home maintaining the responsibilities of home I could be happy. You see, after being with men and you know as well as I do that I don't date regularly and up 'til lately it's really only been a handful. So, hell I'll take them any way I can get them."

"Yeah, for awhile no man stood a chance with you all wrapped

28

up in what's his name. Boy, had your nose wide open. What's his name? Oh, yeah, Jesus. That was the only man in your life. What happened?" Alexis laughed.

"Don't even play with something like that, Alexis LeBrandt. You should know better. If your momma could hear you now. Blasphemin' and all. But seriously I am happy to share in a man's life; to just be an integral part of it—I don't have to be a dominatrix. I've been on my own almost my entire adult life—well at least when it came to bein' the provider. Even when Marshall was there he couldn't scrape two peas together long enough for us to get a bite. So, being independent is really nothing new to me. I just wish I had your financial prowess to go ahead and put together a portfolio like you're doing but I don't and when you're maintaining a household and trying to raise two kids on your own you have to make the necessary sacrifices. I just thank the Lord that he gave me the strength to get through the rough times. There was a time that I really didn't think I wasn't going to make it. But through it all, I never doubted myself thanks to my faith in the Lord. Never. If there was one thing I was always confident of, it was the fact that my kids were going to eat and have a roof over their heads and I sure as hell wasn't depending on some man to provide for someone that I brought into this world," Monica said adamantly.

"I feel you there, girl." Alexis laughed.

"You know I'm gonna handle mine. Still and all, I've always had this gnawing hunger to have a man in my life. I'm not sayin' at any cost. Trust me I've been there and done the man at any cost thing on a number of occasions and it was always a mess. Hell, I don't need no man to add any more weight on me. I've got enough weight on this tired-ass frame as it is. But I really do wonder, at times, what it would be like to have a good man around for companionship. You know just for the gentle warmth of his caress. I don't know that I'm any different than ninety per-cent of the women I know and I understand what you're sayin' about our society being male oriented. There's no doubt that I'm a victim but the fact remains that a person always wonders about how the other half is living and I've always been curious, or *inquisitive* as you so aptly put it about how it would be to be married. I mean really married or at least to have a relationship where the other person is as committed to me as I am to him. I really would like to have that experience at least once in my life. And no matter what I do it just seems to keep eluding me."

"That's because you're looking for it." Alexis murmured.

"Whatever. Maybe you can't empathize being that you've been fortunate enough to have been happily married. Like it or not you can sit back and make a subjective statement because you've been there and know what it's like."

"And you can't? You act like the entire time you were married it was hell. I can remember the times when you were tickled pink. There were months when I was out there floundering around trying to find myself—wondering if I was on the right course changing majors—trying to figure out if I was sellin' myself short by pursuing a teaching career or wondering if I should go into law. I'd call you and you were so busy playing the good housewife, the good mother thinking you were Betty Crocker; baking cookies and having brunches and shit that you couldn't bother to answer the phone. Some friend you were," Alexis teased.

"You need to quit", Monica said smiling glibly. "I'm not gonna lie. The first couple of months *were* pure heaven but when Mandy and Marshall Jr. came into the picture that was the end of that."

"And you did everything that you could to make it work?" Alexis asked.

"Everything that a twenty-one year old knows how to do. Hell, I'll readily admit that I was crazy in love. I wanted more than anything in the world for my marriage to Marshall to work. I guess some things just aren't meant to be. It took me a long time to come to the conclusion that all things aren't meant to be or totally within a person's control. You don't know how long I blamed myself for Marshall's misfortune. I kept telling myself that if I had just done more, if I had been more attentive to his needs, if I had just forced him to talk to me and tell me what was bothering him, what was eating away at him, what caused the sudden change in him then things would have been different. I went through all of that shit. And then I found the Lord. And it was the Lord that made me realize that I was only human and I was not solely responsible for everything that occurred. The Good Lord let me know that I'd done everything that I could possibly do but when another person with a free will of their own is involved there is only so much you can do. I had to come to grips with that and my faith in the Lord helped me do just that. Truthfully speaking, I gave all that I had to give and that's all I can possibly do I've got to be satisfied with that at this juncture in my life.

It's a funny thing though, I listen to the men that I'm around when they talk about their wives. Half the time they're telling me these things because they want to get into my pants so I have to weigh what they say. And every now and then they have a tendency to lie."

"For sho," Alexis added.

"But do you know what I've learned over the years? I've learned that in every lie there's some element of truth, so I listen. Nine times out of ten they, all tell me the same thing. It's basically the same story you're telling me about James—only from a male perspective.

Here they are at some out of the way dive with a woman that they would haven't given the time of day too a few years ago when they were in their prime but since they're not and they're wives shapes are starting to look like mine I'm not looking half bad. How do they say it? I'm doable. Like I said a few years ago when they were in their prime, they wouldn't have given me a second thought or a third one either for that matter. But see the whole time their wives are sitting home in a housedress and slippers while I'm out here in the mix, a career woman, on the prowl trying to shape my shit into something desirable and spending any little extra bit of change to get my nails and hair done and doing the best I can with what I got ol' girl's sitting at home on the phone, thinking she's holdin' it down. Meanwhile, her old man's out here with me just wishin' his lil' Violet who used to be a size twelve and done blossomed into a size twenty-two would get herself together and at least try to get glamorous on occasion. But his little Violet don't know that and she ain't bright enough to realize that and seems content to just sit home knowing that she's got her man locked down. She ain't even thinking that there's someone out there that might just find her man attractive. And she ain't even considering taking the time and the initiative to spruce herself up. And meanwhile, I'm just plodding along. It's like the tortoise and the hare baby. The whole time they cruisin' along and countin' their chips I'm gainin' on 'em," Monica laughed.

"You are certifiable," Alexis laughed.

"No, I'm being real. If they stop for a second and turn their heads the only thing that they're gonna find is that I'm right there waiting for them to slip up so I can grab a piece of happiness for myself. But they don't take the time to think. God said he helps those who help themselves and if they slip up I sho' am going to help myself to their man.

Most of the time they married for security and now that they're secure they don't even bother to wonder what their man is thinking or feeling. I'm tellin' you they better watch their back," Monica said.

"Ooh you're starting to scare me now. Though I don't know why since I haven't had a man I could call my own in close to a year," Alexis joked.

"*Oh, please!* You're one of the few sistas I know that comes out of the house everyday to a fan club. You've got so many that you don't know what to do with 'em. Some of us are out here fightin' to get one good man and you're up here kickin' them to the curb like you used to do your old rag dolls. Now, can I finish tellin' my story, thank you very much?

See, the thing is I used to look like what they have at home.

32

Walkin' around in curlers and slippers but their men don't know that. Since they only see me at work or at school that means they get to see me at my best. While they're wives are sitting they're loungin' with their feet up watching TV and chatting with their girlfriends on the phone I'm workin' everything at my disposal and entertaining their men.

I guess because I'm a big girl and they ain't exactly Joe Quarterback themselves no more they figure that I'm easy pickings. And since I'm single I guess they think I'm in desperate need of a man—any man and they can just bowl me over with a couple of stiff drinks and a stiff dick—excuse my French but that's the way they make it seem. Most of the time they try to be gentlemen, but hey, in the end it all comes down to the same thing." Monica laughed. "They just want the punanny," Monica laughed.

"Don't get me wrong. They don't want to own it. They just want to lease the shit on a short-term, no frills basis. Hell, most of them would rent the shit by the hour if they could. That's just how triflin' these niggas are nowadays. Anyway, that's the impression I've been getting as of late."

"Tell me you're not serious?" Alexis laughed.

"As a heart attack," Monica laughed.

"They obviously don't know you, Alexis surmised. "Don't they know they can go broke trying to get you drunk? I don't know of any woman who can handle her liquor as well as you. It's almost like you're immune to the shit," Alexis laughed drawing the attention of the other Starbuck's customers many of whom had come and gone in the time the two friends had been there.

"C'mon, Monica let's get out of here. I've got to drop off some papers at my attorney's office. C'mon and take a ride and finish tellin' me your story on the way".

The two women climbed into the dark blue Mercedes 350SL and were soon caught up in the busy midday traffic. Alexis looked like she was born to drive the two-door luxury car as she wove in and out of traffic disregarding the other motorists completely.

"Anyway," Monica continued, "most of the guys I've been seeing are from the office or from school. Most of them are married and pretty up front about that before we go out. Usually, they start off like we're going out as friends—you know everything's on the up-n-up—purely platonic and all that but by the time they get finished ordering drinks—mind you we're only supposed to be going out for one drink— but by the time they've finished ordering, we've had six or seven apiece and they've told me everything from the time they played little league baseball to their disenchantment with that 'ho' at home.

By the time the waitress brings the bill I must look like a toss up between Halle Berry and JLo, 'cause all they keep telling me is how beautiful and understanding I am. Then they want to know how I can understand their position and their needs when their wives don't have a clue, I mean no earthly idea about what it takes to keep a man happy.

That's when I smile and turn on that little girl charm and watch them wriggle and fight their inner demons which tell them to go ahead and proposition me. At the same time they feel guilty about the way they're feeling knowing that they have a wife and a house full of rug rats waiting on them at home. Then there's the simple fact that if everything goes the way they want it to and they can make it past the thought of their wife and their kids and get lucky enough to spend a few hours in some fleabag hotel with me they start to wonder what's going to happen when they have to face me in the office tomorrow.

About this time they usually take a good hard look at me and try to see through the haze from the smoke and the liquor and begin asking themselves why they hadn't seen or noticed me before. The liquor's working now and all their inhibitions are gone and their ego's out of control and their libido's stuck on high. That's when they get to squintin' real hard and really trying to size me up.

You can almost see their 'lil chimpanzee sized pea brain at work by this time and then they take another look to see if I'm really *that* big. By this time, they've lost all control and I know they're gonna proposition me and I'm sittin' their thinkin' how humorous and how boyish these clowns are but I still try to reserve an air of dignity and respect for their drunk asses.

It's around this time when they come to grips with what they think is about to happen that they have to get the final confirmation from who else but themselves so they excuse themselves and get up and head to the men's room but not before they tell me to order another round or two just to let me know that an eighty or ninety dollar bar tab ain't shit for a true gigolo. Hell, that's it. That's when I know they're going to come back thinkin' they're Denzel or Billy Dee or some other playa playa.

That bar tab in itself is the final confirmation. That bar tab tells them two things. First, it tells them that with the money they've spent on me that I should surely know by now that they're serious about me. Hell, why else would they spend that kind of money on somebody they can see and talk to at work everyday for free unless I was special in some way?

The bar tab's also confirmation that I'm ready for anything. Either I had to drink that much to allow a married man to get between my legs knowing full well there was no future in the whole charade or maybe I had to drink that much because I was embarrassed with the thought of him seeing my fat Black ass. After all, in his mind he's doing me a favor to sleep with anyone my size anyway. Finally, he tells himself that if he hadn't been drinking and didn't like me and I wasn't humorous and a good friend and co-worker he wouldn't even haven't given a thought to providing me with a charity fuck.

At the same time, he's still feeling guilty as hell and not sure if he should make his move or not but those rosy red lips that are smiling at his drunk ass from across the table have his boy Petey's name written all over it and he can already feel himself coming.' Monica laughed.

"Girl you're a trip," Alexis laughed.

"Hold up 'Lexis, I'm not finished yet. Anyway, I grin some

more before I throw that cleavage up on the table that makes his wife's titties look like two mosquito bites on an elephants ass and now I've got him really shook up and now he's wonderin' just how big and dark my nipples really are and ain't no way in hell to find out but to proposition me.

At the same time he's looking to see if anything's happened over the course of the evening that tells him I'm ready for him to fuck the hell out of me but the only thing he can come up with is the time our knees accidentally touched under the table before I excused myself and went to the ladies room. He's not sure if that had been a mere accident or if I was trying to make a pass at him.

By this time the alcohol's got him sweatin' and starin' at me. And my sitting there, looking good enough to eat, ain't much helpin' his thought process which was pretty limited to begin with if you ask me.

Meanwhile, I'm just sitting there watching him squirm and I offer absolutely no assistance when it comes to what he should do since I pretty much know what follows and have come to the decision many years before and several dates prior to this one that his demons must be dealt with by him and so at this point I turn to the side letting these gorgeous thunder thighs with the these beautiful full figured legs attached dangle in the aisle to quicken the process since I'm a little bored now and after the Patron's given me a pretty nice buzz by this time. The only real question left at this point is if we're going to be friends tomorrow or if I've lost another friend and co-worker.

That's his cue. Time for small talk is over. No more debate on whether Obama has a real chance or not. He doesn't know it but I do. He's not sure if I'm getting fidgety or if I'm ready to go but he's still fighting those damn demons. He's not sure whether he wants to continue to be the faithful husband or if he wants to add a little flavor to his menial and mundane existence with my fine ass that he somehow overlooked up 'til now.

Funny thing though, my opinion never comes into play. You see in his eyes I'm just the recipient of his charity and so he excuses himself and makes his way to the bathroom to make the final decision on whether or not I meet his qualifications. He needs to find out without me influencing his decision whether I am truly worthy enough of sucking his shriveled up middle-aged dick or not. Ain't that a bitch?

Anyway, he heads off to the john confused as hell but already certain that I'm going to be his tonight. I can picture him standing there in front of the sink washing his hands and staring in the mirror talking to himself, reassuring himself, convincing himself that he is after all a man and well—hell I wasn't what you might call hard on the eyes and the body was definitely doable. Besides who would know? If Violet or Clarisse or Mary Sue Beth would stop walkin' around in that damn robe lookin' and actin' like she was eighty and spruce herself up every once in awhile and stop lookin' and actin' like she was eighty and suck his dick on occasion like she used to do when they were dating and she was trying to get him on the permanent he wouldn't be here now.

Far as she was concerned, what could he say? What the hell. It was free and he hadn't had his dick sucked in who knows how long and of course like I said he was doing me a favor, making this sacrifice. Hell, if he weren't drunk he wouldn't even consider it. Besides if I was opposed to letting him have his way with me then why in the hell had I come? She knew the deal. At least she was supposed to know when she accepted his offer to come out for drinks. There was nothin' wrong with bein' pillow pals. Smiling he conceded. Yeah, he guessed he'd do it."

"You got the shit down don't'cha girl." Alexis laughed. "And here you are askin' me for my advice. So what happened when he came out of the john?"

"The fool came out hemmin' and hawin' and stutterin' and carryin' on so I just looked at him and smiled with these big, voluptuous, ruby-red lips he'd been staring at all night, laid that cleavage down right there on the table in plain view so he could see everything I wanted him to see and smiled and said, "Honey is there something you want to ask me?"

"And did he?" Alexis asked narrowly missing a bus pulling out from the curb.

"Yeah, he finally did," Monica smiled.

"And..." Alexis asked now sitting on the edge of her seat in anticipation.

"I told him the politest way I knew how that I was celibate and was waiting for the right man to come along and that I wanted the same thing that he wanted but with someone that was going to be there for me on a full-time basis. Then I thanked him for sharing and giving me insight on what it takes to be a good wife."

"And?" Alexis questioned.

"And what? You know men—he hasn't spoken to my ass since."

Chapter 2

As much as she hated to admit it Alexis missed the heavy footsteps in the middle of the night that drummed a staccato beat of security. She missed the hard driving sound of his urinating with the force of Zeus at six a.m. as he woke cussin' about the flavor of the toothpaste and the boss man he was about to go see. She missed the hustle and bustle and the excuse me's as they bumped into each other trying to get ready for church on Sunday mornings and the afternoon picnics following the service. She missed the crazy, atmosphere that had been her home on Super Bowl Sundays when all James' friends would force themselves into the tiny living room to watch the game while she fixed her own super-sized, super-spicy, version of hot wings and carried a steady flow of chips and dip to the crazed men whoopin' it up in the next room. She missed the deep passionate voice of solace that her man would afford her after a trying day in the classroom. Much as she hated to admit it Alexis missed James LeBrandt.

The palatial condominium with the black and white marble floors loomed large before her as she dropped the brown weather beaten leather briefcase and her coat on the Queen Anne chair in the foyer and stared at the five thousand dollar baby grand piano that stood naked and alone in the middle of the living room floor. Making her way over to the piano Alexis LeBrandt dropped the stack of mail on the piano seat and moved to the bay window with the bench seat, where she sat down and breathed a deep sigh of relief that was of no relief at all but only let her know just how tired and alone she was. Staring out of the high rise across the city she couldn't help but think that after all the hard work she'd finally arrived. But in reality she felt no better than when she was in the tiny three bedroom home staring at James as he dozed in his easy chair. Fact of the matter was that Alexis LeBrandt was not a happy woman.

Bad as she hated to admit it, her friend Monica's words held some truth although she would never let her know for the simple reason that her friend was already to subservient, to dependent on men for her happiness. And Alexis LeBrandt truly believed that a person's happiness was the responsibility of that person and no one else. How many times had she let some man come into her life with their sweet talk and grand ideas and given in to them only to be left crying, hurt and alone to pick up the fragments of her tattered heart. No one understood why she'd married James. 'Not Alexis LeBrandt they'd say'. Not Ms. Right, Ms Uppity stooping to marry some lowly mechanic. Don't even seem right.' But the truth of the matter was James was all she needed to complete her, to help define her as a woman, to give her the security she needed so that she could go out into the world and pursue her dreams and her goals—of which she had many.

Fact of the matter was James was her stability. Behind every successful woman was a good man. James gave her everything she needed. He put her on the throne and crowned her queen. When in doubt and having misgivings about this or that—he was there to slow her down and guide her on the proper course of action. As much as she hated to admit it she knew that one of her biggest shortcomings was the fact that she was impatient and impulsive by nature. Most women were and she hated this flaw in her character but after years of addressing the subject she had gained no more patience than when she started trying to overcome her deficiency. Enter James LeBrandt and the art of decision-making.

Though long, tedious and often painstakingly tough for her to endure in the beginning James always ended—or at least almost always ended up making a wise if not well thought out decision that would ultimately help in her meteoric rise in her career as well as her financial dealings. Not one to pursue such activities himself his wisdom behind the scenes was invaluable and despite her qualms about his career path and lack of initiative, Alexis LeBrandt admired his patience and resolve but most of all the wealth of inherent down-to-earth wisdom and prudence he displayed.

She also liked the fact that James LeBrandt had a sort of inner peace that allowed him to just sit and observe a situation with a quiet ease and hardly a concern while the world spun crazily, out of control around him. It was this quality that she admired the most and despised the most in her. She hated being so goal oriented, so driven, so damn obsessed and passionate about everything she encountered.

Sitting on the window seat she smiled as she thought of the way she used to burst in the house at 2204 Oakmont Court and just jump into whatever the latest hair-brained scheme it was that attracted her fancy and guaranteed her financial security for the next three lifetimes.

James would only laugh, as he picked up the youngest of their three children clutching at mommy's skirt tails for attention and yelling, 'Mommy's home'. In all her excitement she hadn't even bothered to acknowledge the kids. And it wasn't until James standing there showing as many teeth as the toddlers vying for mommy's attention said, 'Give mommy a kiss and ask her how her day was', that she realized that she hadn't even seen the children. All the time, he'd be using his free hand to rub her back in an attempt to soothe her. Then slowly methodically he'd whisper in that big ol' rich baritone voice of his that reminded her of daddy so much that it was scary, to slow down and catch her breath.

Grabbing her coat and hat he'd guide her over to the recliner, make her sit and before she could start chattering away again he'd put a finger to her lips to quiet her and gently push her down and recline the Lazy Boy.

Once seated and still overly anxious to tell the latest bit of breaking news James would smile and then shush her again and make her wait. Oh, how she hated that. He did the same thing when they

41

made love. She'd be right there. Right there on the boiling point about to bubble over and he'd stop and make her wait. God how she hated that. Right when she was on the verge of exploding he'd stop or get up and light a cigarette or go to the bathroom. She'd be right there. Right there and he'd just stop on the best damn downstroke in the last millennium he'd stop cold. Not pause but stop.

Of course his prolonging the whole affair only made her want him that much more and she had to admit that it was okay for him to cover the same ground again and retrace his steps as long as she was allowed to finish this time. Sometimes he used the same tactic three or four times in the course of an evening which frustrated her beyond belief but Lord knows when she did come there were fireworks and explosions that made the Fourth of July look like Palm Sunday. At least that's what it seemed like to her.

When she finished screaming and crying and wiping the tears from her eyes she'd peek out the window to see if the neighbors had called the cops. And James would hardly utter a word—just lie there and smile one of those silly, boyish, 'thanks for the compliment, 'boss' smiles before rolling over and going to sleep.

Oh, how he used to frustrate her but when she came in the door all wound up after waiting all day to share this special thing—whatever it was—with her man and she was put on hold for what seemed like an eternity.

Pushing her down in the easy chair his finger against her lip in an effort to quiet her, he'd leave the room, return with a glass of her favorite Chardonnay hand her the glass and then kneel before, her slip off the six inch heels that were killing her back so, send the kids out of the room, pull off her pantyhose, whistle in appreciation and then return to the floor where he'd begin to gently knead the soles of her feet with his thumb and forefinger until the glass of wine was empty and her head was nestled comfortably in the chair's headrest.

"You were saying?" he'd ask.

By this time whatever it was that been so earth shattering didn't hardly seem as important and her home life would continue without the chaotic madness and excessive baggage that she experienced everyday in her quest for financial success and acceptance in Detroit's darker version of the Wall Street crowd.

Now six months after the divorce, she was on her way to becoming completely acclimated to her former hometown, which, though a far cry from the Big Apple, had an overabundance of opportunities for a Black woman with her drive and desire despite a fledgling car industry and a tremendously high unemployment rate.

A sister with money and the right connections could make waves if she just knew the right people and had a little luck. James on the other hand, was a homebody at heart and was sure that the move back would not only be a better environment to raise the kids in but might help to quell Alexis's penchant for the fast lane.

It had just the opposite effect. Instead of her becoming resigned to her new position that required more of her time since she'd been named a full-professor, James and the kids saw less-and-less of their mother. Since their return to Detroit she seemed in James' words, 'possessed', so was her desire to get a foothold in the Detroit landscape.

Despite the happy home which she had helped to create it simply was not enough to keep her satisfied and she was determined to make her mark on Detroit by hook or by crook even if it came at the expense of her family.

James had accompanied her at first out of nothing more than loyalty and love for his wife but soon grew tired of the phoniness and unethical practices he met in his dealings with her associates. And though rarely outspoken and controversial he commented one evening after dinner with Alexis's new cohorts that these people may have financial creditability and certain expertise when it came to turning a dollar but one thing they sure as hell didn't have and that was a moral conscience. What they were, he concluded, were financial piranhas that would just as surely devour her as the next guy if it meant them making a dollar. It wasn't long thereafter before

James was content to give her a kiss on the cheek before adjusting her blouse or her scarf and sending her on her way with a kiss on the cheek and a wearied, 'Be careful'.

One thing was for sure, however and that was that this was not his scene. A local boy James just couldn't understand Alexis's constant need to hit the streets in search of new ventures when she had an adoring family waiting at the doorstep for her to return each evening.

By now the kids had grown accustomed to their mother's erratic behavior and with Chris a senior at UNC down in Chapel Hill, Nicole completing her senior year in high school and already accepted into Duquesne in Pittsburgh and Michelle the baby right on her heels there was absolutely no reason for Alexis to come home. Recognizing this James decided there was no reason for him to come home either and so instead of working part-time at Penny's he went back to his full-time gig with the hopes that the extra money would be enough of an incentive to curtail Alexis's chasing a dollar during her every free moment.

In all actuality there was little reason for the woman he loved to be out there at all. If she had stopped right then and there, just long enough to take a moment to think as he had in her absence or taken the time to sit down and talk to him about their assets she would have realized that with the rental properties and the stocks, compiled with their IRA's they could have lived quite comfortably into the middle of the next century. No, it wasn't the money that was the issue. It was the fact that Alexis had—as Alexis had always had—something that drove her that would not let her relax and continually told her that enough was never enough.

He'd been cognizant of it early on in their relationship but was sure that she'd mellow with age and they'd be content to fill out the remainder of their days in wedded bliss enjoying each other's company and perhaps a trip or two to the Caribbean each year to soak up some rays while his buddies sat back on the Great Lakes in January freezing their asses off. At least that's the way he saw it.

And he would have been glad to have flaunted Alexis off down in the islands with her bikini on and bring back the pictures to show the fellas at work.

At forty-two she was even more attractive than the skinny little girl he'd brought home to his momma twenty years earlier. She'd filled out better than he could ever have expected and had a set of jugs and an ass that just wouldn't quit and kept eighteen and nineteen year old men who could care less about Sigmund Freud or psychology signing up for her classes. That was one of the reasons that the community college was so quick to tenure her and make her the department chair. Besides being sharp as a tack when it came to her subject area—her classes were always full with a waiting list at the beginning of each and every semester. It had been no different at Medgar Evers University in New York. No different at all.

At first the attention his wife would attract from the opposite sex bothered James a little but he was a man whose constitution was not easily shaken and he quickly came to a resolve that served him well for the duration of their marriage.

Lying in bed next to him one night not long ago and after what had been a particularly trying day in which James had called to say he was picking her up from work to do some shopping since there were no groceries in the house they drove home each sharing the other's day at work.

Stopping at the local grocer James had as James had always done decided to wait in the car while Alexis took her time perusing the lettuce for hardness and the tomatoes for softness. It was something that he could not comprehend and after having one of the worst arguments of their entire marriage he decided that when it came to shopping with her he just as soon wait in the car.

Now James watched as his wife exited the store in her usual mini skirt and heels. These two items pretty much comprised the mainstay of her wardrobe. And she made it a point to wear them in spite of the season or the temperature. Whether it was thirty or thirty below you could bet you last dime that Alexis LeBrandt was going to be wearing the shortest mini skirt and the highest heels she could possibly find. And this day was no different bringing about the usual amount of wolf whistles and passes from men. No, this day was no exception and two young teenage males sporting dreads and baggy jeans were so persistent about walking this middle-aged mommy of three to the car that after having no luck dispelling them she told them that since they so insistent on walking her to the car they should at least carry her bags which they politely did.

Funny thing about the whole situation was that James would always park as far away from the store as possible and tell Alexis that it was better that she walk the extra few steps than for him to have his car door dinged up when the truth of the matter was that James still liked to watch his wife's ass jiggle when she walked. The farther away he parked, the more he could watch it jiggle. After twenty years of marriage he was still as infatuated with her as the day they first met.

When the two young boys got to the car and saw James', big brown frame hunched over reading the sports section of the paper they were visibly shaken. When all six foot-seven feet of him started rising from the car to put the groceries in the trunk they were down right scared. Alexis watched, tickled by whole the affair. James now used to this type of behavior from complete strangers smiled, and thanked the boys who dashed off after handing him the bags.

Later that night Alexis confronted James around the incident and was surprised to hear him put everything into context so methodically, so logically and so calmly that it disturbed her. It was obvious that someone before had asked him the question, as his answer was too pat and left her wondering.

"James, does it ever bother you the way men act towards me," she asked putting her papers on the oak nightstand next to the bed.

"And how is it that men act towards you, baby?" James countered as he turned the page of the paper pretending to feign indifference to her question.

He was exhausted and hardly wanted a discussion on the way

men react to a woman that flaunts her stuff so she can get just that reaction. He wondered why women played such silly cat and mouse games even after they'd been caught. *Whew.* Talk about the male ego. He wanted to tell her the truth—wanted to tell her just how he was feeling –wanted to ask her why she felt compelled to walk around the streets baring her ass so that men could constantly tell her how fine she was when she had absolutely nothing to do with the way she looked. But he wanted nothing more than to see the news before closing his eyes and going to sleep.

Tomorrow was Friday, payday, and he was going on a fishing trip with a couple of buddies from work. They'd planned the trip three months earlier and the last thing he wanted to do now was get in an argument with Alexis and ruin his and his buddies' weekend; so he did his best to patronize her without being too obvious.

"James LeBrandt! You hear me talking to you. Put that paper down now and answer me!" She screamed only half joking.

"Sorry, babe," he said calmly. "Didn't mean to ignore you. What was the question?"

"I asked you if it bothered you for men to constantly flirt with me in your presence?"

"Hmmm. That's a tough one. Kind of a lose-lose situation. But to tell you the truth, I think it's rather flattering that other men desire you but if you're asking me if I feel threatened then I'd have to say no—not in the least." His male ego beginning to bare its' prickly hairs. "You see, babe, it goes back to something my father told me some years ago about women. He told me that it's impossible for a man to possess a woman. So I guess I figure that if you're here with me it's because you want to be. That's not something I can control. And when you don't want to be here there's nothing I can do in that situation either. If you wanna stay you'll stay and if you decide to go then you'll go. Ain't too much I can do either way should that situation arise. Those are things that are beyond my control and I've learned over the years that you can't worry about things beyond your control." James said as he rolled over and turned off the light on his nightstand glad to have wriggled free once again. There would be no CNN tonight.

Chapter 3

When a person gets ready to go there's nothing you can do about it. That's what he'd said; Alexis LeBrandt lamented as she stared out the big bay window across the Detroit city skyline.

"Well, we'll just see about that, Mr. James LeBrandt," Alexis smiled as she got up to shower and change before starting dinner.

She'd met a handsome young broker that definitely had his sights on her when she was in New York but aside from a dinner date or two the relationship had been purely platonic—well at least it had been for her.

Philip Dalton, on the other hand, seemed to have all intentions of pushing up on her regardless of her refusals. Still, she'd managed, though barely, to keep him at bay—well at least then she had. She'd come at him with the, 'I'm happily married thing', and when that didn't work anymore she simply asked him to stop calling. He ignored all of her weak rebuffs since their last meeting prior to her leaving New York.

Not only had he ignored her, he'd gone to the ends of the earth to let her know that he was more than just a little interested, sending roses, carnations and flowers she couldn't even pronounce to her office and arousing suspicion on a weekly basis until she finally had to call the FTD man and tell him not to waste his time since she would not be accepting anymore deliveries.

When the flowers stopped the e-mails started arriving on the average of five or six a day and she wondered when he could possibly have time to be this hotshot broker everyone was clamoring for if all he ever did was e-mail her. She even thought about calling the newly formed Homeland Security Department and reporting him to them since he had all intentions of messin' up her homeland security. Still, he refused to be dissuaded.

Now, in the six months since James had decided that he no longer required her services she'd grown not only tired but also extremely bored. And for no other reason than that she returned Philip's rather witty e-mails and began to wonder if maybe Philip wasn't just what the doctor ordered to break up the monotony that was becoming her new life in the post- James era.

Alexis LeBrandt hadn't really realized how much she depended on her ex-husband during their marriage but she was beginning to realize it now. She missed the evening back rubs and the foot massages and his easygoing manner that made even the worst situations seem bearable. She even missed his quiet but firm reprimands when she said something off-color or totally out of line to one of the kids. What she did not know then was that he was the balance, the only real stability she had in her life. Night-after-night, as she lay tossing and turning, unable to sleep as she had for the better part of the last month she also realized that those things weren't the only things she missed.

Right then and there, she knew she needed a plan to win her baby back but right now all she could be could concerned about was the e-mail that graced her lap top stating that Philip Dalton would be arriving at Detroit's Metropolitan Airport on Flight 704 at 8:30 p.m. The airport was less than an hour away from the hi-rise and she'd been so busy thinking about James that she hadn't even thought about what she was going to prepare for dinner.

In reality she had little interest in Philip when she was residing in New York and to tell the truth she really wasn't too particular about seeing him tonight but after the tips he gave her about a fluctuating market and the tip on the Wachovia stock splitting, dinner was the very least she could do.

Martha Stewart had just done a six-month stretch for committing the same crime and she was a White woman. Imagine what they would have done to Philip Dalton, the young, handsome, Black whirlwind if word had leaked of his sharing insider information. The Wachovia tip alone had netted her close to twenty grand and the stock was still growing. The way she figured it, twenty grand was worth at least one home cooked meal. Besides it was Friday night and for once she had no plans and would enjoy the companionship of both an intelligent and attractive young man. Furthermore, who knew just how valuable Philip could be down the road especially with her being a novice and all in the market.

What bothered her though was the fact that he hardly knew her and yet he was so adamant in his pursuit. God was he persistent. As strikingly handsome as he was with those tall broad shoulders, hazel brown eyes, and an I.Q. to match there was no question that he could have just about any woman he desired. And there were plenty of beautiful women at his beck-and-call wandering Manhattan's crowded streets.

Alexis wondered if her sole appeal was their age difference. Throughout history older women have always enamored young men. The idea that they were older and wiser and therefore knew the ropes in and out of bed was nothing new and had been around since the ancient Greeks. Perhaps that was it. But what really bothered her though was that he was one of the few men that she couldn't figure out.

At twenty-four he was hot, white hot, a supernova in an area where Blacks and Black men especially, were hardly visible. Along with the fact that he was both brilliant and handsome was only part of his appeal. The fact that he was being courted by some of the oldest and largest firms on Wall Street didn't hurt either. And then he was handsome to boot and traveling in high society was also a feather in his cap—at least to the womenfolk.

Why he'd chosen to pursue a middle-aged, married woman not only puzzled her but frightened her as well. That and the fact that he was the first man that *she'd* found herself attracted to in the entire time she'd been married.

Never, not once, had she ever even considered cheating on James in their twenty-year marriage. That was until she laid eyes on the boyish, handsomeness of Philip Dalton whom she just happened to meet while ordering a martini at Commuters Café in the World Trade Center before its untimely demise. She was having trouble getting the bartenders attention and was unsure whether she'd have time to get it down before her train arrived. Her anxiety must have shown and Philip, not one to see a lady wait in vain—especially a lady as fine as Alexis LeBrandt—summoned the bartender, placed the order for her, paid the tab and invited her to join him at his table. She'd been glad for the invite. Standing in front of a lecture hall for close to three and a half hours can be quite fatiguing especially in six-inch heels. And today for some reason or another she was truly exhausted. She only hoped that because she'd accepted his offer he wouldn't come off like some raving lunatic.

Instead, he was quite the gentleman, seemingly content to introduce himself and let it go at that. Surprised that he was so aloof made her inquisitive and it was not long before she was the one asking the questions she'd so hoped to avoid herself. It was just the thing that she hoped *he* wouldn't do and here she was all in the man's business.

Still, he appeared cordial and hardly seemed to mind her line of questioning and pleasantly surprised her with his honesty and candor. It seems, he'd graduated first in his class at Colgate at the age of nineteen gone to London for a year to travel and get his life together and ponder his future. Two years later, at the ripe old age of twenty-one, he returned to the jungle, as he liked to refer to Wall Street with a Master's degree in Corporate Law. First year back in the states he took the bar and passed it with flying colors. Now he worked for one of the oldest and largest brokerage firms in the financial district and was content for now but really didn't like the whole cutthroat scene that Wall Street posed. He'd been there for three years and was on a five-year plan, which left him two years to decide his next move, but ultimately he hoped that it would be in an overseas venue. He was crazy about London and hoped to return just as soon as he could with the hopes of working in some capacity or another in international banking or something or another along those lines.

Still, she listened and was quite impressed with this young man's vernacular as well as the fact that he like so many of the young people she came into contact with every day had a clear cut goal and plan for his life. He liked Hemingway and Hughes but wasn't opposed to a corny western by Louis L'Amour and had in effect read everything that the western writer had ever written. He was a jazz aficionado but enjoyed reggae and was crazy about that new wave of music coming out of London called drum and bass. She hardly knew what he was referring to by this point and was quite certain that she'd missed her train but felt not only renewed and invigorated by his conversation that she continued pressing hoping that he was in no rush to leave.

They argued, playfully, over Zane's worth as a writer and questioned the absence of Black male writers on the scene today. It was well after seven p.m. when Philip Dalton glanced at the Rolex on his wrist and acknowledged that he was running late for a previous engagement but would gladly continue their conversation over dinner the following evening.

They'd been chatting for over two hours and not once had she thought about calling home. That was something she did automatically if she knew she was going to be late. Now as she fished for the tiny Nokia cell in her bag she felt a pang of guilt she hadn't in her married life. How could she have forgotten? She smiled and remembered that she'd left the cell on her desk to recharge and was suddenly glad she had. Her attention returned to Philip and she wondered if Philip might be able to give her a little free advice on the stock market since that was his field of expertise. Maybe dinner might not be such a bad idea after all; she contemplated then quickly changed her mind.

Alexis remembered the conversation as if it were only yesterday and smiled at the thought.

"So, Mrs. LeBrandt, is it?" He asked as he gathered his laptop, coat, hat and gloves and began to put them on, his eyes never leaving hers.

"Mrs. LeBrandt is correct but feel free to call me Alexis," she smiled. "It was a pleasure meeting you Mr. Dalton and thanks again for the drink."

"Does that mean you're not going to even entertain the idea of sharing an evening over dinner with me?" He queried; his disappointment more than a little obvious.

Alexis rubbed the thumb of her left hand against her wedding band nervously. There was something that made the offer extremely tempting though she could not pinpoint exactly what it was that so appealed to her to say yes.

"I'm sorry, Mr. Dalton. That's not to say that I didn't enjoy our conversation but I don't know how I could explain my going to dinner with such an attractive young man as yourself to my husband."

"I'm sure you can think of something. If not, simply tell him that you've met a gentleman who just happens to be a broker that may be invaluable to us in our investing ventures. If you like bring him along."

"You are quite the surprise, Mr. Dalton. But my husband is quite my opposite and simply hates the idea of talking shop over dinner. But since you were quite the gentleman in inviting him then perhaps I might just reconsider your offer," Alexis smiled as Philip grabbed her coat and aided her in putting it on.

"Here's my card she said reaching into her overcoat. My office hours are between one and two. Call me then and I can let you know if I have some free time on my agenda. If you get my secretary just leave a…"

Before she could finish, a very tall, very stately woman of close to six feet and darker and more beautiful than any woman Alexis had ever the occasion to see in the entire time she had been in New York appeared before her. Alexis had to admit, that New York had some of the most beautiful, some of the most striking, some of the most glamorous and elegant women she'd ever seen.

After being in the city less than a month she'd finally come to grips with the fact that she hardly stood out anymore but was just one of millions. Now before her stood a woman that exceeded even those standards. Alexis stood speechless, her mouth open as she stared at the woman before her. She was striking. Suddenly self-conscious she gathered herself together as the dark woman with the closely cropped haircut kissed Philip on the cheek then turned to face Alexis and extended her hand.

"Naomi," she said.

Still speechless by the eccentric beauty that stood before her she somehow managed to take hold of the woman's limp wrist and shook it.

"Nice to meet you, Naomi," she managed to whisper. "Alexis—Alexis LeBrandt," she stammered.

The woman smiled widely showing the widest smile and most perfect teeth Alexis had ever seen.

"I just love your city," she continued. Her smile was as infectious as her personality. And now she knew why Philip hadn't jumped to attention the way most men did when they met her first time. Philip was playing ball in another league altogether.

Naomi continued her chatter going on and on about New York.

"It is such a vibrant place with so many sights to see—quite lovely—I must say," she added.

The accent was noticeable immediately.

"English, I take it?" Alexis inferred.

"Actually, I am Nigerian by birth though I grew up in London so I guess, yes, that makes me English. How could you tell?" she smiled, "...although there is considerable debate going on right now about foreign Blacks being considered English citizens."

Philip interrupted as he gathered his things together. "Did you have any difficulty with my directions?"

"On the contrary, I found your directions to be quite good. Although, I did get a little turned around Broadway. But I don't believe that had anything to do with your directions, Philip. It was more so with me staring at all those wicked buildings," she said turning her smile toward Alexis who was still somewhat taken back by the woman's beauty and charm.

"When I did get a little out of sorts and had to turn and ask somebody I found New Yorker's to be absolutely, *brilliant.* I have *never* met a people so polite and helpful. New Yorker's are absolutely the bloody best. They really are. Shall I tell you about my day?"

"Absolutely," Philip   added, "and by all means."

Seeing this as her way out Alexis extended her hand in an attempt to make her leave. With such a woman, Alexis's interest in Philip was aroused for the second time that evening but she hated being the third wheel and it was getting late.

"Well, Philip, you have my card, feel free to give me a ring when you have the time. It was exceedingly nice to meet you, Naomi. I do hope you enjoy your stay in our fair city."

"Oh, no! You mustn't go, yet, Alexis. I do so wish to talk to you. I've been here all of a week and all I've done is sight see and take rolls and rolls of pictures. I've yet to really sit down and speak with a New Yorker outside of asking for directions. I hardly have a sense of what makes you Americans tick. I'm sorry maybe I shouldn't have said that. I have been feeling rather cheeky though lately, a bit full of myself, you know. I guess I'm just tryin' to do too much in too little time. Sorry. But I would like you to stay and at least have a drink with us before movin' on. The que at the bar is not that long and we can sit awhile while Philip, dear, gets us a drink. You will be a dear and get us a drink won't you Philip? I haven't been to a pub since I left London and could really go for a Mai Thai. Philip is so watchful of every little thing I do that it's hard to do almost anything," she laughed. "Like an overprotective father…"

Philip   placed his coat and hat on the chair smiled at Naomi before making his way to the bar. Alexis smiled before turning to Philip.

"Mind if I use your cell, Philip? I left mine at the office and really need to call my husband and let him know I'm going to be late," saying it loud enough so that Naomi could hear and not get any misconceptions.

"No problem, it's in my coat pocket," he answered politely.

"He is such a dear, isn't he?" Naomi said pulling her chair up to the table.

"That he is," Alexis, commented, already sorry she'd accepted the young woman's offer. Upon Philip's return the conversation was light and from what she gathered the young woman was not only beautiful but also extremely bright, a good match for Philip and was only in the states for a few weeks. It seems Philip and Naomi had met at an Economics seminar while both were attending Oxford, became friends and after dating for some five or six months Philip had been invited to come and live with Naomi's family until his return to the states.

Her parents trusted Philip and were happy, to say the least, when he reciprocated by sending for Naomi to visit him in the states. They were no longer dating but she was still deeply infatuated with him.

Still, she commented. 'There is so much to do and see that she could hardly even contemplate marriage or children at this juncture in her life. Dating had been fine while they were in school. They were the best of friends and enjoyed each other's company. She enjoyed showing him her London but they had goals in and of each other and neither could see standing in the way of the other. So for the time being they remained the closest of friends.'

For some reason, Alexis LeBrandt felt relieved at hearing this admission and when Naomi was finished she again made her leave. This time she made it good. But the appearance of Naomi had only aroused her suspicions even more and though she was a flirt, a bonafide tease, who had over the years practiced her craft until she'd become something of an expert and though she had dismissed Philip's overtures she was flattered by his invitation to dinner. For the first time in a long time she felt something for a man aside from James and subconsciously hoped that he would call.

And call Philip had. So many times in the next several weeks that Alexis LeBrandt, the bastion of confidence, felt threatened. Not that he had been anything but gentlemanly and polite to a fault on their dinner date but frightened by the fact that she obviously felt attracted to this man that was young enough to be her son.

Truth of the matter was that Alexis LeBrandt was so adept at procuring whatever it was she wanted with some friendly conversation that often bordered on the obscene that she had most men eating out of her hand within a few short minutes. But when it came time for her to go to the next stage, which usually meant casual sex Alexis LeBrandt was at her best at wriggling free of the subtle but obvious overtures and not once in her twenty year marriage had she ever been anything but faithful which was what enamored and frightened her so much when it came to Philip Dalton.

She loved James. Of that there was little question. But familiarity breeds contempt. And over the years she'd not only grown content but also somewhat hostile when should could not get him to follow her lead and make the most out of the very boring, mundane life he seemed so content with, whereas Philip on the other hand, embodied everything she'd ever wanted in a man.

His career goals were clear and concise. From what she'd seen in the very beautiful Naomi his tastes and social life were not too shabby either. Smooth and sophisticated she fantasized about him often after their first date and seemed almost compelled to accept his next invitation.

On the Path train home that evening she caught herself smiling broadly and wondered what it was that had her feeling like a high school cheerleader on her first date with the captain of the football team. She was giddy though she couldn't understand why. She'd never felt like this when she'd been dating James. And later that night, when James threw that big paw of his in her direction and eased up on her she felt a vague sense of guilt, which worsened even more when he entered her already moist and throbbing chasm and she closed her eyes and saw Philip. She remembered jumping up from the queen size bed and rushing to the bathroom where she remained for the better part of the next hour sobbing gently and staring in the mirror wondering what in the hell she was thinking. That same night she came to the conclusion that she would not, as much as she wanted to, see Philip Dalton again.

The days following her decision, she was anything but happy. Ignoring his phone calls and erasing his voice mails before listening to them the days dragged on and instead of making her usual rounds after work, she bundled up and braved the cold February winds and made her way home and to bed where she slept fitfully until the following morning when she would once again drag herself to work and go through the motions.

As much as she did to dispel James' concern and assumption that he'd hurt her in some way she couldn't help but break down in tears each time he attempted to apologize. Her own guilt was eating away at her and when there was nothing else she could do to augment that nagging feeling of deception that was slowly taking control of her life she called the only person she knew that might be able to ease her suffering.

When Monica could offer nothing more than an I told you so, about always dabbling in unchartered waters and finally being dragged down by the undertow of her own indiscretions, Alexis LeBrandt made up her mind that it was time to make a career change and immediately began to test the waters in her hometown of Detroit.

The move proved a little too late, and she repeatedly cursed herself for being so impulsive in her decision-making, going against her very constitution, and allowing someone and especially a man half her age to remain rent free in her mind for more than the time she was in his company.

At first, being back home in Detroit seemed horrendous for Alexis LeBrandt though there was the possibility of becoming a big fish in a small pond, Detroit was no New York and had little to offer her culturally.

Refusing to be limited by the proposition of a city that was no more than a blue-collar mill town, posing as a city; Detroit seemed worse now than when she'd left twenty years ago. The unemployment rate was at an all-time high and Blacks seemed worse off than before the King years.

Still, not to be denied, Alexis LeBrandt pushed harder than ever to use Detroit as a launching pad for her career. Her disenchantment with the Motor City only drove her to explore the infinite amount of deferred dreams that often manifest themselves in middle-aged people with half of their lives behind them and only the thoughts of their ultimate demise ahead of them.

Pushing harder than ever and constantly comparing James with the young, Philip Dalton she spent less and less time at home and even more time hob-knobbing with the nouveau rich hoping that one day she would one day be able to jump on a plane and find her way to a chalet in the Alps or the French Riviera. Her dreams within her reach, her goals within the realm of possibility, Alexis LeBrandt abandoned James, the kids, and all the values she'd grown up with in pursuit of those very lofty and ostentatious goals.

Showering quickly, Alexis sprayed a light misting of Estee Lauder on her naked breasts and smiled. Rummaging through hundreds of garments it soon became obvious that even though she had a suit for every occasion she really didn't have anything suitable or appropriate for entertaining at home. When she and James had been lounging around the house it didn't seem to matter what she wore. A housecoat and a pair of flannel pajamas were her customary attire and she'd never even thought about dressing for James unless—well, she'd never thought about it. She thought about her friend, Monica's comments about men and their complaints about their wives and smiled. She wondered if James masked those same thoughts but there was no time to think about that now. She'd have him back in the fold soon enough and this time he'd beg her to stay.

It was true though. She went out, dressed to a tee everyday for the man and her students. But when she got home, well she'd never felt the need. She always assumed that he'd always be there and now that she was looking through her closet she realized that she didn't even own anything halfway sexy or entertaining or that could be enticing enough to be called eveningwear. Yet, he'd never said a word.

Well, nights like these would give her the time she needed to perfect her craft and despite her attraction towards Philip, James was her husband, the father of her children, and the only man she'd ever slept with. He was the only man she'd ever felt comfortable with and despite all of his shortcomings he was if nothing else, a good man and though he didn't know it at the time she would soon have him standing on his hind legs performing tricks for her again before this chapter was over.

The evening with Philip was only a precursor, a chance to perfect her craft without crossing the boundaries and a way to hone her skills for the only man she had ever really wanted.

Chapter 4

It had been close to seven months since she'd seen Philip Dalton. In that time she'd had a chance to get over him to put whatever it was that he possessed neatly in her round file of things to do labeled 'enigmas and other shortcomings' still waiting to be resolved.

Eventually deciding on the bone-white evening dress that hung loosely, and flowed when she moved, as if a brisk, northwesterly wind were blowing in off of the Great Lakes every time she took a step she glanced at her figure in the mirror hoping to convince herself that it was neither too sexy, nor too enticing and realized that everything she owned was either too sexy or too enticing.

Not wanting to prove too inviting though, she went easy on the mascara and decided it in her best interest not to wear anything more than just a foundation to cover those ugly crows' feet that were becoming more and more noticeable around the corners of her eyes in the last few years.

She still had no idea of what to do about dinner and thought about running down to The Fresh Market and picking up one of their rotisserie chickens she so adored and wondered if she would have enough time. Glancing at the clock and realizing she had little option she grabbed a pencil, jotted a short note letting him know she'd be back in a minute, grabbed her coat and headed for the door.

Returning home she breathed a sigh of relief that he'd not yet arrived but that was short-lived as he knocked no sooner than she'd gotten in the door. Dressed in a charcoal gray suit, black knit shirt and black suede loafers, Philip Dalton looked like anything but the Wall Street broker he was. She was used to seeing him conservatively attired—always in the traditional blue or black suit and beige London

Fog that led every one to distinguish the Wall Street broker as the countries, uniformed financial dictators.

She was weakened by his appearance and wondered why she had chosen once again to open up a can of worms when she knew that she had no answer for him. Still, she was glad she had and hugged him graciously—just long enough to let him know that he was missed and not too long as to know that it was more than anything but two old friends meeting after a brief hiatus.

"Lovely place you have here Alexis. But then I knew it would be. Knowing you I knew that it would be exquisite. I just knew that. It's really good to see you. I hope I'm not being too forward when I say this but you're even more beautiful than I remember."

He was grinning that little boyish smile that Alexis remembered so well from their first meeting at the café and Alexis grinned likewise.

"Thank you so much. You do know the right things to say to a woman don't you?"

"I don't know about all that. A few heartfelt sentiments that probably don't amount too much in your thesaurus of compliments coming from my gender I'm sure. Just the best I could do in your presence so awestruck am I by your elegance."

"Oooh, you do have a way with words, Mr. Dalton. Tell me more. It's been awhile since I've had a man of your intellect verbalize such things in such an eloquent manner. Sure beats a wolf whistle and 'I sho am feelin' them jeans, girl,' both laughed and Alexis continued, almost gushing. She was at that moment very glad she'd invited him to visit her while on his stay.

"You don't look too bad yourself," she continued trying to dissuade any further comments about her appearance.

"So how was your flight," she asked.

"Not bad, a little turbulence leaving the city, but nothing to speak of after a few martinis."

"Oh, I'm sorry. I forgot my manners. One of the things that comes with age. You have a tendency to forget."

Now. There she'd gotten the age thing in. She was working her 'thang' now. She had to keep him in her element and not let him dissuade her with those drop-dead good looks, eloquent speech and boyish charm. Had to keep everything on the up n up and on center stage where she could control things so things didn't get out of hand. He was playing in her ballpark now and one thing was for sure. There would be no home runs of any kind hit tonight.

"Anyway, can I get you something to drink? I know you must be tired after your flight. It's usually not the flight that bothers me so much as the preparation and the anxiety that comes along with it," she commented in an attempt to break the silence and make conversation.

"No, like I was telling you, the flight wasn't really all that bad. I hate to fly. Always have. Do you have any vodka?"

"Smirnoff's or Grey Goose?"

"Grey Goose is fine. Only a thimbleful. I love it but it doesn't always love me, and mixed with airplane food it could have me howling for half the night."

"So you ate?" She asked, half hoping that he had since the baked potatoes she'd just put in were going to take the better part of an hour to cook. She could have used the microwave but she never trusted anything that usually took an hour being done in a matter of seconds.

"Didn't really eat, just some peanuts. Couldn't mess up my appetite with you fixing dinner and all. I had about four bags though of those little salty beer nuts. I love 'em but they don't love me. Every time I eat 'em I pay the price but it's my weakness. What can I say?" He said smiling and unbuttoning the suit jacket and relaxing into the deep recesses of the leather sofa.

Handing him the drink as she sipped her own she smiled.

"Is that good?" Taking the glass from her hand his eyes still on her he mumbled, "Very good, very good indeed. In fact much better than I remembered," he said sipping the vodka and staring at her.

"So how many numbers were you able to acquire on this venture

Mr. Dalton? I'm sure every stewardess on the plane was fighting to service your section," Alexis grinned.

"You obviously haven't flown lately. I don't know where they're recruiting the help from these days but most of 'em look like they're just happy to be employed. Stewardessing used to be a pretty elite little job. I don't know what happened but the airline standards certainly have changed." He stated casually and rather matter-of-factly.

"After meeting Naomi, I should have realized that a mere stewardess would hardly meet your qualifications. How is she anyway?"

"Last I heard she was fine. I haven't heard from her since she called to tell me she'd arrived home safely. With her modeling career and working on her masters degree and all she doesn't have much time for anything aside from pursuing her dream. She's pretty driven but I assume she's okay. She's a very talented girl you know."

"I gathered that and very beautiful as well."

"Her real beauty is on the inside though. She has an innate inner beauty that few women possess. There's no gloss and floss about her. Everything that she is emanates from the inside. I guess that's why you two remind me so much of each other."

Alexis knew this was somewhere she didn't want to go but her curiosity would not let her avoid it. Once again he'd lured her in before she knew it or could do anything about it but she had nothing to lose. She was neither married nor on unfamiliar turf. She was at home and even though she was alone with this man she hardly feared him. He had too much to lose to put himself in a compromising position that would ultimately jeopardize his career. Besides there was no need for him to do anything stupid when he could have the most beautiful women in the world with just a wave of his hand.

What did frighten her about him was the fact that he held an almost magical spell, akin to a charm or some kind of voodoo hex that drew her into wanting to know more and made her feel queasy any time she got too close to him. The fact that he could get under her skin with simple conversation and leave her wondering, guessing and acting like a fifteen year old schoolgirl bothered her to no end. Always in control, poised and reserved she could feel herself being swept away by the gentle breeze of his unassuming candor again. And again she could not pull back.

"There is no way that you can compare Naomi a beautiful twenty-four year old woman whose future lies before her with a middle-aged mother of two whose seen better days."

"I hardly believe that any more than you do but I don't think we're talking about the same thing, Alexis. What most attracted me to Naomi when I was in London was not her physical beauty, the way she carried herself or her English accent, which I must say, I did find rather appealing. It wasn't that at all."

"Then what was it Philip?"

" I'm not exactly sure. London has some of the most beautiful women in the world. I hate to say that with the majority of the women there being White," Philip laughed. "Funny thing about London—there are no sistas—or brothas either for that matter. I saw this one brotha over there with an Oriental girl and I could look at him and tell he was from New York just from the way he was dressed but I still had to ask him where he was from. When he said Brooklyn I wanted to run up and hug the brotha. I mean that's how few of us there are over there. Like I said, there are no sistas. None whatsoever.

But the racism is so subtle or maybe I should say it's just not as blatant as it is over here that I guess I let my guard down after awhile and started seeing people as human beings. Here, I saw only Black women. In fact, here I felt like I was only allowed to see Black women.

In London I saw women. There were women from every country in the world over there, and it took me awhile to admit it, you know coming from the Big Apple and being unbelievably loyal, it really took a lot for me to admit that London is truly the center of the world and has the most beautiful women of any place I've ever had the occasion to visit. I mean beautiful and receptive as well," Philip said glowingly.

"And in the two years over there I'm sure you had the time to receive quite a few of them," she remarked wondering why in the hell she was being so smug, so childish, so mean-spirited and was almost sorry she had said anything.

Philip ignored the remark and continued as if she hadn't said anything at all.

"You'd be surprised at the opportunities that made themselves available for the taking but I guess the truth of the matter is that no matter how much I opened up; I guess I still felt the inherent effects of America cause I could never feel comfortable with the idea of dating a White woman whether it be England or anywhere else. I guess they've done a job on me. So, to answer your question Alexis I really didn't date although the opportunity was there for me to. I guess I just couldn't bring myself to do it. One day, maybe I'll feel differently but I can live with the decision I made. I just wish I could have made decision of my own free will but this shit is ingrained far too deeply. I've thought about that one a lot.

Still, if I *had been* dating frequently I might not have gotten the opportunity to meet Naomi. And that would have been a tremendous loss. I learned more from Naomi and her family than I could have ever learned at Oxford."

"You still haven't answered my question, Philip," Alexis mumbled as she curled her feet up under her on the loveseat facing Philip.

"I'm sorry. I thought I had," he grinned. "Grey Goose has that effect on me. It makes me ramble. Age I guess," he said smiling in an attempt to make light of her reference to her own age.

"What was it that you wanted to know?"

"You were saying that beauty was somehow not what drew you to Naomi," she muttered. "Then you went off on a tangent of sorts about England and the like."

"Oh, I'm sorry. What I guess I was attempting to say is that

Naomi and you have an inner-quality, an inner beauty that I find lacking and don't get me wrong, I know I'm generalizing, but too often I run across women after work in bars that are quite attractive to say the least and for some reason they feel like that in itself is enough to turn a man on," he said as he finished off the glass.

"And it's not?"

"Not hardly. I guess what I'm trying to say is that there are so many beautiful women out there that after awhile their beauty is not the major criteria for my choosing them. It becomes old hat after you've dated a few and become comfortable with yourself. It just seems to me that there's more than just trophy hunting, if you know what I mean. After awhile, you get to the point when you get tired of waking up next to Miss New Jersey, Miss New York, Miss Delaware and Miss Coal City, North Carolina and find that there's a significant lack of cerebral tissue matter. You start to wonder if in His creative magnificence and infinite wisdom God may have simply put good looks in its stead.

When I was younger and a novelty on campus because I was so young or maybe it was because I was an American and a New Yorker to boot the women would pretty much flock to my dorm room because I was, like I said different, an anomaly. I didn't really think about it much at the time and I must admit I had some fairly good times and was pretty active socially during my freshman year but by the time I was a second semester sophomore my priorities changed and I got tired of deadening my senses so that I could be comfortable with a slug in bed. I just got tired of the whole scene. I needed more."

"So you began dating ugly women with more cerebral tissue?" Alexis laughed as she poured Philip another glass of vodka and made her way to the kitchen to check on dinner. "Go ahead I'm listening."

"It's funny that you say that because I've found that many of the women that I've had the chance to meet that weren't exactly what you would refer to as knockouts had more to offer in an enrichment sense. It was like they didn't have their looks to fall back so they worked harder to improve themselves overall. I don't know if that's true or carries any merit but that's just the way it seems to me."

"And men?" Alexis questioned.

"I don't know. I don't date men." Philip laughed.

"I know that silly. I was just wondering if you thought that handsome men were also shallow since they could depend on their looks as well," Alexis asked.

"I don't know but since we're generalizing, I will make this comment about the men that I know. If I were a woman with anything going for me at all I wouldn't even bother to date," Philip said.

Alexis laughed out loud; loud enough for Philip to hear and he turned quickly following Alexis around the kitchen with his eyes.

"I'm sorry; did you need some help around the kitchen? I should have asked earlier but you had me so wrapped up in my own conversation that I didn't even think to bother to ask if you needed any help."

"No, I'm fine," she replied.

"You sure? I'm a pretty good hand around the kitchen."

"No, I've got this. Trust me it's not much, certainly not much for someone who's just traveled seven or eight hundred miles and been forced to eat beer nuts for the past two hours but I was running late and this was the best I could do on such short notice. I should be the one apologizing. But no, Philip, I don't need any help unless you can make these potatoes cook a bit faster."

"Don't worry about dinner, Alexis. I'm really not all that hungry anyway. I saw a few rather posh restaurants on the way here coming from the airport. If you like we can gout and grab a bite or we can order in. Chinese would be fine. Would you like that? It'd save you some time and some trouble."

"Wish you had said something earlier," she laughed as she stuck a fork in the still hard potatoes. "No, I'm just about finished now. Like I said it's not much. What I would really like is for you to continue telling me about men. I liked what I've heard so far but its funny coming from another man. Go ahead. Continue." Alexis said, nonchalantly still trying to poke a hole in the rock hard potatoes.

"I wasn't sayin' anything that might be considered profound. Like I said I don't know too many men other than those I work with and I make it a point not to socialize with those cats outside of work. I like to keep that on a professional level--you know--on the job, so I can't really tell you too much about men other than those I know are mired in mediocrity and are or at least seem willing to stay stuck there like pigs in mud and since I can't understand it and I don't choose to live that way I leave them alone because I've never been one to bite my tongue or hide the pity and contempt I feel for them so I basically leave them alone.

The only other man I know, outside of work and in depth, is my father and he epitomizes what a real man is to me. Aside from him there aren't a handful of men that I know personally that I can honestly say that I respect for the men they are. Now there are men all throughout history that have my utmost respect but very few if any that I come into contact with on a daily basis that I would give the time of day to."

Alexis laughed again.

"My sentiments exactly but you haven't told me why and I'm curious to know. I really am. You're a bright, well-traveled, articulate young man and I'm really curious to know why you would make such a generalization about men and be so adamant about it," Alexis challenged.

"Sounds like I hit a nerve."

"Not at all," Alexis replied. "I haven't said much because I am in almost total agreement with everything you've said so far and you've said it with such precise diction and made it a point to express your sentiments so well that you leave little or no room for me to expound on anything you have to say. You almost sound like a jilted lover," she laughed tilting her head back, as she laughed loudly at her own gruff attempt at being humorous.

"Women are not the only one's who are jilted," Philip replied.

"I guess the vodka's talking now and I am a bit bitter and I guess I am feeling a bit jilted but it's not been by a lover per se. It's life in general I suppose. I've lived in New York City or the surrounding area almost all my life and was told, no better yet brainwashed into believing that I lived in the greatest city, in the greatest country in the world. I walked around maintaining this arrogance that by being there apart of all of the hype that that in itself made me better.

I was always leery of traveling to different places when my parents asked me to accompany them when I was younger. But I looked at it from the point of view that nothing could ever measure up to New York and I didn't have the foresight that traveling in itself was a reason in itself to go.

Anyway to make a long story short, I finally convinced myself that I had had it up to here with the racism and anywhere I decided to go at the time was better than here and like I said I was shocked to go to London and find that it was light years better in that regard when it came to racism. Well, relatively speaking that is but more importantly I was shocked to find that the lies that had been sold me about the United States being the greatest place on earth were not necessarily true.

Don't get me wrong. I am patriotic to a fault. But different things appeal to different people for a variety of reasons. I'll give you an example. Stop me if I get longwinded and start to bore you," Philip laughed.

"Now you see why I tried to slow you up when you started pouring that last shot and here you are pouring another one."

Alexis, slightly tipsy herself, poured the vodka with reckless abandon.

"Stop! Stop! That's good right there." Philip shouted. "Are you forgetting that I still haven't checked into my hotel yet? Sometimes I have a tendency to get on my soapbox and get to preachin' and forget all about what I need to do, the time, and everything else I'm supposed to be doing. But let me just say this.

I have to preface what I'm about to say by telling you briefly

74

about my father. He's a literate man, an English professor who taught at Columbia briefly and authored or co-authored a few books in his time. My father loves the literary word more than he loves life itself. He loves the beauty of the written word whether it is Chaucer, Melville, Shakespeare, or Ellison. He loves the images and emotions that a man can evoke through language. But his love for the arts doesn't stop there. It covers the canvas. He enjoys de Tocquellville, as well as Picasso, and the great architects. I guess in essence he just has a love for beauty and the arts.

He follows politics like his life-blood depends on his staying abreast and reads four to five newspapers a day and can recite Poe as easily as he can King and Kennedy.

He can tell you about their lives as well as every writing by any black writer from Countee Cullen to Richard Wright and he's traveled pretty extensively and is as familiar with the history of the Jews as he is with that of the Japanese and while his brothers were buying the latest model Cadillac he was traveling to Paris, Johannesburg and Dakar. The whole time, I was watching and listening and questioning and wondering how in the world one man could possess so much knowledge. *I'm still wondering*. It's a tough yardstick to measure up to but there it is. That's my standard.

At the same time he's keeping up with what the Knicks and the Mets and the Jets did last night and I'm saying wait a minute. The next minute I'm arguing with him about Jefferson being a slaveholder and he's showing me the wisdom and brilliance of Jefferson, John Adams and Mark Twain behind their obvious infractions. Then I turn to my next door neighbors' daddy and the best he can do is try to grunt out the score of the Knicks game after just watching the damn thing for the past two hours. He farts, burps real loud, then laughs as if that were funny while the beer can falls to the side of the easy chair to join the other five and he nods off to sleep until the cute little girl young enough to be his granddaughter comes on television in front of the new Buick LaCrosse and he opens his eyes just wide enough to see her little skinny ass, grabs his nuts and decides it's time for a new car. Ask him who Melville or Twain are and the look he'll give you a look that will make you feel like you're the one in the bubble. Those are the way I see American's and especially men. Thick, obese, ugly, slug like beings; alive only because someone told them they were—with no goal in life except to eat and procreate and work so they can eat some more. It makes me angry just to look at them; to see them wasting they're lives away and so I leave them alone to play amongst themselves while I seek others like myself where good is not good enough and better can be better still. I seek those same attributes in a woman," Philip threw down the rest of his drink like a western gunfighter getting ready to draw.

Alexis stood, clapped, and cheered and Philip being the ham he was, stood and took a bow.

"Not that I deserved all of the applause but I thank you still." He remarked grinning.

"Said so well. So well Mr. Dalton. God, I wish my friend Monica could have heard you but I may have had to wrestle her down just to keep you in my company. She would have loved to hear that. We had almost the identical conversation just the other day. Don't think I'm trying to flatter or seduce you but you are truly wonderful. Beautiful, baby..." she said before he interrupted.

"Feel free to flatter and seduce me anytime, Ms. LeBrandt and if that's what it takes then perhaps I can come up with a better soliloquy to quicken the process. After all, it's been six or seven months since we first met and that's the first time you've uttered such complimentary words," he was smiling now and she knew that she'd used a bad choice of words in his regard but felt much more at ease knowing that they were at least on the save wavelength.

"Sorry about the choice of words..." she said.

"Don't be sorry," Philip   replied.

"I've just never heard it put quite so well and never would I have expected to hear anything like that coming from a man," she replied. "But everything you've said is so very true. I don't know if it's just applicable to men though. I know a lot of women who are mired in mediocrity as well.

It's a funny thing and I can't explain it even though I would have to agree with you about America though. I really don't think America is concerned with the pursuit of excellence anymore. Nowadays it seems like the goal is mediocrity. Mediocrity is in. That's why Obama is so damn popular right now.

While half the nation falls into a dark blue sea of melancholy and mediocrity the smart people are striving for excellence and using these unfortunate idiots out here to do their bidding and doing the dirty work that they feel is beneath them. You see it everywhere. People sit at home and eat. This country is the only country on the planet that has a problem with obesity. And do you know why?" Alexis asked.

"I'll tell you why," Philip said as he sipping the vodka slowly. "Because instead of Americans moving and doing and experiencing and creating they sit at home and gorge themselves and stare at the tube all day long as if they are gaining something or adding to the world around them.

Nine times out of ten, they are so lost in their own little ordinary lives they don't know a world exists around them. My trip was so enlightening in that regard. It let me know that there were other people in the world. They weren't like us, like Americans, isolated from the rest of the world and then isolated even more by choosing to stay in their homes glued to their TV's.

It's funny that you mentioned obesity. Because the whole time I was in London I have yet to see someone overweight; let alone people suffering from obesity. If any people should be obese, it should be the English since there's a pub on every corner," Philip laughed.

"All this talk about food is making me hungry," Alexis added. "If the potatoes aren't done yet then I'm calling out for pizza. That okay with you? I could put them in the microwave but I really hate using the micro. Just seems something wrong with x-rays cooking my food for me. I'm sorry. Just one of my quirks," she added.

"I hear you. I don't even own one myself. Never liked 'em. Same sentiment. Pizza's fine. I just hope it's good. No chains I hope."

"*What?* Like Pizza Hut or Domino's? Be serious, I lived in New York; still consider myself a New Yorker. Do you think I could ever lower myself to eating that slop again?"

They both laughed and while Alexis made her way to turn off the stove and make the phone call to order the pizza, Philip found the bathroom and relieved himself but never once did he look into the mirror and try to convince himself or wonder if Alexis LeBrandt was doable.

God he felt good. The Grey Goose warmed him to the bone and he hated the fact that he still had to check into a hotel but he knew as long as it took him to get an invite to Detroit that it would take her even longer to even consider his spending the night. He grinned at the thought and hoped that he could still make a good enough impression on her that the possibility of him spending a night or a weekend in the near future wouldn't be altogether out of the realm of possibility.

They returned to the living room at the same time and he caught her by the arm as she staggered to the side.

"Are you alright?" He asked his concern showing.

"Yeah, fine. I just called my girlfriend, Monica. She's a mess but I really want her to meet you. You'll have to excuse us but we don't get a chance to come into too contact with too many brothas of your caliber and I need to get her to look you over before I decide what I'm going to do with you," she said, the alcohol definitely talking now.

"You sure you're not calling her over because you feel like you need a chaperone?" He asked grinning.

"By no means if anyone may need a chaperone tonight it's you. You haven't met Monica, baby. And I can't remember the last time either of us had a man this close. Not a real man, anyway.

There are always plenty of dogs out there ready to pounce and chase after anything moving. Could be a bus passing and they're on it. Long as it has a hole, they're good to go. But a real down to earth, thinking—feeling man—now that's a rarity." She laughed but her demeanor changed quickly and Philip hoped that Alexis wasn't one of those people that drank and then got downright nasty and ornery.

"You've got a lot of bitterness and hostility when it comes to men. Is it because of the divorce?" Philip asked knowing he was treading on thin ice now but these things he needed to know and he knew of no other way to find out than to ask. Aside from that the thought of a husband or a jealous boyfriend interrupting an otherwise pleasant evening wasn't beyond his comprehension. Although he'd never had it happen to him the jilted lover shoots innocent man was a pretty common occurrence and never out of the range of possibilities, especially when involved with a woman of her stature.

Alexis LeBrandt was a bombshell. And Philip knew that men would often go to extremes to hold on to a woman as beautiful as she. To top it off she had her hand in every thing that could possibly turn a quick buck and she played hardball with the big boys. She was tough but there was always someone tougher and a simple miscue in her dealings could spell trouble not only for her but anyone connected to her. Although he hardly knew the intricacies of her personal and financial affairs he didn't want to be caught holding the bag when the shit hit the fan.

"My husband is a dear. You can't find a sweeter, more understanding man. He's a wonderful father but he is the epitome of all that you said when you were alluding to the typical man being mired in mediocrity. I guess you could call him old school. He believes in a woman being a mother—which I'd like to think I was—but he also believes in the traditional role for women. You know stay at home, mind the children, clean the house while he brings home a modest income. You know the deal. Go to Yellowstone Park during the family's summer vacation, feed the bears then come home and resume your housekeeping duties while he spends his time in the driveway changing the carburetor, the spark plugs or some other shit on the car. I'm not saying there's anything wrong with that. He just married the wrong woman. When I couldn't live up to my end of the bargain he decided it was time for me to go and gave me my walking papers.

We still talk, mostly about the kids and he seems content and worry free. I'm pretty sure that after awhile he'll find someone closer to his ideal woman than I am and we'll all live happily ever after."

"And you're okay with that?" Philip asked incredulously.

"Have to be," she said sipping another shot of vodka. "Well, at least until he finds his ideal mate then I'll probably snap the hell out and try to rip both their heads off," she laughed.

"And you don't hold any animosity towards him," Philip asked, surprised that she was taking the divorce so coolly.

"No I can't really say that I do. Rejection's not an easy thing for me to deal with. But To be truthful, I'm not exactly sure how I really feel or what I intend to do yet. It's really difficult at times being the person I think I am with this entire ego but for right now, I'm content, I suppose. Funny thing. When I was in high school, I was a cheerleader and every guy in school had the 'hots' for me. Anyway there was this one guy that asked me out from the time I was a freshman up until I was a junior. Eventually, and I guess because he was so damn persistent I agreed to go out with him but for whatever reason—he never did tell me—but I think it was because I wouldn't put out, he dumped me and I was crushed. I never really liked him but it ate me up that this boy dumped me, so I spent the better part of my senior year enticing him to go out with me again. As soon as he did I broke up with him. I'm having similar feelings now and I know it's childish and all but the worst thing about the whole ordeal—well, aside from adjusting to not being with someone you've spent your entire adult life with is the fact that they're not there in your life anymore—is the fact that you've been rejected. That's tough."

"I imagine it is." Philip replied.

"That and the fact that I'm not entirely comfortable being alone with a man since I've never been with anyone besides James." This was something she'd never told anyone and was surprised herself to hear this confession roll from her lips.

Philip, on the other hand, was elated to be making such headway; especially since she'd found the courage or the warmth between them to have finally gotten to the point where she could openly talk about sex to him. It was the first time in seven months even though they hadn't spoken for most of that time. Still, it was an admission that he welcomed and hoped to follow up on when the doorbell rang interrupting the mood.

Philip really hoped that it was the deliveryman with the pizza so he could pick up the conversation where they'd left off, but a tall, very attractive, heavyset woman appeared before him instead. She stood close to six feet and in her heels looked Philip straight in the eye when Alexis introduced them and he stood a shade under six-two.

"Monica, I'd like for you to meet one of my good friends. Philip's the young dynamo I was telling you about. The one that has all the ladies in New York so shook up they can't think straight. Philip Dalton this is my oldest and dearest friend, Monica Manning."

"Nice to meet you, Monica." Philip replied in kind.

"I can see why he's got all the girls panties in an uproar. Handsome devil ain't cha?" Monica said circling Philip and checking him out from the rear as well as from the front.

"Strong shoulders, good buns—let me see your teeth," she said finally completing the circle and peering over her bi-focals while rubbing her chin as if in deep thought.

"This Mandingo here—just might do," she said as if he were standing on the auction block. "What'll you take for him," she quipped. "Two grand? That's a pretty hefty sum for an uppity Negro. Boy looks uppity and sho nuff like a runner to me. Last five or six bucks I done had like him, all been runners. Can't understand

stand it neither. I always treats my niggras better than fair. And wit' respect. Hell, I feeds 'em, keeps 'em dressed pretty good and loves 'em just 'bout all da time. Ain't gonna hardly find a better massa or missus than me and dey still act like fools. I do declare. You wouldn't believe da luck I done had wit' my niggras dis year. Lost six so far and it ain't even March yet. Niggras ain't even had a taste a da fields yet. Mostly just lyin' up getting' lazy but somethin's spookin' em. Can't unnerstand it either. All I been doin' wit' da last few is tryin' to see if they can handle the task of breedin' my wenches so's I been testin' em out on myself to make sho and two or three days a solitaire confinement with me in da backroom a dey shack and here dey go up and runnin' fo' da hills soon as I turn my head. Got hounds chasin' two down—right now as we speak.

A lil' lovin' from me and dey gone. Just like dat. I swear dey don't make 'em like dey used too. Still and all, I guess two grand's a pretty fair price for a buck in his condition. Looks like he could be trained to be a pretty good breeder. Got all the physical qualities. Two grand is a hefty sum, fo sho but I guess it ain't bad for a physical specimen the likes of this ol' boy. Sho you won't accept seventeen five? I would feel a whole lotta betta with seventeen five if he got ta running before I broke him in good. No? Okay. Well, I guess I'll take him. Where do . 'on? Befo' I do that though I'm a gonna need to take him in the back to cneck him out thorough like. Gotta make sure everything's in workin' condition you know. Things ain't always what they appear you know. Won't take me long though. No more than about fifteen or twenty minutes dependin' on what kinda shape this here boy's in,"

By the time Monica had finished her charade all three were in tears.

"I told you she was a mess," Alexis said to Philip who was still in stitches.

"I would have never dreamed," Philip started to say before Monica interrupted again.

"You didn't tell me he was all that and a bag of chips, Lexis,"

Monica said interrupting Philip though her eyes never left him.

"Something's got to be wrong with him. He's too pretty. Sit down honey so the questioning can begin for real this time. You know Alexis's much too sweet and much too much of a woman to get down to the nitty gritty and I guess that's why she called me. I guess I'm the icebreaker. Now tell me honey, are you married."

Philip laughed at the woman before him then sat nervously as he was directed and watched as both women sat on the loveseat, all eyes on him.

"Don't be nervous, honey. I was sitting home alone as usual sipping a little Paul Masson when Alexis called and told me she had something for me—ummm—to see—not actually for me—so I'm a little tipsy but she seemed so enamored by you that I just had to come and take a look. When Alexis let's a man shake her rock, hard image I've got to come see what's up. Hope I'm not embarrassing either of you but I'm not in the presence of such fine, young men with any regularity so I'm gonna milk this one for everything he's got. Sure hope you're bringin' more to the party than just them Denzel good looks. I'm so tired of playa playas without all the goddamn good looks in the world and not an ounce of cerebral tissue that I could cry. You know sometimes God endures His children with an overabundance of one attribute and then denies them another. You have all your toes boy?" Monica asked grinning like a Cheshire cat.

"I believe so," Philip replied grinning nervously.

"You believe so? You mean you don't know? Alexis didn't I tell you not to get me out of bed for another good-looking mute. He's good lookin' sure but I don't do the mentally handicapped, baby. And this boy ain't even sure if he's got all his toes or not. Wrong week for me, honey. I do handicapped and mentally retards on the second week of every month. The twitchin' down there ain't quite that bad yet. Now let me ask you one mo' time. Are you sure you have all your fingers and toes?"

"Well yes, at least the last time I looked I did", Philip answered grinning, broadly.

"Well, at least he's not mute," Monica joked. "And damn he is cute. What's your plans for him cause if you just gonna string him along and play games with him like you do all the rest of them fools then you might as well give this one to me. The landlord comes up to on my way in the door tonight to tell me that we don't have any heat tonight. Coldest day of the year and the furnace is on the blink. I'm sitting up there freezing and had to drink a half a bottle of brandy to get the chill out my bones and you sittin' up over here in a heated apartment with a bed warmer that you don't know what to do with." Monica laughed.

Alexis was visibly embarrassed and apologized to Philip who thought the entire affair was quite comical. Just then there was a loud knock at the door.

"Hope that's not another one of your lady friends here to check out brotha man. If it is tell 'em we already have a panel in place. Now where was I?"

"You were asking Alexis what she was going to do with me because you needed a bed warmer," Philip replied almost in tears now.

"That is correct. You're okay Philip. A little young for my tastes but you'll do fine right through here. I see you've got a sense of humor and everything. I like that.

Now I don't want there to be any misunderstandings. Sometimes words get misconstrued and I don't want that to happen in this case because I couldn't stand another disappointment at this particular juncture in my life so let me break it down to you so there are no misunderstandings. A bed warmer is usually someone who warms a bed. That is true by the standard definition. In my case a bed warmer is expected to perform other functions that may be considered above and beyond the call of duty and in my case and since I am what polite men like to refer to as a full-figured woman, when they are trying to seduce me I may need to give you detailed instructions if you've never been fortunate to act as a bed warmer for a woman with my rather unique attributes."

Before she could go on to describe just what it was she needed, Alexis walked in with the pizza and three glasses of ice.

"Monica, I can hear you all the way in the kitchen. Would you please behave yourself? You're embarrassing me. And you can't tell me that you only drank a half a bottle of brandy when you're acting like this. I've known you since third grade and I've never seen you drunk and especially off no half a pint..."

"Who said anything 'bout half a pint? That was your assumption. When I said I drank half a bottle I was referring to half of the fifth I had. And it's still cold as hell in there with no heat.

Anyway, where was I, sweetheart? Its Philip ain't it? Well, Philip, I'm sorry. I don't usually act like this. I'm usually much more ladylike than this," she said smoothing the front of her dress down over her thick thighs in an attempt to appear ladylike for the sake of her friend. "There now. How's that? Better?" She asked glancing at Alexis for approval.

"Yes, that's much better," Alexis, said trying to hold back her own tears.

"Good. I'm glad that we're all on the same page. Now back to you, Philip. Are you married?"

"No." he answered still grinning.

"Then you must be gay," Monica, questioned her face serious as the four on Mount Rushmore.

"Monica!" Alexis yelled angrily, *"That's enough now. I'm gonna send your ass back over there to that apartment with no heat if you keep it up? Goodness! If I knew you were drunk and going to be downright obnoxious I would have left you at home to freeze. Now stop it. Do you hear me? I would never come over to your house knowing you were having company and try to embarrass you in front of them. Stop it. You're making an ass out of yourself,"* Alexis said the seriousness in her tone obvious in the furrow of her brow.

"Oh, girl you know I'm just having fun. I didn't mean to

embarrass you. If I did then I apologize to both of you. I really am truly sorry," she laughed. "Is that acceptable?" she asked turning to her girlfriend.

"Fine, Monica."

"Okay, again I'm sorry if I overstepped the boundaries—Mr. Dalton is it?" Monica asked.

"Philip's fine, Monica," he replied.

"Whew! Glad that's over. Now Alexis would you mind going into the kitchen and getting me some more ice and another Pepsi so I can explain the details of being a bed warmer and the intricacies of what a full-figured woman needs to make her feel truly satisfied. I really don't believe the needs are the same as for you little anorexic bitches and I'm not really comfortable sharing these intimacies with another woman around. Might want to wash a load of clothes while you're in there too since you're the only one offended by my little pickup routine. You see I'm not really drunk but I want Mr. Dalton—It is Mr. Dalton—to think I am in case he's one of those low lives' who thinks he can take advantage of a woman if she's intoxicated. I am tipsy Philip and I have been known to let men take advantage of me under theses circumstances so don't be shy. Just do with me as you please. Don't worry about being too kinky either. Kinky's fine. Actually the kinkier the better if it will somehow take my mind off of freezing in that icebox that's supposed to be my apartment," Monica said trying her best to hold back her own laughter, "In all seriousness though Alexis is not and I say this with all sincerity hardly ever infatuated or fond enough to talk about a man unless he is someone very special and she speaks rather fondly of you Philip and understandably so. She's everything that she said you are and if I wasn't her best friend I'd do my best to swoop you up and make you my boy toy if I could. I'm just as old and settled as they come but I read a lot of Zane and pick up ol' crass stuff like that and throw it out their every now and then so they think I know what the hell I'm talkin' about when I really don't know shit.

And since I hate being the third wheel I give you my stamp of approval, my certificate of authentication and my blessing that you can make my girlfriend open up her eyes and make a wise decision when it comes to a man like you with like values and interests. I hope she can see the light this time and I really truly hope you are the person you appear to be. She really does deserve some happiness in her life. And with that said I'm going to get my overnight bag out of the car and find the guest bedroom and call it a night. See you good people in the morning. You are spending the night aren't you Philip?"

Well, I hadn't planned on it. I made reservations at a hotel out by the airport," before he could finish Monica interrupted.

"*Nonsense!* Alexis wouldn't think of it and neither would I. There's another bedroom on the other side of mine. Grab your bags and follow me," she said staring past Alexis who was rolling her eyes callously to let her know that she hardly approved of letting a strange man reside in her spare bedroom but Monica looked right past her and pushed Philip down the hall.

"Think I'd better check with Alexis to make sure it's okay though," he muttered.

"Oh don't be silly! Here you've flown all this way to see her and you think she'd let you stay in a hotel. She's crass but I would like to believe she has more feeling than that. Tell him it's alright 'Lexis," Monica yelled.

"Certainly," she replied. "Couldn't have you stay in a hotel after traveling all this way," she repeated the smoke flowing from both ears.

"You don't sleepwalk do you, Philip? If you do; when you come out of your bedroom make sure you make a quick right and then another right. That would be my bedroom. Extend your left hand. Turn the doorknob. And walk right on in.   Don't worry, I'll guide you from there," she laughed.

"Don't worry about a thing darlin'. Just remember you're among friends and in good hands." Monica laughed. "I'm usually not this outspoken and I really hope I haven't embarrassed you Philip. You'll find me to be quite the opposite tomorrow. I'm usually really quiet and reserved—pretty laid-back. You'll see. Hope I didn't offend you," Monica muttered extending her hand as a peace offering.

"It was quite nice meeting you Monica and thanks for everything. Everything. I really didn't want to have to go through the rigmarole of having to check into hotel tonight." Philip said grasping the woman's hands in both of his.

"I know that. Alexis is sweet. I love her to death but she would never have asked you to spend the night. Proper protocol and all that shit. She really doesn't have that much faith in men. I guess it has something to do with the way they approach her. And over the years it's taken its toll on her. Made her a little cold and callous I guess. But she's got a good heart. You've just got to be patient with her. Give her some time. She'll come around. And if she doesn't and you get frustrated trying to wait her out just remember I'm in the next room," Monica giggled and headed for her room. "Tell her I said goodnight. You two need some time alone and I'm truly bushed. Tell her I said goodnight."

"Goodnight, Monica," Philip said placing his overnight bag in the room and heading back to the living room.

Alexis sat on the loveseat in the same position he left her, holding her head in her hands and staring into space.

"Did I interrupt you?" Philip inquired.

"No, not at all. I was just wondering what I was getting into." She replied.

"I don't understand."

"Neither do I. Here I am a forty two year old woman who thought I knew men and I feel like a little schoolgirl with a crush. It's just not me. I hardly know you and here you are spending the weekend with me. I've never slept with another man besides my husband and here I am contemplating making love to a man half my age—a man young enough to be my son.

I usually take pride in playing my cards close to the vest and always being in control and here I am sitting here spilling my guts.

I can't believe this. I have students your age." Alexis sighed, took a sip of the vodka and continued her confession. "Funny thing about the whole thing is that I've never felt like this before. I made it a point not to. Always thought that falling in love and all that was for syrupy little tarts. I guarded myself against that. Always regarded love as weakness and I've always been one to pride myself on being strong. And I still don't know why I feel like this. Maybe you can fill in the blanks. I sure hope so and I suggest you start now. *Right now!* At this very moment I'm torn between grabbing you by the hand, leading you down the hallway to my bedroom and throwing your ass out for making me feel this way. I don't know this feeling and until I can come to grips with it I'm not sure that throwing you out is not the better option. So, for your sake I hope whatever you have to say at this point Philip is pretty damn convincing 'cause it is cold out there." Alexis hesitated. "I believe I was finished," she said staring past Philip at nothing in particular.

"I really don't know what to say," Philip replied.

"For a man that can articulate better than any man I've ever met I suggest you say something before your ass finds itself at the Radisson."

"I don't know what you want me to say, Alexis. I've never been put on the spot surrounding my feelings for someone before. Didn't ever have to give an itemized list of the reasons for me wanting to be with someone other than that there's a connection; a stirring within me that makes it hard not to be around you. Whatever it is and like you I haven't pinpointed exactly what it is—it won't allow me to function at my usual capacity. So, I felt compelled to come see you to have those same questions answered so I can continue living my life as I used to. I spend half my day thinking about you and I don't even know you. My productivity at work has diminished and I'm no closer too answering those questions than you are. I thought maybe spending some time with you could answer some of those questions," Philip paused briefly and stared over at Alexis looking for some sign of compassion anything.

"I've never been in love Alexis so I'm not sure what it is. But from what I understand and the feelings that I've had as of late, and am experiencing at this very moment there's a chance that maybe for the first time in my life, I may be.

I'm not real sure if I've articulated my feelings in a way that would ease the way in which you feel about me but if I need to get a room until you find out and can put some of this in order then that's fine. Just do me a favor and sort it out so that I can understand what's happening as well. I guess what I'm trying to say is that whatever you do, keep the line of communication open so that I'm not in the blind. I need to know what's happening as well. Now, if you would still like for me to leave, then I'll do just that. That is if you're sure that's what you really want me to do."

Alexis LeBrandt looked up into Philip's eyes and a shudder went through her entire body. Bending to kiss her she placed her hand in front of his face and turned her head to the side to avoid his kiss.

"I think it best you leave Philip," she whispered.

"Are you sure that's what you really want," he replied not at all taken back by her rejection.

"That's what I want," she replied holding firm to her resolve despite the weakness she felt in her knees and lower torso.

"I'll be here for the weekend. Perhaps we can have dinner tomorrow," he said, as he went to the room to grab his overnight bag. "Will you be a doll and call me a cab?"

"It's on its way," she replied.

"And dinner?"

"Call me tomorrow and we'll talk about it. Right now all I want to do is sleep. I don't want to even think about what tomorrow may bring."

"I'll call you tomorrow, Alexis," Philip said as he made his way out the front door. "Sorry, if I've done anything to upset you," he said apologetically.

Alexis did not bother to answer and closed the door behind him, putting the double latch and bolt lock on before heading to the bathroom door and slamming it behind her.

A loud, clear strong, voice rang out in the darkness.

"I told you to make a right darlin! I'm right here! Come on in," came Monica's voice amidst peels of laughter. *"So that's your weakness. You can't follow simple directions. I knew you were too perfect,"* she said laughing at her own attempts at humor.

"Monica, hush, before you wake up the neighbors. Ain't nobody here but me," Alexis screamed from the bathroom.

Monica laughed.

"Don't you think I knew that? You don't *honestly* think I'd invite your man into my bedroom and I'm nothing more than a guest at your house. Now, if the roles were reversed and we were at my house—well then—that might be a different story. Besides, it's too goddamn cold out to be getting thrown the hell out over some man. You know I'd never do that anyway. Men are a dime a dozen but good friends are hard too find," Monica said turning over and looking for her cigarettes on the nightstand.

Sitting up in the bed she pulled a Newport from the pack, lit it, inhaled deeply, then turned the pillow to the cool side and stared at her friend who seemed a lot older than she did earlier that evening. Alexis who usually looked a good ten years younger than forty-two seemed to have aged right there before Monica's eyes and it was obvious that something was wrong.

"You put him out didn't you?" Monica asked knowing full well that Alexis had. That was her m.o. Lure 'em in and then just when they showed some interest and looked like they were willing to go to the ends of the earth for her she cut 'em off like a sport fisherman who loved to fish but hated the taste of seafood.

"What was it this time? Too bright or too young? Damn girl, the boy had everything in the world going for him. I sat there in the living room and tried to find some flaws and couldn't. Did it just to show you that maybe this was the one," Monica said breathing a deep sigh of relief.

"C'mon 'Lexis! Don't you want to be happy? You know just last

week I was reading an article in Essence or Esquire. I can't recall which one it was right now but that's neither here nor there. The whole article was about how some people enjoy being miserable. They actually derive pleasure out of being in pain, all the time. I am seriously beginning to believe that that's your calling in life. I'm beginning to believe that you get some pleasure out of being miserable. It's almost as if you enjoy walking around with that fake smile when inside you're just waiting for something to go wrong so you can say I told you so. Life's a bitch and then you die. Is that what you do?"

"I don't know Monica. I really don't know what the hell's wrong with me. I guess I've just been hurt so many times by so many triflin', no-good, low-down, dirty dogs posing as men that my defenses come up before I really even give them a chance, anymore. I don't know," Alexis commented as she found a spot on the edge of the bed.

"Please! Don't forget that I know you Alexis. I'm not just some newborn that happened along in the middle of the picture and doesn't know what time it is? Remember, that I've known you all your life and nothing's changed in the entire time we've been friends. Ever since that kid—you know—Mr. All-Star Basketball Sensation—dropped you when you were a freshman in college and you came home crying and actin' all suicidal; you've run anytime someone gets close to you. Since then—and that was almost twenty years ago—you have never let a man get close to you. And in comparison to the shit that I've had to endure with men I must say in all fairness that you've had some pretty decent prospects who were willing to do anything including lick the soles of your feet just to be in your company. And they're a whole lot better than anything I've had the chance to come across that's for damn sure. And most of them were sincere or at least they appeared to be. But you'd never know. You chased them away before they even had a chance to make some noise. Am I lying, 'Lexis?" Monica said as she ground the cigarette out in the ashtray.

"No, you're not lying," Alexis managed to whisper.

"So, don't ever mention anything about you wanting a good man and someone to love you for you when you start running like Flo Jo every time they come within striking distance. You don't want a man or a relationship all you want to do is bitch about what you don't have. I know women—myself included—who would die for some of the opportunities that you've tossed to the curb. Now tell me. What is wrong with Philip? The man has called and sent you roses and e-mails ever since you've left New York and even flown to Detroit to see you and you go and throw him out.

I can understand the situation in New York with you being married and all but from what you've told me about your relationship in New York Philip never even attempted to cross the line. From your own account he was nothing short of a perfect gentleman."

"That he was," Alexis agreed.

"And who told him you were divorced? I mean it wasn't on public notice like Bobby and Whitney when they decided to throw in the towel. *Please* tell me how he came to find out when he's in New York and your ass is here in Detroit," Monica asked visibly angry now.

"I told him," Alexis muttered.

"*No shit, Sherlock!* And why in the hell was it so important that you let him know this bit of insignificant bullshit unless you were opening the door to his inquiries?" *You had to know that's what you were doing,"* Monica screamed.

Alexis dropped her head in acknowledgement.

"Yeah! You knew what the hell you were doing but do you know why you did it?" Monica asked hoping to find an answer for the bizarre behavior. But there was no answer forthcoming.

"No I guess you really don't know why you do the things you do. You really don't know why, do you, 'Lexis?"

When after several minutes there was still no answer forthcoming Monica proceeded.

"I'll tell you why you told him of the divorce, 'Lexis and you may hate me for saying it but after watching you over the years sometimes I wonder how you've managed to stay alive this long. Somebody's gonna sho' nuff kill yo' Black ass one of these days. I'm tellin' you this not only as a friend but because I really and truly hate seeing what you're doing to some awfully good brothas out there. I know that if I'd been in a couple of their shoes; I would have whooped your ass a long time ago. Trust me girlfriend. You're living on borrowed time as it is. You can't walk around and treat people like shit because of your own inadequacies and expect them to respond favorably to whatever you do or say. Do you feel what I'm sayin', 'Lexis?"

Alexis shook her head in agreement almost as if she were afraid that if she looked her friend Monica in the eye she would turn into a pillar of salt. Yet, she listened.

"You can't continually treat people like shit, 'Lexis, just because it's happened to you. Hell, it's happened to me numerous times. It happens to everybody. That's life, honey. That's just the nature of the game. It is what it is. But you're not supposed to grow bitter and dish it out before it hits you. You're not supposed to look for the hurt and defeat, sweetie.

Each time you set foot out the door, you're supposed to be putting your best foot forward and hoping if not expecting to bring back the crown jewel. If you go out there expecting to lose and be hurt or dish out some pain on some unsuspecting innocent like Philip then you might as well keep your ass in the house, baby," Monica mumbled as she pulled another cigarette from the half empty pack.

"I guess you're right, Monica," Alexis said, hoping to end the conversation right then and there.

"Well, if you agree that I'm right then why is your ass still sitting here? You know as well as I do that the only reason you put Philip out was because he was starting to get to you. You know as well as I do that you were feeling something for the man that's why you invited me over here in the first place. You just wanted me to see first-hand what had you squirming in your chair over for the past seven or eight months," Monica laughed, hoping she could lighten the mood.

"But he's so young. He's only a couple of years older than Chris," she said looking for an escape clause.

"Ain't nothin' but a number, baby. That man's been places you only wish you could go," Monica laughed.

"But..."

"But hell! Splash some water on that tired mug of yours and find something provocative and get your ass down to the Radisson before he finds someone else to replace your ol' tired ass," Monica laughed. "Shit! It wouldn't have been me. I would have put your tired ass out and been hollerin' when he stepped through the bedroom door. Would have been doin' jumpin' jacks and bends and thrusts and every other aerobic move I knew to get into position for that beautiful specimen of a man. The whole time you were tryin' to throw him out I was in here thinkin' of how many ways I could let him in. There wouldn't have been an orifice untouched when he left. I would have been like; did you try this one yet, baby? Let's see if we can squeeze it up in here," Monica laughed at her own joke and got up pulling her robe around her large frame. "C'mon, you simple heifer, let's go see what you've got to throw on that says I'm sorry for bein' a dumbass."

As much as Alexis wanted to reply she knew that Monica was right. She didn't need Monica to tell her or to rub it in. She knew as soon as Philip left that she'd made a mistake. She was regretting it already and rushed at the attempt to find something appealing to curtail her having to formally apologize for being as Monica so aptly put it a dumbass.

Alexis thought about wearing the white outfit, that James used to like so much but decided against it since she deemed it to formal and dinner—well—what had amounted to dinner was over and it was quickly approaching ten o'clock and whether Monica called it a booty call or not she was not going to some man's hotel room looking like she was on a mission from Satan whether she was or not.

Late night rendezvous' were not her thing so she stepped back and put a touch of makeup on while Monica shuffled through the closet looking for something she deemed appropriate for such an occasion.

"Damn girl, as crowded as this closet is there's not a damn thing in here that gives a hint of anything but power lunches and business dinners. It's like someone took the word fun right out of your vocabulary and out of your wardrobe too. *What the hell has happened to you*? This ain't like you," Monica commented as she rummaged through the closet.

Alexis LeBrandt shrugged her shoulders in a gesture of futility and dreams gone astray. Monica ignored the gesture and continued on her mission to find her girlfriend something suitable before she lost her nerve and changed her mind.

"Oooh! This is cute! Looks like a little Barbie doll outfit. What size is this—about a two? I couldn't get my left leg into this thing but it is cute," Monica commented as she pulled the little black, skin-tight, spandex outfit off the hanger. *I ain't never seen you in this before,"* Monica beamed.

"And you never will," Alexis shot back grabbing the outfit from her girlfriend's hand.

"Oh, stop being such a little futty dutty, 'Lexis. **You** obviously bought it for some special occasion. I don't know what it was but there ain't no sense you letting it go to waste."

"I bought it for James. Something to wear around the house to spice things up a little is all."

"And I'm sure it did," Monica laughed.

"But that was then and this is now," Monica retorted. "James is history and if this 'lil ol' rag could arouse the fire in James with his old tired self just imagine the response you'll get from Philip. *All you've got to do is throw it on and stir the embers, honey. Then just sit back and watch the fire burn. Just stir the embers baby,"* Monica chuckled.

"I am not wearing that hoochie mama outfit outside of this house in front of any man that's not my lawfully wedded husband,' Alexis protested.

"And how pray-tell are you going to get him to be your lawfully wedded husband if you don't stop being so damn uppity. You know what they say nowadays, honey. It ain't all in what you know it's how well you blow. Well, at least that's what they tell me but then you sure can't go by me," Monica laughed. "I've taken all the advice that one woman can take on what it takes to get a man and still ain't got one," she mused. Tried sex therapy, aromatherapy, counseling and sodomy.

I sat with a group of suffering, desperate, women just like me, for six months trying to overcome our sexual phobias and learn what it takes to please and keep a man. And when it came down to it in the end; here we were, twelve desperate women with bananas and other phallic shaped instruments in our hands, repeating a mantra that went a little something like this. "Do you want the man? How bad do you want the man? Well, then sistas you know what you gotta do. You either gotta blow or you gotta go. Now how bad do you want the man?

We'd all sit around and laughing and chanting as we sucked on bananas and cucumbers and all kinds of other wild shit but we learned not to be so damn stuck up—you know—so damn puritanical. And I'll tell you something. After Marshall it wasn't nearly so hard for me as it was for some of the ladies simply because now I had a choice as compared to when Marshall was around. When Marshall was around I had to because he said I had to. Now I did it because I chose to and because, hell—to be honest, honey I probably like sex and a little lickin' and suckin' as well as any man out there— that is—if it's done right. Do you feel me, hon?" Monica added.

"Monica! Lord knows, I don't know what's happened to you since I left town but you are as certifiable as anyone I've ever met. No wonder you and Marshall got along so well. You're both crazy as hell. Now you're up here trying to dress me up like 'Supa Ho', and send me out to the wolves so I can get my brains fucked out and I'm supposed to like it. Is that what you're tellin' me?" Alexis laughed as she fumbled with the zipper that was so tight she was sure she was going to zip herself up in it as well.

"Here, stand still, girl let me fix that mammy-made do of yours," Monica said as she put the finishing touches on her friend's hairdo.

"Damn you look good, sweetie. I ain't never really given it much thought before but you'd better count your blessings that I'm strictly dickly. I'm serious, 'Lexis. The way you look tonight you might even turn a few women's heads. I swear girl, if I *had a shape like yours, spandex would be my middle name."* Alexis was forced to laugh at her girlfriend's comments.

"Do you really think it looks good? Actually, you wouldn't believe where I found it." Alexis grinned.

"Probably at some little boutique on 5th Avenue when you were up there in the big city hob-knobbin' with the big wigs," Monica replied as she brushed her girlfriend's bangs to the side and out of her face. "There, now that's better. Sexy, but still with an air of innocence. You look ready for anything but the bangs give you an air that says you're still somewhat reserved. I learned that while taking this beautician and cosmetology class," Monica said matter-of-factly.

Alexis laughed.

"Is there a class that you haven't taken?" She asked while Monica put the finishing touches on her makeup and outlined her bottom lip in black lip liner.

"Not really. Actually I'm glad I did. Gives me a chance to put some of the things I learned to work even if I have to do it vicariously. There now—how do you feel? Do you feel like you can have any man in the world right now?"

"I wouldn't say all that," Alexis mumbled in an attempt to be gracious if not humble.

"Well, you can," Monica said in an attempt to bolster her friend's ego.

"You know Monica, getting a man has never been a problem. It's keeping them that's been an enigma to me," she said.

"Well, you're not alone in that regard but we'll cross that bridge when we come to it. Right now you need to get a move on. It's getting late and we don't want Mr. Dalton to fall asleep on you or pick up someone on the rebound. Isn't the Radisson that Five Star Hotel where they just opened that new jazz club?" Monica asked.

"I believe it is," Alexis replied.

"Girl, you'd better get out of here before he gets to wandering around and finds himself someone who doesn't have your hang-ups about men," Monica chirped as she pushed Alexis towards the front door. "If I wasn't so drunk I'd tag along and see what that clubs all about."

"Maybe you should."

"No, then you'd have a reason to cut out early and knowing you, you'd find a way to come downstairs for something or another. And trust me I don't need any help when it comes to men unless you've got the secret to making them stay put and I believe you said that was one of your shortcomings too. Now go on, get out of here. Time is of the essence. Especially in your case. How old are you now, anyway?" Monica laughed closing the door behind her. "Good luck, sweetie and don't be afraid to let your hair down. Just remember, it only hurts the first time."

No sooner than Alexis was out the door Monica began dressing too. The idea of a jazz club could only mean one thing and that was a mature crowd and a mature crowd meant men. Pouring a shot of tequila she rushed to the bedroom and threw on the outfit she was saving for tomorrow and headed for the elevator stopping only long enough to make sure that Alexis hadn't had second thoughts and wasn't milling around in the hallway or down in the lobby. Seeing that the coast was clear, Monica winked at the doorman and headed for the brand new red Volvo illegally parked in front of the exclusive, East Side, hi-rise.

Chapter 5

If there was one thing Monica hated more than anything about the Detroit after hours scene it was the crowds and commotion and nerve wracking congestion that always seemed to be a necessary but unwelcome part of the whole ordeal. A block away from the Radisson the traffic was already congested beyond belief and it wasn't even eleven o'clock.

With all the urban renewal supposedly taking place in the inner city as a way of rebuilding downtown you would think that someone—anyone connected with the downtown revitalization, hauling in those six figure salaries and calling themselves city planners would have had the foresight to foresee this logjam. It was the same everyday as Monica fought her way to get to work but tonight was especially congested in part due to it being a Friday night and the club just opening a month or so ago.

In another month the in-crowd would have moved on to the next newest craze and the Radisson's jazz club would be what was intended initially; a jazz club for the jazz aficionado. But not tonight. Tonight the Radisson was the place to be and Monica only wondered why it had taken her so long to happen along.

She made it a point to go out once or twice a week to expand her horizons and her circle of friends. One week it was Oprah's book club, the next she was taking ballroom dancing lessons at the Latin Club downtown. When she wasn't learning the cha-cha or the rumba or the Latin hustle she was areobicizin' it at the YWCA or volunteering her time with the Friends of the Library. But ever since she was in grade school and she heard Debra, Hubert and Ronnie Laws taking turns on flute, Monica had been in love with woodwinds. She loved jazz. She loved the fact that she could listen to the same exact piece time after time and find little nuances the next time that had completely escaped her on her first listening and become enthralled all over again as if she were hearing the piece for the first time. That was the beauty of it. And six weeks or six months later that same piece would hold something new and fresh and endearing and she often wondered why she hadn't heard it that way before. From the Law's she went to Jimmy Smith and then Coltrane and Miles stockpiling records as she went and wondering how come her peers could not see the ornate beauty and intricacies that was jazz.

She had always been alone in her love for the music but she hardly seemed to mind. Being alone was nothing new to her and she knew that when she entered the Blue Note at the Radisson that she would again be alone with just her love for her music to keep her company. She assumed from the crowd of pedestrians that passed her on the busy sidewalk while she sat in traffic, horns blowing madly in the cold Detroit air, that most of those passing by on their way in with their two piece Versace suits and shirts made of Egyptian cotton weren't there for the music anyway but only because it was the latest chic spot in town.

Most of the jazz clubs she'd been to were like that. She remembered visiting 'Lexis in New York only a couple of months earlier and venturing out on her own to the Village Vanguard down somewhere in Lower Manhattan to catch Oscar Peterson. A longtime fan of the now elderly pianist, she'd never been quite that excited and was even more elated to find the line a block and a half long to see the world renown pianist who happened to be one of her favorites. The line had moved quickly and before she knew it she was out of the frigid February air and in the warm confines of the Vanguard waiting patiently for Mr. Peterson to emerge.

At the time, the crowd had been relatively subdued. Well, at first they were. By the time the second set had rolled around the liquor was in full effect and she had to strain just to hear him play. By the time, the pianist had started into the second song of the set it was hard to tell who was more discouraged by the crowds rudeness, she or the musicians on the tiny bandstand. She remembered wanting to jump up in the middle of the crowd and tell them all to, 'shut the hell up' but thought better of it and simply grabbed her shawl and left. The next day while leafing through the media guide of the paper she noticed a small musical review where a music critic who was also in attendance remarked on the unruliness and impoliteness of the crowd in the midst of such greatness.

For Monica this was nothing new and for a time she hadn't bothered to go at all but hell, who was she hurting but herself and so she continued her forays into this hole in the wall and that and often came away feeling like the more dilapidated and out of the way the joint was, the more astute and polite the crowd was. And it made sense.

Those that really loved the music for what it was had no problem searching every nook and cranny and every backwoods dive to pay homage. But those that weren't interested in hearing the music and were more interested in being seen themselves wouldn't be caught in a back alley juke joint. No, the Radisson was the place to be. It was Detroit's new hot spot and the word jazz just gave it an air of authority since jazz was cool thus making anybody associated with it 'cool'.

Watching the thirtyish looking crowd full of youthful verve and mindless chatter pass by her Monica wondered how many of them had ever heard of Dizzy or Groove Holmes or even Duke Ellington for that matter. Say jazz and they think Kenny G and Boney James. What the hell do they know? It was at that very moment, a moment of condescending clarity that Monica considered turning the car around right there in the middle of the street—traffic cop or no traffic cop. Catch me if you can, she thought, smiling to herself. But her smile was quickly replaced by a scowl when she realized that she could neither move forward or backwards—let alone make a U-turn. For all intensive purposes She was stuck and seeing no alternative course of action she inched forward at a snails pace along with the cars in front of her until a mere thirty minutes later she found herself in the midst of a host of flashing lights and sirens the like of which she'd never seen before.

She'd been sitting there the entire time and hadn't noticed anything unusual and she thought she'd seen everything. Then just like that, in a tear of screaming bedlam, sirens and flashing neon lights surrounded her like she was Pablo Escobar.

In truth, they weren't actually surrounding her but it sure as hell felt like it. There were so many police appearing out of the clear blue that it seemed like they were surrounding her. It was either that or the president's motorcade was arriving.

In any case, they were everywhere and whatever it was that was going on, one thing was for damn sure; what ever lay up ahead had to be a tragic situation at best. Inching forward gradually, the scene thickened and it was not long before she noticed several ambulances in front of the hotel. 'Black people', she thought to herself.

An officer stood in the middle of the street diverting traffic away from what was obviously turning out to be a crime scene from what she could ascertain. Approaching slowly, Monica rolled down her window as the policeman gestured for her to make a right away from the melee. When she was close enough she stuck her head out of the window and inquired.

"What happened?"

"Hard to say," he said. "Looks like a shooting but we're not really sure at this point."

Monica was shocked. *A shooting?* A few minutes earlier and she could have been right there, smack dab in the middle of all of the hullabaloo. For once she was glad she'd been late and then it hit her like the crushing blow of a sledgehammer against a sheetrock wall and everything inside her crumbled. The idea that 'Lexis was in there, in the thick of the shit, in danger and possibly a victim raced through her mind.

'My God! What if something's happened to her? It's all my fault. I'm the one that insisted on her going. She didn't really want

to go. I had to insist. What was I thinking? I can barely run my own life, let alone give somebody some advice on how to run theirs. I should have kept my mouth shut and minded my own business but when have I ever been able to do that? When? I should have known better. As much shit as I read in the papers these days about the crime and violence right here in the downtown area you'd think I know better than to expose my best friend to this shit. Hell, nobody's safe these days. Nobody's immuned to the madness. Oh my God! What have I done? Lord, I hope nothing's happened to my girl?'

Monica swung the Volvo around in the middle of the next block, despite the police doing their best to divert traffic, found a parking spot, then rushed hurriedly around the corner hoping that all her fears and assumptions would prove false and 'Lexis would be laid up with Philip in some suite oblivious to all the goings on around them. That was the best case scenario.

Arriving at the front of the hotel moments later, Monica encountered a police blockade. A tall, handsome, young Black patrolman stood on the outside of the police barricade, a radio in one hand, barking orders for everyone to disperse but his orders fell on deaf airs as the throng of people moved forward pushing against the blockade in hopes of gaining entry. He had his hands full—that was for sure--but little did he know that he hardly had experienced anything. Monica was approaching quickly with only one thought in mind and that was that her girlfriend was someone in that hotel and for all she knew was in grave danger or—God forbid—maybe even... No, she couldn't think like that—couldn't even entertain such a horrible thought. Anyway, she didn't know what the proper procedure was but one thing she did know was that she wasn't winking or flirting or even pretending like she might drop some drawers for some rookie cop trying to get to 'Lexis. What she was going to do was walk straight past that cop and find her. And she didn't care how big he was or what normal police procedures were, she was going into that hotel and bringing Alexis out one way or another. No sooner had she come to this realization and decided to make her consternation a reality she heard a familiar voice calling her name.

"Monica," recognizing her friend's voice immediately and turned breathing a deep sigh of relief as she saw Alexis's hand waving in the air hoping to get her attention as she made her way through the crowd of nosy onlookers and guests locked out of their hotel rooms.

"What the hell is going on?" Alexis asked.

"The hell if I know. I just got here. I thought about what you said when you were leaving though and thought I'd get out of the house and come down and check out the happenings." Monica said, very much relieved to see her friend.

"Well, there is certainly a lot happening and from what I understand; none of it is too good," Alexis replied.

"You ain't lying. I certainly would have never expected anything like this though. The cop at the corner said there'd been a shooting or something. I was just worried about you getting caught up in the whole she-bang; innocent bystanders always have a way of buying it even though they ain't got shit to do with what's going on. The thought of you getting caught up in some shit after I forced you to come down here had me worried sick," Monica commented still trying to see what all the ruckus was about.

"You should know by now that you don't have to worry about me. I'm a big girl now. I think I'm pretty capable of taking care of myself," Alexis shot back even though she was grateful for Monica's concern.

"Hell, ain't nobody said anything about you not being able to take care of yourself. But I'll tell you like my daddy useta tell me. 'A bullet don't know nobody's name.' Monica started to say more but was cut off in mid-sentence by her girlfriend's shrill scream.

"Philip!" she shouted. *"My God! In all the confusion, I totally forgot about Philip,"* Alexis shouted as she headed towards the police officer who now found himself at the far end of the cordoned off section of sidewalk towards the end of the street where E.M.S.

workers were loading someone into the back of an ambulance while another crew rushed back inside.

The sound of the siren and the haste in which the ambulance made its departure only further worried the now near panicked woman in the skintight outfit. Pushing feverishly through the crowd followed by Monica she shouted at the police officer.

"Officer, I need to get through. My boyfriend's inside. I need to see if he's alright," she screamed over the other voices.

"Sorry, lady I can't do that," he yelled back.

"But…"

"Sorry lady, those are my orders and from what they tell me I don't think you want to be anywhere near the inside right through here. Haven't been inside myself but from what they tell me it's no place for a woman. Sorry!" he said as he raced to stop an older gentleman from going under the barricade.

Alexis made her way alongside the barricade going step by step with the handsome, young cop. The two men were arguing now. It was obvious the young cop was doing his best to restrain himself while the older gentlemen shouted and raged calling him everything but a child of God as he tried his best to force his way past the barricade.

"Boy, you'd better let me through before I have your badge," he shouted as the cop tried to restrain him with causing a panic or incurring a lawsuit in the process. The entire time he was doing his best to reach for his radio to call for backup but with the man doing his best impression of a mad bull the young police officer had everything he could just to contend with the older gentleman.

Alexis was struck by the racist tone of the older gentleman as he referred to the officer as boy and saw this as a golden opportunity to help herself and immediately went to the cops defense, assured him that she was not reaching for his gun, grabbed his radio and followed his instructions for summoning back up. No sooner than she finished transmitting the message three or four cops appeared and in a matter of minutes had completely subdued the older gentlemen who now appeared quite reserved as they led him away in cuffs.

"His daughter's inside,' the officer said turning to Alexis and wiping his brow of sweat. "He's just a little worried is all," the cop told Alexis in a vain attempt to reassure himself for having the man arrested. "Still, there's a proper way to go about things and that is *not* the way. Wanna thank you though," he said looking at Alexis as though he was seeing her for the very first time.

"You're pretty quick on your feet," he said motioning to two gentlemen and clearing a space so they could get through. Alexis looked at him puzzled. How could these two just pass through while the rest of us... Her bewilderment obvious, he smiled at her and said, "Homicide detectives," almost as if he were reading her mind.

"The name is Officer Davis, 105th Precinct. And yours?" he asked as he let another group of gentlemen through the barricade. "Forensics," he stated to Alexis matter-of-factly.

"Oh, sorry," she said still puzzled and more than a little worried by this time. "My name's Alexis—Alexis LeBrandt. Glad that I could be of some help, officer. Now maybe you can be of some help to me. You see Officer Davis..."

"Excuse me Ms. LeBrandt, the officer said as he rushed down to the other end of the barricade to fend off some newcomers before returning with his radio in one hand.

"Say Sergeant, you wanna get me some help out here. We've got an awful lot of anxious people out here. Can you get somebody out here to field some of their questions? I've got a quite a lot of hotel guests standing out here with nowhere to go. Yes sir. Yes sir, I can do that sir but I don't know how long I can keep the guests at bay. It's getting late and they have nowhere else to go. Yes sir, I'm doing the best I can," he said before turning back to look at the young lady who seemed insistent on following him from one end of the barricade, step-by-step.

"Ms. LeBrandt is it?" he asked. "You were saying?"

"Yes, Officer Davis. I was hoping that you could find some way to allow me to get to the front desk so I can inquire about the welfare of my boyfriend."

"Hey, I appreciate the help you gave me a little while ago but there ain't no way in hell I can let you enter a crime scene without the proper credentials. Sarge would have my badge. Besides, like I said, from all accounts it's pretty gruesome in there."

"I understand, Officer Davis but maybe I can make it worth your while. How 'bout I treat you to a drink when you get off this shitty detail?"

"Sounds like you're trying to bribe me, Ms. LeBrandt and you know I could never accept a bribe but what I can suggest is that you try calling your boyfriend's room and see if all's well. I'm pretty sure the switchboard's still up and the operators are pretty isolated so they're shouldn't be too much of a problem getting through."

"That's just it though, officer. I don't know what room he's staying in."

"Well, I don't know what to tell you, Ms. LeBrandt. Although if you wouldn't mind me offering a little advice. I think your best bet would be to go ahead home and just sit tight. Nine times out of ten he's all right and will be calling you just as soon as things die down to give you the scoop. That's about the best I can tell you. Hope everything works out for the best and I'm sorry. Just wish I could do more."

Alexis's head dropped in utter resignation. The one time she needed the charm to work it hadn't and then she thought of herself in that silly get-up that Monica had insisted on her wearing that made her look like a South Side hooker and she felt even worse. Turning to walk away, she heard someone call her name and recognized the officer's voice.

"Call me a hopeless romantic but anyone willing to go through what you just did to get the whereabouts on their boyfriend must really be worried and really be in love. Wish my ex-wife had felt like that. We'd probably still be married. Look, walk around to the employee entrance and ask for Sergeant Wilcox. Tell him Officer Davis sent you to him and tell him what you need. He's kind of gruff but ignore that. He's a softee on the inside. He'll tell you what you need to know about the whereabouts of your boyfriend."

"Oh, thank you so much, Officer Davis. You don't know how much this means to me," Alexis said feeling a little more relieved.

"No, I really don't know how much it means to you but if things don't work out between you and errrr–what's his name–don't forget that drink you promised Officer Ricky Davis of the 105th Precinct. Just you remember that," he said smiling before rushing to fend off another group trying to crawl underneath the barricade and gain entrance to the hotel by the front door.

Waiting patiently, Monica followed Alexis through the crowd. The street was far less crowded and Alexis dug through her pocketbook until she found the little Nokia and called the hotel. No answer. She then tried the number on the tiny piece of paper that Philip had given her and after letting it ring for several minutes decided that the whole cell thing was a waste of time. She'd never liked the damn things anyway and could almost never reach anyone when she really needed to. No sooner had she disposed of that thought and threw the cell into the clusterfuck that was her pocketbook the phone rang.

"You called?"

"Philip! Oh my god. Is it really you, Philip? My God, where are you? I've been looking all over for you. Where in the hell have you been?" she screamed.

"Well, the pizza was good but when I left your place I still had a craving for something and being that it was my first time in your fair city I decided to get out and do a little sightseeing and grab a little late night snack. What's up?" he asked seemingly unaware of the events that hard taken place at the Radisson.

"I honestly don't know. I decided to stop by your hotel and apologize or at least attempt to apologize and when I got here there was nothing but police. They're all over the place. Where are you?" She asked, as she slowly came to grips with her emotions which only a moment ago had been on the verge of panic. Now she was doing her best to mask them but it was obviously too late as the concern in her voice was far too apparent.

"I'm right behind you," he said, *"and let me tell you; I'm lovin' that outfit. Do you hear me? I'm lovin' it! No wonder you're so durn conscious about keeping everything under wraps. My God! If the boys on Wall Street could see you now you'd have half of New York flying to Detroit. My goodness! Thank God you don't dress like that on the regular. I don't know if I could fight off the competition. And you say you were comin' to see me? Aren't I the lucky one? I don't know what you had in mind and I don't know what's goin' on here but let's not let any of that get in the way.*

Alexis laughed and breathed a deep sigh of relief at the same time.

"I wasn't particularly crazy about the accommodations when I checked into the room. Not for what I'm paying anyway, so if it's okay with you let's cut through the chase, save the chit-chat for tomorrow and hail a cab or are you driving?" Philip asked in a playful tone but Alexis knew that only the tone was playful.

"Where are you?" she said, her tone changing from worried suitor to self-conscious flirt. Suddenly conscious of her outfit that had brought Philip out of the closet in a way she'd never known before she suddenly felt a warm glow coming over her. She knew the outfit was enticing. It was meant to be but that combined with her unbridled angst made her an easy target and she could hardly recoil now though she was still trying hard to mask her indignity.

"Where are you?" she repeated trying in earnest to change the subject.

"I'm right here, darling. And the only reason you're here is because you had second thoughts about throwing someone as persistent and adorable as me out after I came all this way to see you. That and the fact that deep inside, you know that no matter how hard you try to fight it there are some things that can't be avoided—like the way we feel when we're around each other and the way we feel for each other. I know it scares you and I can understand that but you have to reconcile yourself to the fact that it is what it is and there's no escaping it. Now tell me. What's the best way for us to handle this thing?"

Alexis LeBrandt was dumbfounded, speechless for once in her life and as hard as she tried to summon the words which always flowed so easily, no words appeared, although she did gasp loudly when Philip appeared out of nowhere, grabbed her from behind, spun her round to face him and kissed her deeply, in front of the world to see, while Monica stood idly watching a love affair unfold right before her very eyes.

And as much as she wanted to be happy for the two and the way the evening turned out, somehow she just couldn't and was surprised to feel a twinge of jealously descend on her like a dark, gloomy cloud on a summer picnic. Not knowing what to do or why she suddenly felt so helpless and so bothered by the couple standing in front of her, she did the only thing she could do; she turned and walked through the thinning crowd and made her way to her car the tears streaming down her face.

Chapter 6

It was close to two months before Monica would see Alexis again and then it was only by chance as she just happened too be shopping at Lane Bryant's even though she'd vowed that she would not shop there again and would be down to at least a sixteen by the summer. And here it was May and she was no closer to a sixteen than when she started that damn low carb diet months ago. She'd starved herself continuously, worked out feverishly at Curves after work on the average of three to four times a week and in all that time and Lord knows it felt like forever the best she could do was shed a paltry twelve pounds. And although she could hardly see the fat leaving anywhere but her ass; making it even flatter than it already was the girls at the gym encouraged her daily telling her that her all of her efforts would soon pay off but after awhile, even they stopped telling her how well she was doing. They knew what she knew. And that was that she was doing everything within her very soul to shape herself into the woman she wanted to be. Yet, despite the cruel and unusual punishment she was inflicting upon herself she was no closer to losing the forty pounds by her June deadline than she had been when she started working out months before.

What it essentially boiled down to was the fact that her physical makeup was just that. It was her physical makeup that refused to let her downsize no matter how much she worked out. Truth of the matter was that she was like every one else in her family. They were all big and not just big but big-boned as well. Much as she wanted to believe Oprah's success stories on Oxygen, the truth of the matter was that Oprah was a little woman that ate herself into being huge, so she could lose the weight.

Her brother had experienced the same problem when it came to his weight and after having both knees operated on because of cartilage damage he'd opted to have that new tummy reduction surgery which cut out a large part of his intestines or was it his stomach with the hopes that that would help in the weight loss department but she hadn't really seen that much difference and if it meant surgery she'd just as well carry the burden of being overweight. Besides she was sure that after everything else she'd been through losing forty pounds by the time the summer rolled around wasn't out of the question. But that was then. Now she wasn't so sure.

One thing she was sure of, however, she wouldn't be a third wheel anymore—sitting around, cosmetic smile glued on her face, watching as everyone around her found happiness with the man of their dreams while she sat idly by, being the loyal friend while they snuggled and kissed happy kisses and tried to disguise their glee in front of her knowing that she would have given anything to be in their shoes at that moment.

When things got really bad they tried to fix her up with their co-workers or friends or little brothers or distant cousins they hadn't seen in a awhile with the hopes that maybe—just maybe there would be some fool out there either horny or desperate enough to fall in love, despite the rolls of cellulite that made her who she was. But up until now that hadn't happened and no matter how desperate the men were that she was introduced to, they would not allow themselves to concede that the best they could do was this oversized woman with forearms bigger than theirs.

After awhile, she stopped going out altogether with friends or anyone else for that matter and resigned herself to the fact that she needed no one and would be better off just being her own best friend. Well, at least until she dropped a few pounds. That was then and in the last two months she'd given up everything in her pursuit to be someone she could be proud of. Just knowing that she'd pushed the envelope, knowing full well that she was doing all that she could in the pursuit of her goals, in the pursuit of excellent and soon she'd have them all swarming like bees on honey and not just to be pillow pals either. No, it was her belief that if she concentrated solely on making herself the best person she could be then she really and truly didn't have time for anyone else and if someone did happen along they'd best come with more than just sex and a pleasing personality. After all the work she'd done and the commitments she'd made to improving herself, mentally and physically she'd be damn if she'd be just some trick for some disenchanted husband just looking to drop his seed. No, that was yesterday. Today she was moving forward and looking to the future.

Yet, in reality her own physicality's remained stubborn and daunting refusing to lend way for her new spiritual growth and the bottom line was that no matter how bright you were or cheerful or pleasant what a man wanted was a slim goody that he was proud to show off like a new suit from Hanes or a brand new Chrysler. What he didn't want to show off were those old battle wounds and scars from the war or even the medal he'd received due to her heroics.

Most men her age, were either too worried about their best years being behind them or the fact that the years they thought that that lay ahead were rapidly flying by now and they couldn't quite get a firm grip on what was going on with the time and the aging but there wasn't a lot of time to be contemplating the plight of the world with the grim reaper gaining on them every day. Hell, they didn't even have the time to spin a good yarn or listen to one either for that matter.

Life was too short to be holed up in house with one woman and some kind of commitment. By this time of their life, if they weren't married then they had been and it only takes a fellow one time to travel that path to know that he doesn't want to travel that road twice when there's only one lifetime to journey. Now all he needed was something glitzy and brash and fine that spoke for itself and said—yeah—he's still got it—even at his age. Having her on his arm would probably do wonders for their psyche but hell who wanted to sit and conversate and have intelligent conversations about the elections in Iraq and the chances for democracy, or the effect of

Arafat's successor on the Mideast when they could sit back in the lazy boy, a cold beer in one hand, a slice of pizza in the other, and a woman half their age in some hoochie mama outfit with a teddy up to their titties and lips that have lockjaw written all over them.

Hell, what man wouldn't prefer a warm behind and a lap dance at halftime of the ballgame when he returned from draining the weasel. Beats a conversation on the Middle East any day.

Of course she could provide a lap dance as well as the next skank 'ho but then boyfriend might wind up with a hiatal hernia and find himself searching for a new Lazy-Boy the next day. No men weren't interested in the knowledge she'd accrued. They could care less how many megabytes the new Dell has or why anyone would purchase a Gate over an Apple based on specs and compatibility with other pc's. No, they wanted a fine, hot, sassy, young woman, who appeared as if she'd been peeled right of the cover of Essence and placed before them to pay homage from a kneeling position. That's what they wanted—what they truly desired. A woman on her knees praying to God—them—while they leaned back and pretended to be oblivious. Meanwhile, she kneels there, between his legs, facing him, her eyes pretending it's hotter than July and he has graced her, blessed her, with a blueberry slushee that she's welcome to suck on until her heart's content.

Monica shuddered at her own thoughts and thought how condescending, how bitter she'd become in the last few months because she didn't fit the mold or have the right body. In a way she hated those little heifers who hadn't achieved a thing in life and were content to get by on simply their God given attributes or lack thereof. And then the thought arose and she wondered if she'd be content to suck a man's dick, fix his meals and cater to his every whim if he occasionally told her he loved her and meant it? Would she do it if he was good to her and he so desired?

The thought frightened her and her principles wanted to scream *'hell no'*. Her ethical side wanted to believe that it take more than that on his part. No, that would certainly not be enough. He would definitely have to have something to offer she thought to herself before smiling and thinking to herself, 'hell, yeah she'd do it'. Who was she fooling? She'd cater to his every need, his every whim without so much as a second thought. Hell, she'd done it before without the man wanting or desiring or treating her good and though she couldn't say she was glad she'd succumbed to that level she'd certainly do it again if she even had the slightest inkling that the relationship had some promise.

She knew she'd become angry, bitter but men were hardly to blame. They were simply society's creations hardly conscious of what it was they so passionately desired or why they desired what they desired. It was simply a manner of someone setting the standards and them promptly following. That was it in the nutshell. They would have never made it with Captain Kirk and the Starship Enterprise who ventured to go where no man had ever been before. No, they were followers.

And since she didn't fit the bill of what was attractive and desirable she was left with the only option available to her and if that meant pumping iron after work and walking for what seemed forever on that damn treadmill then by God she'd do it. Lord knows, if that's what it took to get back in their good graces then by God she'd have to resign herself to the fact at hand and get to steppin'.

The more she walked on that treadmill, headphones on, with Sade crying about lost loves and broken promises, the more withdrawn she became. She seldom got out anymore and except for church and dinner with Bridget and her mother on Sundays she remained pent up in the house reading or walking around the house partially nude and constantly glancing in the mirror to see if there was any change at all. And if it weren't for momma insisting that she be on the ladies Juneteenth Celebration at church next month she would haven't been caught dead in the mall now. There was not a time that she stepped into that place that she didn't recognize someone she knew, whether it was an old classmate, co-worker or a church member. And at this point she didn't want to see any of them.

At first, her decision to avoid people was in her eyes a good one. She'd go through a much disciplined routine feeding both her mind and her body with everything she could to promote a stronger, more intelligent and of course more streamlined Monica. Besides who would miss her anyway? And then when they'd least expect it; the unveiling. My wouldn't they be surprised by the newer sexier, sleeker, streamlined version of her own self replete with glamour that came with buying the best in name brand suits and designer bags. She'd show Detroit just who Monica was. And those same pathetic creatures that hadn't seen fit to give her the time of day before, would be standing in line, begging her to let them entertain her. That was the plan anyway.

As she made her to Lane Bryant's in the mall she was cognizant of everyone around her and the men who were proud to be seen with their significant other. It especially incensed her to see the young lovers snuggled up whispering naughty nothings to each other and she found herself grimacing every time she saw them.

Monica wondered if she were losing it. She knew staying in was only adding to her anxiety but she'd vowed not to appear until she had accomplished what it was she set out to do and that was to be utterly and insatiably desirable to every man she came in contact with. The hell with her body type and the genetic pool and whatever the hell the chromosome was that said she had to be obese. She'd rearrange the DNA if she had to but she would lose the weight and become physically desirable if it killed her. And without surgery, too.

But it hadn't happened as of yet and she vowed that she would not buy another stitch of clothing if it had to come from Lane Bryant's. But here she was and who should she meet of all people but 'Lexis. Monica had been avoiding her calls for close to three months now. Content to let the voice mail do its job. She felt no animosity towards Alexis. Then again, maybe she did. 'Lexis always seemed to have it going on, never being more than a size six at any time since she'd known her. Walking around touting that little figure that kept the guys drooling Monica had come to almost despise her especially since Alexis turned more good looking guys away in a week than Monica had the pleasure of meeting in a year and here she was always crying and bitching about something or another. The little spoiled bitch didn't know how fortunate she was. When they'd go out to eat at this restaurant or that, Alexis would gobble down the entree as if it were the Last Supper while she sat there at the same table feeling all self-conscious and wondering if people were staring at her or the food on her plate or her table manners or just staring.

At times like these she'd always eat slowly, picking at her food like she wasn't really hungry in an effort to show whoever was dining with them that she wasn't a slob or glutton but no matter how she tried to play it off the thought was always there that people were staring, wondering if she were going to drop her head slam down in the plate and root around like a wild boar or something. Not knowing if they were really staring or if she was becoming increasingly paranoid she stopped going out altogether and though the weekly afternoon lunches or dinners had become pretty much of a ritual since Alexis's divorce she just couldn't do it anymore and she didn't want to hear her friends lectures on being confident in one's own abilities and strengths despite the odds. She'd heard enough of 'Lexis's self-help speeches to last a lifetime. Yeah, she was certainly good at dishing out the advice but let a minor fluctuation manifest itself in the ever so proper Alexis LeBrandt's life, like her actually being attracted to a man for something other than for her financial benefit and she was Calamity Jane bordering on the verge of a nervous breakdown. Stupid, pathetic bitch. What was it that her father used to tell her about, 'one man's sugar being another man's poison' or something to that effect.

Anyway, she had no use for Alexis LeBrandt right now, running around town flaunting her little, tight ass, and taking advantage of the suckers who didn't have the smarts to see her for what she truly was which was nothing more than a little, selfish, conniving, golddiggin' bitch intent on having her fifteen minutes of fame and fortune at the expense of any gullible idiot with a dick out there. Monica had had a lot of time to think about her friendship with 'Lexis during her workouts and the time she spent at home and this was the conclusion she'd arrived at.

At first, she'd missed the daily phone calls but after awhile she realized that she was nothing more than a sounding board and excuse for 'Lexis is to hear herself talk since James was no longer there to fulfill this role for her. She wondered how he was surviving without 'Lexis and promised to call him when she got back to the house. After all, they'd been friends long before 'Lexis and he met and come to think of it she was the reason they'd gotten together anyway.

Now outside of Lane Bryant's there was no doubt about the figure approaching her grinning from ear-to-ear. And if there had been any question all she had to do was glance one time at the skin tight mini, pumps and that walk that always cried out, 'take me this instant' to know that it was Alexis.

"I don't know if I should speak to you or slap you," Alexis laughed genuinely glad to see her and then hugging her as if she just escaped from the clutches of Al-Qaeda.

"Where the hell have you been and why on earth haven't I heard from you? Do you realize that's it's been close to three months since that crazy night down at the Radisson," 'Lexis screamed pretending to be angry. "You know that shit ain't right, don't you?"

"I know. I'm sorry, babe. I just had so much on my mind and all that…"

"So much that you couldn't pick up the phone and call me to at least let me know that you were alright? Did I do something to offend you? If I did then I am truly sorry but the last time I remembered either seeing or speaking to you was on Philip's first visit and you seemed fine then."

"You're so right. That was the last time I talked to you. Look 'Lexis, there really isn't much to say. No, you didn't do anything to me. It's just that I have a lot going on in my life right now and…"

"So much that you can't even say hello? This isn't like you Monica. We've known each other since…"

Though standing there staring Alexis right in the eye Monica had long since turned her off choosing not to entertain any of her ramblings about friendship and how long they'd been friends and all the usual bullshit. She remembered when Marshall was around and he'd made the observation that the only reason Alexis hung around with her was because she never had to worry about her upstaging her in any fashion since she was no threat. She didn't know why that particular thought had popped up at this occasion but it made sense. For as long as she could remember she'd been Lexis' patsy, her sidekick and well, frankly she was tired of it.

"Hey Lex, I'm really in a hurry. Gotta meet momma," she lied. "Do me a favor, give me a cal when you get home and we'll set something up for this weekend," she said as she hugged her girlfriend tightly before turning quickly and heading to the parking lot. 'The hell with Lane Bryant's. I can do this', she thought to herself not paying any homage to the tiny woman who had been babbling away about something or another and who now found herself still standing in the middle of the entrance to Lane Bryant's surprised beyond belief.

Monica didn't know how to feel as she left the mall by the rear entrance. She was too preoccupied with her own thoughts to listen to Alexis' idle chatter. Nothing had changed in the thirty-five or forty years since Alexis had moved onto her street but perhaps Marshall was right. Maybe she wasn't anything but a sidekick to make Alexis feel better about herself but the truth of the matter was there was no one out there making her feel any better about herself and it was due time she put herself first and foremost. She had goals—things she wanted to do and accomplish—things that 'Lexis took for granted like yesterday's old newspaper.

There was Alexis' husband James for example; a good man who she'd had the pleasure of introducing to 'Lexis at a church bazaar some years earlier. He had the patience of Job and been more than tolerant withstanding 'Lexis' wrath and petty idiosyncrasies for as long as any man possibly could. She never understood how he did it. In Monica's eyes James was no more than a doormat to Alexis when it came right down to it. And to think she had initiated the whole affair.

Checking her voicemail when she arrived home later that evening Monica was surprised to find a message from Alexis. Having grown accustomed to the constant chatter that seemed to need no one on the other end to create what most people regard as conversation she deleted the message and dialed James instead. He seemed genuinely pleased to hear from her and she thought it funny that after a rather prolonged conversation that neither of them mentioned Alexis at all. It was almost as if they were picking up where they left off before the introduction that had caused him so much heartache. By the time the conversation was over, a good hour or so later, they'd agree to meet for lunch at the Blue Marlin Restaurant the following Tuesday.

The following days never seemed longer for Monica. Work, school, and then long hours at the gym proved almost more than she could endure but she forced herself to follow the routine and did so diligently while at the same time starving herself to death. By the time, Tuesday rolled around and she was to meet James for lunch she was having some rather serious doubts and counted herself a better woman than to date her best friend's husband even if it were her ex. Sure they'd been friends but this man had shared a bed and better yet a life together with her best friend for the last twenty years and like it or not and despite the way she was feeling about herself and Alexis the whole affair just didn't seem right.

Of course, there had been times and more than just a few where James had picked her up from shopping or the airport but that was different. Alexis was always aware. And even when her car had broken down she'd called Alexis first before soliciting James' help. But this was different and she had to stop and wonder what her intentions really were. She really and truly had no reason to be angry with 'Lexis. They'd fallen out countless times over the years over pettiness but had always managed to reconcile their relationship despite their differences. And she couldn't lie to herself. Alexis had always been a tease, a gold digger who preyed on good men's weaknesses. She'd known this for as long as she'd known Alexis. But the years had taken their toll on her and she hated to see the same ol' same ol' and especially when good men were in such short supply. Besides those games were for highschoolers; not for a woman, a grown woman with kids in college rapidly approaching fifty years of age. When did the games end? When would she learn, if ever, that people were not put here solely as a stepping stone for her to reach her goal in life.

"Much as you'd like the rest of us to believe it the rest of the world does not revolve around you Ms. LeBrandt," she heard herself say aloud.

It was at that very moment—that moment of clarity that happens once or twice in everyone's life that Monica knew that something was wrong—something was terribly wrong not only with those around her but more importantly with something within her as well.

Still, unable to pinpoint whatever it was that was driving her, forcing her to act in such a manner she poured herself a half a glass of brandy and decided, despite having second thoughts that what she needed more than anything was a night out in familiar surroundings with close friends and no strings attached and since she hardly felt like apologizing to 'Lexis and rehashing the drabness that had been her life over the last few months since they'd seen each other, James would have to do.

She just hoped that when she did get around to apologizing for what amounted to no more than simple jealousy, on her part, Alexis would be understanding enough to forgive her. Right now though she had only one concern and that was getting out of her drab little apartment that was fast becoming a prison.

James had called earlier in the day to say lunch was no good and dinner would be better and now she was glad he had. It had taken her the better part of the day to get where she wanted to be with getting her hair and nails done and was pleasantly surprised to find that the dark blue suit she'd been wearing as a dress uniform for the past two months was suddenly too big for her. Perhaps things were paying off. She had always had a tendency to be too hard on herself and maybe things were getting better after all, but just in case they were not she turned the bottle up, poured herself another shot of brandy and smiled as she searched for something a little smaller and a little tighter. She still had to shower and stripping naked and looking at herself in the full length mirror did little or nothing to assuage her already poor self-image but where yesterday she would have been particularly hard on herself the brandy would not allow her spirits to be down. Showering quickly she placed the bottle of brandy on the top of her vanity, sipping liberally while applying her makeup.

By the time James arrived on the scene Monica was more than just the social butterfly and was damn well near drunk but had the resolve and fortitude to hide the fact. She was genuinely surprised at how good the years had been to him and even more surprised that he really and truly looked better than he had at any time in his life. They hugged briefly and Monica was for the first time in twenty years self-conscious about hugging James. She didn't know if it was guilt or not but James didn't seem to notice and kissed her as he always did on the cheek before spinning her around in the living room and commenting on how good she looked.

"Damn girl, are you getting better looking with the years or are my eyes deceiving me? Talkin' about the years agreeing with somebody. How in the hell did I let you sneak by me when we were in high school. They say young and dumb and I guess they weren't lyin'. What the hell have you done to yourself," he asked appreciatively.

There was no doubt he was sincere and a warm tingle ran through Monica's body and she wanted to ask herself the same thing looking at James. He was one fine man but then Alexis never did mess around with any ugly men. The mere thought of her friend swept through her in almost the same fashion as James' comment had but she quickly dispelled any thoughts of wrongdoing or guilt and vowed that this was a night where two old friends were just getting together for old times sake.

"Any thought of where you might like to eat?" he asked.

Well, that in itself was a first. Usually her male friends tried their best to corral her into naming the cheapest, most inexpensive dive on the outskirts of Detroit but they never left such an open ended question up to her to respond to and right away she recognized the fact that James' wasn't like the rest of those idiots. He'd known her—well—as long as she could remember and they'd always been close. And even when his parent's moved out to the suburbs James had always found his way back to her house to visit. It was only since the marriage to Lexis that they'd grown apart. And that was largely in part to Alexis being insanely jealous of any woman within fifty meters of James even though he meant nothing more than an old piece of scrap metal to her. Not to upset her friend and to give them some space she stared clear of them when they were at home unless it was a special event like one of the kids birthdays or something of that nature and James not to upset the hen house kept pretty much to himself as well. But with Alexis out of the picture there was no more need for pretense and both seemed the better for it.

"The Blue Marlin's fine," Monica replied remembering the question.

James was the first male—well—outside of family that she'd had over and she was a bit nervous about entertaining at home since it was her first time but didn't want seem rude or ill-at ease with a man that used to sleep over when her parents thought it too late for him to travel home alone. Besides she was in no rush to sit in some high falutin' restaurant while other women gaped at she and James the way they used to do trying to figure out why such a fine hunk of a man would be caught with the likes of her when he could surely have them. James never seemed to notice when they were younger and from the looks of thing he hadn't changed much at all despite having to suffer through twenty years of pure hell with Alexis.

"Oh, how rude of me, come in and have a seat James. I'm not used to entertaining. I guess I forgot my manners," she said, smiling. "Would you care for something to drink?"

"Whatever you're having is fine," he said staring off into space. "I like the place Monica. You know you always did have nice taste. Remember that blue floral arrangement you did back when we were in high school when I couldn't afford to buy my mother a Mother's Day gift?"

Monica smiled. "Boy you remember everything, don't you?"

"How could I forget? Do you know that was one of the few times that I can remember that I really and truly couldn't get momma a gift. It's funny though; in all those years and all that money I spent trying to find her just the right thing—you know—the perfect gift—that's the one gift she holds closest to her. It is beautiful though."

"Don't tell me she still has that old thing?"

"Does she still have it? She goes to the floral shop every couple of years and drives the salespeople crazy trying to make sure that when something breaks or falls off that they replace the piece with the exact same color and tint. You wouldn't believe her but then you know how she is."

"Still a mess huh? I've been meaning to get over there and say hello."

"Yeah, she'd like that. She still blames me for not scooping you up when I had the chance. Wish I had listened. You know what they say. Mother knows best."

Monica blushed deeply and smiled but made no comment.

"She's got a touch of the gout that acts up every now and then but she's still tough as nails and feisty like you wouldn't believe. I just hope I'm like that when I get to be her age."

"You and me both," Monica acknowledged.

Both laughed and Monica felt good to be around her old friend again.

"Say Monica can I ask you a serious question?"

"It's never stopped you before," she said knowing that no matter what she said once James had a drink in him he was hardly ever quiet and here he was holding out his glass for another.

"I just need to know one thing," he said deliberately and Monica knew that it wasn't about the bouquet or her having good taste in the decorating department.

"I just want to know if 'Lexis put you up to seeing me tonight. You know so that she could say I was unfaithful."

Monica was immediately taken back and had to catch herself before answering. Finishing off the bottle before she answered, Monica gathered herself as best she could and replied simply, "You know better than to ask me that, James."

And then without as much as another word he leaped from the sofa and said, "Thank you, Jesus!" Then toasted her glass and sat back in the same spot on the green and gold loveseat as if nothing had transpired at all.

Monica wondered if she'd either had too much liquor or was in a time warp. Unsure of either, she headed for the bar and cracked open another fifth of brandy passed the pack of Newport's to James who took one and offered her a light in return.

She'd cut back enormously but when she'd had too much to drink they were the first things she reached for. The second thing was a man. Glancing over at James she wondered just how he would be in bed and then caught herself. For better or worse this was Alexis' husband and she was eyeing him like fresh meat; all dressed up and ready for slaughter. This time she didn't ask and filled his glass to the brim with brandy. James drank the shot eagerly and it was soon obvious that he was tipsy.

"I never could drink you know," he said laughing as the liquor took control. "By the way, where's the bathroom?"

"Second door on the left," Monica answered taking a deep drag off of the cigarette and eyeing James' well shaped buns as he made his way down the long, narrow, corridor on his way to the bathroom.

"Umph, umph, umph—what I could do with that," she muttered to herself. "The hell if I'd ever let something that fine walk the hell away." she grinned.

"By the way James, why'd you ask me that question?"

"What?" He shouted from the bathroom.

"About 'Lexis sending me?" she asked.

"Well, she's always been kind of jealous of our relationship. I'll never forget the night we were lyin' in bed—you know—just chillin'and watching television and out of the clear blue she asked me if I'd ever slept with you."

"No, she didn't!" Monica said her surprise showing clearly.

James laughed. "That was my reaction too. Of course I told her that I hadn't. It kind of puzzled me though. But you know me. I didn't really pay it that much mind at the time since Alexis is always asking something or another that was pretty much out of line. And I thought that was the end of it.

To tell you the truth, *I was a little surprised* that she would ask me something like that but then again if you know Alexis then you know all the tough talk and the gruff manner is just a façade. She's really nothing more than a very insecure little girl at heart that needs constant reassurance to make her life seem credible. Anyway, after she asked me if I'd ever slept with you she asked me if I would be totally honest with her. And since I've always tried to be totally honest with her I had a rather hard time with her next question which was like a cold slap in the face to me. Do you have any idea what she wanted to know?"

"No, what?" Monica asked, though she really didn't want to spend an evening talking about Alexis.

"She asked me if I would have had the opportunity to sleep with you would I have?"

The statement shook Monica but there was little she could do other than play out the hand he dealt her.

"And you said?" She asked ready to run and hide but she gathered herself together and tried her best to remain composed and...

"And I said *absolutely* but the occasion never arose and I'm happily married to you so why all the questions about Monica. That wasn't long before the divorce and I think it did more harm than good. There's too much given to that honesty makes a good relationship crap. But what I think it did was let her know that despite everything she had going for her on the outside she really didn't measure up to you in a lot of ways. I don't know if I'm making my point or if there is really a point to be made but her inner failings, her insecurities about you and a lot of other things really brought about the downfall of our marriage. I don't know if you know but she really lacks self-confidence and I really truly and honestly believe she's jealous of you. And with good reason I suppose. You're bright and attractive and well I guess I really didn't help matters much for me to let her know how I felt about you."

Monica was both stunned and elated by James' impromptu confession. Speechless, she tried to remain humble and play it off the best way she knew how with a bit of witticism but heard her self say instead, "And you honestly meant that?"

"There you go with the honesty thing again. So far it's cost me a marriage. Now it's about to cost me a friendship", he laughed. "But yes, to answer your question, I have always felt that way. I just never wanted to jeopardize our friendship so I left it alone. I figured it's better to be some part of your life than to have no part in it at all. Besides I don't know I'd have done if you'd rejected me."

Monica was speechless. This time her attempt at humor fared a little better.

"Why James LeBrandt I never knew you had a crush on me. I never thought you could see that far ahead with you looking over your shoulder all the time to see which little heifer was trying to track you down. It's flattering to know though." Monica said not knowing where to go with the conversation.

"Monica?"

"Yes, James," she said hoping to end the conversation and get going while the going was good. What more could she ask? For whatever reason he'd chosen to flatter her with this line was fine by her but there was nowhere else to go with it and she was content to know that he had at one time felt this way about her.

"Monica?"

"Yes, James," she answered wondering why she had invited him in at all.

"I want you to know that my feelings haven't changed."

"I'm really flattered but I really don't know why you're telling me this. Anyway you look at it; it's a no win situation. I mean let's just look at it hypothetically. Alexis and I, despite our annual fall-outs are like sisters. I've known her almost as long as I've known you and in all that time we've never crossed paths when it came to men. I don't think I could do that to her or any woman I considered a friend. It's just not done. Well, let me correct that. It is done. But I won't be the one to do it. It shows nothing if you ask me. At least not ethically." Monica said hating every ethic and principle standing in her way at that moment.

"I understand what you're saying, Monica and I respect you for what you're attempting to do but you and I both know that we felt something a long time ago. And that same feeling is upon us right now as we speak. Tell me you don't feel something between us, Monica. Besides I'm not married anymore," James pleaded.

"You will always be married to Lexis as far as I'm concerned James. For better or worse until death do you part. And if you don't consider yourselves married in each other's eye; you're both still very much married in mine. Do you have the faintest idea of how a woman's mind works?"

"I'm afraid not but I have a feeling you're going to tell me," he said, sighing impatiently.

"Can we talk over dinner? If I've waited forty-five years to find out how a woman's mind works, I think I can hold off another forty-five minutes," he joked. "May I have one for the road," he asked sticking out his glass for her to refill it.

"No sir, I really think it's important that we have this conversation right here and right now before we go anywhere. Do you realize that a woman can divorce a man and it means nothing—absolutely nothing when it comes to that man seeing another woman? Divorce or no divorce, she will lose her mind if she even thinks that the man she slept with, her ex is seeing or better yet sleeping with another woman. In a woman's eyes that's sufficient justification for manslaughter. And you more than anyone knows that all of Alexis' bricks ain't in the wagon. She wouldn't think twice about slicing your neck or mine either for that matter. With the contempt she has for your gender she probably wouldn't expect anything less from you but she'd sho'nuff look at me as someone worst than Judas himself for betraying her trust."

"You probably do believe all that but the fact of the matter remains that life goes on in spite of Alexis. There's no betrayal. At least I wouldn't look at it from that perspective. I can't. Life goes on. Alexis was a chapter in my life that I neither cherish nor regret. It was what it was and now it's time to turn the page, as they say. And the fact of the matter is that we have to go on living. We're both adults that have some feeling for each other and I hardly think it's fair to let someone who's decided that she no longer wants to be a part of my life to interfere with my future," James said.

"Don't get me wrong, sweetie, I understand your sentiments exactly and I think you're absolutely right. There's no reason you shouldn't go on with your life and if your ex had been any one other than Alexis there's no doubt that I would have entertained the thought but being that things are what they are I guess we'll simply have to settle for dinner. Are you ready," she said tilting the glass skyward and finishing the remainder of the brandy in her glass.

"Ready as I'll ever be," he said. "You might want to grab a jacket, Monica. The temperature's supposed to drop."

James waited at the door while Monica grabbed her jacket and threw it around her shoulders as he'd done so many times before in years past. Only this time he held her shoulders in his large hands and turned her around slowly, gently and said, "Monica, I want you to look at me. I mean really look at me," he said staring into the deep recesses of her eyes as though he were searching for something and she, without knowing, held the key.

"Yes, James," she said and began to feel herself weaken.

"Tell me, Monica—tell me at this very moment in time that you don't feel something very special between us?"

Monica stared up at the large man towering over her and shuddered.

"How can you deny this feeling?" he said as he bent down and placed his hand under her chin lifting her head so her mouth met his and before she knew what had hit her he embraced her wrapping one arm around her shoulder and led her to the sofa where they sat their lips never leaving the others.

In her mind she knew… She just knew. But the warmth of his embrace clouded her every thought and her tongue fought to find his. He was leading now and she bit down hard not knowing what to expect and then she felt his lips on her neck, nibbling, then sucking gently. He smelled of musk and the smell of his cologne and the heat rushing through her limbs let her know that it had been far too long. Her hands grabbed his head as she fought to find his mouth and tongue again.

The room was dark now but she was too hungry, too longing, too desperate for love, to worry about being reserved or lady like. Pushing him back onto the sofa, she struggled to grasp every bit of his tongue and sucked on it hungrily the way she had been taught, assuring him that there was more to come in that regard if he just kept making her feel like she did at that moment. How she hoped he wouldn't stop. She prayed that he'd continue until…

James seemed to realize her need as well as his own and though he tried to appear casual, he cursed under his breath and felt the beads of sweat explode on his forehead as he fought to undo the buttons on her blouse as she pressed into him still fighting to gobble up every inch of his tongue.

In her clutches, he had to admit that he had never met a woma.. so strong, so passionate, so desperate and as starved for love as she and he truly wondered if he'd be capable of meeting her demands.

Monica was aware of James' probing hands and the thought of Alexis was no more than a mere afterthought now. In the back of her mind she knew this was nothing short of the worst type of betrayal and the thought brought a smile to her face if only for an instant. Tomorrow she'd deal with her conscious but tonight she needed more than anything to be wanted, to be needed, to be loved and if it meant her putting her morality on the backburner tonight and paying the piper tomorrow then pay she would.

As James played with the back of her bra she was suddenly aware of his intentions and was glad that she'd worn her new bra. Of course, she hadn't expected anything like this but the snaps in the front not only were easier for her but they made the whole ordeal easier for James as well.

Seconds later she felt the snap open and the pressure from the tight fitting forty-two D cup released allowing her to breathe a deep sigh of relief but the pressure remained. He was in control now and she wondered if she were being too aggressive as she reversed the roles once again and forced him back into the couch where she could gain some leverage. It had been a chess game at first but now it was clearly a monopoly and she owned both Park Place and Boardwalk.

She could feel herself trembling and wondered if it was possible to orgasm without actually… If it wasn't she was damn sure close to something of that nature and when she felt her nipples spreading under his touch she wasn't counting out the possibility. When he grabbed them and tweaked them between his thumb and forefinger she knew that an orgasm or something closely resembling one was not only clearly in the realm of possibility but close at hand.

With his free hand he grappled, tugging her belt hoping to unleash the treasure within. He was struggling again as he had with her blouse but by this time there was no denying his intentions and he fought to find room between the snug fitting jeans and her skin. She wondered if helping him would suggest that she was too easy and decided against it in his quest to get to know all of her.

Again she thought about principles and ethics and Alexis and then eased to the side and spread her legs ever so slightly, discreetly, hoping he wouldn't notice that she too wanted him there but moreso so he would have easier access to her treasures once his hand slid down into her pants and between her legs.

My God it felt good and even better when he managed to slide two and then three fingers up in her. It had taken him some time, more time than she'd ever have imagined for him to navigate her belt buckle, the jeans and finally her panties, which were now drenched but she refused to move to aid him in his efforts so as not to appear too easy.

This continued for some time and his eventual success only served to give him proper license to lead her to her bedroom. Embroiled in passion he found himself sweating profusely after spending what seemed like hours bringing her to the brink of a climax with his hand. She was thrashing and hovering over him now and her tongue felt like a vicious current, a whirlpool, sucking everything in its midst and drawing his passion to a yet before, unknown level.

He was struggling now and felt himself sweating profusely from every pore. His arm and wrist both ached from the constant in and out motion. Relaxing the motion in an attempt to tease her and bring her to the verge of a screaming climax; James paused several times, waiting, watching her relax to the point where the arch in her back was gone and she was seated again.

Then when it appeared that she was lucid and on the verge of relaxing he'd ease his hand back up into her moist vagina and lead her as close to an orgasm as he dared before dropping her off again, unfulfilled. Over and over again he teased her, bringing her to the very brink and each time she would spread her legs slowly, each time a little wider, hoping that he wouldn't notice. She wished that she'd worn that dress she started to wear—the one she had complained about being too big instead of these tight black jeans he was having so much trouble navigating.

Again and again he would start, then stop, and then drop her off into a sweating, broiling, soaking mess of passion, rage and frustration that she seemed to both love and hate at the same time.

She made no mention of how she felt about this and James suspected that she was unable to gather her thoughts or her emotions into any coherent thought and when it appeared that her eyes were no longer glazed over in pain and pleasure and agony and frustration he'd begin again.

By this time, his wrist and forearm were both quite sore and limp and the idea of her smothering him in her haste to take his whole hand inside of her stopped him cold. Her moaning excited and frustrated him at the same time and the ever growing bulge in his pants now burgeoned on exploding in anticipation but she made no move to indulge him or his mounting needs and he wondered if perhaps her lack of empathy had been passed on to her by his ex-wife.

Now it was Monica who felt betrayed and she had a hard time understanding why he would stop just when she was oh so close. Hell, he had to know that she was almost there. As much as she'd tried to give the impression that she was and could be ladylike in lieu of everything he *just had to know* that he'd found her weak spot and reduced her to nothing more than a horny middle-aged woman starving for a man's touch. She was exactly what all the guys said she was. Nothing more and nothing less. She was a woman with insatiable desires that had a hard time finding just the right man to fulfill her needs. It was obvious from the way she felt at that very moment that James was just the man who could fulfill her wants, her needs, her desires. So why was he teasing her? He certainly had to know how badly she needed to release all of those pent up feelings. He had to have known how long she'd worked to be in just this position.

All the little girl dreams of a happy marriage and a two car garage with the little one's running around tugging on her apron strings had eluded her simply because she was overweight and men just didn't desire big women—well—unless they needed to relieve themselves and a whole lot of men didn't even want that from her.

The truth of the matter was that in most men's eyes, all she could do in the bedroom was perform oral sex. It had taken her awhile to realize it but it wasn't until a male friend told her this that she actually came to grips with this cold hard truth.

By the same token Monica refused to let her size deter her from doing what she wanted and aspired to do regardless of their constant denials. At one point, she'd even gone so far as to try the personals over the internet but that hadn't worked out well either and when she showed up at a rather chic night spot to meet one guy she'd met while surfing the net he took one look at her and made it known in no uncertain terms that she didn't quite meet his criteria for what he desired in a woman and abruptly excused himself.

Despite being, for lack of a better word, horny all the time she'd made it a point not to give into the one night stands, empty proposals and pleasuring a man just so she could say that she had a man. Well, that is except for times like now when she didn't think she could go another day without sex but how often had that been.

In her eyes it had been too often and although there were times she saw possibilities and had hopes that one of them would call back the next day simply to talk or even reminisce about the night before they seldom did. The one's that did call waited, sometimes more than two weeks and she knew then that it was nothing more than a booty call and would usually cut the conversation short and wind up masturbating or with her face buried in a wet pillow asking herself why.

There had been that one guy, the African, whom she'd slept with, although, once again, it went against everything she believed in. She hadn't actually cared for him but each time she showered and looked in the full length mirror as she got dressed for work she knew that her options were somewhere between slim and none, so she'd endured him for as long as she could with his antiquated views about the roles for men and women.

Still and all, he was fairly good in bed and he was a man and though she wasn't in love with him she was certainly in love with the idea that he unlike most of the brothers she knew wasn't too much interested in how she looked but more interested in burying himself in her every chance he could. Size meant nothing to him—nothing at all—as long as she allowed him to stay up in her he was happy. And for her, the bottom line was; he was there.

The fact that she couldn't understand almost anything he said didn't matter either. She really wasn't listening, anyway. She was just glad that she had someone around who looked at her and desired her for whatever the reason.

Now here was James stopping, right when she was at her peak—well—almost at her peak and she wondered if in her haste to feel good she'd been too aggressive. Perhaps she'd let him see just how starved she was and any man that knew that he could have his way with her. Even James. But there was no way that she was going to allow James LeBrandt to have his way with her without paying the cost. She hoped she wouldn't be forced to spend another cold, lonely night alone in her bedroom with her worn out purple dildo with the simulated veins fantasizing about the last real one she'd had but she would if she had to and before she'd let a man just walk in and demean her.

Embarrassed she looked at James and wondered what he was thinking. Now she was glad she had muffled the screams she wanted so badly to unleash. At least she'd held on to some of her dignity and then was sorry she had if she'd let it go she would have surely orgasmed by now. At the time, she really hadn't been thinking about her dignity or what James thought for that matter but more of the neighbors and now that she was sitting there wishing she'd screamed so she could have released all that pent up aggression that had been building for the last seven or eight months she hated herself for always worrying about what other people thought.

Now look at her. Clothes all rumpled and wet and the sweat from her underarms was spreading like wildfire making massive stains on her blouse. Her vagina was sore and throbbing and begging for more and she had no idea what he was thinking.

James looked at Monica to see if he could translate the emotions he saw in her face but could not distinguish anything. Her face was clearly flushed and her dark brown cheeks appeared red before him. Her eyes distant, he wondered if she was ready to love him the way he needed to be loved or if she were still feeling some regret over their actions.

No, she couldn't possibly have regrets. She had been too warm, too receptive, too hungry not to want to pursue the night ahead of them. But when he stood up and tried to pull her to her feet and lead her to the bedroom at the end of the hall she refused.

Well, at least, at first she refused. And there was something to say for that. A few minutes later, with the steady rhythm of his hand and fingers again working there way in and out of her soaken vagina, all her convictions became a thing of the past and the next thing she knew she was the one standing and leading him down the long narrow hallway into the master bedroom.

Chapter 7

It was very unusual for the morning sun to catch Monica Manning still in bed but this was no usual morning and Monica did her best to hide from the suns rays that shone brightly through the twisted pane in the blinds like an unwanted guest. She'd been planning to have that blind repaired and even thought about replacing it but with her hectic schedule she just hadn't gotten around to it. Now she was suffering because of her negligence and responded in the only way she knew how; by pulling the comforter over her head. Lifting her arm she felt a twinge of pain run from her arm straight down to her leg and shrieked in horror.

Sitting upright, the pain spread straight through her body and she wondered if she might have overdone it at the gym and then memories of the night before came cascading in with the vengeance of Hannibal's armies and she turned and buried her throbbing head in the pillow and tried desperately to recall the events of the night before but to little avail.

She could remember bits and pieces but for the most part what she saw were only scattered sketches which hardly painted a complete picture. But what saw she didn't like and thought of Dr. Fielding warning her about blackouts which result in temporary memory loss if she continued to drink heavily. When he first mentioned it, she'd laughed it off and chalked it up to him being a tea totaling little English faggot and washed the thought away with a beer and a couple of shots on the way home from his office. Now she was forced to admit that his prognosis did hold some merit. The last few times she'd been in the presence of the opposite sex and alcohol the combination had not proved—well—beneficial to say the least. She'd ended up sleeping with Kyle, one of the mail room clerks, from the office, whom she used to smoke a little weed with every now and then in the parking lot at lunchtime.

They'd been friends for as long as she'd worked there and that was close to fourteen years and the thought of sleeping with him never so much as crossed her mind. If she had a type, and she had to admit she didn't when it came to men—but if she had—he was certainly not it with his short stocky, Poindexter glasses wearing self. But on the day her car had broken down and she needed a ride to and from work he was her first and last best choice and he, being the friend he was, agreed with little or no reservation.

On the way home, she suggested they make a quick stop at Darryl's for a drink. Three hours later, and more than a little inebriated, she ended up seducing him and then screwing the hell out of him in the backseat of the parking lot. There had been other times—more than she cared to remember and it had always been the result of having too much to drink and too little in the way of self-esteem but it had been a while since she'd had an episode like that.

Now, laying there, the sun playing peek-a-boo through the cracked pane in the blinds and insisting on her getting up on this Saturday morning she thought about what Dr. Fielding said about alcoholism being a progressive disease and the blackouts becoming more and more frequent as she fought to remember the events of the night before.

Turning her head away from the sunlight she felt the throbbing in her temples and her body felt ravaged as pain shot up from her lower extremities to her pelvic area and brought forth a mirage of images she hardly cared to see. Suddenly, there was Marshall standing there in the bathroom door with the light on staring at her. She could remember though vaguely, his standing there, a glass of brandy in his hand. She remembered marveling at the finest physical specimen of a man that had ever graced her presence. He was finely chiseled and cut to perfection and as she lay there, smiling, she thanked God for having blessed her on this night.

Moments later, James noticing that she was now awake, grinned back before sliding his briefs to his ankles and stepping out of them, revealing that dreadful sight that made her tremble in horror as she glanced down at the monstrosity dangling between his legs. She'd never in her life seen a man so well endowed and thought for a minute that he had to be a contender for the Guinness Book of World Records. And then it dawned on her that his revealing of those thirteen or fourteen inches could only mean one thing. Panic filled her eyes when she came to the sudden realization that he had all intentions of putting that thing inside of her. But there he was seducing her and the rest was a blur.

As the events of the night unfolded she remember counting to nine before passing out in a sore but blissful exhaustion as a result of his licking, nibbling, sucking and slurping areas of her body she hardly knew existed until then.

Over the course of a few short hours, he'd exposed her every weakness, and she no longer worried about the neighbors as she screamed and cursed and moaned and then begged him to stop before shouting, 'fuck me baby' and an occasional' work my pussy'. *Damn that man was good!* Monica smiled at the thought.

When he'd slowed down to a steady, rhythmic lapping of her clit with his tongue in an effort to let her unwind and regroup before taking her back up the long incline to her apex, she lay there wishing, then praying that he would stop all the foreplay and just bear down on her and suck her clitoris hard and hungrily releasing her from his teasing.

After three or four times of climbing and then falling she found herself screaming, then begging for him to stop torturing her with his tongue and just let her come. But it was to no avail. He seemed like he was on some covert mission to drive her completely insane.

Soaked by this time, a large imprint of her body staining the sheets she could feel the tears cascading down her cheeks. Never had a man gone through so much trouble or relinquished so much time in an attempt to please her and though she would be forever grateful she had one thing on her mind at that moment and that was to be released from his hold if he was just going to tease her.

It had gotten to the point where it was almost unbearable now. Grabbing the edge of the bed Monica tried to slide to the floor and free herself from his grasp but he was too strong, too intent and he simply grabbed her thighs in what felt like a vise grip and ignored her pleas and continued to suck lightly on her throbbing clit.

Falling on deaf ears and since crying appeared to be of no avail Monica abruptly changed her tactics and began moaning in earnest. This seemed to turn him on even more and coupled with, 'baby, is that all you've got' and 'sweetie, you can do better than that', he upped the stakes and began slurping and sucking her so fast and so hard that it was only a matter of minutes before she was sitting straight up trying to force her entire vagina in his mouth so hard did she climax. That had been the final time and she could remember grabbing the back of his head in both her hands with such force that she could literally hear him gasping for breath as she felt one long, deeply intense orgasm after another rush warmly, freely through her love forsaken body. She smiled thinking back to the night before. So, this is what the girls in group had been talking about when they referred to multiples.

She'd passed out for a second time after the last cataclysmic eruption and had no earthly idea how long she'd been out but a flicker of light had awakened her and she awoke with a mouth as dry as the Mojave Desert itself. Her first thought was to get a glass of cold water from the bathroom and continue her dream.

Instead, she found James standing there and when he noticed that she was awake, he pulled down the tiny, thong like briefs he was wearing to finish the job he'd started before she'd passed out on him.

At first glance, Monica made up her mind that there was no way on God's green earth that James LeBrandt was going to even consider making love to her with…

And for the first time since he'd arrived she thought of her girlfriend. Only this time there was no contempt but a tremendous amount of respect when she thought of the five-foot-two inch Alexis accommodating such a massive man as James without so much as a whimper. Not that Alexis was one to kiss and tell or even suggest something as personal as her sexual affairs with her but Monica could just imagine Alexis looking at James for the first time and wondering what the hell she had gotten herself into; then shrugging her shoulders and accepting it as just another challenge before making the best of a bad situation. Or maybe, just maybe that's what separated James from the other guys pushin' up on her all the time.

Everyone wanted to know what the attraction had been between the laid-back, unassumingly aloof, James Le Brandt and the very outgoing up-beat career-oriented Alexis LeBrandt. And the funny thing was that during the twenty year union no one knew anymore now than they had then. Well, except for Monica who now believed she knew the key to Alexis' infatuation.

Still, she'd never been the thrill seeker or the go-getter that her best friend was and she surely would have turned down this challenge even as much as she longed for a good roll in the hay every now and then. Yet, this was a bit more than she'd bargained for. The problem that she was encountering though, was again, one of principles—not that she'd been a stickler for principles up 'til this point. But the fact of the matter remained that not very long ago, James LeBrandt had taken her to heaven and back and one good deed naturally deserved another. He hadn't been shy or the least bit hesitant when it came to loving her for the better part of the night but now it was her turn to satisfy him and well—truth of the matter was she just wasn't too sure that she could please him or accommodate him. Although, she could always...

Before she could entertain the option she felt James—all of him—greet her, first gently and then with all the rage and passion of Spain's annual running of the bulls. She met his first tryst with a blood curdling shriek of pain that would have brought the cops calling at any other time except that it was a Friday night and the whole building was alive and jumping and her screams blended into the cacophony of sounds like the second clarinet in a New Orleans big band. After the first few thrusts, she was riding the crest of each wave like a seasoned veteran and fielding each thrust with a thrust of her own that made the recent tsunami seem like a mere ripple in comparison. Loving each minute, she found herself locked in a union like she had never known before and prayed that this night would never end.

By two o'clock that morning she'd lost count of just how many times she'd come but Lord knows, in all her life she had to admit that she had never been so completely and utterly satisfied by a man and she counted her friend Alexis a fool for dismissing this diamond in the rough.

Yet, despite all the props and accolades concerning James' performance there was no denying the fact, that as good as he'd been they could never see each other again in this light. And maybe he'd been right about sleeping with her in the past and ruining a beautiful friendship since now they had no relationship.

Again the sun shone through the blinds and every time she turned her head to avoid it, her head banged beyond belief. She was glad James wasn't there now although she did wish he had had the common decency to at least say goodbye. A kiss on the cheek would have sufficed but to wake up and find him gone without so much as a farewell was tantamount to him leaving twenty dollars on the night stand like she was no more than a common call-girl.

Still, she had little conversation for him. What was there to say anyway? 'Thanks James. The session was off the hook and you performed well beyond my wildest expectation but I'm sorry at this juncture we're unable to use your services. Now don't take the dismissal too harshly, my dear sir. As I said your performance was well above our current standards. In fact, you performed at an exemplary level Mr. LeBrandt. It's just that–well—we are experiencing some in-house crisis that must be resolve before we take on any new full-time clients. But don't be disheartened, Mr. Le Grande; I'll make sure to keep your resume on file and your performance chart within easy reach and should I come across anyone seeking someone of your rather unique talent and expertise I will make sure that I refer you with a glowing recommendation. I hope you understand the nature of your dismissal. It would simply be a conflict of interest on my behalf if I were to go on seeing you or opt to retain your rights at this time. Have a pleasant day Mr. LeBrandt and I wish you much luck and success in all your future endeavors'.

Monica smiled at the thought before becoming very sullen and morose when she thought about losing the best friend and sex partner she'd ever had. And despite the countless number of men she'd had either the pleasure or horror of sleeping with there was no question in her mind that they all paled in comparison to Mr. James LeBrandt.

Monica reached into the drawer of her nightstand, grabbed the bottle of extra-strength pain relievers and shook two from the bottle. Moments later she stood and felt her body sway to the right. It had been some time since she'd had a hangover of this magnitude but was not at all dismayed by it. It wasn't the first time and despite what Dr. Fielding had to say it probably wouldn't be the last. What she needed was nothing more than a hot shower and a cup of Folgers and she'd be good to go. Not to sound cliché ish but she would let no moss grow under her feet. There was still far too much to do and too little time. And just because she felt a little bruised and banged up there was still plenty to do. She'd encountered a lot the night before. Been places she'd never even perceived and enjoyed every minute. Gone was the guilt and the doubt. And for the most part she considered James just another chapter and was ready to proceed on with her life and her goals of self-empowerment.

Gathering her underclothes and spreading them out neatly on her bed, Monica went to the hall closet and grabbed the yellow jogging suit she was so fond of and the ironing board although her thoughts continually reverted to the evening before in spite of her trying to stay focused on the day at hand.

In that time, though, she'd come to two conclusions. The first was relatively easy. No matter how much guilt she felt; Alexis could never know what had transpired. And secondly under no circumstances could she ever let anything like that take place again. She was disappointed but not distraught; having learned a long time ago that her life was nothing but a work in progress doomed to be marked with mistakes and bad judgment. She'd also learned along the long, hard rocky road that was her life that she could spend an eternity beating herself up over her misdeeds. It was only recently that she'd come to the conclusion that reminiscing and feeling guilty hardly atoned for anything and the best thing she could do was to learn from her mistakes and that way she wouldn't be apt to repeat them.

Monica remembered doing something utterly idiotic in high school and dreading the fact that she had to face her father that particular evening when he got home from work. She loved her father more than anything else in the world and never wanted to be seen in a negative light in his eyes but confident that the news had already reached him, she dragged herself in to the house to face the music and was surprised to find that he was hardly angry but simply chalked her latest faux paus up to not thinking as well as being young and impulsive.

He hadn't even chastised her as her friends had warned. She'd felt so stupid, so dumb standing there in front of him waiting for his latest lecture. Instead he simply told her that people and especially young people were prone to make mistakes and it hardly made them dumb. They were only dumb if they failed to learn from those mistakes. She'd carried that message with her throughout her life and the rough times and it had served her well. And even though she had been close to seventh heaven only a few short hours ago, she knew that that evening could only be a one time tryst not to be repeated again under any circumstances.

Monica felt that it was important that she let James know exactly how she felt and if it meant losing his friendship then so be it. It was something that just had to be done and done now before she relaxed her resolve and let him ease his way back into her heart.

He'd been right about one thing though. She did feel a strong bond between them and always had. She'd just never had the self-confidence to tell him how she really felt about him. To Monica, James LeBrandt was in another league and she often wondered why he hung around with her with every girl on the east side of Detroit chasing him down. When the dust had finally settled she'd introduced him to Alexis and a few months later they were married.

Picking up the receiver Monica dialed the number she had dialed so often over the years and waited as the phone rang. The voice mail answered abruptly and Monica was shocked to find Alexis voice still on it. She felt a large swelling in her throat and a nauseousness in the pit of her stomach when her girlfriend's voice requested a message be left at the sound of the tone. Hanging up quickly Monica found herself seated on the sofa in the living room rummaging desperately through her pocketbook, her mind in shambles as she sought to find the pack of cigarettes.

No sooner was she seated than the doorbell rang. Knowing that it could only be Bridget or momma this early on a Saturday morning, Monica pondered the thought of answering the door then realized that her car was parked directly in front of the building and not answering only meant one thing to Bridget and momma. It could never mean that she had company or gotten up early and gone out with a friend or. Oh, no! If neither of them had spoken to her in a day or two it only meant one thing and that was that Monica was in trouble.

She remembered the time not long after she and Marshall had separated and she'd started dating this nice guy from somewhere around Champagne and he'd come to spend the weekend. Not wanting to be interrupted she'd parked their cars around the corner and not in her usual spot.

Anyway, she and this fella whose name escaped her now were

shacked up for about three or four days just lying around eating and talking and making good love 'til they got tired of eating and talking which was on the average of every fifteen minutes or so. In any case, she'd made the cardinal sin of taking the phone off the hook for the weekend so as not to be interrupted. Her mistake however, was not telling anybody about her plans. She'd been close to thirty then and really felt no need to. Little did she know?

When she and ol' boy finally did get up to go out and grab some groceries the house was ransacked. They said daddy had gone in and felt the toothbrushes to see if they were wet and the light bulbs to see if they were still warm like he was a member of CSI or Law and Order or some shit.

When they finally did catch up with her they gave her the tongue lashing of a lifetime about how they were so worried and how anything could have happened to her in this day and age. Oh, yes and lest we not forget how irresponsible she was for not having the decency to check in and let them know she was alright. So, she knew now that despite the fact that she was in no mood to see family or to go on some wild goose chase or shopping extravaganza at a Home Depot for hours on end for door hinges or table mats—she knew she had no choice but to open the door and entertain their whims.

Opening the door Monica was shocked to find a highly pressed preppy looking James s LeBrandt with a smile that filled the entire doorway posed in front of her. Monica couldn't help but smile despite the vow she'd just made.

"Mornin'. You were sleeping so soundly when I got up that I hated to wake you", he said stepping past her with a kiss on the cheek and a bag full of groceries. "I just ran out to get a change of clothes and to pick up a few things," he said emptying the bags on the kitchen counter before she had a chance to speak.

"Somehow we got sidetracked last night and missed that dinner I had planned for you so I thought I'd fix you one of my world famous breakfasts' to make up for it," he said smiling. "Where do you keep the bowls?"

Monica pointed to the cupboard over the sink before saying anything.

"James dear, I think we need to talk,"

"Talking is good but if it requires me to think then I must tell you I think a lot better on a full stomach and I don't know about you but between last nights missed dinner and this morning I seem to have worked up quite an appetite. Hope I didn't interrupt any plans you had for today but if you have time I'm going to show you a day of days. If not we can try again tomorrow but I must tell you that I've got everything planned just for you and I think you're going to love it. How long will it take you to get dressed, baby?" he said as he found the potato peeler and rinsed four nice sized potatoes over the sink. "Hope you're hungry."

She hadn't realized it at the time but her stomach would not let the fact go unnoticed and when the smell of the bacon made its way from the oven she reconsidered breaking the news and opted to wait until after breakfast to break the bad news to him.

"Have you showered yet?"

"No," she answered coyly, "In fact I just got up. James look, last night was beautiful..." she started to say.

"Yes, it was and trust me; last night was just the beginning of many beautiful days and nights. Last night we were just getting to know each other again and I know you were a bit apprehensive and probably even feeling somewhat guilty about the whole affair but trust me I thought about all of that and I think we can work this whole thing out but let's worry about all of that later. Right now, though, you need to get a move on. We've got an appointment at eleven and its nine-thirty now."

Monica had never known James to be so talkative, so driven or so adamant but she heeded his suggestion and found her way to the shower where moments later she was basking in the surge of warm water and smiling at the thought of once again having a man around even if it was only for one more day.

Rinsing the soap from her body, Monica heard the bathroom

door open. Pulling the shower curtain back she was surprised to see James standing there smiling and also felt a bit apprehensive about having him see her naked. Last night had been different. It had been dark and he'd been unable to see her but this was different and she suddenly felt very self-conscience about having him see her now. She'd been losing weight gradually and he'd noticed. It made her feel good and was one of the high points of the evening but she was by no means where she wanted to be and she really hated him seeing her in this light. In her mind she was still overweight although over the years she'd learned to mask it well. And even though she had all intentions of ending this charade before another day passed she only wanted him to have the memory of the night before and not regret sleeping with someone who didn't have the self-discipline to even maintain her own weight.

Monica pulled the shower curtain back quickly and shouted. *"Get out James!"* And then realizing how harsh this must have sounded quickly added, *"Can't a girl have any privacy?"*

"Not when I've waited this long to be with this girl. Sorry, hon, but this has been long overdue." And with that said James tore the curtains back to Monica's ultimate disgrace and stood there staring at the woman in front of him.

If she could have Monica would have melted like a grain of sand and been grateful to have been washed down the drain along with the last bit of her dignity that had just been usurped by this godlike specimen of a man that stood before her.

Speechless she stood there while he grinned broadly. She wondered whether he was smiling at her or laughing at the image she presented and felt a cold hatred welling up inside of her for this man she had felt so much for a little while ago. But when he began to loosen his belt and slowly strip in front of her she knew the smile that he wore was only in anticipation of what was to follow. And she couldn't help but thinking of all those nights she'd fantasized about making love in the shower.

In no time at all, James was completely naked and standing

beside her. Turning her to face him, he pulled her head forward and kissed her gently, taking one lip between his two and then the other nibbling gently on each separately. The water was warm and felt good rolling down her chest and between her legs. And she suddenly came to the conclusion that she had to have him at least one more time before letting him walk out of her life but the choice was no longer hers to make as he wrapped first one leg and then the other around his waist and lifted her up pinning her to the wall of the shower. The cold tile against her back was nothing less than exhilarating and his smooth gentle thrusts so different from the night before assured her that what he said was true and that last night presented the last obstacle before them and now that they had transcended every obstacle she knew that for the first time in her life she could truly say how it felt to be made love to.

The warm water beat against her face hiding the tears that flowed freely as she wrapped her arms around his shoulders and buried her face in his neck. She could hardly feel anything now but the idea that she was falling deeply in love.

Chapter 8

Alexis had no idea what was going on. She had turned with the idea that Monica was still standing there but after searching the sea of faces around the front and side of the Radisson Hotel for close to a half an hour Alexis had given up her search in vain and was forced to agree with Philip that Monica must have bumped into an old friend or gotten bored with the scene and left.

Alexis knew Monica better than that and was sure that something had triggered her friends' sudden departure. After twenty years, she knew her girlfriend well enough to know that she wouldn't just up and leave unless something was bothering her. When she returned to her hi rise and found Monica's clothes gone she knew something was askew but had no idea what it was.

In fact, she'd been more outgoing and upbeat than she'd ever known her to be laying out her clothes and teasing Philip endlessly for much of the evening. So, for her to disappear was really out of context. Still, Philip might be right. Hell, as hungry as Monica was to get a man—any man—she'd probably gone with the first guy she'd met having two legs and two arms. Alexis laughed. She loved Monica but had to admit that when it came to getting a man Monica couldn't catch a man if her pussy were stocked choc full of beer and ballgames. Alexis laughed out loud at the thought.

Men just weren't Monica's forte and even the sorry, no-good, do nothin' guys Alexis wouldn't think to give the time of day to who were always whinin' and cryin' about winning the dusty dick award would take one quick look at Monica and count themselves as a shoo-in for next year's award as well.

She'd spent the night with Philip that night, entertaining him for the better part of the night at some little oyster bar on the outskirts of

Detroit proper and even let him spend the night but after all that and all his pleading and talk of a future together she just couldn't bring herself to make that move and had even gone so far as to lock her bedroom door in case he thought her denial was a case of playing hard to get. The next night Philip fared no better. And although he had to admit that it was one of the best weekends he'd had in a long time he had to admit that it could have been better if she would have only let him into her heart.

They promised to meet again the following month in New York and pick up where they left off and they had to and extent but much to Philip's chagrin they also left off in the same place. It would take time she'd told him. That's all; just time. After twenty years of being with one person Alexis found it difficult to suddenly abandon all those crazy feelings. And right now that's exactly where she was; all jumbled up, trying to cope with James' rejection, the divorce and the fact that her kids blamed her for walking out on their daddy. It was all a bit much to just let go and though the marriage had been over for some time the shock of receiving divorce papers in the mail didn't necessary bring about closure as much as she wanted them to.

And what could Philip know of closure or divorce? In her eyes, he was still wet behind the ears. He'd never known a partnership as strong or as completely devastating as the one which had ended the longest friendship she'd ever known with a stranger asking her to sign some papers as culmination. It was hard but she was handling her business nonetheless. If he wanted her he would have to wait and Lord knows she didn't know how long it would take. The wounds were still fresh, and still painful. But she was handling in spite of it all. And without the help of group meetings for divorcees at the local church or therapy or even Monica who always had a way of bringing some light into the dark. And speaking of Monica where in the hell was she.

She'd been calling her for months now and to no avail. She'd left messages and even stopped by the house on several occasions.

The first couple of weeks hadn't bothered her so much. Monica had always been on the moody side and in the summer when they'd be sent off to camp, and Monica would get homesick or boy sick or just sick of everything and everybody in her midst including 'Lexis and Bridget, they would tease her about being bi-polar and getting the good doctor to see about prescribing her something to lift her spirits but the next day she'd be just as chipper as the day is long. She'd been that way as long as Alexis could remember—up one day and down the next—but never this long. Even when they had been separated by states or countries did they go this long without talking to each other.

There were even periods of time when and argument would last for weeks, sometimes months but they'd always managed to work things out. But as they got older the arguments had been few and since being in New York this was the first time they'd gone without talking at all. Funny thing about it was that nothing at all had occurred and after weeks of trying to find a reason Alexis decided that she had enough to worry about without worrying about this little fat heifer not speaking to her. Still, it bothered her. First James and now Monica.

It seemed like the only good thing about her life was Philip but he was so far away that even with her long distance calling plan she couldn't be calling him on the regular and e-mailing and instant messaging were just to impersonal. Besides what man wanted to hear about problems between two girlfriends or the latest gossip from the old neighborhood. Certainly not Philip who was in Charlotte one day on business and Atlanta the next. He hardly had time for her conversation let alone her petty issues concerning Monica.

One thing she was glad about though and that was the apparent attentiveness he showed her when she spoke of James and her divorce. She wasn't quite sure she would have or could have been that understanding but at this point she had no one else to talk to and for some reason James was on her mind more and more. When they'd first split he'd called her everyday just as he did when they were married but after a time he'd stopped calling and she assumed that he'd moved on. But the more she thought about it the more confident she was that James could never live without her. When the phone calls stopped coming she began to worry and Philip's presence didn't ease her anxiety in that regard. And when the kids came home from school and went to stay with their daddy first and then came to stay with her and were happy to report that daddy must have a girlfriend since he didn't come home last night she found herself to be nothing short of devastated. So he had moved on. The thought angered her to no end and bothered her even more when her daughter accused her of being jealous. Jealous? In order to be jealous she had to have loved him and though she loved certain attributes he possessed she had never really been in love with him the way it had been drawn up and presented to her.

There had never been the sparks and although he had certainly lit her ass up on a number of occasions in the bedroom it had never really been like what she imagined it would be with the knight in shining armor shit coming to sweep her off her feet and make passionate love to her that would have her head in the clouds and make her swoon at the mere sight of him. No, it had never been anything like that.

When she asked Philip if that's how it felt to him—falling in love—that is. He assured her that that was exactly what it felt like when he was in her presence. She was a princess in his book and he knew how it felt to be on cloud nine and in seventh heaven at the same time weeks after seeing her. Only thing he still wished for was for was her to be passionately in love as well. They both laughed and she wondered if he was tired of hearing about James yet. Having too much time on her hands without Monica and James around she wondered how long it would be before Philip grew tired of her antics too and would find a way to dismiss her as well.

But if she needed any of the three at this point in time it was Philip. He was close to a genius when it came to the market and by way of e-mails and faxes he was showing her how to play the game the way the big boys did. She was now spending more time hovering over the NASDAQ and Wall Street Journal than her lesson plans and the benefits were accruing rapidly.

Over the last month she'd made a bundle with Lockheed thanks once again to Philip who was quick to advise her that with the current administration and their penchant for war anything that had the smallest connection with the military industrial empire was a goldmine. It made sense but she would have never known if it wasn't for Philip. He not only told her what to invest in; he told her how to invest so she could see the dividends almost immediately.

And all she'd been doing as of late was robbing Peter to pay Paul. There was no long term investment strategy. It was simply a case of dropping a ton over here just as it was about to take off, catch it while it was soaring but don't be greedy. Pull it out before it peaked and wait for another hot tip and throw it on something else. At least that was the gist of it in layman's terms.

Alexis had complete faith in Philip's judgment and sometime around the time when she saw her dividends reach the quarter of a million mark Alexis grew a tad bit apprehensive and entrusted Philip with the power of attorney and let him work her portfolio as he saw fit though she followed his every movement as if she were doing the actual investing herself. And she loved what she saw. The hobby had quickly turned into an obsession and she had to admit she loved following the fluctuating market more than just about anything these days. Then again there wasn't much of anything else these days.

Every now and then she'd get the itch to see James to ease her cravings but she thought better of it and was sure that if she gave him a little taste it would kill the overall plan which was to hold out until he came back to her on his hands and knees begging for her to take him back. The problem was that as time went on she found herself wanting to crawl back to him instead and apologize for her own stupidity. The longer they were apart the more she appreciated what he'd meant to her life. But that wasn't the only problem. The other problem was that he hadn't called her in months.

Oh, Philip was still there, still hanging around waiting in the wings but he was no longer patient and the thought of him being anything more than a good friend had dissipated enormously from the first time he'd come to see her.

Now when he was in town, which seemed like every other weekend he just naturally assumed that the guest bedroom was his and she no longer felt compelled to lock her door. They'd usually stay up 'til the wee hours of the morning just talking and going over the market. And needless to say they enjoyed each other's company, he more than she, but the thrill was gone in her eyes since all she now saw was James.

She'd seen James on a few occasions since the divorce. Calling him several times to see if he was home before dropping by the house to pick up something or another she really didn't need and he'd always been more than glad to see her or so it seemed but he'd changed. No longer did he jump to see her. Most of the time he was outside in the garage tinkering with something or another on that ol' beat up '57 Chevy always trying to see if he couldn't add just a little more pep to its step. He'd roll out from under the car, give her that big infectious smile of his, tell her that the backdoor was open and to help herself to whatever it was that she needed before sliding right back under that tin hobby of his that superseded life itself. 'Lexis always made sure that she was dressed to the nine on these visits wearing the tallest heels and the shortest dresses she could lay her hands on.

She'd usually call and hang up on him just to see if he was home, then pretend to stop by just because she was in the neighborhood so he wouldn't get the impression that she was coming over because she missed him.

Once, she'd called prior to her stopping by and he'd picked up the phone so quickly that all she could do was speak. When she found out that he was working on the car she opted to up the stakes. It had been close to a year since she'd had sex and was really beginning to feel the strain. *Damn she needed some!* Knowing full well that James, like every other man she knew was weak for a good pair of stilettos, some ruby red lipstick and some cleavage; she dressed accordingly then opted for no stockings or panties, replacing them with baby oil instead so that she glistened from head to toe.

She hoped that he was in his usual position underneath the car so when he looked up he could get a full view of everything he was missing. She grinned at the thought as she stared at herself in the full length mirror. If she knew her man and she was damn sure that after twenty-two years of marriage that she knew James she knew that it would be next to impossible for him to turn her down today and that would just be the first step in her plan to have him crawling back to her.

Alexis wondered if he would try to take her right there in the garage, in the front seat of the Chevy or if he would have the strength and the discipline to wait and escort her into the house before raping her sweet, little, brown ass. And then she thought about James' manhood entering her as he'd done so many times before.

Considering how much time that had elapsed she realized that she might not be able to accommodate him as readily as she had in the past and pulled out the baby oil again and began lubricating herself once more. Only this time, the application was internal.

Smiling as she parted the lips to her vagina to apply the baby oil she moved one leg up onto the sofa to gain easier access and found herself thinking of James and began massaging even more vigorously. Before she knew it both legs were up and the six inch heels were digging a deep imprint in the leather cushion of the sofa.

Her eyes closed, she thought of the day not that long ago when she and James had attended Chancellor Philbin's faculty luncheon at the college and she'd worn his favorite cream-colored camisole with the matching fishnets and garter belt underneath that black Jones of New York suit he adored so much. She knew it wasn't appropriate but it made her feel sexy and anything that would add some spice to one of those stuffy lunches for those bourgie—ultra-conservative—stuffed shirt, academics was more than appropriate if you asked her.

James loved the outfit and insisted on letting her know it before they left home but she'd put him on hold. In the car on the way over to the university she'd teased him at every stoplight pulling her skirt up and telling him to watch as she parted her lower lips and rubbed her love button lightly while sucking on one finger and then two as if they were popsicles on a sweltering July afternoon.

He'd pulled the car over on the dusty road outside of the university on more than one occasion, as her colleagues rode by on their way to the luncheon. Laughing and grinning like a schoolgirl she'd ease out of his grasp complaining about him messing up her hair and rumpling her clothes. Then, as soon as he'd pull the car back onto the highway she'd begin masturbating again just to tease him. Again he would pull the car over and this time he was so heated by her exhibitionism that she could not get him to move the car no matter how much she begged and pleaded.

They were quite late now and she feared she was going to have to give him some right then and there right outside of the university entrance if they were going to make it at all. If it hadn't been for one of her colleagues stopping to see if they were having car trouble she honestly believed they would have missed the luncheon altogether although with the way James had been making love to her lately they certainly would have known she was in the vicinity.

The luncheon had been held in one of the first houses to be built on campus and she had to admit that it was a rather charming old house with the high ceilings she so adored and stairs so worn and rounded that they cried out when too much weight was put upon them but overall it was a charming home; the kind that befits a chancellor.

Of course, all eyes were on Alexis when they arrived and she welcomed the attention. James enjoyed it too—only making her stock rise in his eyes. Though not all of the professor's wives were as fond of 'Lexis as their husbands' tended to be they appeared cordial. Crowds of professors, the majority of whom were men hovered around the tiny, brown bombshell discussing everything from nuclear physics to her feelings on reparations for African-Americans. But her eyes never left James who always commanded a small crowd of his own and who never felt completely at-ease at these functions since he had maintained little or no interest in politics, the latest gossip or sleeping with another man's wife no matter how discreet they tried to be when they offered him the punanny.

By the time lunch was served and the chancellor took the podium the only thing James and Alexis were starving for was each other. And when 'Lexis dropped her fork under the table and James bent down to pick it up; he found Alexis hard at work with a champagne glass tucked firmly between her legs. Grabbing his head roughly she removed the glass and tried to replace it with his baldhead. Trying desperately to force it between her thighs Alexis laughed out loud, drawing even more attention to herself, when he jerked his head away from her grasp and returned to his seat looking hot and bothered.

'Lexis remembered him whispering, telling her, that, 'she wasn't right', and being more than a little upset with her antics and though he didn't exactly voice his opinion she knew James well enough to know that he was more than a little frustrated. He was angry now. Alexis only hoped that she could diffuse his frustration. And feeling more than a little kinky herself she knew that she'd better take care of it now or the ride home would be as unpleasant as the ride there had been pleasant.

"Give me five minutes and then follow me," she whispered in his ear before excusing herself from the table and making her way down the hallway and up the stairs.

James had no idea where she was going or what she was up to now but waited a minute or two before promptly excusing himself as well and making his way in the direction he thought Alexis had gone. When he couldn't find her in the bathroom at the top of the stairs he was at a loss but continued to open door after door until he found his wife standing nude in the middle of the room at the end of the hall.

"Come in sweetie and lock the door behind you," Alexis said as her husband swung around to see if anyone else had followed.

"Are you crazy?" he whispered, smiling but at the same time aware that the wrong person happening in on this scene would not only mean his wife's termination but the end of her career as well.

"Come here, lover," she said. "I've got something special for you."

James moved forward, and although he was more than a little apprehensive he followed her lead. When he was directly in front of her, she reached into her bag; found the tiny tube of chocolate-cherry, X-Scream, edible lubricant, pulled him to her then dropped to her knees, unzipped his pants and applied the gel to his already hard member before gobbling up both James and the lubricant in one fell swoop. The loud slurping noises that usually excited James and hastened his climax now only served to slow him down.

"Baby, they can hear you," he said nervously.

"Let them, baby." She said slurping and slobbering all over him.

"Good God baby can we save some of this for later on tonight?" he begged still worried about someone walking in on them.

"Relax. Trust me, sweetie, there's not a man down there, including the chancellor, who wouldn't mind trading places with you right now. Now feed me baby, I'm starved."

And again she took him in her mouth sucking just the tip of his penis now and gripping the lower half of his shaft, tightly and sliding her hand up and down, in unison with her mouth since she knew this was his weakness. Seconds later, she felt his body become rigid. Certain that he was on the verge of exploding she let his rock hard dick fall from her mouth and leaned back arching her back high in the air and pulling her skirt up to her waist before applying a dab of lubricant to her already moist pussy and rubbing it feverishly in a small circular motion. James loved to watch her masturbate but there was no time for that now but after feeling him in her hands and her mouth she needed to feel him in her pussy.

"Come on lover, it's waiting for you," she whispered between moans.

James obliged and entered her slowly and before either of them could feel the other they were both coming in tremendous waves that he thought could surely be felt throughout the entire house. Finished and spent, they rejoined the reception, separately and decided to leave early.

James thanked the chancellor, shook a few hands and explained that Alexis was feeling a bit under the weather and was waiting in the car. They made love three more times before they reached home and once more in the garage after they arrived.

Now here she was sitting on the sofa on the verge once again, reminiscing about James when she should have been there.

Alexis glanced at her watch and realized that it had been some time since she'd phoned James and hoped he was still at home. Of course he was. The lube job she was applying to herself was soothing, relaxing and satisfying most of the time but it could in no way compare to what James could do. Jumping from the sofa Alexis grabbed her car keys and headed for the red Mercedes 350SL outside.

Moments later Alexis stepped into the early evening and into a nasty drizzle which made it seem even colder than it was. The weatherman said it was forty-two degrees but the wind coming in off the lake always made it seem ten degrees colder than it actually was and she had to wonder what had ever made her come back to Detroit to live in the first place. Lord knows, it certainly wasn't the weather. Now she wished she hadn't been so damn cheap and gone ahead and paid for one the parking spots in the garage below the building. At least she wouldn't have been getting soaked now.

What had previously been a light drizzle was now turning into a torrential downpour and she could feel the sticky clumps of no run mascara running down the sides of her face.

'Nobody but a fool or a love sick puppy would be out in this kind of weather,' she thought to herself then smiled when she considered herself the latter and trudged the block or so more towards her car.

It was a good thirty minute ride but she could do it in twenty if she jumped on the expressway and traffic was on her side. Surprised to find the traffic relatively light for this time of day she soon had the Benz up to seventy-five with hardly an afterthought. Another three or four minutes and she'd be pulling up in the driveway and have James on his knees begging her to come back home.

Grabbing a tissue from her bag to wipe the dark streaks of mascara from her face Alexis tilted the rearview mirror to see the oily mess and could not believe her luck. Approaching rapidly from the rear, lights flashing was a state trooper. She truly hoped he wasn't following her though something in the back of her mind and the numbers on the odometer told her he was. Glancing down at the dash she could hardly believe she was doing eighty-five. She'd meant to get that damn thing checked but in her mind she knew she wasn't getting around this one. It had stopped raining by the time he pulled her over and she wondered if he would have if it had still been pouring. Sure he would have—cops were assholes. Probably get out with one of those cheap ass plastic slickers and one of those plastic condoms for his hat and still give her a summons.

She needed another ticket like she needed a hole in the head. This would make four in the last six months and the insurance company was already threatening to drop her if she got another one. What had she been thinking? *Damn.* Still, she didn't feel like kissing his ass to avoid another one. Probably wouldn't do any good, anyway. Probably one of those hard-nosed, I'm just doing my job sorts anyway. The hell if she was going to hike her dress up and smile all pretty for this mother. In fact, she wasn't even going to give him the benefit of looking at him. Just give me the fuckin' ticket and let me be on my way.

Easing the car over onto the shoulder of the road Alexis

considered her options again—only this time the anger was gone. She really couldn't afford another ticket. Waiting for the officer to get out of his patrol car she thought about selling the damn car and getting a Hyundai and maybe bribing the cop. Since neither were viable solutions she did the only thing she could do in her position. She pushed the seat back, crossed her leg and waited for the officer to approach the car and cite her for speeding. She would not utter a word in objection and just hoped he'd be quick about the whole affair so she could be on her way.

Hearing the door of the patrol car slam, Alexis reached over and grabbed her purse and proceeded to rummage through it before taking out both license and registration. She then rolled down the window with her eyes and face still fixed on the road in front of her and handed the officer the necessary paperwork without so much as even glancing in his direction. From his hand she could tell he was Black and she felt a little relieved but at eighty-five miles an hour it didn't matter if he was blue or gray.

"Ms. LeBrandt is it?" he asked.

"Yes, officer," she replied stoically the anger obvious in her voice.

"Ms. LeBrandt, do you have anything earthly idea of how fast you were going?" he said in that matter-of-fact way they have of rubbing salt in the wound and making matters worse than they already were.

"Yes, officer, I know how fast I was going. Did you ever think that it was because I might just be in a hurry to get where I was going?" she asked not the least bit concerned about the ticket now but simply wanting to be on her way.

The officer ignored her and continued writing as Alexis now with both hands on the steering wheel stared straight ahead. She wished now that she hadn't worn that tight ass little dress. Something less revealing would have made her feel a little more comfortable as she felt the officer give her body the once over. She wondered if this couldn't be tantamount to some kind of police harassment but could only blame herself.

It was drizzling again and he had neither yellow rain slicker nor condom for his hat and she prayed he'd get soaked. What was taking him so long anyway? License plate, registration number and speed he clocked her at were all he needed.

She wanted to turn and ask him if he was writing a bestselling novel but she refused to turn and look in his direction though she could feel him giving her the once over for a second time and wondered what fool would stand in the cold and the rain to stare at a woman's chest. 'Stupid fool'.

"Are we quite finished here, sir," she asked hoping to speed up the pace some.

"Just about," he said handing her driver license and registration through the crack in the window.

"So you live on East Manchester?" he said.

"I believe that's what my license says," she replied curtly hoping to dispel any future conversation which may have led to some cheap pick-up line.

"That's good. That means you're not too far from Bentley's. A couple of the fellas and I play there every Thursday and Friday evening and I believe you promised me a drink," he said never changing his tone.

'*Okay, that's enough*', Alexis thought and only wished she'd left the mini-cassette she used for taping her lectures in her pocketbook. Now he was definitely bordering on sexual harassment but she had no way of proving it without having him proposition her on tape. So, she did the only thing she could do and ignored his comments and said, "*Officer, please! Would you just tell me what this is going to cost me?*"

"Well, if I were citing you for speeding then it would probably cost you somewhere in the neighborhood of two hundred dollars with court costs and the like but I've always been a firm believer in one hand washing the other and you did save my neck outside of the Radisson some months back. Still, and all you did promise me a drink if I'd let you through the partition and this time I'm going to hold you to it, Ms. LeBrandt. Now would you like for me to pick you up at home or do I have your word this time that you'll be at Bentley's on Friday night?" he asked smiling.

Alexis' head swung around in disbelief.

"How've you been Ms. LeBrandt? I always wondered if I'd see you again. In the brief time we talked you left quite an impression on me."

Alexis was shocked to see the young handsome cop from some months ago and was immediately ashamed of her calloused behavior.

"Oh, my God! It's you," she screamed. *"Damn! Talk about a stroke of good fortune. Damn I can't believe it's you. I certainly am glad, too. I certainly couldn't afford another speeding ticket. Tell me how have you been?"* she asked with a sigh of relief.

"Much better now that I've seen you," he said flirting openly now. "Guess I'm alright considering the tongue lashing I just took."

Alexis dropped her head in embarrassment.

"Guess I was kind of a bitch, huh?" she acknowledged.

"Kind of…" he replied, smiling at her.

"I'm sorry. It's just that…"

"No need to explain—I understand and believe me I've heard far worse. Anyway there will be plenty of time to explain later," he said handing her a pink sheet of paper.

"What the hell is this?" she shouted wondering why in the hell she'd let her guard down when he was summonsing her anyway. Why that low-down dirty son of a bitch she thought to herself the anger showing in her face.

"Calm down, Ms. LeBrandt. It's not what you think." He tried to explain but she was having none of that now as her rage boiled over.

"All that shit about one hand washing the other and you're still going to give me a ticket?" she asked heatedly. *"That's why Black people can never get ahead. They're so busy trying to get one up*

that they can't see who they're working for or who they're hurting. Damn you. I don't know why I thought you were different. Can I go now?"

"Yes mam," he said dejectedly, "but I need you to sign the back of the warning first. You see I 'm obligated to issue a warning or something anytime I make a traffic stop. It's just a procedure to insure our safety and yours. The paperwork itself is supposed to aid in unnecessary stops to cut down on racial profiling and sexual harassment and that sort of thing."

"Oh! I am sorry," she replied. "Where do I need to sign?" she asked suddenly feeling very stupid.

Taking the clipboard back from her, and tearing off her copy, it was obvious that her latest tirade had taken its toll and she wondered how cops did it with the constant abuse they received. She hardly knew what to say now but she didn't have to worry he was finished with her and her attempts at an apology.

"Sometimes its better to listen to the whole of something before we jump in; that way we can better understand what's going on, Ms. LeBrandt," he said not wanting to appear smug or hurt over her latest discourse. The rain was coming down much as it had earlier pelting her windshield and the officer.

"Have a good evening, Ms. LeBrant," he said before making his way back to the patrol car. "The directions to the club are on the back if you're interested," he shouted as he got in the car.

Alexis wanted to say something but didn't know what. She wanted to kick herself for being so goddamn impulsive all the time and thought about the numerous times James had tried to get her to slow down and think before she spoke. Now here she was—just finished apologizing and needing to again. And for what? Because she never gave herself a chance to hear something in its entirety. God, she hated that in herself. And here he was giving her a break and she'd all but cursed him out. He was just a cop and she'd never really had any use for them—but hey—a cop wasn't necessarily a bad person to have on your side. How stupid could she be?

Still, he'd given her his card and the directions to the club so she could still apologize besides she owed him at least that much and made it a note to keep Friday open. She just wished Monica's sorry ass would act right so she could drag her along. She hated going to some new dive alone and if this was a place cops hung out it was probably a dive.

Watching the officer's patrol car roll away, headlights flashing in hot pursuit of another lawbreaker speeding down the highway, Alexis wondered if they would fare as well as she had. Alexis still ashamed of her own behavior bent over and picked up the pink warning ticket in the passenger's seat next to hers.

Embarrassed by her own behavior Alexis knew she had no choice but to make up for her rudeness and was surprised when a business card fell from the warning citation reading, Officer Ricky Davis, Private Investigator. The job description intrigued her greatly and she wondered when he found the time to do that and play in a band after chasing bad guys all day.

Well, she would certainly find out on Friday but right now she had more pressing matters at hand—matters which after eight or nine months she could no longer postpone. Ironing out the wrinkles in her dress and reapplying touches to her make-up once again. Alexis started the car and headed home.

Minutes later, she pulled up in front of the modest brick and stucco Tudor style house she used to call home, breathed a long deep sigh of relief and thought of Terry McMillan waiting to exhale. She hadn't understood exactly what Stella was going through at the time but upon seeing James' long legs sticking out from under the Chevy truck she knew she could finally exhale too. She was finally home and all the chaotic madness that was the world suddenly faded and she was once again at peace. Just seeing James had that effect on her.

Hearing the car door slam, James slid from underneath the truck and smiled broadly as Alexis made it a point to straddle her ex with the hopes of shaking him up.

"Good God, woman!" he said with no choice but to look up her skirt. *"I see, ain't too much changed with you. I see you're still makin' it a point to come out of the house half-dressed or should I say half-naked."* he chuckled. *"One day, somebody's gonna snatch your 'lil ass up and that's gonna be the end of you,"* he laughed.

"I was hoping that might be you but you're a little slow on the draw. I figured you'd have me on the front seat of the truck by now. What's a girl gotta do these days?" she laughed just glad to be in his company again.

"Sorry, can't today babe, I'm on a kind of a tight schedule but I left the paperwork you asked for on the kitchen counter. Be careful though, I'm remodeling the kitchen and it's a mess in there to say the least. By the way did I tell you how good you look? I've gotta admit you're still holding it down, Lex," he said grinning widely at his former wife before sliding back under the truck. It was then and at that very moment that she suspected that James had to be seeing another woman.

The mere idea of James, though totally unfounded and unsubstantiated seeing someone else, not calling and not wanting to see her ate at her like nothing ever had before. Divorce or no divorce, he was, like the inscription read, hers, until death, 'do us part,' and this she believed.

In the entire time they'd been separated she had not once thought about sleeping with another man—well, actually the thought had crossed her mind—but it had only been a passing thought incurred by too much alcohol and of course Monica's whorish prompting. But the fact remained that she hadn't. Her sentiments always remained solely with James and only with James. She didn't know if it was because he was the only man to ever reject her or because he was the only man she'd ever slept with. Neither was hardly a matter of concern right now though. What did concern her at this point in time was the fact that he remained hers pure and simple.

Yes, he was to remain hers to do with as she pleased and divorce or no divorce—they'd made a pact—a union under God's eyes which was binding and indestructible not only in her eyes but in God's eyes as well.

There was little doubt that she'd made some mistakes when it came to their marriage. There was no denying that. But the fact still remained that James belonged to her. The fact that she had a gnawing and insatiable drive to chase her dreams was hardly grounds for a divorce. Hell, he knew that when he married her and if he knew that then and accepted it then, then why was it that he had such a hard time accepting it now.

Everything she did, she did for her family and that included James along with the kids. There wasn't a paycheck in the last twenty years—not one that she didn't bring home and lay down on the kitchen counter for him to do with as he pleased. Because he chose to bank it instead of invest it or live more than frugally was not her fault.

Now sitting there in the driveway pretending to look over the paperwork she'd just picked up she stared at James, well at least what she could see of him on the dolly sticking out from under the '57 Chevy, Alexis wished for one of those nights back when she'd felt it ever so necessary to try one of her crazy schemes. She'd give it all back for just one night—just one night—but how would he know if she couldn't tell him and right now her pride refused to let her tell him how she really and truly felt.

Alexis wondered if her staying home more would have made a difference. But then she'd always—but always made it a point to ask him to go. His choosing not to go was not her fault and after awhile she simply stopped asking him but she would very well have stayed home if he'd only insisted. He'd known since high school that she was a flirt-hell—everyone knew that. It was just one of many flaws in her character. Now, more often than not, it was a means to an end. In any case, the going out was nothing. For the most part they were no more than business meetings at best. And he had to admit that she'd compiled quite an impressive portfolio from her so-called extra-curricular activities.

There were the houses from the real estate ventures, then there were the stock options and the fact that both kids college tuitions were thanks to her, paid in full.

Financially she'd made sure that they were set for life. They could travel virtually anywhere in the world on a whim and that was all as a result of her late night liaisons as James so aptly referred to them and seemed so opposed to although he said nothing. Maybe— just maybe she wouldn't have fared quite so well with him tagging along but she'd certainly done her best to make him feel welcome. It was his decision not to go so why blame her? Why fault her for wanting more out of life than sitting at home fighting the temptation of being the newest cast member of <u>Desperate Housewives</u>. For her it had been all about improving her lot and providing financial security for her family and she'd certainly achieved that. She had never been degrading or considered herself condescending but her idea of enjoying life entailed more than simply sliding underneath a beat up ol' truck every night after dinner to adjust a carburetor or a cammy or something or another she'd never heard of before. She tried to learn about cars and what it was about them that so intrigued him. But he'd never taken the time or the interest in anything she did.

Even when he had the balls to finally file for the divorce it was so obvious that he'd wanted for who knows how long and they'd met at his lawyer's office to discuss the terms of the settlement and he'd countered all her allegations with those of his own never once did she count her marriage as being over. Not for one minute! Even when she appeared in court on that dreadful day and signed the divorce papers making it final she never once believed that it was finally over but James simply crying out in the only way he knew how to respond to her cry for a little space. That was all it was. She was sure that he hadn't really meant for it go this far.

Truth of the matter was that they talked more after the divorce was final than they had in the previous five years. At first, he called everyday and then just like that the phone calls stopped altogether.

She'd been so busy at this time with work, the new apartment and learning the ins-and-outs of the market that she really hadn't noticed but aside from Philip and Monica no one else called her on the daily.

Now as she sat pondering what had gone wrong in her life and in her marriage in the front seat of her car in what used to be her driveway, a myriad of jumbled thoughts, none of them good, swept through her mind.

She wondered what the hell had happened to the relationship that this man who at one time so adored her didn't even have the time to look in her direction anymore. And when he did she could see the loathing and contempt in his eyes. Now staring straight ahead, so absorbed in her own troubles, Alexis didn't notice James approaching the car.

"You okay, 'Lex?" he asked, his obvious concern showing.

Startled to find him standing there she answered abruptly and it was quickly apparent that there was something wrong although James had no idea what it was that was deeply troubling her.

"Do you wanna come in and talk about it?" he asked.

Still, in a daze she turned abruptly as if she were seeing him for the first time and without thinking, snapped, "No, I don't want to come inside James. I just want to know if you ever think about how anyone else feels besides yourself?" she asked apropos of nothing.

Bewildered by this line of questioning but knowing her well enough to know that an incorrect answer could lead to an argument James pondered her question carefully before submitting an answer which could leave him cursed out and babbling for forgiveness from her wrath.

"What are you talking about, Lex?" Repeating the question or feigning like he didn't understand always bought him some time in the past to size her up and he hoped it would do it now.

"What do you mean, what am I talking about?"

Ahh, yes he'd been right. She was angry, seething and he wondered why he'd ever approached the car in the first place.

"You know as well as I do that the only reason I got dressed this way was to come and see you,"

"Could have fooled me. That pretty much looks like your normal attire, if you ask me," he said and was sorry he had as soon as the words left his mouth. At times like this the best thing he could do was not saying anything at all—just nod his head in agreement and make sure that he kept eye-to-eye contact to let her know that everything she said was of the utmost importance and that the earth and the planets very rotation was dependent on what she had to say next.

"The hell with you, James LeBrandt. You know I don't dress like this everyday. The only reason that I got dressed like this was to come and see you and you act like this," she said.

James really wished she hadn't gone through all the trouble if she were going to act like this but he kept his eyes fixed on hers and said very slowly and calmly as though he were on the bomb squad of S.W.A.T. and had a live one ready to detonate.

"I act like what?" he said feigning ignorance and wishing whatever it was that was bothering her wouldn't include him as well.

"Why James, don't play dumb with me. I got all dressed up for you and you act like you don't even see me."

By this time he had had quite enough.

"What is it that you want me to do, Alexis? You want me to do somersaults or jump through hoops just because you greased up your legs and decided to leave your panties at home. C'mon girl I know you. I've seen you from every view there is, baby. When you first got here and before you went in to the house I made it a point to tell you that you looked nice just so I wouldn't have to go through this shit. I figured I'd fed your ego enough for one day but I guess I didn't. I really don't know what it takes and to tell you the truth I really don't care. I'm not in the business of feeding your ego anymore, Alexis. There just ain't enough hours in the day for that," he said feeling himself growing angry. "What more do you want from me?"

Alexis could feel his anger growing too. Anytime James called her by her full name she knew it was time to back off, recoil, think, reassess and consider changing the game plan. It would be quite hard to diffuse him now and no matter how angry he got she needed to get where she was going and he was an integral part of her achieving her goal. But James was hardly finished and she was truly sorry that she'd chosen to take the game plan she had. He continued.

"What you're really saying without trying not to be so blunt is that anytime you get the whim you can come over here, half-dressed, throw your little hot body in my face and not ask but demand that I screw you. That's what you're really talking about when you say 'fulfill your needs'. Come on, let's be honest Alexis. That's what you're really talking about. Isn't it Alexis?"

"And if I am?" She said glad that he'd had the balls to call a spade a spade and let the cat out of the bag though she figured that she'd made that pretty clear when she pulled up and straddled him in the garage and showed him she was panty less. He was no nuclear physicist but he couldn't have possibly thought that her virtually throwing the pussy at him was the prelim to a discussion of world news tonight.

"And if I am?" she repeated hoping to hurry this along so he could nail it a couple of times and relieve some of this pent up aggression, and release some tension so she could be on her way.

"And if I am'" she repeated a third time hoping she had him now.

"And if you are what, Alexis?"

"If I am asking you to cater to me and take care of my needs—my physical needs—then so what—what's wrong with that? You should be glad and welcome the fact that I still want you baby. You know, James, whatever differences we've had in the past and I must admit we've had our share; our sex life has always been something truly special. I could never in a million years have asked for more from you in the bedroom."

175

She knew she had him now. She'd been around enough men to know that their sexual prowess was a source of great pride since they all envisioned themselves as being Don Juan behind closed doors.

"That's one thing I have always said. You have always been great in bed, baby," she added waiting for him break out in that broad smile she'd come to know so well but much to her chagrin there was no smile this time.

"Who told you that our sex was great, Alexis. And how the hell would you know anyway, if, as you say, you've never had the opportunity of sleeping with another man? What the hell do you have to even compare it with"

Alexis was shocked by this latest discourse and the shock showed clearly on her face.

"Well, you never had any complaints before." She added still stunned by this latest revelation. But he was hardly finished.

"And how would you know how I felt about us in bed anyway, Alexis? Everything was always about you and how you felt when you were here but most of the time you weren't around enough to know how I felt about sex or anything else for that matter," he replied. He was digging in now. Ready to get grimy, gully even as he readied himself to go toe-to –toe with a woman who considered herself far superior to him in every way.

Alexis had never seen James so adamant and so strong in his convictions. Knowing James as she did Alexis realized that everything he did required considerable thought and it was obvious that he'd spent considerable time thinking about this; hardly reveling in what had prompted the end of his marriage. Twenty years with Alexis and now he was feeling like a veteran picking the scabs of dried up old war wounds that remained sore. Festering now and oozing pus in small droplets those old wounds hurt more now than when they first inflicted.

On unfamiliar ground, Alexis was hardly used to asking, let alone, begging for sex. Things certainly had changed over the past few months. Usually it was she who was doing the rejecting and in all honesty she couldn't remember James ever having turned her down before if she was in need although she had on several occasions when they were first married when he was under the impression that that thing of his was supposed to be permanently inserted in her. If she weren't moving then it was just naturally supposed to be in her. At the time she stayed hurt and raw but over the years she'd picked up a few tricks of her own to quench his desire and save herself from his constant onslaughts. Now it seemed that the tables had turned and if it wasn't enough that the tables had turned to the point where he not only no longer desired her but he had her almost begging him to make love to her or at least screw her if he couldn't see fit to make love to her.

"James darling can't we put the animosity aside for once and just go inside and discuss this?"

"Look baby, If you wanted to go inside to talk then that would have been fine but the truth of the matter is—and I really don't think you're hearing me is that James LeBrandt is no longer here to just satisfy your needs. I'm pretty sure there are quite a few men out there who wouldn't mind doing just that but I don't fall in that category anymore. Do you feel me? Look, why don't you solicit one of your business associates to scratch your itch, baby? I'm sure there's quite a few that have been waiting in line to do just that if they haven't already. Seriously speaking though Alexis, it has taken me quite some time to gain closure on you and I, and I'm not about to let you open up my heart so you can go treading all over me again. It hurts too much."

"So, what you're trying to tell me is that you have absolutely no desire whatsoever to sleep with me? Is that what you're saying, James?"

"No that's not what I'm saying at all. You're not listening. I didn't say that."

Alexis breathed a deep sigh of relief knowing that there were still hope and was confident that if she stepped it up a level she could still have him despite all the anger he was getting off his chest for her not staying in touch as much as she probably should have over the last few months and just showing up. James continued but Alexis wasn't listening at this point so fixated was she on getting him in the house and wearing his ass out for having her go through all of this.

"So you do still have a desire to be with me?" she asked grinning broadly.

"Look Alexis, I've tried to explain the situation the best way I know how. Maybe I'm not as eloquent as you are with words. I'm no college professor. I'm just a good ol' boy one step removed from the plow—just a good ol' meat and potatoes country bumpkin who likes the simpler things in life and maybe you can't understand someone being content to be that way so let me put it to you like this.

Much as I may want to sleep with you, Alexis—I can't. I just can't. Those days are long gone for me. They simply don't exist anymore. They're simply a memory nowadays. I've moved on and I hope that you can do the same as well."

Alexis was both shocked and hurt at the same time.

"I can't believe this. I really can't believe what you're telling me," Alexis said, her eyes welling with tears. *"I really can't believe this. Is it that I don't appeal to you physically anymore James?"*

"No, it's not that all. You are a beautiful woman and you certainly appeal to my senses. I'm not blind. I'm just hurt. But now that the healing process has begun I don't want to reopen old wounds is all. Not a hard concept to understand."

It was beginning to drizzle again and Alexis was tempted to take James up on his offer to go in the house and follow him into the house to continue their discussion. If there was one thing she hated more than anything was being rejected. And not only had he rejected her he'd turned her down so coldly that she was more determined than ever to have her way with him.

All she had to do was get inside. Once inside, she'd grab her favorite chair in the living room, prop one leg up like she used to do when she knew James was on his way home from work and had

had a particularly long and trying day at work, then wait 'til she heard the garage door open and begin stroking herself as if her very life depended on it. She thought about it but today was different somehow. She'd never seen him quite so strong, so adamant in his conviction. And if he turned her down again his rejection would kill her.

Gazing at him through the open car window, Alexis suddenly realized that in the months since they'd spoken he'd somehow this was not the James that she'd come to know and take for granted. He'd changed. And she had to admit that she liked the transformation— the new and improved James LeBrandt—so strong in his beliefs, so resolute in his resolve. Still, there was nothing on this earth that Alexis LeBrandt could not possess with her own resolve if she truly desired it, including James.

Alexis smiled as the old adage came to mind. Desperate tactics require desperate measures or something to that effect. Raising her skirt to her waist, Alexis parted the lips of her vagina with her left hand before taking her right hand and slowly rubbing her already throbbing clitoris with the other as James looked on in disbelief.

"Alexis, please! You know how nosy the neighbors are. You can't be sitting out here in the driveway doin' that," he said though his eyes never left her crotch.

Ignoring his pleas, she continued.

"So, this is what I have to resort to now, James? I told you to invite me in," she said continuing the circular motion with her index finger and enjoying James' reaction. She was beginning to feel it now and James' facial expressions only served to turn her on that much more. She knew she had him now.

"Damn, baby, can't you finish it for me. Just rub it for me," she moaned. Beads of sweat were beginning to form on the top of her lip and on the bridge of her nose as they always did right before she came.

"Please finish it for me James. Please baby! Just rub it for me!" She was shouting now and James turned to see who if anyone

was watching.

The drizzle had turned into a hard, pelting, spring shower. The cold water seemed to bring James back to his senses. Anxious now to get out of rain, he eyed Alexis who was still working feverishly to keep his attention and listened as she moaned and then whispered.

"Please make love to me James. Please darlin'. You don't know how badly I need to feel you, to have you hold me."

"I'm sorry baby. I just can't," he replied emotionless.

"Please baby," she said begging now.

"Sorry baby but those days are long gone. I told you that. What is it that you don't understand? I'm finished playing with you Alexis. Finished."

"You can't be serious, James. Here I am sitting putting on the performance of a lifetime for your benefit. And you're going to ignore me—the woman that got down on her knees for your ass for twenty years. The woman who had your children, who raised your children, who is sitting in the driveway of what used to be our house, masturbating because you won't give me fifteen minutes of your precious time," she said now angry that she'd stooped to such a level and still gotten no response or at least the response she was seeking.

"Look baby, this conversation is going nowhere. Let me get in the house and out of the rain. You take care of yourself, you hear, Alexis," and with that said he turned, picked a wrench lying in the yard and walked away.

Alexis had never felt so utterly useless and unwanted in her life as she watched the only man she'd ever come to have a semblance of passion for walk away and out of her life. Pulling her dress down in anger and opening the car door she screamed loud enough for the entire neighborhood to hear.

"James LeBrandt!"

Turning to see what was wrong now. He bent over picked up the remainder of his tools dropped them into his toolbox and stared at her as she opened the car and stood facing him.

"James LeBrandt I have one question for you and I want to answer me honestly."

"Yes, Alexis?" he answered.

"James, in twenty years you have never ever turned me down. Never! I'm just curious to know one thing."

"Yes, Alexis?" he answered his finger on the garage door opener.

"Just tell me one thing, James. Are you seeing someone else?"

"Goodbye, Alexis," he said pushing the button and watching her figure fade as the garage door closed.

Still, he had to admit as he watched her legs fade from view that she was still one fine woman.

"Why you smug, selfish bastard" he heard yell from the other side of the garage which was now closed completely.

Several neighbors hearing the commotion stood in the doorway watching the woman they'd all come to know as Mrs. LeBrandt standing in the pouring rain ranting and raving like never before.

"You remember this, you bastard, I made you what you are James LeBrandt and I'll be damned if I let some other woman reap the benefits. If you won't sleep with me you won't sleep with anyone," Alexis screamed as she opened the car door. *"I'll see you dead first. Just you remember that! I'll see your ass dead first."*

It seemed like the entire neighborhood had assembled behind closed doors and blinds and peep holes to watch the theatrics and though she saw blinds and curtains move she hardly cared.

James, on the other hand now wished he'd given this crazy love sick woman something to tide her over instead of having her creating the scene in the driveway of his house in front of his neighbors.

One thing was for sure. It wouldn't happen again and as she she knew left his first order of business would be to obtain an order of restraint against one Alexis LeBrandt.

Chapter 9

If James' first order of business was to obtain an order of restraint the Alexis' first priority was to find out who in the hell the little heifer was that had laid claims to her man.

Not since grammar school had Alexis considered grabbing another female up and giving her the thrashing of her life. And that hadn't worked exactly out as she'd hoped, that's for sure.

Of course there had been a boy involved. There always was. His name was Lil' Marky Davidson. Well, that's what everyone called him anyway. And Lil' Marky was the man in third grade. Light-skinned with wavy hair and a Roman nose was what made him different from all the rest of the boys who looked like her with their dark complexions and peasy hair. No, Lil' Marky was different, with his light, olive skin and light eyes and that in itself was enough to make him the heart throb of every little nine year girl at St. Josephs.

Alexis had never been much interested in boys up until Lil' Marky entered the scene and asked her, by way of Monica to lunch. She preferred jumping double-dutch with her girls but with Monica's prompting she agreed and on the following day she remembered asking momma to make her sam'wich which always consisted of the same thing. Everyday since she could remember momma made her a bologna sam'wich with a big glob of salad dressing. But the night before, she went to momma and asked her if she could make it extra special since she was going to be sharing Her sam'wich with Lil' Marky Davidson. Well, she didn't exactly tell momma why or that she had a lunch date but she begged her not to push down on the bread so much when she cut it in half 'cause she hated those fingerprints momma always left in the Wonder bread and she figured Lil' Marky would probably laugh at her when she told him that her momma always fixed her lunch for her and those were her fingerprints in the Wonder bread.

She was pretty sure Marky made his own sam'wiches since he was pretty much of a man in her eyes although he didn't have her daddy's height or his build. But around St. Josephs he was recognized as a man. After all, Lil'Marky Davidson was twelve years old although he was still in third grade. But that was only because he was from one of those other countries that bombed the Trade Centers and since America didn't like that too much they put him in the third grade and said it was because he didn't speak right good English but daddy told her the real reason. And even though America didn't like Lil' Marky Davidson too much, everyone at St. Josephs thought he was pretty cool because for one he was older and he was different from the normal kids. Monica said it was because he was more mature than the rest of the boys in their class—whatever that meant. And he was tough. Nobody but nobody at St. Josephs messed with Lil' Marky Davidson. *Nobody.*

Now Monica had somehow gotten the word that Marky was interested in her best friend and made it a point to let the rest of the school know it as well. And somehow, as was the custom St. Josephs—well at least as far back as anyone could remember—when a boy and a girl liked each other and wanted everyone to know that they went together they shared their lunch at recess and that's why on the night before her first big date when momma made the lunches it was so important that she made sure that momma didn't press down too hard and leave the imprint of her fingers in her sam'wich.

And although momma didn't understand why all of a sudden it was so doggone important, she did her best to comply with Alexis'; wishes and even went so far as to cut the crust off the bread which 'Lexis used to fuss about so.

The next day, Alexis found herself sitting alone in the schoolyard—well—alone that is except for Monica who insisted on coaching her on the do's and don'ts of eating a bologna sam'wich in front of the opposite sex when trying to make a good impression.

Listening intently, Alexis nervously watched as Lil' Marky Davidson hung upside down from the monkey bars on the other side of the playground not looking in her direction but obviously pulling everything out of his rather limited repertoire in an attempt to impress her. And although she was impressed she certainly wished he'd get on with it so she could join her girls before recess was over.

With most of the lunch hour now gone and Marky still swinging like a chimpanzee, Alexis had finally had all she could take of the charade and pushed Monica and her advice aside and headed over to her girls who were jumping double-dutch and having the time of their lives. Before she could join the long line of girls waiting for their turn Alexis felt a tap on her shoulder. Turning to see who it was she was quite surprised to look into the eyes of Lil' Marky Davidson.

"Wanna share my lunch with me?" he asked.

Glancing over at Monica for the go-ahead she could see Monica beaming with pride almost as if it was she Lil' Marky was asking out.

Alexis smiled, showing the big gap and her missing front two teeth and said, "Sure Marky, I'd love to share your lunch with you," just the way Monica told her to say it.

Sitting there on the concrete bench at the picnic table at the far end of the playground Alexis suddenly understood why Monica had pushed her into this latest tête-à-tête and she was certainly glad she had. This beat jacks and double-dutch by a landslide. Lil' Marky Davidson was certainly the gentleman and though he wasn't much in the way of conversation, he did compliment her on her two missing front teeth and no one had ever done that before, telling her that it helped give her an air of maturity that separated her from the rest of the third grade girls who still had their baby teeth. The sound of his voice made her tingle all over and although neither one of them exchanged another word she knew right then and there and at that very moment that following Monica's advice had been the right decision after, all.

Just as she was about to consummate the union and hand Lil' Marky Davidson half of her bologna sam'wich without the fingerprint or the crust a hand swooped in and knocked the sam'wich her mother had taken the time to prepare so diligently to the pavement below.

Stunned by the intrusion, Alexis looked up to see her arch-rival and the bully of St. Josephs, Martha Grimes standing over her.

"Here, Marky," she said handing the twelve year old a piece of her own lunch.

"Ain't nobody want no nasty bologna sam'wich. Here, Marky take half of mine. My momma don't never make my lunch. She say she ain't got no time to be makin' no sam'wiches and it don't make no sense when she can get the real thing—even better at Subway.

Lil' Marky Davidson seemed pretty entertained by the whole chain of events and was used to having women fight over him but Alexis was beside herself. The mere thought of someone knocking that sam'wich which momma had worked so hard to get just right to the ground was too much for her to take.

Alexis jumped up from the from the concrete picnic table and before she knew it she had a handful—well maybe two fingers of the girl's hair since Martha was basically bald. Anyway Alexis got to grabbin' what she could of the girl's hair and was doing her able-bodied best to rip what little she did have from the girl's scalp when all of a sudden and in one fell swoop Martha Grimes, the bully of St. Josephs, flipped Alexis around some kind of way with all intentions of slamming her head into the concrete picnic table when Monica arrived as she always did right in the nick of time and proceeded to whip the living stew out of ol' Martha Grimes.

Alexis grinned as she recollected her childhood memories and only wished that Monica were here for her now as she traveled home from seeing James. In tears she dialed Monica's number as she'd done so many times in the past few months hoping and praying that her girlfriend would answer the phone but as usual there was no answer. Monica was the only one she knew that could answer her questions and give her the kind of advice she was so desperately in need of at this point. When Monica didn't answer she thought of stopping by her house but it was so far out of her way and if she wasn't answering the phone then she probably wouldn't answer the door either. So, that was out.

Alexis wondered what was eating at Monica but she really didn't have time to worry about that right now. James was seeing someone and she meant to get to the bottom of it with or without Monica's help. Placing the cell phone back in her bag, she couldn't help but notice Officer Davis' business card. Private investigator—well that was one way of going about it and getting the answers she was so desperately searching for. She wondered if she was making too much of the whole situation with James but there was only one way to find out and since Monica was refusing to answer her calls her only other option was Officer Davis at this point. She just wished she hadn't been so combative, so abrasive, so goddamn rude when she'd addressed him. He'd been more than nice on both occasions when she'd had the pleasure of encountering him though she could hardly say the same for herself.

Now she needed him because after all that was his line of work, his specialty. And she only hoped that with an apology and a smile they'd be on level ground again and he could waylay all of her fears.

There was still the chance that James wasn't seeing anyone and was just hurt by her actions. She could deal with that. With the proper amount of love, devotion and a little TLC she was sure that she could alleviate all of his hurt, fears and animosity and bring him back into the fold but if there was someone else in the picture—well then—that was a different story altogether.

A woman had a way of turning a man's heart and head around; making him think that he hadn't experienced life at all but had merely been existing, stumbling headlong into a sea of oblivion until she happened on the scene. A woman could make a man believe that with her arrival came everything that he'd ever deserved in life;

everything he'd ever desired and ever craved for on a silver platter. And a man—especially a man like James LeBrandt would swallow all that she told him, hook, line and sinker almost as if she were the second coming of the Messiah himself.

If that was indeed the case, then Lord knows, Alexis had her work cut out for her. No longer could she count on Monica coming to her rescue as she had in grade school when she decided to snatch what's her name up by the roots of hair. No, now the matter required careful deliberation, some significant thought and a bit of planning. If there was another woman involved she had to know what attributes ol' girl possessed that she lacked.

Yes, she was sorry she'd been so rude when she'd spoken to Officer Davis but he was certainly going to be of the utmost importance now.

Chapter 10

Monica couldn't believe James. Not only had he been thoughtful enough to bring breakfast but afternoon delight to boot. The shower scene still had her head spinning and her body tingling now here they were on Fifth and Main window shopping.

All thought of her dismissing him were forever a thing of the past and she decided at the checkout counter in Macy's waiting for him to pay for the two hundred and fifty dollar Gucci bag that he insisted on her having that there was no conceivable way she was going to let him walk away as long as he desired to stay.

Alexis was another story. Monica just hoped she'd understand. After all, as the saying goes, one woman's trash is another woman's treasure. Maybe just maybe she'd feel good about Monica finally finding some happiness in her life. But knowing Alexis, nothing ever came easily and there was no reason aside from wishful thinking to think that Alexis would be happy just because she and James had found some happiness with each other. No, that would be too grand a supposition. Still, Monica reasoned; it was all in how she approached the subject and all she really had to do was appeal to her human side if she had one.

After a lovely afternoon of window shopping where she gawked and James bought, Monica felt even more compelled to bring up the ordeal with Alexis and though both agreed that they would not allow Alexis to in any way stand in the way of something as beautiful as this, she needed to be told and Monica agreed that it was she who needed to be the one to tell her. And just so this would not stand between them, they argued at Monica's behest that they would not see each other until this had transpired.

Arriving home later that evening, Monica had trouble deciding which part of her date had been better; the all-night lovemaking exhibit or the exhibit of love he'd shown all day. One thing was for sure. James LeBrandt was the total package and she had done absolutely nothing to show him what she could do or how she felt or what she had in store for him. Still, so intent was he on pleasing her that it didn't seem to matter to him. But now that the day was over and she'd insisted that he let her take care of the business at hand, things didn't seem quite so sunny on the horizon. She had no idea how she was going to break the news to Alexis but break the news she must.

She considered coming right out and baring her soul to her girlfriend; knowing that as many times as Alexis had attempted to contact her she'd be glad, if not ecstatic to hear from her. Then perhaps she'd set up a lunch date for old times sake followed by a confession which included her take on how difficult it was to get a man followed by an impromptu mentioning of how she'd just happened to see James and how good he looked with the hopes of eliciting Alexis' response so she could get a feel for her sentiments.

At this point, she hoped Alexis would turn the conversation to Philip and the rest of her attaché of eligible bachelors and maybe—just maybe—see fit to suggest that she and James get together. That was the best possible case scenario. If there was no suggestion of the sort forthcoming she could always throw out the possibility of taking James out for lunch and see what reaction that would solicit. Anyway, it couldn't hurt to try and after giving it considerable thought and two glasses of Hennessey later, Monica picked up the phone.

An hour later, Monica put her head back on the futon in the den and smiled. There had been no mention of James or Philip either for that matter and she had to admit that it felt good to talk to her girl again.

On Wednesday of the following week, which just so happened to be Ash Wednesday, Monica met Alexis at their favorite hangout which just happened to be Starbucks. The two women embraced as if they hadn't seen each other in years.

The conversation moved through its usual channels and after two espressos and a chocolate mocha latte Monica found Alexis in high spirits yet not once did she mention Philip or James. And it was Monica who finally brought up the subject of men. Still, she was careful almost deliberate in approaching the subject of the men in Alexis' life. Hopefully, something would trigger some mention but as it was getting late and there was still no mention Monica took it upon herself to steer the conversation.

"So girl, how's your love life?" Monica asked.

"What love life? The closest thing I have to a love life is that little pink vibrator I bought at that lingerie show Bridget threw last year. Sits right there in the bottom of my nightstand. Love it too. Never argues, never talks back and never lets me down in a pinch. Don't have to worry about shit. Don't have to support nobody. Don't have to feed it. Don't have to buy nothin' but those lil' Enegizer batteries. They're 'bout the only ones that can keep up with a sista, ya know. And trust me I give them a run for their money every chance I get. I keep it on high. I guess I wear out a pair every other day or so. That 's the closest thing I have to what you'd call a love life since I don't know when," she laughed.

"You wouldn't have a problem with your love life if you weren't so damn particular," Monica replied.

"It ain't about being particular nowadays girl. It's about being careful. With the SARS and the STD's and the Aids and every other little three letter word floating around out there just looking to put a sista six feet under my Energizer bunny suits me fine for the time being and when I do find that special someone that makes me wanna drop my drawers you can believe me I'm gonna take all the spontaneity out of that shit. Gonna drive his ass down to the clinic and get him tested and poked and scanned and pricked 'til I'm satisfied that he's a virgin or a goddamn monk. But until that day comes my Energizer bunny will do just fine," Alexis commented as she sipped her latte.

"A little short in the way of conversation though, I'm sure?" Monica quipped.

"No, not really. About the same caliber as most of the men I've dated lately. In fact he's better than most of the men I've been seeing," Alexis laughed.

"But you gotta admit, there ain't nothin' like the real thing," Monica infused.

"Girl, if I had the real thing and it didn't make a buzzin' whirring sound I probably couldn't come anyway," she laughed. "Hell, by the time I get finished at night I ain't gotta worry about aerobicizin' shit. Sometimes, I walk in drop my coat and my briefcase start at the doorway and by the time I'm finished the batteries are on low and I'm tryin' to drag myself to the edge of the bed so I can pull myself in. I can work the hell outta of a pussy baby. Gotta keep that lil' bitch in shape so she'll still be able to handle her business if I ever do find her a man," Alexis chirped. "Sometimes I get scared that I done stretched it so far outta shape that it may never spring back." She laughed. "But there I am right back at it the next night diggin' away again trying to see what other mysteries and secrets that little treasure chest box holds. Everyday it's something new. So who the hell needs a man?"

"So, whatever happened to what's his name; the accountant from New York—the one you kicked out the last time I saw you?" Monica asked, hoping that they were still an item.

"Oh, you must be referring to Philip. Stock broker, baby—not an account. He's doing fine. I see him off and on. He flies in about once a month; sometimes more often than that but don't get it twisted; it ain't that kind of party. We're just friends. I usually put him up in the guest room next to your room but like I said it ain't that kind of party."

Monica's face dropped when Alexis mentioned *her room*. She could never remember Alexis happier than the day she took Monica to the mall and had her shop 'til her heart's delight at Bed and Bath and Pier 1 telling her to pick out anything she liked. Monica was happy to oblige assuming that she was only helping Alexis decorate her newly purchased hi-rise condo but when she arrived like all the other guests for the housewarming a week or so later she was not pleasantly surprised but shocked to find a large sign across the doorway to the guest bedroom next to the master bedroom which read, Monica's Room. Inside she found every bauble, do-dad and piece of bric and brac that she'd picked out along with balloons, a bottle of champagne and a fruit basket with a card that read, For My Best Friend, Love Alexis.

The thought of Alexis setting up a room for her ate at Monica making it even more difficult to break the news to her now but she knew she had to. There was simply no way to avoid it.

"Alexis do you realize that we've been here for close to two hours and you haven't even mentioned James," Monica said finally.

"What's to mention? We're divorced and I guess the idea, the reality has finally begun to settle in is all," Alexis replied almost too nonchalantly for Monica's tastes. No she was definitely hiding something avoiding the subject—hedging though Monica had no inclination as to why other than to save face. And any other time she would have let the whole issue die at this point but she had too much riding on Alexis to just let it go.

Truth of the matter was Alexis was still smarting from her own self degradation and James' denial in front of the world to see. She'd been so angry after the whole driveway incident that she couldn't have driven more than a block or two before she was trying to solicit the services of Officer Ricky Davis.

Still on duty he'd agreed to discuss the matter on Friday, at the club but until then she was to say absolutely nothing to anyone. Those were his instructions. For some reason and she hadn't completely understood his reasoning but when he made it a point that if she wanted him to represent her and handle the case then she wasn't to whisper a word to her mother, her father, her children or anyone else she had her druthers. When Alexis asked what the big deal was with all the secrecy he simply asked her if she wanted him to handle the investigation or not. And so up until now she had said nothing.

What Officer Davis didn't realize was that aside from James and Monica there was really no one else who she confided in anyway. And since James was the subject of the investigation and Monica had all but gotten ghost at the time there was no one else to tell anyway.

Oh, she could have mentioned it to Philip but lately he'd been rather testy whenever she mentioned anything about her divorce or James. She knew he was jealous of her relationship with James or what was left of it. And from his own mouth he believed that James was the only thing standing in between himself and her master bedroom. With a quarter of a mil riding on Philip's shoulders in the market she needed for him to believe that she was his for the taking when the time was right.

But now as Alexis sat across the table from her best friend in Starbuck's on this gloomy Wednesday afternoon she realized that officer Davis wasn't the only reason she couldn't tell Monica about the episode with James or her suspicions. She was embarrassed for one and the idea of James dismissing her so casually still wasn't sitting right with her. Besides it wasn't something she wanted to discuss with Monica or anyone else for that matter. Neither did she want to talk about her marital problems with a complete stranger like Officer Davis and now she really wished she hadn't called him but what troubled her more than anything else was the simple fact that the man she'd been married to for twenty-two years could be seeing another woman. That bothered her to no end and if Officer Davis had a means of finding out who this triflin' little bitch was she'd tell him anything he wanted to know.

"Alexis honey, where are you? Wherever the hell you are you sure as hell ain't here today. You sure they didn't put somethin' in your latte? You just left me. Are you sure you're okay, baby?" Monica asked, a look of genuine concern showing on her face.

"I mentioned James' name and you just left me girl. Are you

sure everything's okay with you two?" Monica asked sensing that this was the time for her to get 'Lexis to come around—maybe open up a little. She knew it wasn't easy for 'Lexis to ever open up and the fact that they hadn't been in contact for months didn't do anything to foster their relationship. In fact, it always had the effect of making 'Lexis less trusting and often times it would take months before they were back on level ground. She hoped this wouldn't be the case this time but one thing was for sure. 'Lexis was troubled about something and whatever it was she wasn't willing to share it even with her best girl.

"Geez, I'm sorry babe. Guess I was in another world. Didn't mean to ignore you. It's just that I have so much on my mind right through here and I really haven't been sleeping well. I went to see Dr. Philbin and the first thing he wants to do is prescribe something and I usually turn him down but I took it this time I think he prescribed Valium or some shit and I've been taking them pretty regularly for the past week and I honestly think I feel worse for taking them. It's like I'm half asleep even when I'm awake or I fade in and out. But anyway, that's neither here nor there. As far as James is concerned I guess he's doing fine. Don't know. Don't really care. Sorry I didn't mean to be rude. I guess he's doing fine."

"So you're over him finally," Monica asked apprehensively not knowing if she were treading on thin ice or not but not knowing how else to find out what she so badly needed to know.

"Damn Monica what's up with all the fuckin' questions about James? If you're that interested in knowing about James give him a call. I was under the impression that you came here to see me to find out how the hell I was doing after not talking to me for three months but instead all you want to seem to want to know about is how James and I are doing. I told you before. Out of sight—out of mind. I mean you know as well as I do that after twenty something years of marriage you don't just forget overnight but I try to make it a point to stay busy and make sure that I keep myself occupied so I don't do exactly what you're trying to get me to do right now."

"And what am I trying to get you to do right now?" Monica asked angrily.

"Tryin' to get me to dwell on some shit that I don't want to think about and can't do a damn thing about. 'Sides there are too many goddamn men out there sitting in the stands waiting to get next to this to worry about one simple motherfucker that doesn't. Do you feel me? If you don't then I can sho' nuff break it down for you ol' skool style the way my daddy useta do so I don't have to hear about this shit anymore. Now try to listen so I don't have to repeat myself," Alexis snapped, the anger showing in her face.

"You don't have to be nasty about it," Monica replied. "If it bothers you that much to talk about it then keep it to your damn self. The only reason I brought it up was because you appeared to be stressed and I was just tryin to find out why. That's all. You don't usually let things get you down so this is all new to me. But like I said if you're going to get nasty 'cause I'm inquirin' about your welfare then keep the shit to yourself. Believe you me I won't lose any sleep over it," Monica fumed.

"My fault," Alexis said ignoring Monica's remarks. "Just listen up for a minute, dammit."

"Go ahead," Monica said, "And watch your tone when you speak to me. I'm not one of your children."

"Damn! Are you going to let me tell this story or what?"

"Go ahead, Alexis. Tell your story."

Alexis began slowly as if she were trying to remember through the glaze of the smoke and the latte and the drugs all brewing to a pitch inside of her.

"You see there was a farmer…" she said.

"Oh Lord," Monica interrupted, "are you going to take me back down on the farm for this one?" she laughed, sighing at the same time.

"Damn would you just listen? Anyway there was this farmer everyone called ol' farmer Brown and he had this chicken coop full of a bunch of ol' cacklin' hens always cluckin' and cacklin' away about this and that, always complainin' and shit to ol' farmer Brown who usually ignored them since all they did was fuss and stay in each other's business. But like I said ol' farmer Brown pretty much ignored them since he knew he was doin' his job and they just fussed to be fussin' since they had everything they could possibly want under the circumstances. All of them were well fed and plump beyond belief."

Monica wondered if Alexis was referring to her but let Alexis continue.

"No other chickens on any of the other farms around were as big and fat or had as much as farmer Brown's chickens but they were still always struttin' around bitchin' and complainin' despite the fact that farmer Brown loved his hens to death.

Anyway, one day ol' Mr. Fox comes around up to his usual no good self and snatches one of them big, fat, sweet, succulent hens from farmer Brown's chicken coop and gets to haulin' ass. Well, farmer Brown hears all the commotion and jumps up from the dinner table and runs outside just fast as his little, short stubby legs will carry him and just in time to see that ol', sly, fox shoot right past him with Mary Lou. You see all of farmer Brown's chicks had names. Anyway, the fox has got Mary Lou in his jaws and he's movin', headin' straight for the woods and ol farmer Brown doesn't make a move to stop him. Meanwhile, all the rest of them hens is in a tizzy and just a cluckin' away and callin' farmer Brown every name under the sun but he just looks at them the way he always does and shakes his head. But they go on and on just a rantin' and ravin' until he starts to get a little angry and tells them all to shut the hell up and where they can go.

Well, they'd never seen this side of farmer Brown so there's a moment of silence and when it's almost completely silent ol' farmer Brown tells them to elect a spokesman and then let that hen share their collective grievances so he can better understand their position on the matter at hand. So, they elect a spokesman and she turns out to be this big ol' white chick and she comes up to the farmer just a shakin' her tail feathers and carryin' on and says, 'Farmer Brown how come you didn't chase that ol' ornery fox what had Mary Lou?'

And ol' farmer Brown didn't flinch one bit. He didn't even bat an eye. He just looked at them chicks all lined up in front of him, hoppin' mad and said, "I'm sorry about that. I know what you must be feelin' right through here. I gotta tell you, I loved Mary Lou just as much as I love any of you but if I'd a gone off chasin' that sly ol' fox chances are that he mighta had a brotha or a cousin lurkin' around and I mighta lost all of you, too."

And with that said Alexis picked up her cup of latte, took a swallow and then burst out laughin' as she looked at Monica's puzzled face across the table.

"What the hell was that all about?" Monica asked the bewilderment still very much apparent.

"Dunno," Alexis laughed. "But someone told me it's a helluva story if you wann ever get someone out of your business and on to a different topic," she said doubling over in laughter again as she looked at Monica.

"Damn, 'Lex I don't know what's been goin' on with you since the last time but I truly believe the stress has been too much on you. I really think you've lost it this time girl," Monica said lighting another cigarette.

"On the real though Monica think about it. It took me a while to figure it out but I guess what I got from the whole thing was that ol' farmer Brown being a wise man and having been in this situation before knew better than to waste his time chasin' after a fox that he didn't have a chance in the world of catching. And even though he loved that chick to death why would he expose the whole hen house and take the chance of losing all of his chicks. You know what I'm saying? Why would he risk chasing a lost cause when there are so many other chicks out there standing around vying for his attention? You see, honey that's how I've had to come to terms with losing James. Guess that's how I've come to view the whole divorce thing in the nutshell."

"And you, Alexis LeBrandt can honestly sit here and look me in my eye and tell me that you're okay with that?"

"Have to be. I talked to him one day this week and he made it quite clear that there was no turning back—no need to cry over spilt milk and all the other stupid, utterly worthless clichés that said leave him alone; it's over. So what's a girl to do? He said he was moving on with his life and I needed to move on with mine. What else can I do but heed his advice? I sure can't make him love me. All I can do is accept his advice; pick up the pieces and move on," Alexis said smiling; the tears welling up in her eyes.

"Well, I give you credit. You're certainly handling things better than even I expected."

"C'mon Monica, think about it. I mean, do I really have a choice? Am I supposed to just stop living because James has decided he doesn't want or need me in his life anymore?"

"I guess not. What can I say? I'm proud of you girl. You certainly have come a long way. The Alexis I used to know would have struck out at the closest person to her and then thought about it later—a nine millimeter in one hand and shotgun in the other," Monica and Alexis both laughed at the comment and Monica suddenly felt a sense of relief knowing that she wouldn't have to worry any longer about being the wrong end of a reprisal. Still, the guilt was there when she saw the pain and the hurt in Alexis' eyes. But then another sense of warmth rushed through Monica as she thought about all the dirt Alexis had dumped upon this guy or that in her quest for fame and glory. Monica smiled as she thought how Alexis must feel now being the recipient. 'You reap what you sow'.

There was little doubt that Alexis was still in love or infatuated harboring or at the very least harboring some type of feeling for James and if she weren't sure before the divorce his constant denials heightened her longing to be with him. Alexis thought of the Joni Mitchell song she'd been so fond of as a kid. How did it go? Oh yeah, 'you don't know what you've got 'til it's gone. Now they've paved paradise and put up a parking lot.'

Even after her admission Monica knowing Alexis as she did refused to believe that she was telling her everything or that she'd just accepted her fate. No, there was still something amiss, there was still something Alexis was leaving out whether intentionally or unintentionally. There were just too many gaps, too many unanswered questions, too many missing pieces in the whole saga to make her story, her surrender, credible.

To begin with Alexis always told her everything down to the most minute detail. There were no parables, or convenient little stories to convey points. She was far too literal for all that shit. She called a spade a spade and if a man ever dumped her then that man was made to pay in some fashion or another. But for her not to even bother to put up a fight outside of the courtroom—no—that was not Alexis LeBrandt. Alexis LeBrandt was more the hair pulling, eye gouging, I'll kill you before I let you leave me type and until Monica saw this she had to believe the situation with James was far from being over. The fact that she'd done everything in her willpower to get her to open and talk about James and only aroused her suspicions more and convinced her that Alexis was up to something.

Later that evening, Monica found herself home alone and more leery than she had been prior to their meeting. She even wondered if James was somehow involved and if Alexis was somehow using him to test their friendship or perhaps setting them both up with the hopes of making another appeal for alimony in court based on James' infidelity.

Perhaps she thinks that I've been seeing James all along and that was the reason I hadn't been in contact with her. All kinds of thoughts raced through her head until she was so fatigued from trying to make any sense of the whole affair that before she knew it she was sound asleep on the futon in the den.

Awakened by the phone she was startled to hear Alexis' on the voicemail reminding her to pick up Philip at the airport. She'd agreed earlier in the day but hated the thought of being a gopher for the ever so popular Ms. LeBrandt and wondered what the hell had prompted her to begin talking to her again anyway. Life, after all, had been much more peaceful, more structured and a lot less hectic than when she was running errands for 'Lexis.

Best friend to Alexis LeBrandt simply translated meant driver, gopher, confidante, third wheel and other condescending thoughts Monica hated to entertain but which her psyche summoned nonetheless.

Monica always remembered telling her children to never use the word hate—that hate was a strong word, too strong a word to use when speaking of another person—any person—but as Monica dragged herself off the black leather futon she knew that if it wasn't hate then she certainly despised Alexis.

And it wasn't Philip. Philip had nothing to do with her dislike for Alexis. Like her, he too was just another pawn in Alexis' whole charade to climb as far and as fast as she could despite the people she stepped on in the process yet it was hard to comprehend just what kind of hold Alexis had on people. Now, here was Philip flying from New York to Detroit on a Thursday night to spend time with a woman who no more cared about him than she did that last pair of torn knee highs she just discarded. And yet he was still commuting with the hopes that maybe she would one day open up to him and respond to him in a way that suggested he was more than just her stockbroker heaping tons of money into her account. Philip may not have known it but Monica certainly knew that if he hadn't hit pay dirt by now then chances were closer to slim and none that he never would but here he was due to arrive in about an hour and Alexis was on her way out of town.

Chicago is what Alexis told her when she'd asked her to pick Philip up and get him settled in. And of course it was on some crucial, can't wait business scheme, something pressing, concerning some real estate venture but who really knew? Sitting her drink down and putting on her jacket, Monica cursed Alexis for interrupting her evening, grabbed her keys, her pocketbook and headed for the airport to break the news to Philip.

The March skies were cloudy and overcast and there was a slight chill in the air as Monica opened the car door and slid in. She hoped Philip wouldn't be too disappointed when she broke the news to him and wondered why she was back in the business of carrying out Alexis' dirty work. It was bad enough she was in bed with her husband and she wondered if she had agreed to pick up Philip out of some subconscious feelings of guilt but then there had been no guilt before she'd slept with James when she was playing the same role. Her thoughts jumbled and distorted, she wondered if she wasn't merely a substitute until Alexis found the time to call James and put him back on her busy schedule.

Perhaps, that's why she hadn't seemed overly concerned with James' dismissal. In the back of her mind Alexis probably figured that she could summon James back at any time. While, on the other hand, all Monica was, with her thick thighs and forty double-D's was comic relief, simply an understudy maintaining the decorum and appearances of normalcy until the star returned.

Sitting outside Detroit Metro Airport waiting for Philip's flight to arrive getting angrier by the minute Monica considered the possibility of being played by all parties involved. The way she figured it she was at best nothing more than a boyhood fantasy for James while Alexis handled some other pressing matters. It was a well-known fact that James had wanted her since high school and told her so on at least one occasion. And of course, Alexis could care less. What was it that she said about James in days past when the question arose concerning James and other women?

'Hell, James can go out every night for dessert as long as he makes sure he dines at home first. As long as he eats here first and handles his business here I don't care what he does afterward,' Alexis had told her.

And if she said that about her own husband then how could she possibly feel about Philip. The more she thought about the whole situation the angrier she became. Well, if Alexis didn't care and was leaving town knowing Philip was flying in then why in the hell should she care about Philip? After all, he wasn't coming to see her. What she needed to do was get back on her regimented schedule and forget about James, Philip and Alexis and get back to concentrating on herself and the ways she could improve her own well-being instead of tagging along on 'Lexis' coat strings grateful for her leftovers.

Monica started the car and waited for the traffic to pass when she noticed a tall handsome figure racing toward the car. Seeing Monica, Philip smiled broadly and made his way to the car, tossing his overnight bag in the backseat before jumping in.

"Monica, it's great to see you," he said not looking at all surprised to see her instead of the woman who was supposed to meet him. "Alexis just called me on my cell and told me to look out for you. You don't know how glad I am to see you. I was already having second thoughts about making the trip and when she told me that she had an emergency and had to fly up to Chicago on business, I was ready to scream. But when she told me that you volunteered to be my escort for the evening I couldn't have been happier. Now we can see if all those invitations were heartfelt or not," he laughed as he reached over and gave her a kiss on the cheek.

Monica laughed.

"Lord have mercy! Please tell me you've forgotten that drunken heifer that was just rambling on as usual about anything that came to mind," she laughed, glad now that she'd waited or at least that he'd flagged her down.

He was just as she remembered him—warm and spontaneous…

"You know what they say about alcohol confessions?"

"No what is it that they say about alcohol confessions?" Monica asked glancing over at Philip.

"They tell me that that's when the real truth comes out," he laughed. "At least that's what they tell me."

"Well, they tell me that you can't believe everything that you hear," Monica quipped.

"That's true. But I'm certainly hoping that since we're home alone that some of what you said holds true—especially as good as you look this evening," he said smiling.

"Oh. No you didn't Mr. Man!" Monica said feigning surprise. *"Here I am picking you up only because my best friend's out of town and you're not in the car a good five minutes and you're trying to do me and my girl,"* Monica shouted grinning the whole time. *"Talk about a dog's dog. Umph! Umph! Umph! You are certainly a mess, Mr. Man. But go ahead anyway. Keep talkin'. I think I like what I'm hearing,"* Monica laughed. "But you know you're wrong—dead wrong. Here, Alexis is sending me to pick you up and asking me to apologize to you on her behalf and you're sitting here flirting with me. That shows absolutely no respect."

"Excuse me for being so blunt but you and I both know Alexis. And you've known her for a lot longer than I have so you know she has absolutely no romantic interest in me whatsoever. I'm no more to her than her stockbroker who she pays a tidy commission to teach her the ins-and-outs of buying and selling stocks on the open market. The only one that ever did have a romantic interest was me and she let it be known in no uncertain terms that there was nothing happening in that direction. What woman would get up and leave town knowing that someone is flying in to see her?"

Monica hung her head in shame that was not her own and continued to drive now sorry she'd even brought up the issue in the first place even if she had only been joking. It was apparent now that whatever had commenced in her absence had left Philip deeply hurt and quite apparently deeply scarred as well.

"I'm sorry," Monica said hoping to ease the pain and end the conversation.

"For what? I feel graced almost blessed to be in your company. At least I know that when I talk to you, you're honest, upfront and for real. I don't know you that well but I know that you're good people and most of the good people I know lives aren't made up of self-serving schemes and hidden agendas. I know as well as you do that Alexis has no interest in me other than what I can do to put another dollar in her pocket," Philip smiled again upbeat after this admission. "If I wasn't her broker chances are I wouldn't even be here this weekend."

Monica was shocked to hear Philip speak in such a forward manner.

"And you still do her bidding for her?" Monica asked a look of astonishment obvious. "When did you come to this realization?"

"It's taken me the better part of a year to come to see the light. I guess I knew it all the time and was in denial but after ten or twelve trips and nothing but the guest bedroom I had to face up to the fact that Alexis is no more interested in me than any other man—well— let me clarify that—any other man aside from James. That's the only man she even pretends to care about and until he's out of the picture or until she really and truly gets over the fact that he doesn't want her I don't stand a ghost of a chance."

"You don't say," Monica said nonchalantly as she wheeled the Volvo into the third lane of the expressway and stomped on the gas.

"I'm sorry I probably shouldn't have said that. That was in bad taste and I do apologize," he said as he stared out of the passenger's window at the buildings that made up the outskirts of Detroit Metro.

"There's no need to apologize, Philip. I've known Alexis all my life and have been having the same thoughts about her lately although I think I've become pretty much acclimated to her bullshit. To tell you the truth and I don't mean to beat a dead horse I'm just a little tired of the way she abuses people and especially the people closest to her. Here you are flying in from out of town to see her and she doesn't even have the common decency to call or e-mail you to let you know this is a bad weekend to come or that something's come up. Then to compound matters she just assumes that I have nothing at all to do and not only asks me to pick you up from the airport but asks me to make sure that you're settled in—whatever that means," Monica said matter-of-factly.

"I'm not real sure either and again I do apologize for our friend but if you have the time and since you did agree to help me get settled in, let's assume that that includes letting me take you to dinner. It's the least I can do for you giving up your evening to pick me up."

"Oh, trust me, Philip now that I've got the 4-1-1 on the whole situation I'm going to make sure that you reimburse me for my evening," she laughed. "Remember the last time you were here and I tried to give you directions and you ignored me. I tried to spell it out to you then. I told you how a woman of my size and dimensions had certain needs. I was even willing to give you a step-by-step run through if need be but you deferred. *Well there will be no deferred payment plan tonight. Tonight is going to cost you. This little hour foray out here to the airport, along with some erroneous decision making on your part that's brought you half way across the country to see a woman that has no interest in you whatsoever is going to cost you a whole helluva lot more than dinner, sweetie,"* Monica laughed.

"You're joking, right?" Philip asked smiling but mildly amused by her candor.

"Hold on let me check my cell and see who called me. But to answer your question; hell no I'm not joking. I'm dead serious and if I do have some time on my hands other than what it takes to get you settled in then trust me you've got your work cut out for you." Monica snapped the cell phone shut. "Nope, nothing that can't wait 'til tomorrow, I'm afraid—*which means you're all mine tonight, sweetie.*"

Philip laughed at Monica's forwardness but was unable to ascertain how serious she was and attempted to change the subject just to be on the safe side.

"That's surprising, Monica. The fact that someone with your looks and vivaciousness has a night free must be by choice?" he said hoping to downplay her attempts at seduction without dismissing her completely and hurting her feelings with his refusal. "I figured your schedule would be booked solid," he continued but she recognized his wanting to change the subject for what it was worth. After years of denials, men trying to creep out the back door before they lay down with a woman her size was nothing new to her.

And although she really neither needed Philip or felt particularly attracted to him at that very moment she was sure that after a couple of drinks she would make sure he was settled in alright.

"My fault, you were saying?"

"I was just saying that I'm surprised that you're free on a Thursday night. Figured your schedule would be jam packed every night."

"And you know it usually is, however, sometimes I have to make time for quirky girlfriends and it just throws everything out of whack," she smiled.

'Yeah, it's jam packed alright she thought. Between Curves and those dreaded aerobics, her little all-girls book club, the little purple toy in her night stand and the television remote she hardly ever had time for anything else.'

"So are we on for dinner or do you want to tease me some more?" Philip asked.

"I guess we're on for dinner since you're not taking my offer seriously," she laughed. "I gathered from the first time I offered you this voluptuous, full-figured body and you turned me down that you liked the sweet, neat and petite type more. But don't feel bad, most men do. Oh, well I guess I'll just have to chalk it up to your loss, honey and keep on movin' on and wait 'til I come across a man that's not afraid of a challenge," she laughed.

"You're a trip," Philip said laughing. "You know one day someone's going to take you seriously and you're going to be in serious trouble Monica."

"Do you have his number?" Monica laughed.

"You mentioned dinner," she said letting him off the hook. No need beating a dead horse she thought to herself when he feigned indifference and chose to answer her flirtation with a gentlemanly politeness that said, 'not interested.'

"Any food preferences? As you've probably noticed I am Detroit's official food and wine connoisseur and its unofficial critic although as you probably are well aware of there aren't many types of foods or restaurants which I would really deem as *bad*. I know a great Turkish place if you like Turkish food, a nice little Japanese steakhouse and a Thai restaurant if you don't mind that burning, gurgling sensation in the morning. Then there's a splendid Italian restaurant that's rather pricey but the veal scaloppini is to die for."

"I see you get around."

"I do my best. I love good food. Let me clarify that. I like food but for some reason food doesn't always seem to like me. Goes straight from the lips to the hips," Monica laughed.

"You talk an awful a lot about your weight to be as fine as you are. I think you're beautiful despite the way you come down on yourself."

"A lot of men think I'm beautiful, Philip, until it comes time for them to make a commitment and then for some reason the thought of coming home and sharing my bed each night doesn't seem quite so appealing." Monica replied.

"I think you're mixing apples and oranges. A lot of men may think you're physically attractive. Others may think you have a certain gene se qua—a certain inner beauty but that hardly means that they want a commitment. Don't you know that that very word will send grown men—Steven Segal—Vin Diesel type men—scurrying like rats trying to find a hole? That word is a no-no in the 'how to be a man handbook', baby. You never but never say that word in or around any man that you may have or are considering having romantic ties with. That is an absolute no-no. And you mean to tell me that you have been thinking that the reason that you have not been able to harness a man was because of your appearance or something about your personality. *C'mon?* Hell, don't you know that the only way a woman's going to get a man to commit is to dupe him into it. Ain't no man in the world gonna walk into hell's kitchen knowing full well that there ain't nothing there but fire and brimstone and an end to their very lives. Well, to men marriage is hell's kitchen," Philip laughed.

"You're really a sweet guy, Philip. Alexis is really making a big mistake this time around," Monica said the smile disappearing as she thought of her friend.

"Does that mean you want to extend your offer again?" Philip said toying with her.

"I might just do that," Monica said, "but first tell me where you would like to eat."

'The first thing I want to do is get out of these clothes and..."

"Oooh that sounds good to me," she said smiling.

"Do you think about anything else?" Philip asked.

"Not much! I used to think about such worldly things as politics and world hunger and euthanasia—you know those sorts of things—but as I got older I've managed to narrow my interests down to the more important things such as the pursuit of a good bottle of wine, good food and great sex—not necessarily in that order. And since I can pretty much guarantee the first two I think it best I concentrate on the third one since I've got your fine ass up in here," she laughed.

"You are a trip woman. But you never know you may just get your wish if you could just pause in your quest long enough to let me grab a quick shower and get out of these clothes," Philip said still staring and smiling at Monica.

"Not a problem. And if you need any help—any help whatsoever with the latter you just let me know."

Monica parked the car in her designated spot with the No Parking sign in plain view, in front of Alexis' building, hit the automatic door lock and led the way into the building. Once inside the apartment she threw on some Miles Davis then threw off her coat like she was in Gone with the Wind and in the fashion of Scarlet O'Hara or Betty Davis threw one arm over her forehead and bending over backwards in an attempt to swoon and faint at the same time said, "Take me now m'lord, Philip. You don't know how long I've dreamed of this night—of standing this close to you—to be in your mere presence, m'lord. Oh, how the fever rages within me. I'm afraid that if you turn away or spurn me m'lord I will be consumed in a fire of desire that will never be quenched. Please, find the mercy, the charity that I know resides in your very being and take me now my love and my lord," she said staring directly at Philip before bursting out in laughter.

"I believe I *am* inclined to agree with Alexis on one account."

"And what is that my darling," she asked still swooning.

"That all the bricks are not in the wagon," he said now doubling over in laughter as she pirouetted across the room to the bar.

Ignoring his comments Monica continued.

"Shall I fix you a drink my love?" she asked.

"Sure," he said attempting to regain his composure.

"And what can I fix for you tonight, m'lord?" Monica asked bowing suddenly and then pirouetting over to him once again.

"Whatever you're having will be fine," Philip said unfolding his overnight case in a vain attempt to ignore her.

"Why m'lord I don't believe I will share in the fatal consumption of spirits this evening."

"So you won't have a drink with me," Philip asked.

"The mere sight of you has me more intoxicated than any wine or spirit could ever hope to achieve and I fear that should I sip even a mere droplet that the combination of wine along with your presence would be enough to render me drunk and speechless in your presence and I would much rather savor the sweet spirit of your presence.

Still, I would be honored if you would allow me to pour you some of Gallo's premium Zinfandel so that I may be easier and more pleasing to thine eye. And it is I that pray that with each swallow you become even more intoxicated than the last and find yourself in such an inebriated state that when you look at me you do not see me as your humble servant girl but rather in a whole 'nother light. In a light as bright as a shooting star so that you can finally and for once see the undying love and the burning passion which screams from my tender loins. A light so bright in it's intensity that you may envision yourself as Othello himself and me but a darker version of Desdemona. Or perhaps you as Marc Anthony and me your Cleopatra. This is how I wish for you to view me tonight m'lord," Monica shouted as she threw herself across the sofa, both arms flung high in the air as if waiting for some imaginary lover to fall into her lap.

Philip still doubled over in laughter tried to gather himself as the tears rolled down his cheeks but couldn't help but fall down on the sofa next to Monica in hysterics at which time Monica promptly got up and returned to the bar and poured them both a drink and returned to the sofa.

"Guess you could tell I just finished taking an English literature class," she said smiling.

"Is that what that was all about?" he said still chuckling to himself as he sipped the vodka rather briskly.

"Yeah, thinkin' about taking a couple of acting classes this fall. How do you think I'll fair?" she asked grinning.

"Head of the class, baby—head of the class."

"You really think so?" she grinned. "I want you to know that you're the first person that has had a command performance," Monica smiled.

"Well, let it be known that I feel honored and intend to repay you in kind at a later date, my fair Desdemona, for making this a very entertaining night so far." Philip said smiling.

"And trust me there's more in store. I'm so much better in front of a large venue. Kinda brings out the real performer in me. Just wait 'til we get to the restaurant. I figure I'll do my Mae West rendition somewhere right after the main course. Whaddaya think?"

"Please don't," Philip said playfully.

"Another drink?" he asked getting up to get himself another.

"Sure! All apart of getting you settled in," she smiled.

Handing her a fresh drink, Philip picked up his toiletry case and overnight bag and headed to the bathroom.

"Give me fifteen minutes and I'll be ready to go so don't get too comfortable," he said winking at her.

"How the hell am I supposed to get comfortable with Mandingo prancing around in front of me? Go take your shower so I can try to pull myself together and try to regain some of the self-esteem you took from me in the car."

"And how pray-tell did I do that?" he asked.

"C'mon Philip a girl damn near throws herself at you. I say a girl because a woman would have too much tact to do that. Anyway a girl begs you to make love to her—okay—maybe make love may be too strong a concept so let's just say—a girl begs you to take her as Luther says—if only for one night and you ever so gently push her aside. I now have no self-esteem left and must still try to make the best of this night in my vain attempts to get you settled in. I have offered you the best that I have to give and you ever so gently pushed me away. And although I may not appear to be distraught my spirit has been broken and is crying out for someone, anyone to make me feel whole again after my tumultuous fall from grace," Monica said dropping her head to her chest in an effort to express her heartbreak and grief.

"Perhaps I can make up for my insensitivity later on this evening, perhaps during dinner if you promise not to begin the second phase or your acting career in the restaurant," Philip joked.

"Oh, do you mean that darling? Tell me you will grant me a reprieve. Tell me you mean that darling and I promise that any Scarlet O'Hara I may have left in me shall be gone with the wind," Monica replied in her best southern accent and once again throwing her hands in the air pretending to be a rich southern debutante awaiting the annual planter's ball.

"Please tell me you mean that darling," Monica repeated grabbing Philips hand in both of hers and staring him straight in the eye.

Philip laughed pulled away and headed down the shower. A moment later Monica heard the shower running and after leafing through the latest edition of Black Enterprise headed to the bar to fix herself another drink. She was feeling no pain and really was enjoying Philip's company. She hoped he was comfortable with her but then again it didn't really matter. She enjoyed his company. He seemed to be fun and not like the usual stuffed shirts Alexis usually hung around with and if worse came to worse she could be content just being in the company of such a good looking young man even if he wasn't hers for the taking.

No sooner had she gotten comfortable on the sofa than the phone rang and Monica who usually hated answering Alexis' phone didn't think twice before picking up the receiver.

"Hey girl, it's me," came the voice on the other end.

Monica recognized her girlfriends voice immediately and felt the anger rise within her although she could hardly account for the mood change.

"Did you pick Philip up on time? Did he have a good flight? How's he doing? Did you get him settled in? Good! Good! I knew I could count on you. That's my girl. Where is he? Oh okay. Well tell him I just called to check on him and I'll see him first thing in the morning if everything goes as planned. My flight's at six so I should be home no later than seven-fifteen, seven-thirty at the latest. You shouldn't have any problems. There's really nothing to worry about if you're planning on staying and I hope you are. I've got him pretty much on lock so you don't have to worry about him trying to push up on you or anything like that. I used to keep my door lock but in all the time I've known him he never made an advance or anything like that so don't worry about anything like that honey. If it makes you feel better just lock your door before you go to sleep. But trust me, I know him like a book and he's a puppy dog compared to the guys we grew up with. Enjoy dinner, honey and if you change your mind and don't feel like going out to eat there's a couple of rib-eyes in the freezer. Gotta go, love ya and I'll see you first thing in the morning."

Monica couldn't understand it but there was that feeling again and as she placed the receiver back on the hook and sat back down on the sofa she wondered why she even bothered trying to understand Alexis. She no longer felt like going out or entertaining or doing much of anything besides going home and getting into her nice warm bed and calling it a night. She'd already planned on calling in tomorrow and the idea of sleeping in seemed all the better now. Philip would be fine by himself and even better when Alexis returned so there was no need for her to stay there. Still, Philip didn't deserve her walking out on him with no explanation. He'd already been through that so she decided to wait until he was out of the shower to tell him she wasn't feeling real well and thought it best she head home.

"Monica, darling would you be a sweetheart and hand me a towel and my shaving kit," she heard Philip call from the bathroom.

Dragging herself from the sofa she hadn't realized just how tired she was. Between the vodka and the melodic meanderings of Joe Sample Monica had lost all of her prior spontaneity and suddenly felt old and worn.

"Monica."

"Coming Philip," she called back.

Moments later she stood at the shower door and handed him his shaving kit and a towel which he thanked her for and although the door was only cracked slightly he noticed a change in the woman's demeanor.

"Everything alright?" he asked.

"Yes, absolutely. Everything's fine, Philip. 'Lexis just called to make sure you were alright and nestled in and told me to tell you that she'd see you in the morning," Monica said repeating her girlfriend's words.

"And that's it?" Philip inquired sensing something askew.

"That's it," she replied.

"And we're still on for dinner?" he asked now unsure.

"Well, to be perfectly honest, Philip, I don't know if it's the vodka…"

"Or the phone call," he said finishing the sentence. "Alexis has a way of doing that shit," he said angrily. "She could fuck up a wet dream. But only if you allow her do so. The next thing you'll be telling me is that you want to head home and I'll be fine until she gets here."

Monica smiled.

"You're perceptive beyond your years. But actually I was going to tell you that she said there were some steaks in the freezer if you were hungry and yes, I was going to head home. Come tomorrow I'll be the third wheel and I don't really like that role. As you saw earlier tonight I'm more inclined to play the starring role and not continually be the understudy," she said smiling.

"Trust me Monica, you are nobody's understudy. You're like a breath of fresh air to me and to tell you the truth I brought Alexis' portfolio to go over her entire account and break all professional ties since that's basically all we have. This was to be my last trip to Detroit and after spending only a couple of hours with you and I hope this is not in bad taste being that she is your best friend but I would love to come back and visit you if only as friends—well—initially as friends. Do you think that I'm being too forward?"

Monica smiled her confidence renewed.

"No, I kind of like the idea but are you sure that's what you want to do or are you just feeling the same animosity I'm feeling and that's just a way to get back at her for everything she's done to you over the last few months. If that's the case I'm the perfect tool to strike back at her. You know how she'll view the whole scenario. Disloyal best friend steals her man when she was out of town."

"Sounds like a good headline for one of those gossip tabloids but I don't have time for that. I'm being totally sincere and I'm not looking for anymore than friendship and I think we've pretty much established that tonight. Don't you?" he asked, "C'mon, no strings attached, just friends. If it develops into something more that would be wonderful. If not then what have we lost?"

"No strings?" she asked.

"No strings," he replied, then added, "Well maybe one," he said smiling.

"I knew it. There's always something attached," she asked, her smile now gone and his widening as he stepped out of the bathroom with the towel wrapped tightly around him exposing every muscle and a slight bulge in the front.

"My God, 'Lexis is a bigger fool than I thought," she said making no attempt to mask her gaze.

"I want you to disrobe right here and right now," he said smiling.

"You don't mean you want me to take my clothes off, do you?" Monica said stunned but still staring at that beautiful hunk of a man standing directly in front of her.

One thing was for sure. For all the negatives she could conjure when it came to her friend, Alexis had excellent taste in men.

"You can't be serious," she said now looking into his eyes to see if he was for real.

"I'm dead serious."

Monica thought for a moment.

"So, all that talk about being friends and what not basically comes down to sex. We can be friends if I satisfy your needs tonight since there's not a chance in hell of Alexis doing that but you'll settle for her full-figured friend and if worse comes to worse and she doesn't tell you what you want to hear tomorrow you can always throw that up in her face. Is that it?"

Philip could see Monica getting angrier by the minute and seeing the need to diffuse the situation let the towel fall from his waist.

"Oh, my god!" Monica said as she stared at the naked body in front of her.

"Didn't I tell you to be careful what you wish for?" Philip said grinning widely now.

Monica was petrified. Her mouth had always gotten her into things she couldn't get out of and this certainly appeared to be one of those times.

"Philip, I was only joking in the car. Alexis told me to make you feel wanted and at home and that's all there was to it. I was only playing sweetheart. I didn't realize that you were taking me seriously." She said pleading now and wondering if he was going to rape her right here in the hallway of her girlfriend's house. Near panic she turned to run when Philip reached out and grabbed her shoulder firmly and repeated the order.

"Take your clothes off, or I'll take them off for you, Monica," he said the smile still glued to his face.

Monica's thoughts flashed back to Marshall and how he had given her the same order before slamming her into the wall for not moving as quickly as he liked. She thought of all the meetings she'd attended following those episodes for battered women. And if it was one thing she learned was that resistance only caused further pain and so without uttering another word she began to disrobe.

Moments later, she was naked and standing there waiting, almost expecting for him to slam her up against the wall before digging deeply into her or waiting for him to punch her in her stomach causing her to bend over so he could mount her from the rear as Marshall had done so many times before in the past but instead he circled her, still grinning as if he'd never seen a fat, naked forty-two year old woman in his life. And then as if someone, somewhere had commanded him to—he stopped and faced her then turned to someone and said, "Well suh, I do believe fifteen hunnerd for this niggra wench is a bit steep but then she does have some pretty good qualities about her. Good childbearin' hips, I see and she seems to be in pretty fair health. Good breasts—firm —not much sag in 'em—looks ta hold a fair share a milk in case any of them sickly wenches goes down. She looks like she could feed d'ere younguns too—if need be. Nice strong calves and a pretty shapely waist. Might make a fairly good field hand if I choose to use her fo' dat but da ways I sees it she's no mo' than a breeder from what I can tell. Still, looks can be deceivin' so if ya askin' fifteen hunnerd I believe da least ya can do is let me take her in da guest bedroom here in da big house and let me give her a run through. Shouldn't take me more than fifteen twenty minutes at mos' if she's a willin'. If she ain't, I don't wan' her. Don't wanna be fightin' wit' no niggra wench o'er da punanny afta a long day a overssin' in da fields. Is ya willin' fo' me to tries ya wench out?" Philip asked laughing.

"Does ya wants me ta try ya out, wench?" he asked Monica. "I promises ta go easy on you the first time out. I never believes in ridin' 'em too hard when I'm first breakin' 'em in," he said smiling and staring directly at her now. "C'mon, nothin' breaks dem in like a good strummin'."

Not completely sure if he was serious or not Monica shook her head and hoped he wouldn't force the issue. And then it dawned on her that he was doing no more than turning the tables on her. This is what she'd done to him while in a drunken stupor when they'd first met. He'd taken it a bit far but with all her prodding, teasing and flirting perhaps she deserved this.

"Okay, well I hopes we can still be friends then. Mind getting dressed? Every restaurant I know pretty much prefers their patrons bein' dressed," he said laughing.

"Oh, I hate you," Monica screamed breathing a deep sigh of relief.

"No, you don't," Philip said wrapping both arms around Monica's body and holding her tightly as she placed her head on his chest.

"You had me scared silly," she said.

"Scared? Why in heaven's name would you be scared? I would never do anything to hurt you."

Monica could feel the bulge growing between them but it bothered her little now and she was almost relieved that he'd left it her choice.

"C'mon Monica let's go to dinner before my friend here has other plans that I can't accommodate."

"And why can't you," she said. "Maybe there's something that I can do to help?"

Chapter 11

"Oh my God! Oh my God!"

The sun hit Monica like a sledge hammer but it was the voice that made Monica jump straight up in the bed and look not into the face of the sun's beaming rays but into the heated face of her best friend, Alexis LeBrandt who stood standing over her like one of Hitler's storm troopers.

Monica sat up slowly wrapping the sheet around her and yawned. She was used to 'Lexis melodrama but at five thirty in the morning this was uncalled for. Here she was just a ranting and raving and carrying on about something or another. Whatever it was, at five thirty in the morning Monica hardly wanted to know.

Ignoring her Monica dropped back down in the bed only to feel something move next to her. This time it was she who yelled.

"Oh, my God!" Monica turned abruptly, the sheet falling to the floor beside her exposing her naked flesh and the figure of the man beside her.

"Oh, Monica! Oh, baby I am so sorry. I should have told you to lock the door but I would have never expected him to..." she said her voice drifting off as one does that feels but can't quite gather their thoughts at that precise moment. A fusion of thoughts entered her mind and then just as quickly leaped from view leaving her standing there wondering, trying to decipher what it was that greeted her eyes as she entered the bedroom that Friday morning. When no clear answers appeared before her she just naturally assumed...

"My God, Monica—what can I say? Are you alright?" Then turning to the body slowly showing some signs of life she addressed him in the only manner befitting this roguish man, this thug who had taken her friendship and masked his own, this man who had

taken her hospitality to mean that he could take advantage of the one friend she had in the world and soil her already fragile being by raping her.

"Philip, how could you, you bastard? Get your ass out of here before I call the police. Monica do you want me to call the police on this bastard? I knew I should have let you stay at a goddamn hotel. That was my first premonition but no, I ask my best friend to pick your ass up and this is how you show your appreciation—by taking advantage of her. Are you okay Monica?" Alexis was in a rage and before either Monica or Philip could reply the woman was gone.

Philip turned to Monica and smiled, then kissed her gently.

"You were beautiful last night baby but not as beautiful as you appear to me this morning," he said kissing her deeply, passionately before standing up and grabbing his boxers.

"I think we have some explaining to do," he said staring at Monica.

"Perhaps I should handle it," he said. "No need to mess up a relationship that's been around as long as yours and Alexis' has. I guess I can be a rapist. It's not something that I'd put down on a resume and it would probably mean us sneaking around for the rest of our lives that is if you still have intentions of us seeing each other. But if I know Alexis…"

"But you don't know Alexis. You don't know that Alexis will blow your goddamn head off if you don't get the hell away from that woman. That is my friend and you have not only taken advantage of her but me as well when you come into my home—my home," she yelled, *"and take advantage of a woman that's like a sister to me,"* Monica could see the tears running down Alexis' face. *"If she's hurt, I'll kill you, you no good bastard,"* she screamed drawing the hammer of the pistol back.

Up until now Monica hadn't said anything but when she heard the hammer click back she knew just how grave the circumstances had become and her silence was doing little to diffuse the situation. Never at a loss for words she found it difficult to find the words at that moment but knew that if she allowed Philip to speak there was more than a good chance that Alexis would probably shoot him.

"Are you okay, Monica?" Alexis inquired her eyes never leaving Philip. *"You can't have me so you take your frustrations out on Monica. Is that it?"* she said waving the pistol at Philip.

Philip moved towards her and began to speak when the first shot rang out, grazing his ear and narrowly missing his head. Stunned, Philip fell backwards on the bed and readied himself to meet his maker.

The shot acted as a wake up call for Monica who was suddenly mobilized and jumped in front of Philip right before Alexis decided that Philip's twenty-three years was more than enough time.

"Alexis! Stop! Have you lost your fuckin' mind? He didn't do anything to me," Monica shouted.

Blinded by her anger, Alexis eyes were still fixed on the man in front of her.

"You're all the same. All you bastards are the same! Move Monica. You don't have to cover for this bitch ass motherfucker. Move, baby I'm gonna make it so this bastard never put his hands on another woman in this lifetime. Now move Monica!" Alexis screamed. *"Ain't a man worth his weight in shit and every time I open up and let one in this is how they act. Well, here's one that won't have the opportunity. Now move goddammi! And then again maybe he will but not in this lifetime."*

"Alexis, put the goddamn gun down and listen to me!" Monica shouted, pleading now. *"Philip didn't do a damn thing that I didn't want him to do. He didn't rape me. If anything, I seduced him. Now put the goddamn gun down!"* Monica screamed.

When she finished Alexis turned and studied her closely trying her best to see if she was defending Philip out of pity for him or to see if there might be some truth in her words. And although she was still not convinced she least listened nonetheless as Monica continued.

"I'm telling you the truth Alexis. Philip was a perfect gentleman

and if anything I seduced him. Hell, we had no intention of hurting you or anything like that, baby. It was just something that happened. We talked about it and flirted a bit and after a few drinks this is where we ended up.

It's as simple as that. I'm sorry if you think we disrespected your home but it wasn't intentional. Honestly there was no malice intended and I am sorry," she added, praying that Alexis in her rage would not turn the gun in her direction.

Searching both their eyes and finding nothing but shame and guilt Alexis lowered the gun and returned her gaze to Philip who sat speechless on the edge of the bed still dressed in nothing but his underwear; the thought of how close he'd come to death still vivid in his mind. The thought of life never as important as it was at that very moment.

"Is this true Philip?" Alexis asked the gun still in her hand.

"You have never known me to be anything but a perfect gentleman, Alexis. How could you ever think that I would do something so bane, so utterly despicable as to jeopardize my relationship with two women who have been as kind to me as you and Monica? *Damn! How could you even think some shit like that, Alexis?"*

"She thinks shit like that because she knows that that's exactly what she deserves," Monica interjected. *"Alexis knows that the way she treats people that it's only a matter of time before her number comes up. It's only a matter of time before someone gets fed up with her shit and decides to take some action. She just hasn't met that person yet is all. That's why she's walkin' around here all paranoid with that damn cannon. But I'll tell you what Alexis—when the time comes for you to cowboy up and pay to the fuckin' piper that piece of steel ain't gonna mean shit. When it comes time for you to meet Saint Peter and ante up on how you lived your life your ass is gonna need a whole lot more than that shit. I'm tellin' you girl that piece of blue steel ain't goin' to mean shit. You've been doin' the same thing, treating people the same way ever since I've known you and trust me you don't have long before your number comes up. The signs are*

everywhere but you ain't reading them. You're too busy worrying about how your ass can make another dollar and buy another condo and parade around like you're the Queen of Sheba to be worried about people or how you got where she is today. That's why you lost James. But you don't see it," Monica said as she grabbed her clothes and pushed her way past the distraught woman and headed out the door.

Alexis hung her head in shame letting the gun fall from her hands. The forty-five automatic hit the floor with a heavy thud. Philip looked at the woman in front of him and sighed. He wanted to hold her, to caress her, to tell her it was okay and that he was alright but he'd heard Monica. And in his heart he knew that despite the love and the desire that he still held for Alexis that there was more than an air of truth to be said for Monica's words and yes, perhaps it was time for him to wake up, smell the coffee and to see the world for what it was really worth. He'd wasted too much time already on a woman that was not his or anybody else's for the taking. Not that a man could possess a woman or even that a person had the ability to possess another but if there was a possibility of that ever happening Alexis was not the woman to be had by any man. In recognizing this, he did what any man would have done in a similar situation. Pardoning himself he made his way past Alexis and rushed out of the room in hopes of catching Monica who was now fully dressed and heading out the front door.

"And you weren't even going to have the common decency to at least tell me goodbye," Philip said as Monica opened the front door.

"I thought I mentioned the fact that I've never had a particular affinity for being a third wheel and after that shit that just transpired I really don't want to be anywhere near that bitch right now. Maybe we were wrong but nothing is that bad that a person has the right to threaten another person's life and—well—this whole crazy-assed scenario has been too much for me. Nothing personal but I just need some time to clear my head," Monica said closing the door behind her.

Philip opened the door as quickly as she'd closed it.

"Hold on Monica, let me grab my pants and I'll be right there," he said. Monica continued walking to the elevator as though she hadn't heard him at all.

Philip headed back into the house with all of the urgency of a man not knowing his fate. Unsure if this was the last time he'd ever see Monica he bolted past Alexis and grabbed the scattered remnants of his clothes which were strewn all over the guest room.

It had certainly been some night. And he'd been quite surprised to learn that Monica's boasting was not all just talk. He'd slept with many a beautiful woman in his college days but could never recall sleeping with someone of her vitality and passion. She made love as though it was the last thing she would ever do. And though he'd become fatigued rather quickly there was no quit in her and each time he thought he would roll over and call it a night she would find another way to arouse him to the point where he found himself begging her to make love to him just one more time even though he was both exhausted and quite sore. To be honest he never would have imagined that he could have actually made love as many times as he did in the course of a night.

By the time Monica decided that she was too spent to go another round the clock read somewhere in the neighborhood of four a.m. Though they'd agreed earlier to go back to their respective bedrooms for the sake of appearance they were both so exhausted that they'd passed out in each other's arms in the midst of a kiss. Philip hadn't given tomorrow a thought but if it was one thing he did know it was that he'd never felt the way he did that evening. Now before he was even given a chance to consider his options Alexis had appeared out of the blue and Monica was running out of the door and out of his life. One thing he was certain of and that was that he'd never felt this way about anyone or had anyone make him feel this way. And it wasn't just the lovemaking. He'd never felt quite so comfortable, so at ease or so completely in tune with anyone in his whole life as he had last night. He'd only wished that they had had the foresight to go somewhere, a hotel, her place, anyplace but in the guestroom at Alexis'.

His ear still rung from the sound of the gun blast but it was of little concern as he watched Monica make her way down the long corridor to the elevator. If there was a concern it was not letting this woman who had taken him places he never dreamed of in and out of the bedroom walk out of his life just as quickly as she'd managed to walk in.

Making his way past Alexis who was now standing in the doorway to the guest room, Philip quickly dressed and headed for the elevator to find Monica gone. Unscathed by her sudden exit, Philip reached the lobby just in time to see the red Volvo pull away from the curb and into traffic. It was then that he was rendered the disheartening realization that not only did he did know where she lived but didn't even know her last name.

Making his way back into the apartment, Alexis picked up the dirty glasses from the night before and placed them in the dishwasher before spraying the glass cocktail table and turning to Philip.

"I guess an apology at this point wouldn't suffice," she asked the tears flowing freely.

"Alexis I don't have time for the bullshit. Save the apology. If you want to do something for me you can give me Monica's number and home address. Other than that save the apologies and hysterics for some other sucker. It's a bit too late for all that now," Philip said gathering his overnight bag and other personal items in a tidy pile on the dining room table.

"Philip, listen to me for just a minute and then if you still want to go to her then I'll take you but just listen and try to understand what it is that I'm feeling," Alexis said grabbing both of his arms and staring up into his eyes.

Philip looked down at the tiny woman who no longer appeared to him as she had. No longer did he see the forty-two year old bombshell that could pass for thirty easily with a body that summoned all men to her like metal to a magnet. Instead he saw a worn and broken, frightened woman whose worst fear in life was of being alone and he suddenly felt some compassion. He was melting before her and sought some resolve in the image of Monica who was still fresh in his mind rushing through the door but then there was Alexis speaking to him again, staring at him, begging him to just relinquish a minute of his time to explain.

"You have to understand the stress that I have on me Philip. I've tried to confide in you and I've prayed that you would understand what I've been going through these last ten months so that you wouldn't give up hope and bail out on me like every other man has done. All I wanted you to do was give me some time to jump over some of these hurdles so that you and I could have some time— quality time for each other in the end. I'm racing around here trying to make a move here and a move there so we both can share the benefits of being financially secure. You can't help but know that I love you Philip. You have to recognize that. I hope you don't believe it's because you do my books for me."

"And you mean to tell me that that's not the reason you let me tag along behind you, Alexis?" Philip replied.

"Why, certainly not," she said raising her voice in disbelief. *"Is that what you truly believe? That the only reason we're in communication is because I let you handle my accounts?"* Alexis fell back on the sofa laughing. When she was finished she went to the bar picked up the bottle of Hennessey and poured herself four fingers and returned to the couch.

"I don't know if that's Monica talking or if you really believe that. With all the brokerage firms right here in Detroit and the contacts I made in New York you can't possibly think that that's why I see you and allow you to stay in my home. C'mon Philip I know you're more insightful than that. If you must know I've been in love with you from the first time I met you. I moved back here because I couldn't get the thought of you out of my head and didn't want to jeopardize my marriage but you see that I'm not married.

I could never tell you because of my own insecurities. All through my life I've had the misfortune of being soft and letting men come into my space and each and every time I let my guard down they end up walking out the door and leaving me heartbroken. My momma used to tell me that I was an attractive girl but then she would always ask me, 'what man wants to buy a cow when he can get the milk free' and so I may have used my so-called attractiveness to lure men in but once they found out that they couldn't get the milk free they always found a way to leave me so I built up a wall around me and I suppose that's why I'm so leery of men but just when I'd gotten to the point that I can trust a man the cycle starts all over again," she said the tears flowing freely again.

"And?"

"And?" Alexis repeated.

"And what does any of that have to do with me," Philip asked.

"Don't you see, Philip? Right when I decide that Philip is somehow different, that perhaps you are genuinely interested in me for the long term then I come home *and find you in the bed with my so-called best friend* and lose all hope again."

"It's been ten months, Alexis—without so much as a kiss and you want me to believe this? If it's your account your worried about I took the liberty of reassigning you the power-of-attorney and have washed my hands of the whole affair. I had the papers are signed and notarized before I left New York. I came here this weekend to let you know that I would no longer be handling your portfolio and you didn't even have the common decency of calling me and telling me that you would be going out of town. But believe I've gotten used to your selfishness and insensitivity to other people's needs. Right through here I've grown extremely tired of it and aside from us talking about the market I have a hard time seeing where you have any interest in anyone aside from yourself." Philip countered his anger showing.

"Now if you would be so kind as to give me Monica's address I'd like to go and apologize which is really something that you should be doing."

"Apologize to her for what? For picking up a man she knew that I had feelings for and bringing him back to my house and screwing him in my bed. I should apologize for that? I know you can't be serious. Ever since we were kids and people you used to make fun of Monica I stuck by her. I was always her friend. I always looked out for her like an older sibling trying to protect her from falling into this trap or that. Now I walk into my house and she's in bed and I don't know if she's been raped or being her usual little whorish self and I'm trying to protect her and you think I should apologize. *You must be out of your John Brown mind!"* Alexis screamed.

"This is not the first time she's sniffed around behind me trying to push up on something that wasn't hers and it probably won't be the last. Let me tell you something you don't know, Philip. Monica has always used sex to try and latch onto a man. I don't know if she feels inadequate because she's big or if she just doesn't know any better but this isn't the first time she's used sex to try to get a guy to fall for her and if I were you I'd be careful. My father used to tell my younger brother when he used to date in high school that, 'you don't step in every hole you see'. And if I were you might want to take heed as well."

"You're offering advice, Alexis? After watching you in action over the last few months, Alexis, I think the only thing that you could probably give me is Monica's address," Philip said deeply disturbed by her latest admission.

"I will not. I'm not going to let you make a fool out of yourself because of one night. And let me tell you something else, Mr. Dalton. You are not the only one's that's made a major investment in this relationship. I have too. I lost a husband and a marriage to be with you and because you don't have the maturity or the perceptiveness to see that is not my fault. But I will not just turn you over to that bitch because of a little one night tryst. I was really hoping that you would be the one that somehow passed the test. I really believed that somehow you were the one that had the foresight to see us on our own private beach in the Bahamas making love beneath the palms under the light of the moon and all that other romantic shit.

I thought that perhaps, that maybe, just maybe you would be the one to somehow make it past the bullshit distractions that face us in our everyday lives. I though that maybe, just maybe you had the discipline to   stay focused on your career until the time was right and we could both leave this rat race behind us and live comfortably and worry free for each other."

"Well, Alexis, perhaps you should have informed and included me in your plans. Perhaps and just maybe you should have taken the time to spell it all out for me so I could somehow see how I had a part in what course *my life* was supposed to be taking. But that's neither here nor there now. It's really too late for all of that and truly and honestly believe that all this conversation is simply coming out of desperation because you are so damn fearful of growing old alone. I don't believe any of this shit you're telling me and honestly wonder why you're wasting my time. I hope it has nothing to do with the fact that you and Monica have something kin to a sibling rivalry and you really and truly don't want her to succeed where you've failed. You know on first impression it would appear that you two were inseparable—the best of friends but now that I look at it from afar you two don't even like each other. Oh, you may have at one time and remained in each other's company out of a need to hold on to the only thing you have of your pasts, of the good memories but I really and truly believe that that's all you two have in common now and as the years have moved on you two have a growing animosity towards each other that almost borders on hatred."

"You don't have any idea of what you're talking about, Philip and again you're in a subject that's way over your head," Alexis screamed.

"Well, that may be so. I don't honestly know. What I do know is that there's a loving, caring, feeling woman that is somewhere feeling used and abandoned who needs to know that a roll in the hay was not just a prelim to the main event," Philip replied.

"But isn't that exactly what it was?" Alexis replied smiling.

"It most certainly was not."

"Well, let's just see. Give me time to grab a quick shower and I'll take you over to Monica's as soon as I get out but first I want you to grab the bag next to my suitcase and bring it here. Don't look in it, just bring it here. Thank you. I bought this for you although I'm not going to show it to you as of yet but I want you to ask yourself two questions while I'm in the shower and I want you to think about them closely. First of all, I want you to ask yourself why I wasted the ticket I had to catch an earlier flight and what I had on my mind when I bought this gift for you? Now will you excuse me Philip while I grab a quick shower? Oh, I almost forgot your gift. Believe me I understand your being upset with me so if you decide you don't want the gift I brought for you I totally understand."

"Alexis, I don't want a gift or anything else from you. Forty-five minutes ago you called me every name under the sun, accused me of raping your girlfriend and pointed a gun at me—a gun, Alexis—and had all intentions of blowing my head off and now you're standing here telling me that that you've always loved me and I guess I'm supposed to act like none of this even happened," Philip grinned sarcastically. "Are you serious?"

"How can I apologize for my stupidity, Philip? Words could hardly atone for the harm I've caused you. Believe me; I understand you being angry with me but if you can just give me a chance to redeem myself..."

"Redeem yourself? Alexis please. You've had close to a year to exhibit the way you feel about me and I have seen little up until now and you think that in the next few minutes you can redeem yourself? C'mon let's be serious?"

"I am serious. Dead serious. Just you wait and see," Alexis smiled. "Give me a minute to grab a quick shower and then I'll allow you to be the judge of my sincerity."

Philip had no choice but to wait. He was uncomfortable and grieved deeply for Monica. The evening they'd spent together had been more than enjoyable and for it to wind up like this was more than he could have ever imagined.

Now, here he was stuck in a situation that left him little choice other than to let things unfold the way Alexis wanted them too. If he had any hopes of seeing Monica again it would be because Alexis permitted him to. She would have to consider it the right thing, the charitable thing to do. Philip realized, however, that there was no way Alexis with her ego and air of superiority would allow him to see Monica unless he succumbed to her wish. She didn't want him. Of that he was sure. But neither did she want Monica to have him either. She would never allow Monica the possibility of perhaps sharing in some happiness while she was mired in such misery. No, he would have to play his cards close to the vest. Perhaps grudgingly forgive her for firing a gun in his direction and then let the whole subject drop and let everything resort to normal until he felt a sharp pain in his ear and let her feel his pain as well as her own guilt.

He would rest during the afternoon and awaken in the early evening and tell her it was because of the ringing in his ear—once again attempting to work on her guilt.

The next matter at hand would be the returning of her accounts. Playing on her ego, he would intimate that she knew enough for her to manage them herself and insist that she sign the necessary paperwork to give her full custody of the accounts. Hopefully, she would get the sense that he needed neither her accounts nor the commission from them.

His subsequent return of her accounts along with his power of attorney making him no longer her representative in any financial matters would ultimately do two things. First, it would insure the break was clean between them and leave her with the sense and the finality that this was the last time she would see him.

And although Philip was positive that she had had no interest in him—well—other than what he could provide in the form of a financial consultation here and there the thought of him leaving her would cause a substantial blow to her already fragile ego. It was not ingenious, this plan, by any stretch of the imagination but only the result of clear observation.

In fact, it was the same identical scenario that he'd witnessed firsthand over the past year or so. She hadn't given James a second thought either, until he'd decided to leave and then his stock had risen sharply in her eyes. And his leaving so close to James' exit and her divorce could only mean one thing in her eyes. And that was, that despite all of her intelligence, her good looks and her business savvy the bottom line was that Alexis LeBrandt did not have what it took to keep a man. And with her disposition that was one thing she would not be able to live with. Not only would she deliver him to Monica that evening she would beg him to return and to take her account back and anything else he desired as long as he didn't leave. It was one thing that he'd come to recognize in Alexis LeBrandt it was the fact that her own inflated ego was her Achilles heel.

There was more to Philip's plan but he desperately needed to run it past Monica but that would have to wait. And if Alexis had only been a little more receptive to both his and Monica's needs he would have never considered such a strategy but as always she was only concerned about how Alexis felt with no regard to either of them and Philip, not to be had was going to make her tow the line from here on out.

First things first though, and so after pouring enough Grey Goose to insure that he would sleep straight through the afternoon and into the early evening Philip emptied the remainder of the bottle into the kitchen sink to give the appearance that he'd had too much to drink. And with that small but inconspicuous move Philip's plan began to take shape.

Moments later, Philip heard the bathroom door close and wasn't sure that he'd poured enough of the vodka down the sink to enact the first step of his plan. There was no doubt that he was more than a little inebriated which was fine but giving the illusion of being drunk was not his intention. Aware that any sign of weakness would give Alexis the upper hand he made his way to the kitchen, leaned over the sink and splashed cold water on his face with the hopes that it would not only clear his head but give the impression that he was sweating as well. He then took a plastic bag filled it with ice, wrapped it in a dish towel and returned to the sofa where he held the cold compress to his left ear which was still throbbing and placed his head on the arm of the so as to appear in obvious pain.

No sooner had he completed this ruse than he heard the sound of Alexis' footsteps making her way down the long hallway and into the living room, at which time he closed his eyes as if this would be an obvious sign of the pain he was suffering and feigned sleep.

"Baby, are you okay," he heard Alexis whisper the concern evident in her tone.

"Huh' uh yeah, I'm fine," he said not bothering to open his eyes.

He thought of Monica's acting debut last night and could feel a smile forming but quickly masked it. 'Wonder what she would think of this performance?' he thought.

"Are you sure you're okay?" she asked again, her concern more than obvious this time but still he did not open his eyes and thought not to dignify her question with a reply. 'Let her think what she wants', he said to himself. 'One minute she's trying to bury me and the next she wants to know if I'm okay.' The thought angered him and he turned his body into the crook of the sofa so as to ignore her altogether.

"Baby, I told you I had a surprise for you," she said. "But you have to turn and look this way.

Philip contemplated the idea for a moment. His curiosity was getting the best of him but he remained steadfast in his defiance. He had to. His whole plan depended on how well he could manipulate this woman who wrote the handbook on manipulation. He never worried about her doubting his sincerity. In a year, he'd been the quintessential ambassador of trust and sincerity. He couldn't have set a better backdrop if he'd tried and as the result she would never give him the credit for having the wherewithal to con her.

No, if his head was down and he could hardly lift it at her command then he was hurting. He had to be. After all, didn't he always do everything she commanded?

Groaning slightly he curled up into the fetal position, wondering just how far he had to go with this charade to get her to understand that he was hurting. And then, by the grace of God, it finally dawned on her that maybe she'd done more damage than she initially thought.

"Philip, sweetheart, are you okay?" she asked.

"My head," he replied whispering so she had to bend down to hear him.

"Is there anything I can do?" she asked. "Do you want me to call my physician? I can probably get him to come over and take a look you; maybe prescribe some pain killers or something," she asked. "My goodness, I didn't know I'd done that much damage. God! I am so sorry," she said her voice teetering and he knew she was on the brink of tears.

Now for the coup de tat, he thought.

"No, I'm sure, I'll be fine. If you can get me two aspirins I'd appreciate that. My ears are ringing."

There that was it. But he wasn't satisfied and added, "Do you think you could help me to the bedroom. I think if I were to lie down it might help some."

"Not a problem. Here, wrap your arms around me," she said.

Philip let his weight fall on her and did as little as possible to help her but after struggling a bit she was finally able to get him in the bedroom and into the bed.

"Let me get you something for the pain, babe. Hold on sweetie, I'll be right back. God, I feel so bad. I don't know I was thinking. I should have known better than to think you could harm a fly. Oh God what have I done?" she said pacing to and fro and muttering to herself. "Oh yeah, the aspirins."

The tears were flowing now and Philip only wished Monica could have been there to see her now. It was the first time since Philip met Alexis that he had seen anything resembling a human side. Her emotion obvious, Philip wondered if it was truly heartfelt or just another act. Lying there he groaned once more before opening his eyes briefly.

Walking away, he was shocked to find Alexis LeBrandt the consummate professional always so nattily attired dressed in nothing but a pair of opened-toed heels and a sky-blue thong.

If he wasn't sick before he was sick now when he realized that in all the time that he'd known her she'd never thought to seduce him until now when she thought, he too, was leaving her.

Philip, at once had mixed feelings. On the one hand, he wished he had held off faking his injury just a little longer to see if her story was for real. Had she really intended on opening up tonight? Had she really taken an early flight home just to spend a little extra time with him? The fact that she'd brought this 'lil outfit back for him could all have been a ploy and then again who knew, she could have been sincere. One thing was for sure, he would never know now and if he gave in now, under the circumstances what would that say about him?

No, he'd found warmth and compatibility with Monica and though he hardly knew her, he knew enough to know that that's where his heart was at that moment and besides she'd left him so sore that had he opted to test the waters with Alexis he wouldn't have been able to anyway. Philip smiled at the thought. He smiled just thinking about Monica and how she'd teased him and caressed him and ridden him from one sweaty, shuddering, orgasm to the next. Each time he thought he was drained and had nothing left she pulled out another trick from her seemingly endless repertoire and had him begging for more despite being both raw and sore.

Now, here was Alexis standing before him almost naked except for that piece of string and with the most well proportioned body of any woman he'd ever come to know. And all he could do at this point was look and marvel. Even if he'd wanted to do something he couldn't have in his condition but hell, how the thought appealed to him just the same.

Hearing the door open, Philip closed his eyes once more. Only this time he was happy to do so rather than be tortured by the sight of this naked beauty; a woman who he had spent the last ten months lusting for. He hated to even think about it. But there it was plain as day. Now that she was *finally* his for the taking he could not partake. The irony of it all disgusted him and he knew he would be unable to sleep though his eyes remained closed.

"Here sweetheart—take two of these and get some rest and we'll see how you feel in an hour or two. How's that? If you're not feeling in about an hour or so we'll try something else; maybe call Dr. Philbin. I don't know let's just wait and see.

I still have a surprise for you but it can wait," And with that said Alexis bent over Philip and kissed him lightly on the cheek. "I'll be in and out checking on you so don't be alarmed," she said on her way out of the room.

"No gun this time, I hope," he said making sure to keep the reason he was in bed fresh in her mind.

"That's not funny, Philip. I'm trying my best to atone for my stupidity," she said. "I said I was sorry," she repeated.

'Not nearly as sorry as you will be,' Philip thought as he pulled the covers over his head.

Alexis waited until he heard the door close and swallowed the two pills Alexis laid on the nightstand and smiled as he thought about the next phase of his plan. Alexis was not the only one with a surprise, he mused before drifting off to sleep.

Chapter 12

Philip wasn't sure how long he'd slept but for the second time that day he was awakened from a sound sleep by something completely out of the ordinary. Only this time he felt an excruciating pain unlike anything he'd ever felt before. He was nauseous and figured that the liquor was having its way with him but the burning sensation he felt in his stomach in no way compared with the sharp pain he felt in his genitals. A stabbing pain that felt as if his very flesh were being torn from him. When he tried to sit up he found that he was unable to, and though everything seemed blurred and fuzzy he was able to make out the shape of Alexis who straddled him and was grinding hard against his pelvic area in an attempt to make him erect.

Sweating, profusely it was quite clear that she'd been at it for some time. He could only guess how long but it must have been quite awhile since she'd had the time to tie both his arms and legs to the bedpost and gag him with his own handkerchief. Every now and then between blacking out and regaining consciousness Philip would hear her cursing in frustration as she continued to grind against him.

Seeing her naked breasts staring down at him he could feel himself begin to emerge from beneath the sheet and saw the smile slowly spread across her face. He cursed himself for not remaining limp and tried to tell himself that this was not the woman for him but between brushing her tiny breasts against his lips and her hand caressing him there was little he could do. Tugging at the knee-highs which had him spread eagled and bound to the four corners of the bed he felt totally helpless. He wanted to tell her that he was both raw and sore but each time he attempted to speak the handkerchief seemed to be sucked in to his mouth even deeper and he was sure that if he continued he'd ended up swallowing it, choking himself and maybe even suffocating. For some reason, he didn't seem in full control of his faculties and was having a hard time maintaining his erection. And though this elated him it seemed to drive Alexis into a fury.

"You mean to tell me that you can get hard for that fat bitch and you can't stay hard for five minutes for me? Well, will just see about that Mr. Dalton. Trust me, baby, when I get finished with you today you won't have the strength to look in another woman's direction let alone think about screwing them. When I think about that fat bitch in my goddamn house screwin' my man I'm sorry I didn't shoot her fat, sloppy ass. She ain't nothin' but a two bit sorry-ass whore. Never did have any respect for herself," Alexis said angrily and to no one in general.

She was still grinding herself against Philip and the brief erection that he had only moments earlier only gave her the notion that it was eminent and all she needed was the right motivation to make it last.

"Baby, tell me what you need me to do for you. You just tell me, baby. Need me to model the outfit I bought for you? Is that what you want? Or maybe you want me to throw this little tight ass up in your face baby, so you can watch it wiggle. Want me to make it dance for you? That's what you want, isn't it?" Alexis asked. "Just tell me what you want Philip…"

'If that was it, you–sinister bitch—how the hell could I tell you with this goddamn handkerchief stuffed halfway down my throat? You want me to talk and I can barely breathe,' he thought to himself as he continued to wrestle with the knee-highs tied to his wrists. She'd tied two to each wrist and double-knotted them to insure his not moving and he had to admit that she'd done a hell of a job before resigning himself to the fact that there was little he could do but hope and pray that she would get bored and it would soon be over.

"So you wanna see my ass move for you don'tcha baby," Alexis asked grinning. "I promise you it will Philip but you seem a little tense so I'm going to go get my baby a sip to loosen you up some. How's that sound, sweetheart. Be right back," she said smiling

Philip couldn't for the life of him understand why it had taken this long to transpire. Two months ago he would have given anything to be in this very same position, Hell, two weeks ago. Hell, two days ago. In fact if she hadn't been stupid enough to send another woman to pick him up and then make sure he was comfortable he might have been alright with this now. But the truth of the matter was that she had sent another woman; and not just any woman but an attractive woman not only with robust features but a robust personality to boot and she had come into his life like a big ol' rough and tumble whirlwind and taken him by storm, ruining him for all who came after. She had him thinking that he'd fallen in love in a night's time then stroked him 'til he was raw and incapable of anything including Alexis touching him there now.

But how was Alexis to know? The thought of communication never entered her mind. She just assumed. And being so goddamn stupid, so oblivious to what was transpiring around her and with him, she just naturally assumed that there could be no one other than her in his life and if there was it was only temporary. When she'd finished with him, all thoughts of anyone else would amount to no more than a passing fancy.

Philip wished he could tell her of his dilemma but his own maliciousness, his own malice and need for revenge left him prone, bound, unable to speak and at her mercy and he prayed that if there was another round she would be gentle in her assault.

Alexis returned minutes later with the bottle of Hennessey, poured a glass for Philip, placed the glass on the night table and then sat on the edge of the bed her back to him and guzzled freely.

"You have to excuse me, baby, I know this isn't lady-like but you have to agree that this has been one hell of a day and it's not even one o'clock yet. I thought about waking you up hours ago but you were sleeping so peacefully that I didn't want to disturb you. Besides I wanted you to save all your strength for this. You know there was a time that I was really, really unsure about you and I, with the age difference and all that but I guess I've overcome that. When it wasn't that it was James.

Monica told me that some people live to be miserable—you know—they look to dwell on the negative and it's funny but it's almost like they get their peace of mind by dwelling on their own unhappiness. I can't really explain it but I guess that's where I was. Funny, me quoting Monica. She certainly doesn't let anything stand in the way of her pursuit does she?"

The liquor was talking now and Philip only hoped that she'd drunk enough to temper her quest to make him happy. Turning the bottle up she guzzled some more before turning and grinning at him.

"Guess what lover? I got the piece of land down in the islands I was telling you about. Isn't that wonderful? I can't wait to start renovating the hotel. Gonna turn it into five units and rent them out as time sharing lots or maybe a bed and breakfast. You're gonna love it. Oh, I can't wait but there's no need to talk about that now. Let's celebrate now and talk about all of that later after I've spoiled you. Just promise me that if I take the handkerchief off for a toast that you won't say a word; not a single solitary word. I want you to have a toast, relax and let me love you for all the time I've wasted. Now tell me you promise?"

At this point Philip would have gladly told her anything if she just took that goddamn rag out of his mouth and allowed him to taste his own saliva once more. Hell, he didn't know what was worse—being shot at or being bound and held hostage.

"Do you promise?" she asked as she took another swig. "Why, of course you do. And why wouldn't you? I read that it's every man's dream to be bound and gagged by a beautiful woman and then be taken apart morsel by tiny morsel until he has nothing left and has to beg for mercy. Is that true?"

Philip stared at the woman sitting on the side of the bed and wondered if she were completely mad.

"Well, I think I've had just about all of this I need. Are you ready for your sip?"

Philip tried to nod but found that he could barely raise his head. He'd had close to half a bottle of Grey Goose but he'd never felt quite like this from alcohol and wondered if the events of the day had him feeling out of sorts. It was hard to explain but he knew there was something wrong—something terribly wrong.

"Hennessey always relaxes me and I guess you can tell from all this idle chatter," Alexis laughed. "Truth is I'm just a little bit nervous. I've never made love to anyone other than my husband so if I don't do something right just bear with me. You can teach me as we go. Anyway, I guess that's why I'm so talkative. Well, that and the fact that it's been over a year since I've done this. But I promise you that if it's time, love and tenderness that makes for good love, I can certainly supply those.

Well, then again—I don't know about the tenderness—I've still got a hatchet to bury concerning you sleeping with Monica so after I convince you that you made a terrible mistake playing with the second string I might decide to resort to a little tenderness but first you're gonna pay. That's why I gagged you when you were sleeping. No need for the neighbors to hear you and I don't want you crying and begging me to stop. I ain't trying to be compassionate right through here. I'm getting ready to pussy whip your ass and put that thing of yours on lock," Alexis laughed.

"Now come here. Let me take this handkerchief off so you can take a swallow. Remember you promised not to say a word. One word and it goes right back on. So I suggest you sip quietly."

Still drunk from the vodka earlier in the day and feeling both nauseous and groggy, Philip didn't want anything to drink but he would have done almost anything by this time to get that damn gag out of his mouth.

Alexis lifted Philip's head after taking another swallow herself and untied the gag. Philip was about to say something when Alexis put her finger to his lips and gestured for him to be quiet. Seeing the gag in her other hand he followed her directions and swallowed the drink the only way he could with her pouring large gulps in his mouth and almost choking him.

"Now, now," she said as though he were a newborn, "that's more than enough. "I would let you finish the glass if I hadn't given you those valiums earlier. The combination could be dangerous," she said before grabbing the handkerchief from its place on the nightstand.

So that was it. That's why he was feeling so goddamn strange. She couldn't possibly have known about the Grey Goose but she could have let him know that they were painkillers instead of aspirins. My God! If she wasn't the devil reincarnate he didn't know who was. Know wonder he had no power over his limbs or his… And then he smiled but it was obvious Alexis took his smile to mean something else entirely.

"I knew you would love it, baby. I've been thinking about doing this for you ever since that night at the Radisson when I thought something had happened to you. That's the night that I knew it was only a matter of time before I would have you just like this—just the way I dreamed—bound to me mentally, physically and spiritually. Somehow, I just knew. I figured any man that goes to the extremes that you did to see me and spend time with me and well—just share time together when sex wasn't a factor had to be a pretty good man. And I guess I was right. I'm not even going to entertain the idea of Monica and you because I know how she can be. She's typical of so many sistas out there starvin' for a good man that they often—in fact—all too often forget everything and everyone around them just so they can grab a foothold. That's Monica. The girl will sleep with anybody if a man just promises her he'll love her. Say the 'L' word to ol' girl and you've got the pussy. It's a damn shame but that's the way it is," Alexis said crossing her thick brown calves.

"Oh, my God! I'm sorry, baby, I'm just a runnin' my mouth. I told you that liquor does that to me. Here let me see if you're ready for me now."

Alexis slid her hand under the comforter and rubbed Philip's penis gently. As lightly as she did it still sent shockwaves of pain up and down his spine. My how it hurt and Philip did his damndest to let her know but with the rag back firmly in place he could do little more than moan.

"Ooh, it's getting there," Alexis said and she was right. Despite the pain the covers rose forming a small tent around Philip's thighs.

"I guess you're waiting on me," she said. "I'm almost ready, baby. Here have another swallow with me lover."

It was more than a little obvious that she was drunk now and cared little about the pills she'd given him earlier or anything else at this point.

Philip, on the other hand had never seen a woman drink quite as much as Alexis had that afternoon and it was more than obvious that whatever skeleton's Alexis was trying to mask were numerous and weighing on her heavily. Whether she wanted to make love to him at all was now a question that Philip had to entertain. And he really had a hard time deciding if she were doing it to convince herself that she did love and want him after all or was it out of some sense of duty for all he'd done for her up 'til that point in their relationship. Or had he'd simply gotten caught up in a rivalry between two women.

"Another drink, lover?" Alexis said slurring her words now.

Even if he could have answered he wouldn't had time to since Alexis all but ripped his head off trying to get the handkerchief off for the second time. Once she'd gotten it off, she lifted his head and poured the liquor into him like it was water. Gulping the first few mouthfuls he prayed she would to stop but she was too far gone and not in control and it wasn't until he began to choke that she realized that maybe it was a bit much.

"Oh, I am sorry, Philip. Did I make a mess? Here let me wipe your mouth." She said smiling.

"Okay, I guess the stage has been set. The magazine says to take your time when setting the stage. Says to let your man savor the beauty of seeing you naked for some time before attempting anything aside from a few light kisses and a whiff of your perfume. S'pozed to heighten the senses and set the tone for some light foreplay. Then I'm s'pozed to stroke you lightly or cover your body with sweet but sensual kisses and then stroke you once more from head-to-toe. *Swear to God.* That's what the magazine said. Want me to show you the article? *I swear to God. That's what it says. I memorized the shit.* And I'll tell you what. It works. They took a survey and ninety-six percent of the women in the article claimed they had a fuller and richer marriage afterwards but I'll tell you what. I don't know about them but it's working for me. We might just have to save the foreplay for another time though 'cause my shit is throbbing for some of you right now, baby. Don't be mad though but I've got to have some right now. I guess I waited too long to go through the whole thing step-by-step so if you'll excuse me it's time for you to cowboy up and give a girl a taste of your fine ass self."

And with nothing else said Alexis stood up on the bed and turned her back on Philip so her ass was in his face, rolled her hips twice and lowered herself onto his semi-erect shaft.

"*Yes, baby. That's it baby. That's my sweet spot. That's it,*" she screamed. *My God, Philip! It's so good—so hard—so, so—so damn good, baby. Oh yes! C'mon Philip! Come for me baby. Can you feel me baby?* She moaned.

Could he feel her? He'd never felt so much pain in all his life and the tears flowed from the corners of his eyes. Each time she slid down on him it felt as though another piece of flesh was being ripped from him. There was nothing he could do now but hope and pray that she would orgasm quickly but it had been a year and she was like some love sick eighteen year old who was making love for the first time so insatiable was her appetite. Several times during the next hour, which seemed like days she would rise and scream.

"*Baby. I'm coming. Come with me, baby! C'mon Philip let it go baby. C'mon baby I can't hold it any longer. That's it move with me baby. Make me come. Good God, you're beautiful, baby but then I knew you would be! C'mon! That's it! Fuck me baby! Fuck me like you did that bitch. That's it! Fuck me good, baby! Yeah! That's it! Oh, my God! I'm coming baby."*

And then—right then and there on the verge of an explosion she would stop, get up, take a sip from the almost empty bottle, relax until the feeling had passed, then lower herself on to him and begin again.

"I told you, you would remember this for the rest of your lifetime, Philip darling and I intend to keep my word.

By this time, Philip withstood the assault on his manhood with little or no emotion. The pills and brandy rendered him all but numb and he could feel himself sliding away in a deep, dark abyss of melancholy. He was no longer angered by Alexis' selfish indifference. He felt sorry for her. And his thoughts moved from blind fury to a mixture of compassion and sympathy.

Over and over again he gazed up at her and listened to her screams of passion and wondered what it was that could take a woman of her beauty and intellect to such extremes. He simply came to the conclusion that she was driven by abandonment and rejection and loneliness. Still, relatively young at forty-two, there was obviously a sense that she was for all intent and purposes a woman alone in an ocean of piranhas and other bottom feeders who cared nothing about her, other than what she could do for them and in time she had taken on these attributes herself as a way of fending off these sharks. And it had taken her a year to finally trust him enough to realize that perhaps—just maybe, Philip was sincere. Then just as she'd come to this conclusion, she'd come home only to find him in bed with her best friend. It was obvious from watching her move up and down, her ass pumping up and down faster and faster that the events of the morning had pushed her over the edge.

There was her ego that would not allow her to be defeated again which told her that she was much too fine and much too bright to lose in another relationship. If she lost this time, and she'd be damned if that happened again, it wouldn't be because she hadn't expended every ounce of strength and love within her. She viewed herself as lovely, a gift from God, a prize for any thinking man and yet the brothers rejected her constantly.

That was except for Philip Dalton. And perhaps she'd been too slow and too rigid in making sure he was the one but he was the one and Monica and no other woman was going to stand between her and her having him. Philip was one brother who wouldn't get away. And she was determined to let him know it. If it meant making passionate love to him 'til he was unable to look in another woman's direction then she would do it. If it meant her flying to New York to spend time with him at every available opportunity, then she would do it. If it meant her ignoring the fact that he'd slept with Monica—well—that would take some time to get over but eventually she'd get over that too. If it meant her having to ride him all day and half of the night to wipe away the thought of Monica, then she would do that too.

Hell, it had been her fault. It was her own insecurities that made her string him along this long. After all, he'd done all one could possibly ask. He'd been more than sympathetic to her needs—flying to see her when she allowed him to and being at her beck and call. And still she wasn't sure. Still, she needed to know. She needed to know if he was sincere.

Hell, half the men she came across appeared to be sincere; always claiming to have her best interest at heart. A few weeks later, they'd disappear all hot and bothered 'cause she hadn't seen fit to drop her drawers in their time. But not Philip. Philip had remained steadfast in his pursuit and now she was giving him something she'd never given any other man aside from James and if it meant her apologizing in the only way she knew how then she would do that too.

Philip came to realize this between the blurred vision of the drugs and alcohol as he watched her ass move up and down in such rapidity that he knew she had been without for far too long. This was for him, of that he was sure but not only was this for him but for her too and he listened while she screamed for him to *'fuck her'* over and over again. Whatever demons she had bottled up inside of her she was intent on exorcising right here and right now. She needed him but not his interference so she'd bound and gagged him so she could have her way, so she could pleasure him and herself without his direction or his input.

"Oh, Philip baby, I'm stuck! Oh, God help me! Philip move your ass, baby. C'mon, baby. You've got to help me Philip! C'mon baby—work it—make me come. C'mon baby! Grind in my pussy baby. Make me feel you baby! C'mon Philip! Make it yours baby. C'mon, baby, make this shit yours. Make it so it jumps when you call it baby. C'mon, do me right, babe. That's it Philip, honey. Grind in it sweetheart! Ohhh, baby, I'm ready! I'm right there! Do that shit baby! Make me come."

Philip watched her sweet, little ass slow to a rhythm as she moved up and down on his penis but it was different now and instead of slamming her body up and down like a bit in a Texas oil rig she rolled her hips on the tip of his penis so he could hear the sweet popping sounds of air as she caught it and then let enough of it go that he was outside of her chasm. She was teasing him now and much as hated to admit it she had him wanting her.

Her fine brown ass was moving so slowly now that he was sure that if he continued watching he'd either come in waves or get motion sickness from the ebb and flow. The thought of Monica and the events of earlier in the day slowly began to melt and fade from view as she began to gobble up more and more of his penis and then just when he thought he was going to lose it she stopped, went back to the head of the class and teased him, taking it out with her hand and using it to massage her clitoris. Damn, she was good and he almost wished he had waited. Closing his eyes, Philip smiled and relaxed.

"Okay, baby, it's time to show mommy what you can do! You've got to move with me Philip! Play time is over she said untying the knee highs from his ankles. No more excuses baby. I want to feel all

of you up in me. Do you hear me? I'm not even going to move. Your pussy's right here, baby but you're going to have to arch your back if you want to get it. Now, c'mon daddy! Show me how badly you want it," she said lowering just the opening of her vagina on Philip's penis and massaging it gently with the lips of her vagina.

Philip had to admit she was good. Where Monica worked at making love and making sure her lover was satisfied. Alexis worked at sex. And though there was a difference—the truth of the matter was Alexis had washed away his defiance and presented a challenge that had him arching his back at unbelievable angles while she giggled and kept her pussy just beyond his reach. Every now and then she'd lowered herself on the tip of his penis with just enough strokes to keep him moving but there was one thing that was certain. Her stock was rising with every missed stroke at the bottom of her vagina and he wanted her more at that very moment than he'd ever wanted anybody. No more thought of Monica or pain or even revenge. Now what he wanted more than anything in the world, more than money and fame and fortune or lying under the warm tropical sun on a beach under a palm tree in Tahiti was to bury himself deeply into the warm chasm of her vagina.

He was sweating profusely now and watching as she sipped on the last of the Hennessey with one hand and slurped on a lollipop at the same time. She was teasing him and advertising what was to come but little did she know that his frustration was mounting quickly and he was once again losing any empathy that had come as the result of the drugs and the alcohol. And then when he'd called her every name under the sun and given up the thought of penetrating her deeply, she dropped the now empty bottle of Hennessey to the floor and lowered herself onto him and until she had taken every inch of his penis into her and slowly began grinding in tiny circles, lifting her ass no more than an inch at a time.

"This one's for you baby," she said turning her head to watch Philip. *"Let me show you how to make love, baby,"* she said smiling.

And with that said and her slow grinding against his pelvic area, Alexis LeBrandt took world traveler Philip Dalton to exotic places he'd never before seen.

When she was sure she'd taken him exactly where she wanted him to go and she was sure he was both spent and exhausted she smiled and kissed him on the cheek. "Was it good for you, baby?" she asked as she cuddled up next to him. "Don't worry we can finish later but you've worn me out. *Six times, Philip. Six times in an hour.* I certainly hadn't expected anything like that. Oh, baby I'm sorry. Let me untie you. I guess it's no fun to sit in the ballpark after the game is over but have no fear we can try it again tonight if you like or you can do me if you feel domineering," she laughed.

"Tell me something honestly, though Philip and don't worry about sparing my feelings," She said looking directly at Philip. Then realizing there was little he could say with his mouth still gagged and bound she began to undo the ties on his wrist and ankles before removing the gag from his mouth. "Was it as good for you as it was for me?"

Philip had already decided that choking her to death as he'd contemplated earlier would serve little or no purpose at this juncture especially in lieu of the fact that Alexis would never have considered that she'd done any wrong. After all the sun revolved around Alexis LeBrandt and the thought that he may not have wanted to be bound and gagged was never even entertained. It was what she wanted to do and his opinion mattered little if at all. His anger subsided along with the pain and he felt little for the woman now lying beside him but contempt although he did his best not to let it show.

In a matter of a few short minutes and before he could respond she was soundly asleep and despite being disoriented and still groggy he managed to gather his clothes and make his way to the shower. The warm water greeting him like a breath of fresh air and though the open cuts stung like hell he managed to endure the pain.

The next thing he needed to do was find Monica's number and after rummaging through her pocketbook and checking the computer it finally dawned on him to check the phone. Recognizing Monica's name, Philip dialed quickly. He needed to talk to her and meet her and do all of this before Alexis woke up and found him gone. She knew he didn't have any contacts in Detroit and the last thing he needed at this point was to have her thinking that he'd somehow managed to meet Monica after the performance she'd just put on for him.

What she was totally unaware of was that even if he had considered making love there was little he could do sexually in the condition she'd left him. Still, he'd rather not have to go through the lying and explaining and as he made his way to the corner where he was to meet Monica he wondered why he hadn't thought about simply calling her when he returned home. It would have been far safer.

Truth of the matter was that he was both hurt and angry and the fact that he had to hide his anger and his frustration only heightened his desire to put his plan into action

In the year or so that he'd known Alexis, he'd watched her closely observing all of her foibles and idiosyncrasies the way a man often does when considering spending the rest of his days with that woman. Up until a week ago he'd liked what he'd seen overall but if there was one thing that Philip recognized as Alexis' Achilles' heel it was her lack of judgment when it came to certain significant matters. All too often, she made decisions that would affect her future without so much as giving them a second thought.

Even Alexis had to admit that her impetuous nature would be the cause of her demise. But it hadn't happened yet. Thank God James had been there to handle the more important decisions that affected their lives and their futures but now that James was no longer in the picture and she'd been forced to put all of her trust and faith in Philip's hands in handling such mundane affairs as investing in her future.

Smitten, from day one, he would have given his right arm for a chance to be a part of her life and if it meant jeopardizing his career then so be it. He'd crossed the line on more than one occasion, passing insider trade tips with the hopes of building her nest egg and enhancing his value in her eyes since it was obvious from the first time they met that she was not obsessed with making money as he was but hording it instead.

His business acumen stirred a certain fascination in her similar to that of a little girl with her first doll. Aside from that, the only other thing about Philip that really sparked her interests beside his striking good looks and the fact that he made a charming escort was his affinity for nice things. Yet, what appealed to her even more was the fact that unlike her he enjoyed making money. After he made it—well—that was a different story. He could have cared less about the money. With more than thirty-five clients, commissions were as common to Philip as changing his underwear and often times he left his commission checks lying around for weeks before opening the envelopes or depositing them.

And whenever she was a little short on a business venture that he deemed a can't miss he would always tell her to hold on or he'd get back to her the next day after he checked his mail to see if there was anything sitting on his armoire or in the post office box that resembled a little extra cash.

On one particular trip to see her, he'd had a premonition—well not exactly a premonition—but he'd stopped by the post office, anyway—just in case. He'd just finished reading an article in the Wall Street Journal earlier in the day where the troops had questioned then Defense Secretary Rumsfeld around supplying the soldiers with better equipment in Iraq.

Philip always on the lookout for something to buy into read between the lines and thought that it might be a good idea to invest in a couple of the companies manufacturing armor plating. And as had been the custom since he'd met her he just assumed that 'Lexis would not be ready when the time came to drop a few dollars on the barrel and so he'd made it a point to stop by the post office where he ended up having to purchase a rather large carry on bag just to carry the accumulated mail.

Alexis was stunned that afternoon to find that he was actually carrying something other than his overnight bag and his briefcase and when she inquired about it and found out that the contents were the last month's mail which he kept putting off picking up they both laughed.

Later that afternoon, after discussing his investment ideas he was not surprised to find that all her money was tied up in an array of ventures and with all the investments he'd made for her she still had no ready cash at her disposal for an opportunity such as this. How many times had he told her that she had to be ready and fluid when the time came. That had been the closest they'd come to an argument and he'd even threatened to let her handle her own affairs.

Together they sat on the living floor and went through the stack of letters and Alexis was even more shocked to find a little over twenty thou in checks; commissions that he'd just left hanging idly around. That wouldn't have been her, Alexis joked. No, sir. She would have been at the post office days in advance—camped out in a sleeping bag like she was waiting for tickets to a rock concert. Either that or she'd be knocking on the post master general's door telling him to get the hell up. Hell, for twenty grand she would have gotten in bed with the post master general and his wife asking; who wants to go first? No sir, it wouldn't have been her. Philip remembered laughing 'til his sides ached but for some reason that last comment stuck in his craw.

Now with close to two-hundred and fifty thousand safely tucked away, thanks to Philip, in just a matter of months, she was not going to let him just walk away and leave her holding the bag. So, with little choice, in her eyes and although she was more than a little leery of giving him total control at the outset, she'd relinquished to him the power of attorney.

But she soon came to the realization that as long as she controlled him and kept him at bay and at arm's distance and craving her there was little to worry about so she put the means at his disposal to do with as he saw fit—that way—when it came time for him to make what he saw as a solid investment the money was there. And in the last month alone he'd netted her close to fifty thousand on a couple of rather shrewd investments and she was at once glad she'd turned over her finances to his better judgment.

Now with a quarter of a million of a dollars in assets on the line and a chance to double or even triple her holdings, Alexis LeBrandt wasn't about to let Monica Manning or anyone else step into the picture and cause him to turn his head and lose his focus in a moment of weakness. As far as she was concerned all his attention needed to be on one thing and one thing only and that was her and her holdings. And if she needed to step up the game and add just a little more in the way of being a motivational factor then she would.

For a quarter of a mill she had no qualms about rockin' his world but if Philip even gave a thought to leavin' her it was rock a bye baby. And when she put him to bed this time it would be for keeps. She had vowed sometime after the divorce that she would never let another man walk out on her. It didn't matter whether she wanted them or not. The fact of the matter was if they had the balls to push up on her and disrupt her life then that man—whoever he was— better damn sure come correct. If she let him into her life and God forbid if she gave of herself he had better have her best interests at heart and prepared to go the long run. She wasn't some common everyday whore to be banged and then bailed out on when they got tired of the pussy. Hell no! This life thing, this marriage thing was something she took to heart even if she didn't do it all that well. The second time was the final time so if Philip or anyone else decided they were ready to play with her heart they better be ready to suffer the consequences if something went awry.

If Philip hadn't been sure how dangerous this woman was before he certainly knew now that she wasn't someone to be taken lightly. If she had the gall to pull a pistol on him under the auspices of protecting her friend then there was no limit to what extremes she'd go to protect what she accounted for as being hers.

Philip knew Alexis LeBrandt was no plaything and if he admired her feistiness before it frightened the hell out of him now. As he waited on the corner counting the minutes 'til Monica arrived he smiled as he thought about something he'd heard Muhammad Ali say once after losing a close fight. When asked about his defeat Ali said, 'that as great as he was there was always someone better'. And after the year he'd had it was time to let Ms. Alexis LeBrandt know that there was someone not just better but far superior at her own game.

It was a dangerous ploy and Philip wondered standing there just how close Monica and Alexis really were. If any word of this leaked back to Alexis not only would his career be finished but there'd be nowhere to run and nowhere to hide. Still, he'd played it straight with her for more than a year and to say he had feelings was an understatement. He'd crossed the line and bared his soul to her and she'd overlooked that always keeping her eyes on the prize and the prize for her was not him.

From the day he'd made that initial investment with Mobil Oil, before the price of a barrel of oil skyrocketed he knew that if he didn't marry this woman she could mean the end of everything he'd worked so long and hard for. Well, that's what he'd thought at the time. But after months of attempting to woo her it soon became obvious that her sentiments centered clearly on his ability to make money for her more than any thought of marriage or commitment. God, what a fool he'd been.

The red Volvo pulled up to the curb awakening him from his daydream. Monica looked vibrant; refreshed though not nearly as cheerful as she had when he'd seen her last night.

Wearing an earth tone dress and a pair of sling back heels with rhinestones she looked absolutely ravishing and he was suddenly aroused. He felt renewed seeing her and the good times he'd had came cascading down like in a myriad of thoughts and ideas. He wasn't sure where they were going but hoped it was to her place. Time, however was of the essence and if they were to go there he was sure he wouldn't want to leave. They needed somewhere to talk and though the idea of going home with her appealed to him greatly though he knew that he couldn't afford to get too engrossed in her company. If anything were to happen he would certainly have to explain his refusal and he had no idea how that would go over.

"Where are we going?" she asked. "And what is this all about anyway? I thought I did a pretty good job of getting you settled in and getting you warmed up for the first team. You pretty much got what you wanted from me so why in the hell are you calling me? I'm quite sure between Alexis and me you should be pretty satisfied. And come to think of it, where did you get my number. I know one thing for sure Alexis damn sure didn't give it to you."

Philip smiled. Monica's anger was apparent but then again if she hadn't been feeling something towards him why had she bothered to come. In a way, he was kind of glad that she was angry—only he needed to direct her anger in the right direction. She certainly couldn't have been angry with him. He'd gone through the same ordeal as she had. Unless she really believed that she really was just the second string and a bed warmer until Alexis entered the picture. No she couldn't possibly believe that. She had to know he felt something for her. After all, he'd gone to extremes to get in touch with her. No, she wouldn't be here if she thought that. But there was obviously more to the picture than what appeared and her anger was almost certainly emanating from the relationship between the two women and that had nothing at all to do with him. Still, he chose his words carefully when he spoke. Monica was essential to his plans and aside from that there was something there that was undeniable and he had to know more.

"I got your number from the caller ID if you must know. It was no small task either. Had to rummage through her pocketbook and logging on to her computer was no easy task either considering I had no password but after an hour or so it dawned on me that it was probably on the caller ID. I don't know how many unknowns I called before I got you," he lied.

Monica smiled. There he was in.

"And where was baby, girl during the whole Easter Egg Hunt," Monica inquired.

"Sleeping like a baby. Matter-of-fact, she was still asleep when I left."

"Oh, so that's it. What's this, some new fantasy to write home and tell the boys about? What you gonna call it—the Detroit Connection? I can see your name up in lights already. The marquee will probably read something like this, huh? Jet setter and big time playa, Philip Dalton sleeps with limo driver until supermodel and world renown film star returns home from filming her latest movie abroad then sleeps with her, until she's knocked the fucked out before calling her limo driver back for another go round of the real good stuff."

"Why are you even going there, Monica? You know good and well that that's not the way you really see me and the reason that you don't see me that way is because you have what few people have and that's the ability to see people for what they're really worth. Call it intuition, call it wisdom—I don't care what you call it—you figured me from the first time you met me. You have the ability to read people and you're honest about what you see. You know damn well that I wouldn't have laid down beside you if I hadn't felt some attraction and I'm not talking just a physical attraction. If it were a physical attraction and nothing more then I certainly wouldn't have gone to the extremes I did to see you now."

"Well, no, I guess you wouldn't have," Monica said smiling, "but there is something on your mind."

Philip lowered his head. Damn this woman was perceptive.

"Yes, I do have something on my mind but it's not something that's troubling me. But I need to get a sense of where you are and how you feel about what I'm about to do before I tell you everything."

"Oooh sounds intriguing," Monica grinned, "you're not connected with the CIA or any terrorists groups are you," she laughed. "Hell, the way you make it sound, it's like you want me to go on some covert mission or try to uncover the location of The Dead Sea Scrolls or some shit."

"Well, in a way it is covert and it's gonna require you to use some of those acting skill you exhibited last night."

"Hold up just a doggone minute. Does any of this involve another man or sex or something along those lines," she asked, "cause believe you me I ain't wit' no kinky shit. What you saw last night was as far as it goes. I'm a one woman man and maybe I'm a little too free at times in my quest for good love and a good lover but hell, I'm just looking for a good strong man and a healthy relationship and trust as you can plainly see if you look closely at the third finger of my left hand I don't have a clue as to how to go about obtaining either," she said joking.

"Could you be serious for just a minute, Monica. I don't have a lot of time and I don't want Alexis to get suspicious about where I am and what I'm doing,"

"So in other words you don't want her to know you're with me?"

"Exactly."

"So, then why are you here with me?" Monica asked.

"I'm here with you because for what I have planned I need your help," he replied.

"Well, before you go any further let me just say this. If this plan of yours is anyway connected with Alexis I'm sorry but I want no parts of it. That's it. I'm being as straightforward and down to earth as I can be but that's the bottom line. I have never been as shaken as I was this morning.

A gun, Philip! The woman pulled a gun out on you and tried to shoot you. I have never experienced anything like that in my life. It took me half the day to unwind and to tell you the truth I'm still not over it. As boisterous and as obnoxious as I may pretend to be—I live a rather sheltered and dismal life. And you know what?"

"What's that?" Philip asked looking down at his watch.

"I like my life. And if I learned anything this morning it was the fact that life is cheap to some people and I value my little existence too much to just throw it away over a misconception," she said a tear rolling down her cheek.

"I understand wholeheartedly," Philip replied.

"Alexis doesn't care about people, or about friendship or about human life. All Alexis cares about is Alexis. Lord knows I tried to be a good friend and all she's done is use me. She could care less about how I feel about anything and I grew tired of it months ago and stopped talking to her. But I've always been a sucker so I let her convince me that we were friends again when I knew in my heart that nothing had changed and what happens? She comes home and can't believe that a bright, young, man could ever be attracted to me and tries to shoot him. No, Philip whatever your plan is I have to pass if it includes her. Anything involving Alexis LeBrandt carries too high a penalty," she said the tears flowing freely now.

"That's all I needed to know Monica," Philip said smiling before pulling her over to his side of the car and kissing away the tears.

"Stop! You're going to make me wreck," she screamed, a big smile stretching across her face.

"What do you mean that's all you needed to know?" Monica asked definitely in a better mood than when he entered the car.

"Well, some things transpired after you left that I really don't care to talk about now but I promise you this, and I hope I'm as good a judge of people as you are but Alexis is going to pay dearly for the shit she pulled today," Philip said angrily.

"That bad?" Monica asked as she parked the car on a quiet side street not far from downtown.

"Worse," Philip replied.

"Couldn't possibly be worse than having a gun pointed at you and having your head nearly blown off," Monica asked quizzically.

"To me it was," Philip said angrily. "There were times I wished I was dead."

"Really?" Monica asked definitely intrigued

"Look, Monica I have a plan but I'm going to need your patience and your help," Philip repeated.

"Like I said before Philip; I'm looking to put as much distance as I can between Alexis and myself this morning and you want to tell me that things got worse and you want me to stick my neck out. Don't get me wrong, I like you. I like you a lot and I don't know how you feel about what went down last night but even if I never saw you again I'd have to chalk it up to one of the high points in my life. And that includes you scaring me to death when you made me strip. To tell you the truth I even enjoyed that looking back on it but we really don't know each other but I do know Alexis and I think you may be getting in a little over your head. She plays hard ball baby and if there's a backlash I don't want to be in the way this time," Monica said.

"Didn't' this morning teach you anything? If Alexis had really been in love with you there's a good chance she'd have shot us both and thought about it later. And like I said, this morning was way too much drama for me."

"So you're turning me down?" Philip asked.

"I'm sorry, babe, but I have to this time. I'm not even sure my seeing you right now is a good thing," she added.

"So we're going to let someone who doesn't care about either of us control our lives and designate whether we can see each other or not? Is that what you're saying?"

"Basically."

"And you can live with that?"

"Pretty much," Monica smiled knowing that Philip thought a lot less of her now for backing down than he had at anytime since meeting her.

"I know what you're thinking. You're thinking about the principle, you're angry because you figure you've been wronged, and you want revenge. Well, I can empathize with you but I am a little older than you are and I've learned that sometimes you have to look at the bigger picture. You have to look at the reason for your frustration and then ask yourself if whatever's causing you such pain and anxiety is really worth you giving this much thought to it. In the case of your girl, the minute that plane taxis on to that runway tomorrow evening all thought of Alexis LeBrandt should be history. Trust me, Philip I've known her for close to thirty years and ever since I've known her she hasn't been anything but trouble. Don't waste your time. Trust me, just chalk it up to experience and move on."

"That's easy for you to say, Monica and I agree with you to an extent but if you'd experienced what I did after you left this morning you may have other ideas on what course I should be taking."

"Perhaps you're right but since I don't know and since you seem hesitant about telling me, what can I say to you other than to say let bygones be bygones. After all if you get right down to it and start being honest with yourself nobody can do anything to you that you don't allow them to do."

"I don't really have time for this Monica but everything isn't always as cut and dry as it appears at first sight.

When you left this morning, I went back to grab my pants and head out after you but you were long gone by the time I hit the lobby. I didn't have your number or any way to get in touch and of course Alexis refused to give me your number so I faked a headache with the hopes that she'd feel a little bit guilty. I figured that by the time the evening had rolled around she'd be feeling so bad—you know—so guilty that not only would she give me the address that she might…"

By the time Philip finished telling Monica what had transpired and showing her the damage Alexis had inflicted she was visibly shaken and close to tears.

"I can't believe her. I really can't believe that she'd go to such extremes for the sake of a dollar," Monica said. She was truly shaken and more than a little angry. "And how she could ever have the nerve to accuse you of rape is beyond me. And you mean to tell me that you never said a word?"

"Not a word. I just found your number and left."

"My God! And the fact that it's not hygienic I guess was not a concern. I guess that was her way of cleansing you of me. Let me tell you something you'll never understand. Alexis has a terrible fear of coming in second even when there's no one competing but herself. I don't know if it has something to do with her enormous ego or whether someone told her that she just wasn't good enough when she was a child but she is always out to prove something – almost like she's trying to leave her mark—her legacy on everything she comes into contact with. It's almost like she's saying people be damned. She's done it to me. She's done it to James and now she's included you among her latest victims. Lord knows I wish I knew what was on her mind. I'll tell you what she needs though. She needs a wake-up call."

"And I intend on doing just that. I'm gonna tell you something that my father used to always tell me. Nothing hurts a liar worse than being lied to. Nothing hurts a con artist worse than being conned. And nothing hurts a thief worse than when someone steals from him. You see Monica; I plan on hitting Alexis where it hurts."

"You know Philip, there's another saying that's pretty applicable at this juncture as well," Monica added.

"And that is?" he asked.

"Vengeance is mine said the Lord."

"The Lord also said he helps those who help themselves and I plan to aid the Lord in his work. After what I went through today, I just can't walk away. I tried this morning. I really did. You were all I really cared about but she wouldn't let me. She refused to let me come and see you. And it had nothing to do with me or you. The way I figured it, it was just the point of her losing again. It isn't that I mean anything special to her. It was just the fact that she feels like she's conceding; like losing a battle of attrition against her so-called best friend. She doesn't have the ability to see you as a person. In truth, I don't think she really has the ability to see anyone as a person but rather like a resume and since yours doesn't stack up to

261

hers on paper she can't understand why I would even be swayed to look in your direction. That's all it's really about anyway isn't it? It's almost like there's a sibling rivalry going on and I just happened to get caught in the middle."

"There's no rivalry on my part Philip. I have my flaws. I drink too much at times and I guess I'm looking for the same thing every other Black woman out here is looking for, a little romance and happiness and perhaps I try to obtain it in the wrong ways but a sibling rivalry with Alexis—I really don't think so. Alexis, on the other hand is simply a control freak. She's all about possessions. Money, fame, men; not necessarily in that order but those are her flaws and she has come to the point in her life yet to know that people can not be possessed. To her you're no more than her boy-toy who she finds to be a valuable asset and trust me even though I told you to walk away and don't look back, you're going to find that that's going to be almost impossible unless you can convince her that she doesn't need or want you anymore. She's not just going to let you walk out the door on her. She's got a terrible thing with rejection. I guess we all do to some extent but she refuses to let that happen to her and I'm getting the feeling that you two share that quality in some regard."

"Maybe you're right. I don't know but I agree with the fact that she needs a wake up call," Philip replied, "And I definitely need your help, in that regard."

"Give me some time and let me think about it and get back to you, Philip. The girl scares me. I've known her for a long time but this morning showed me that I really didn't know her nearly as well as I thought I did."

"I understand."

"Give it some time, Philip. Think about it and then give me a call and let me know what you intend to do. You have my number. Now let me get you back before she decides to blow your other ear off," Monica laughed.

"Not funny," Philip said smiling.

Monica turned the car around and headed back in the direction of Alexis'.

"Do you have any cash on you?"

"No, I left my wallet and everything back at her place," Philip answered wondering what Monica needed with any money. "Why, do you ask?"

"Thought I might drop you at the little grocery down the block from her house so you could pick up a few things for dinner to cover yourself in case she's awake and you need an alibi when you get back."

"See, I knew you were the one," he smiled.

"And what is that supposed to mean?" Monika asked somewhat puzzled.

"Well, they say that behind every good man there lies a good woman and I just think that you may be the one," Philip said smiling.

"You're a mess, Philip. Now look behind your seat and grab my pocketbook. There should be a few dollars in there. Take that and grab some groceries and make sure you get a good bottle of wine. She can't drink wine at all—a couple of glasses and she'll be out like a light. Trust me. That way it'll give you a chance to heal. Then again if you're working on making her feel guilty you might want to show her the damage she's caused. Although I can't believe I just told you to do that," Monica said her smile all but gone now. "And do me a favor. Hand me my cigarettes while you're in my bag. There in the brown cigarette case. Make sure you work on her guilt and just proceed as normal and don't give her any reason to arouse her suspicions or you may be looking down the barrel of that gun again. Be nice and bide your time and get the hell out of there before you think about bestowing any type of retribution on her. Like I said, go home, clear your head and sit down and ask yourself is this really what I want to do and then call me."

Philip smiled. There was another side to Monica. Aside from the jokes and the clowning and the boisterousness there was a quiet practical side that he was suddenly attracted which only helped him

263

to understand Alexis' jealousy even more now. She had good reason to be jealous and he had reason to want to know Monica even more so now.

"Even if I change my mind and come to my senses and realize this is a foolhardy thing to do and a total waste of time as you would have me believe, can I call you or better yet see you in a couple of weeks? I'm supposed to be in Miami next week or else I'd say next week."

"I don't know. Call me and we'll talk about it. How's that?"

"Well, that's not exactly the response I was looking for but if that's the best you can do then I guess that will have to do. It's not as if I was asking you to come and stay with you—you know? No ball playin', jet-setter just flying in to hit it and quit it and write home and tell the boys as you said... I was thinking more along the lines of me flying in or perhaps me flying you to New York for a weekend on the town, no sex. Nice hotel, maybe dinner and a play, some shopping..."

"Hold up, just one minute. Let me clear some things up. This may seem a little forward for your tastes but if I come to see you or you come to see me let's get a few things straight. I have a voracious appetite and it's just not for food—if you get my drift—so there will be no need for a hotel and second of all, you couldn't come see me next weekend anyway in the condition you're in. Hell, it's gonna take you a good two weeks for you just to heal and to be honest with you I'm gonna have to have a doctor's note before I go anywhere near that thing the way it looks right now," Monica laughed as she returned to her loquacious side. "Seriously though, you may want to see a doctor and gets some antibiotics just to be on the safe side. It may cause you a little embarrassment but then it's better to be safe than sorry."

'Will do," he said as they pulled up in the parking lot of the Super Wal-Mart.

"And be careful," she said as Philip leaned over to kiss her. "Any chance of you coming my way next weekend?"

"Not much," Monica said smiling. "You need to give yourself some time and me too. This is all a bit too fast for me."

"Well, in my business if you jump on an opportunity when it's presented to you a lot of the times you don't get a second chance."

"You just keep doing what you're doing, Mr. Dalton and I'm pretty sure you'll get a second chance," she said smiling and leaning over to meet him halfway.

Philip stepped out of the car gingerly. It was still painfully sore and any time he moved it sent shivers of pain through him.

"Sure you won't consider me coming to spend the weekend with you, next week? I'm pretty sure I can get someone else to represent me." he asked again before closing the door.

"No, I won't consider it but let me tell you where you made your mistake."

"Where's that?" he asked puzzled.

"You shouldn't have asked me. You should've just showed up," she said smiling. "I'll see you Philip," and with that said Monica Manning put the Volvo in drive and headed for the expressway and home.

Alexis was still asleep when Philip returned. It was somewhere around eight o'clock when Alexis finally awoke.

"What time is it?" she said as she came into the kitchen looking as though she'd been on a three-day drinking binge.

"Seven forty-five," Philip replied.

"Oh my, goodness, don't tell me I've wasted the whole day," she said. "Any coffee ready?"

"Yeah, I made a fresh pot but that was this afternoon," Philip replied.

"Mind fixing me a cup, hon?" she asked.

"Not a problem," he replied trying his best to be cordial.

"You are a sweetie pie. Listen. I've got to run out for awhile but I shouldn't be in too late."

"Business, I'm sure," Philip countered a sarcastic air in his voice.

"Do I detect a hint of jealousy?" Alexis said smiling.

"Perhaps," Philip lied.

"Never any need for that baby. I'm yours for as long as you'll have me. Besides after this morning you should never ever question my love. I thought I proved that to you," Alexis said smiling not waiting for any response. After all, what could he say?

Far as she was concerned he had nothing to offer. She had pussy whipped him and made sure that he was locked down, locked up and chained to her all in the matter of an hour with the best lovin' any man could ever want.

Now she had to go and she knew that he was jealous but she didn't have time to explain and was not at liberty to discuss the situation—well at least not at this stage. Still, she hadn't had to answer to anyone since her daddy and she wasn't going to start now.

"I love you, Philip," she said kissing him on the cheek as he handed her the coffee. "Could you put it in the microwave? I'm running late and I need to grab a quick shower. I shouldn't be home later than ten-thirty or eleven. If you get hungry there's some veal in the 'fridge," and with that said she headed for the shower and moments later was on her way out the door.

"We can finish what we started when I get back," she said smiling as she grabbed her keys and the coffee.

"I don't think so," Philip said.

"And what does that mean?" Alexis asked.

"After what you did to me, I think it's gonna be quite some time before we'll be able to do anything," Philip replied showing Alexis the damage she'd done in her haste to make him hers and hers alone.

"My God Philip I'm sorry I didn't know. Why didn't you say something?

"Kind of hard under the circumstances," he replied.

Alexis spent the next half an hour apologizing and insisting he let her put peroxide on it and remain with him instead of going.

266

But after insisting that he would be fine he eventually was able to convince her that there was little she could at this point.

Heading towards the Club Bentley, Alexis couldn't help but think of her early morning tryst with Philip. She was truly sorry. She really was but that had never occurred before. And after awhile she was convinced that it was probably more to do with Monica's fat, greedy ass and let it go at that. Hell, he was a big boy. He'd heal and at least now she didn't have to go through that shit again for awhile. As far as she was concerned she was more than satisfied and was good to go for another month or two.

As far as the sex, there was no way she could really assess his performance with him being tied down and all. Fact of the matter was, he was nowhere as big as James but he would do for now. Still, he was a nice replacement for her little purple toy that was already showing signs of losing its shape and wearing out and given a free reign there was really no telling what he could do in bed. But now was neither the time nor the place to think about Philip or what type of potential he had when it came to scratching her itch. He could never replace James. Even with all of his skills in the marketplace, he could never—not for a minute replace her James whose dick seemed to somehow curve to the shape of her pussy and make her howl with the best of them.

And if James even considered leaving her for another woman she was going to nip that in the bud before it had a chance to develop into something that might ultimately threaten her happiness.

It was already eight-thirty when she arrived in front of the club. A dimly lit little hideaway on the wrong side of town and she was immediately glad she'd decided to go casual. Actually, she hadn't decided but with Philip losing focus and sleeping with Monica she certainly didn't want to give him too much to concern himself with and so she'd dressed down.

Entering the front door of the club, she was surprised to find a doorman, a coatroom and a relatively chic ambience. Despite her initial misgivings about it being on the wrong side of town and the dismal appearance she had to admit that it was nicer than many of the so-called up-scale places she'd been to downtown.

Still, she hated venturing out into unchartered waters without knowing anyone or anything about the joint and having some low-life thug following her around for the better part of the night, which was a pretty common occurrence. Paying the cover she was even more surprised to find a rather subdued mixed crowd and a rather swanky atmosphere of well dressed patrons that made her feel out of place and now she understood why the doorman had given her a disapproving look when she asked if Officer Ricky Davis was performing. Now she knew that dropping his name and his card were the only reason they'd probably let her enter at all.

There was obviously a dress code and jeans were not the customary attire. Grabbing one of the few unoccupied tables in the rear she ordered a double Glenfiddich which she hoped would relax her and make her feel a little comfortable.

The alcohol seducing her, Alexis checked out the crowd with the hopes of spotting Officer Davis. Nowhere in sight, she wondered if he was in-between sets and decided to wait until nine before calling him on her cell. She didn't want to give off the wrong impression and seem overly anxious and then again she didn't want to sit there half the night and he not show. The stage was empty and many of the crowd seemed to be enjoying a quiet dinner while others sipped cocktails and chatted among themselves while Sade played in the background giving the tiny club a warm glow.

Enjoying the soft music and the stiff drink, Alexis felt a light tap on her shoulder. Waking her from her thoughts, she turned and looked up at the tall, dark gentleman to her rear recognizing him immediately although he certainly didn't look the same way in uniform as he did now. The uniform hardly did anything to enhance his physique but the charcoal gray turtleneck with the gray blazer and charcoal grey trousers forced her to take a second look.

"I hardly recognized you out of uniform," she said smiling and standing to shake his hand.

"Well, I certainly recognized you," he said, smiling as well, "For a minute I didn't think you were going to show."

"Wouldn't have missed it for the world after the way I treated you. I had to at least come and apologize. I sure wish you'd told me how nice the place was though. I'm sitting here in jeans, feeling all out of place and everyone else is dressed to the nines."

"Take it from me, Ms. LeBrandt—you look as good as anyone in here and I say that with the utmost respect. May I call you Alexis?"

"You most certainly may, Mr. Davis."

"And it's Ricky since we're being informal but now keeping it on a professional basis; what exactly is it that you need me to do? I'd like to get the gist of what it is that you need my services for since we go onstage in about fifteen minutes. I'm hoping you're in no hurry. I'd like for you to hear us play and while I'm onstage I can mull the whole thing over and see if I can be of any real service to you. You mentioned something about your ex being involved with another woman? Tell me something? Are you involved in a divorce proceeding at the present or just separated?"

"I've been divorced for close to a year now and was separated for a couple of months before that," she answered wondering if his line of questioning was professional in its intent or purely of a personal nature.

"And who was it that petitioned for the divorce?"

"My husband." She answered dropping her head in embarrassment.

"And the grounds?"

"Irreconcilable differences," she said.

"Would you care to explain?" he said taking out a small notebook and jotting down a little something here and there at different intervals.

"There's really nothing to explain. I'm a go-getter and James is basically a homebody. More or less the traditional type that believes a woman is supposed to cook, clean, raise the children and maintain the home. You know—the barefoot and pregnant thing."

"And you?"

"Well, I have some real estate ventures that keep me fairly busy as well as a budding interest in the stock market and I'm a department head at the university which gives me a pretty full schedule."

"So basically your plate is full."

"Basically."

"Any children?"

"All grown and in college."

"And your husband's occupation?"

"He's an instructor at the local community college and a full-time auto-mechanic at J.C.Penny's."

"How long have you two been married?"

Alexis had to think about this one.

"This year would have made twenty-two years of what I thought was a happy marriage."

"And have there ever been any occurrence or suspected incidences of infidelity?"

"Never, I've never even slept with another man," she lied. "And I know James has never—well—I don't believe he's ever…"

"So why do you think he is now and why inquire close to a year after the divorce has been finalized. What do you have to benefit except for the fact that if he is you'd only be rubbing salt into a wound that appears to be healing rather well?"

"I'm just curious to know, Ricky. I really thought that our separation was just a temporary situation. I just thought we both needed some space and I tried to accomplish all of the things that I wasn't really able to do because of the constraints of being a so-called good wife. I never expected to be served divorce papers and I fought it. Eventually I gave in to his demands but I knew—in the back of mind I just knew that we'd manage to overcome all the legalities, the mud-slinging and all the other bullshit and be a couple again."

"And why don't you think that's a possibility now?"

"Well, after talking to him over the last couple of weeks, I can tell something's different, something's changed."

"And you think that's due to someone else being in the picture?"

"Just call it a woman's intuition."

"So what happens if you find your premonition to be true?"

"I really don't know but at least I'll know what I'm up against. If there is someone else in the picture then I can better assess my position and know what course of action to take in winning him back."

"And if you can't?"

"Then I guess I'll just concede."

"And hope that means bowing out quietly or else you may be looking at charges of harassment. I'm not sure if you know it or not but he's already taken out a 50B on you."

"Excuse me? What in the hell is a 50B?" she asked incredulously.

"You probably haven't received the papers yet, but he's filed for a restraining order which does not allow you to come within a certain proximity."

"Why that dirty bastard." Alexis commented under her breath.

"That's why I need to take all that you say into careful consideration but if I should decide to take the case and you overstep your legal boundaries I'll be the first one to come and look for you because then you're bringing me into a quagmire that I'd rather avoid.

In any case, if it's curiosity that's driving you and I see this a lot, my rates are one hundred and twenty-five dollars an hour and surveillance can be both time consuming and extremely tedious. And that does not include expenses. If I decide to take the case which I'm pretty sure I will I'm going to need a retainer of five hundred dollars and need you to fill out this form telling me his habits and some other rather pertinent information so I can see what I'm working with.

So, while I go do my thing I want you to seriously consider what you're doing and ask yourself the tough questions. Ask yourself if it's really worth it to find out what your ex-husband is doing in his spare time? And if by chance he is seeing someone do you really want to know who it is? In more instances than not this doesn't do anything more than stir up a can of worms. But that's not for me to decide. I just provide a service. If you're not interested in sitting through the set just give me a call sometime in the latter part of next week and let me know what you decide. It was good talking to you, Ms. LeBrandt."

And with that said the very formal, very debonair, Officer Davis who insisted on being called Ricky stood up, shook her hand and made his way to the bandstand.

Alexis impressed by his professionalism had to admit she was pretty taken back by his demeanor. Oh, he had been all that he'd been on their first two meetings but he was so much more than she'd perceived and she had to admit that she was somewhat intrigued by the fact that he hadn't even tried to hit on her and it sparked an interest that made her sit through the opening set.

Alexis arrived home little more than two hours after leaving and the rest of the weekend proceeded without incident. Philip returned to work that Monday feeling both tired and spent. Upon his leaving she literally begged him to reconsider keeping her as a client and he told her he would consider it. When she asked him to keep her as a mate, he smiled, hugged her and told her he would consider as well.

Since then the phone calls had been steady and continuous with her even proposing that she come to New York the following weekend to spend some time with him. When he told her that he was to be in Miami on business for the remainder of the week she'd even gone so far as to phone his secretary to confirm his story. This angered him a little but it also let him know that the tide had turned in his favor. He wondered though if she were more afraid of losing him as her broker or just feared being rejected once again. Of course, it hardly mattered why she was so adamant in keeping him around as long as she was intent on doing so. If she had plans for him at this point that was fine. What she didn't know was that he had plans for her as well.

Chapter 13

Back in New York, Philip was able to relax and by Wednesday Monica's advice flooded his thoughts. He found himself, much, as he hated to admit, it once again, entrenched in his work, the thought of Alexis LeBrandt a distant memory at this point. He had two accounts, the one in Miami, and another, which would net him close to a hundred and fifty thousand, and he was intent on closing both.

Still, Monica remained on his mind and he picked up the phone on more than occasion to call before placing the receiver down. Calling her would only make him ache to see her and there was just too much else on the agenda than trying to woo another middle aged woman desperately hoping to fall in love.

Hell, New York had too many bright, beautiful women, readily available who would die for a chance to date a twenty-three year old stockbroker on top of his game. But as he buzzed the intercom to ask Sharon, his buxom secretary to try the 313 area code. He was somewhat surprised when the otherwise, quiet, soft-spoken, Sharon responded.

"Mr. Dalton, I've been trying Ms. Manning, all morning and all I keep getting is her voice mail. She must be at work. Do you have her work or cell number? She's obviously not at home."

A little taken back, Philip did not answer at once and then replied.

"Hold on let me see if I have her cell."

It was mid afternoon before Philip was able to reach Monica and had to admit that hearing her voice lifted his spirits some. There was nothing new on her end but she was glad that he called anyway since it gave her the sense that Philip's interest had been genuine.

Still, she found herself at a crossroads and had to admit that it felt good having two men in hot pursuit. James had called her earlier and seemed almost frantic since he'd been trying to reach her all weekend only to get the answering machine.

Monica loved the idea of two men wanting to share her time although she knew a decision would have to be made quickly. Still, it was no easy decision. For once, and both appeared more concerned about her general well-being than a follow-up sleepover. She couldn't account for the sudden interest but never one to look a gift horse in the mouth she soon found herself overwhelmed by all the attention.

When James called again she found that the only way she could get off the phone with him was to promise him that she would attend one of Tyler's Perry's plays and have dinner with him on Wednesday night.

Still, she was somewhat skeptical about his role in the whole scheme of things. It was all a bit much. Only a week or so before she'd been bored to tears. Now she was hard-pressed trying to recall being in such an enviable position which made it easier to put her suspicions about James on hold. At least for now she'd go along with the whole affair, despite not having told Alexis, and just let the whole scenario play out.

Even so, she wondered if she really cared about James. After all, she had similar feelings about Philip and wondered if there wasn't some underlying animosity towards Alexis that was spurring her on. She hated to think so after telling Philip that vengeance was a waste of time and emotions but here she was agreeing to see James again.

Fact-of-the-matter was that two men had never courted her at the same time that seemed to really care for her as a person. Lord knows it felt good. Besides they always ended up leaving her in the end so why not enjoy the time they wanted to spend with her while it lasted. She had no crazy ideas about marriage or even a relationship for that matter but for now their pandering to her every wish would suffice. If Alexis found out well, she'd just have to cross that bridge when she came to it.

That was Monday. On Tuesday she was having some serious questions about the whole affair and decided that if there were two men such as these who were interested in her then there had to be at least one other man out there somewhere who had similar interests and wasn't somehow connected to Alexis. She'd agreed to see James but this time she assured herself would be the final time. No matter how she saw it, it was unethical. And Alexis despite all her flaws and unscrupulous dealings would never ever have stooped so low as to even consider dating her ex's. And here she was calling herself a child of God and always going on about doing the right thing; up here sleeping with not one but two of her best friend's men. Despite her misgivings and the pleasure she felt each time her phone rang she knew that she had to let Philip know as well.

It had been no easy task telling Philip but he had taken it surprisingly well considering. He still insisted her taking his home and office numbers just in case she might be in the Big Apple and needed somewhere to rest her head and though she had no intent on using it she entered her cell phone as a keepsake nonetheless.

Telling James on the other hand would not be nearly as simple. First of all, she didn't want him to get the wrong impression and second of all she didn't want him to get the impression that she was milking him for a play and dinner so she called him to check and see if he'd already purchased the tickets. He'd been ecstatic to hear her voice and went on-and-on about how he'd waited in line for close to two hours to get the tickets only to find that they were sold out when he finally got to the box office window. Monica breathed a sigh of relief. But he wasn't finished. Seems that since he knew what a big fan she was of Madea he just couldn't help but seek some other means and so he tried his credit card but that hadn't worked either and so on his lunch break he'd gone back down to the theatre and was lucky enough to have bumped into a woman who couldn't make the show because of an illness in the family who sold him her tickets at the regular price. And second row at that. He was ecstatic and at that point Monica didn't have the heart to tell him. And so on Wednesday evening, prompt as always, James showed up at her door knocking. Monica made sure that her attire was dressy but not provocative by any means. The last thing she wanted was James to get all hot and bothered and have any thoughts about coming in and spending the night. No, there could be no low cut dress exposing any cleavage or splits that traveled northward like hurricane winds and her lipstick she made sure was not that damn ruby red that most men found so enticing. Instead she wore the chiffon dress with the floral print her mother had given her years ago that seemed to move farther and farther to the back of her closet and a pair of two inch heels that screamed, 'not tonight honey, these dogs is too tired' and greeted him with a friendly kiss on the cheek that said, 'sorry, baby, it's that time again'. James, however, was hardly demurred by her attire and even went so far as to make the comment that she had never looked good.

"Alexis always thought that less was better but you know there's a time and a place for everything and although I never told her sometimes wearing more is more of a turn on than less. It leaves more to the imagination," he said as he wrapped her shawl around her and closed the door behind them.

Monica, on the other hand, was shocked by this latest revelation and wondered how in the hell she was going to dissuade James from coming on any stronger than he already was.

The play had been everything that she'd expected. Tyler Perry was even better than she could have ever imagined in his role as Madea and dinner was even better. There were several moments over the course of the evening where Monica thought that there might be a time when the conversation would reach one of those uncomfortable silences between first dates when she could inform him of her decision but there had been no lulls or uncomfortable silences to speak of and so she decided to wait until they reached the apartment where he would invariably try to kiss her goodnight or attempt to come in and have a nightcap. Trouble was she liked James. They had a history and were from the same neighborhood, knew a lot of the same people and were both anything short of citified. And well, they just felt good in each other's company which made them friends first and lover's only as a culmination of their friendship. In short she really liked James and was at once sorry she had ever introduced him to Alexis. Either that or she was just plain sorry she'd invited him back into the fold. Nevertheless she had to do something. And that something meant she'd be once again home and alone or at Curves Gym and in school or some other place she would rather not be standing, praying, hoping that Mr. Right would happen along when he was standing right there in front of her.

As they reached the front door of her apartment, James suddenly reached out and grabbed her and kissed her abruptly on the cheek.

"Best date I've had in years, sweetie. I would ask to come in for a nightcap but it's already eleven-thirty and I've got to get up and meet the man in the morning."

Monica was shocked and had to laugh at her overly inflated sense of self-worth that just knew this man was going to try to force his way in just to get into her panties. This week had been full of pleasant surprises and she had to admit that James was once again the most pleasant of all.

The following day was Thursday and Monica was having trouble concentrating on work. She'd always made it a rule not to date on weekdays since it inevitably affected her work the next day.

If it was a co-worker or school mate then a weekend usually gave whoever it was, at that particular time, a chance to mull the whole affair over and regroup from his crash landing before returning to work or class, to face her after embarrassing himself in his pursuit of the punanny. But James was not a co-worker and had been so damn persistent that she had acquiesced. Still, she'd made it a point not to drink more than a glass of wine with dinner and although she felt refreshed and well rested with not even a hint of a hangover she still had trouble focusing on anything other than the night before. She wondered if James was having similar thoughts but found her thoughts rudely interrupted by a co-worker informing her that she had a package in the lobby.

Monica was glad for the interruption. Here she was, at work thinking of James, instead of going about the task at hand and here it was the day after the night before when she was supposed to be ending the madness but instead, here she was dreaming about her best fiend's husband. That was it. The long walk to the lobby gave her time to regroup and get her thoughts together. No matter how much she cared for James the simple truth was that she had to put a stop to it all. She'd let it go on long enough and she saw no way out but to call him when she returned to her desk.

Approaching the receptionist desk, Monica was surprised when Mrs. Dailey the elderly receptionist bent over and handed her a bouquet of roses and for the first time in her life Monica had little or no idea who had sent them.

What made matters worse was that the card enclosed simply read, 'thank you for being you'. There was no signature or return address listed and Monica wasn't sure if it was Philip or James but the thought warmed her just the same. Embarrassed by the sudden attention and stares from her co-workers, Monica made her way back to her desk only to find a message from James LeBrandt obviously calling to see if she'd received the flowers but then again, what if it wasn't he who had sent them? What if it had been Philip? Monica decided to play it cool and call him without mentioning the bouquet, which would only make it harder to tell him what she had to say anyway.

Dialing his cell, Monica rehearsed her lines. Two men in one day. She had to smile and as much as she hated to end what had all the makings of a beautiful relationship she knew the choice was hardly hers to make.

"Hello, James? Yes, I got your message that you called," she said.

"Listen, sweetie, I'm in between classes and I can't really talk right now. I've got two students waiting outside of my office but I've got a bit of bad news. Well, it's not really bad. More disturbing than bad but I wanted you to know. I was trying to get in touch with you earlier but they've got me running around here like a chicken with its head cut off. Anyway, I want you to know that I really enjoyed last night and I sent you a little something just to let you know what a difference you've made in my life over the past few weeks and I hope that what I have to tell you doesn't change any of that. Maybe I'm being selfish but I haven't felt this alive in years."

"The news James. What is it that you need to tell me?"

"Okay, I hope you're sitting down for this one," he said hedging.

"Go, ahead James. Just say whatever it is that's on your mind."

"Well, Alexis just called me to inform me that she's had a private investigator tailing me and that he followed us or better yet me last night and she knows I've been seeing you."

"No, she didn't!" Monica screamed alerting the whole office to the fact that the bouquet of roses wasn't the only thing new in her life.

"I'm afraid she did although that shouldn't mean a whole lot as far as we're concerned but I have a sneaky suspicion that she's going to be calling you next since I just got off the phone with her and she's fit to be tied. Called me everything but a child of God. And then went on and on about how you slept with her broker over the weekend but I didn't pay it any mind. She'd say anything as angry as she is right now. I just chalked it up to spite but I wanted to alert you so you know what to expect. I'm kind of glad it's out in the open myself. Now you don't have to worry about sneaking around behind her back or betraying your best friend. Listen, I've got to go but I'll call you when I get off. Love you, sweetie."

The news was startling and left Monica with chills. She knew that Alexis was up to something when she'd met her at Starbuck's last Friday. She'd always been secretive but never played it as close to the vest as she had on Friday. Monica had an inkling that something was wrong but couldn't be sure. But since they hadn't had talked in about three months it was a little difficult for her to pinpoint the problem but now she knew and only wished she hadn't been the focal point of Alexis' wrath.   To be caught in bed with Philip was one thing. James was, on the other hand, a completely different story.

If Alexis had any heart at all, this is where her heart lay. And where she'd disregarded the previous affront there was sure to be a price to pay for this latest indiscretion. Monica wondered if Alexis would call her as she did James or make it a point to stop by her job and embarrass her in front of her co-workers and decided it best that she avoid an ugly situation and take the remainder of the day and head home to sort things out. No sooner than Monica had gathered her belongings and filled out her request for sick leave than her secretary who appeared even whiter than usual summoned her.

"A call for you Ms. Manning. I told her you were on your way out the door but she wouldn't take no for an answer. I don't know who it is but she's being very rude."

"Thank you Sarah, I'll take it in my office."

Sarah may have not known who it was but Monica sure as hell did and wasn't looking forward to a confrontation with Alexis but knew that if she refused to take the call, Alexis would harass Sarah for the remainder of the afternoon and Monica was a stickler for keeping her personal life separate and apart from her career.

"Monica Manning here. How may I help you?"

"Baby girl, trust me I am not the one that needs the help. What the hell is wrong with you?   Saturday morning I walk into my house—my house—and find you buck-naked and in bed with my so-called boyfriend who I asked you to pick up and get settled in. When I said settled in, I didn't necessarily mean for you to sleep with him. What in the hell is your problem? But no! I overlooked that when I should have taken your ass out right then and there but I let it slide 'cause you know as well as I do that Philip really doesn't mean that much to me. If you get off sleepin' with somebody else's leftovers then that's something that you have to deal with, girlfriend. But hell, you know as well as I do that that showed no respect at all. And for

your fat ass to be lying up in my guestroom—well, hey—that just shows me what kind of woman you are. I was angry. But more than that I pity you. I look at you and realize just how hungry you are to have a man. Seems like all a man has to do is toss a promise your way and you'll spread your legs.

I've never in my life seen a woman so damn desperate. You're really desperate and you don't even try to hide it. You have so little self-esteem that you let everyone see just how desperate you really are. What man do you know that wants that? You really are pathetic. But I don't have to be you so what the hell do I care if you want to be known as a cheap whore and an easy lay all your life. But when I find out that you're fuckin' my husband as well as my so-called lover then I'm comin' after you one way or another baby. I'm sorry Monica but I just can't let this shit slide. Not this time. Somehow—someway—you're going to have to atone for this shit"

And with that said, the phone went dead without Monica ever having said a word. But then what could she say? Alexis was right to an extent. And she had every reason in the world to be angry. But they'd been friends and friends did not intentionally hurt each other the way Alexis had just done. Not over some man. Sure she'd slept with James but they were divorced and Alexis showed no interest in him whatsoever.

She'd asked her what the situation was long before anything had taken place and yes she did have problems. And all of those things Alexis had said were true about her being pathetic but she'd never intended to hurt her. It just happened. And everyone involved knew that Alexis wanted no involvement with Philip so what was the big deal? It certainly didn't warrant her calling her place of employment and threatening not only her livelihood but her life. That was childish, high school shit and she was neither up for playing these silly assed games nor appreciated being called a fat, pathetic, whore by a woman whose sole interest in life was to use those closest to her. And the more Monica thought about the gall of Alexis the angrier she became.

To chastise her as though she were a child was one thing. To have her followed was quite another. No longer did she feel apologetic or guilty about her liaisons with Philip and James. Instead she felt a deep-seated anger that went beyond reason and no sooner had she walked through the door and hung up her coat then she was on the phone.

"Philip?"

"Monica here. What do you need me to do?"

"What's wrong, baby?"

"There's nothing wrong, Philip just another run-in with our friend, is all. To tell you the truth, I kind of expected it. She just called me a little while ago at work and blessed me out, is all. Typical Alexis. Like I said, I expected it. I'm just tired of it is all."

"Want me to call you this evening when you get home?"

"I'm already home. I left work a little early."

"That bad, huh?" he asked.

"No, that had nothing to do with it at all. I wasn't feeling all that well before she called and decided to take some personal time," she lied.

"I'm sorry to hear that. Anything I can do?" he asked.

"Yeah, you can make her pay for the misery she seems to so enjoy causing people."

"She must have really struck a nerve this time. Wasn't it you that was telling me something about vengeance being the Lord's or something to that effect?" he laughed.

"Look Philip, there's only so much a person can take. And I don't have time to rehash everything. If you need my help in bringing this witch down and making her accountable for all the pain and misery she keeps causing then let me know." And that said Monica placed the phone back up on the receiver and sat there staring into outer space.

Seconds later the phone rang.

"Okay, Monica this is what I need for you to do. We're going to work this one step at a time so we don't get in our own way and we've got to go slow. This could take months but what I need you to do right now is to apologize to her."

"Apologize? Are you out of your mind? For what? For not treating you the way you should have been treated? For not enjoying you for the person you are instead of running a game on you so she could fatten her nest egg? For having you traipsing back and forth under the guise of her wanting to be with you? Come on Philip wake up?"

Philip laughed and Monica caught herself.

"She really got to you, didn't she? I don't know what transpired but I can see she really got to you this time. Now you know how I felt on Saturday when you were preaching those wonderful words of wisdom.

Well, I don't have any words of wisdom or passages from the bible that I'd like to refer to when Alexis' name comes up, unless you're interested in hearing me quote, 'an eye for an eye'. You know here on Wall Street I'm in a dog-eat-dog situation everyday and it can become ruthless at times. But one thing you have to do if you're going to become successful among the sharks is to make sure you play everything close to the vest and never let them peep your whole card. That's the same thing we have to do if we're going to have any success in dealing with Alexis. And the first thing I need for you to do is to be humble and apologize so you can gain her trust. That way you'll be privy to all of the information I need to break her down. Now do you suppose you can do that?

You might want to give her a day or two to settle down before you approach her or you may even want to put on one of your command performances and just break down and let her know how sorry you are and how much you value her friendship. Now can you do that?"

Monica thought about it briefly.

"I've got an Oscar winning performance in me and I believe I'll debut it tonight. Call you when I get back."

At six fifteen Monica sat outside of Alexis' apartment building in her usual spot waiting for her friend to get home. She still had her key but wanted to test the waters in the open instead of being caught in the apartment with Alexis when she had no earthly idea what state of mind she might be in.

Seeing her pull up across the street, Monica got out of the car and walked across the street to be out of earshot of the doorman in case there was an altercation but Alexis appeared congenial even in a rather jovial mood. At least that was Monica's first impression.

"I know you're not coming here to talk to me about anything. You've got a lot of nerve even approaching me after the shit you've done," Alexis began. "And to think I considered you my friend. And after all these years, how could you be so low, Monica?"

The anger was clearly apparent in Alexis tone and Monica knew that what lay ahead was no easy task and it would take an award winning performance just to keep her cool.

"Baby, I'm sorry. What can I say? I've mulled this thing over and over in my head all week and I was just too embarrassed to call. I didn't know what to do. I even called James to talk about it since I figured he knew you better than anyone else."

"So you slept with my husband to get to know me better? Is that what you're telling me? Now that's a hoot. And what did that tell you?"

"Alexis! Stop it! I know you're not insinuating that I slept with James?"

"And you're going to tell me that you didn't."

"I wouldn't even dignify that with an answer."

"You need to in lieu of the fact that you slept with Philip, you goddamn whore."

Monica had to do everything she could not to reach out and slap the black off the tiny woman she had once referred to as her friend but Philip told her that it was paramount that she stay in control of her emotions and always consider who and what she was dealing with. 'The means justifies the end", he'd told her. And right now she truly hoped so 'cause she had no intentions of being too many more of Alexis' ho's.

"Alexis, a whore is someone that sells herself for something. I have never sold myself for anything other than the possibility of some happiness."

"Precisely! And for you the price of happiness is a man. Any man! That would be fine. But you have no discipline, no rules, and no regard for yourself. It doesn't matter that that man belongs to someone else or not. You've told me as much yourself. But I never thought that you'd lower your standards to the point that you have the nerve to sleep with someone that I was seeing. But then why should I be off limits? I thought I could trust you because, after all, we were supposed to be friends. At least I thought we were but, it turns out that you're nothing but a low-down scandalous ho." Alexis screamed loud enough for the doorman to hear.

Monica dropped her head. There was that word again. And it cut through her with all the sharpness and precision of a machete opening old wounds that she'd thought had finally healed.

"Tell you what Alexis," Monica said forgetting her promise to Philip, "I ain't goin' to be too many more of your ho's."

She knew she was coming undone and straying from the plan but Alexis had a way of bringing out the worst in her and she'd had just about all she could take. Still, if she'd said nothing—well—that wouldn't have been her. So, she chalked it up to 'keepin' it real', swallowed hard and made another attempt at reasoning with her girl.

"Look, Alexis, I'm here because I did wrong. I admit that."

"No shit Sherlock and how long did it take you to figure that one out?" Alexis quipped angrily.

"It took me awhile," she said calmly. "But I didn't know how to come to you and apologize. I didn't think you had any interest in Philip. Well, that's how it appeared to me and I think he was a little bit frustrated with you not giving him the time of day and well one thing led to another and a few Mai Tai's later I found myself knee-deep in some shit I couldn't get out of because of me runnin' my mouth. And for that I am sorry but I really and truly didn't think you had any interest in him. I actually thought you'd be happy on two accounts. First of all, I thought you might be happy for me especially if anything came out of the whole thing other than another man taking advantage of my desperate ass and getting me to spread my legs as you so aptly put it. And second of all I thought me taking him off your hands would just allow him to do what you want him to do and that's your investing and your books. Hopefully, that would give him two reasons to come to Detroit. 'Cause you know as well as I do that he's a gold mine but he's not going to keep jeopardizing himself and traipsing up and down the road if you don't eventually give him some." Monica said smiling.

She'd hit a nerve and she knew it. Alexis didn't know she was so transparent but had to smile. Monica knew her as well as anyone and maybe what she hated most about Monica at that moment was that they were cut from the same cloth and it was extremely hard to put anything over on her.

"And you thought about all of that before sleeping with Philip?" Alexis asked smiling. "Or was it the fact that you refuse to listen to Dr. Philbin and take his advice and stop drinking?"

"I can't lie. I guess that had something to with it as well but tell me the truth Alexis; tell me you have an interest in Philip?"

"Come on in the house, ho and I'll tell you about it and you can tell me what the hell you were doing out with my James." Alexis said turning to make sure the alarm system on the Beamer was activated.

Once inside and seated, Monica felt a little more at ease.

"May I have a drink," she asked.

"I don't know why you're asking me now. You didn't ask Saturday night when you and that asshole sat here and drank up all my good liquor. Tell me, Monica? What would you have done in a similar circumstance? I'm going to tell you. My first impression when I saw you two in the bed was that I should blow both your asses away but then I thought about it some more and just knew that he must have taken advantage of you because you would have never allowed me to just walk in on you like that and allowed me to catch you with your pants down. I said my girl's too much of a lady for that too happen so I jut knew he had raped you and I was stunned when you told me that you had initiated the whole thing."

"Alexis, stop. There's no need to rehash the whole thing. I was there. Remember? The problem that I'm having with the whole thing is that I don't understand why you're so angry with me."

"I'm angry with you because you never once talked to me about my relationship with Philip. You never asked me where we were or where we intended to go with our relationship. You never thought that maybe I might still be undecided in lieu of the fact that I am just now starting to get over my divorce and get some closure."

Monica interrupted. She was tired of the bullshit—tired of the weak-assed snow job Alexis was trying to administer. She was no novice. She'd known her for the better part of thirty some odd years.

"Stop it, Alexis. This is me you're talking to. Do you remember you and I sitting in Starbuck's last Friday. I believe it was you asking me to pick Philip up from the airport? Do you remember me asking you about your love life and you telling me it was non-existent and that when you needed some good lovin' all you had to do was turn to your nightstand and get those two Energizer batteries working? Do you remember any of that?"

"That does not give you any right to assume that because I'm not sleeping with Philip that I don't have any interests in him."

"I'm sure you do have an interest in him 'Lexis but it's not a romantic interest that's for damn sure. You don't want Philip for any more than what he can do for you. All you want to do is string him along and tease him and give him the impression that maybe there's a chance of you two being an item down the road."

"And if those are my intentions what the hell right do you have to interfere in my plans?" Alexis yelled. "And I guess your fat ass thought it the Christian thing to do to enlighten him around those facts."

"I didn't have to enlighten him around anything, Alexis. Philip is very perceptive. He knows what you're doing and he also knows what type of person you are. I'm just telling you what he confided in me."

"And you never agreed or added anything to the conversation?"

"It wasn't my place to. Besides he sees you for what you truly are. He's just so strung out over you that he doesn't know which way to turn. He can't even walk away for fear that you'll threaten to turn him in for the insider trader tips he's been giving you."

Alexis smiled.

"I swear, I didn't give him that much credit," she laughed, her mood suddenly changing. "But now that he knows there's no need to continue this stupid charade. He's all yours if you want him but you should know this since you think you know me so well. I would never turn him in for compromising his ethics."

"Compromising his ethics?" Monica said the disbelief showing in her voice. *"He loves you Alexis. That's why he took the chances he took."*

"And he'll keep taking them as long as he's painted this sordid view of me and I won't say a word to discourage him," she laughed.

Her laughter angered Monica who had everything she could do now to remain focused on the task at hand.

"Alexis do you care anything at all about Philip or that young man's future?" Monica asked.

"Sure, I do. I never asked Philip to do what he was doing? Honestly speaking, I really don't care to know anything about it. He thought that money was the key to my heart and so that's the road *he* chose to take. I have nothing at all to do with that. *Nothing.* That's what I was trying to express to him when we first met but because of his age I guess he wasn't fully able to comprehend. Hell, a lot of men are enamored by a big butt and a smile. I knew then that that's all it was and I tried to dissuade him but he kept trying to push up on something he wasn't ready for.

He has an aptitude, almost like a gift for making money and I admire him in that regard but aside from that he's like most men in that he has a weakness. And so he decided to use his aptitude to get what he wanted. Whose fault is that?"

"But you led him on."

"Didn't you just hear me say that I tried to dissuade him? He would not be dissuaded. He kept following, kept pushing and now this is the position he finds himself in and you wanna blame me. *Girl please.*"

"But if you recognized this why didn't you tell him?"

"Monica, Philip is a grown man and if he can't see the error of his ways then who am I to tell him. I have two children that are damn near his age and when they were growing up I did the best I could trying to show them right from wrong but there's a time when they assume the role of adulthood and there's no more that I could tell them."

"So you see this man throwing his career away trying to win you over, trying to win your heart and you won't speak up?"

"Look Monica I'm tired of the holier than thou attitude. Philip is a grown man with a mind of his own. You told me that when you first met him. If he chooses to toss his career away then that's on him. If he chooses to travel back and forth from New York to Detroit every couple of weeks who am I to dispel him? I'm cordial. I treat him well and enjoy his company."

Monica shook her head in disbelief. She wanted to play the role Philip had asked her to play and say, "Sho' you right and go on girl, I feel ya', but she was in no mood to and settled on another drink instead.

"Look, Monica, you know me. I'm not Shrek or some evil ogre you paint me out to be. I'm not saying anything like, 'if Philip can't hang with the big dogs he needs to get on off the porch'. Nor am I saying that things only happen that you allow to happen to you. Philip knows what he's doing I'm sure—or at least—I hope he does.

At this point in my life I enjoy his company. Maybe I can't give him what he needs as far as love or romance are concerned because my heart just isn't in it or maybe because I don't know what the hell that is. But if you feel as deeply as it seems you do about him then I sure wouldn't stand in the way of your happiness.

But one thing I will say is that I don't want you interfering in my business relationship with him. You may get to the point that you might decide that you care enough about him to want to protect him from himself. You might get to the point that you might want to sit down and have a little chat like we're doing now and advise him on the pitfalls of being unethical in his trading practices. You might want to do that. I wouldn't suggest you doing that. You want to love him, fine. You want to fuck his brains out, fine. You want to pander to him and take care of him and raise him, fine. But do not get in the way of my business dealings with your holier than thou advice on the semantics of what's right and what's wrong.

And please explain to me while we're having this little chat; what the hell you're doing with James."

Monica was stunned. She couldn't believe that she'd not only been handed Philip on a silver platter but she'd also been given the rules on how to play the game. She was surprised that Alexis hadn't told her what position in the Karma Sutra she was to use when making love.

She was seething, burning inside and she wondered how she had ever considered this cold, unfeeling woman to be her friend. It was true. All the things she and Philip had discussed concerning Alexis' cold, calloused selfishness. It was all true. Alexis cared about nothing and no one but herself. Neither Philip nor Monica mattered in her eyes and she made that perfectly clear tonight.

"You look puzzled, Monica," Alexis laughed. "C'mon you know me. I'm doing the same thing they do to us. They come along out of the clear blue see something they *think* they want, push 'til they get what they think they want and then when they grow tired of it they move on. And ninety-nine percent of the time our dumb asses are left standing there trying to get our pantyhose up, our girdles in place, and wondering what the hell just happened while they're off seeking some new victim. Well, I'm not doing the pursuing. I'm not dropping any drawers either and once I have what I need then I'm moving on as well," she laughed. "Now tell me about James."

Monica forced a smile. When she thought about it she had to admit that there was really nothing new in what Alexis was telling her. Only thing new was that she'd become involved. Many times over the years they'd sit around and laugh about the same things Alexis was telling her now but for some unknown reason it all seemed distant and foreign now like an ocean had come between them. No longer did Monica see the humor. Now all she saw was contempt but not only for Alexis but for herself as well and truly despised not just Alexis but the person she'd allowed herself to become.

Monica smiled in an attempt to show Alexis that she understood. She could afford to be bitter. There had been countless Marshall's in her life. And too many times when her drinking had left her prone and helpless she'd wake up to find her clothes on the floor beside the bed and whoever it was on that particular night, long gone; she being no more than a distant memory at best.

How many days after the night before did she sit by the phone hoping and praying that they would call her? Then crying her eyes out when they didn't. Did that make her a ho' for trying to give them what they wanted most and the best thing she had to offer? Her only hope was that while they were there they would find other reasons to love her as well. Was she ho' because she needed to feel the warmth of another body next to hers?

Sure, she was guilty of all of those things and she'd been crushed on more than one occasion by the weight of knowing that no matter what she offered they had no desire to stay in her presence any longer than the act itself required them to. It hurt as much now as it had when she came to the realization that men did not desire her or care to be with her for anything other than the time it took to relieve them. Then they too were as fleeting as the wind. But in spite of this, she'd come to love herself for the person she'd become. Despite her numerous flaws and shortcomings she had over the years come to love herself even when it seemed like no one else did. And so it was difficult for her to understand how Alexis, with all of the attributes she so desired had become so insensitive and so heartless.

Why hadn't she noticed it until now? The thought disturbed Monica and she wondered if it was true about birds of a feather flocking together then abruptly rejected the thought. No, she had just been lonely. She was so lonely at times that even Alexis' presence appeared better than none at all.

Maybe unconsciously she did wish to be like Alexis with her sultry looks and penchant for drawing men. Maybe that had been the attraction but now after listening to her for the very first time she no longer aspired to be like her or even near her for that matter. And if Philip hadn't requested she befriend her she would have made her exit long ago.

"So, tell me about James."

"What's to tell? I can tell you that I didn't appreciate you calling me up asking or better yet accusing me of sleeping with him." Monica said matter-of-factly.

"Well, need I remind you that this is the same week that you were caught in the bed with Philip."

"Need I remind you, Ms. LeBrandt that I am the sole reason that you carry the surname LeBrandt? I do believe that I was the person that introduced you two," she added.

"Anyway, what's the story?"

"I told you there is no story. As you know he was my friend long before he was your husband and being that I considered us *friends* and knew that you were angry at me I thought he might give me some insight into how to approach you around the whole Philip thing."

"And?"

"And he had two tickets to that new Tyler Perry play and it seems that someone stood him up so he asked me to go so he wouldn't just lose his..."

"And?"

"Oh you know how I feel about Madea. Girl, Tyler Perry was off the chain. *Loved it! Talk about...*"

"Girl, I don't give a damn about Tyler Perry. I wanna know who the ticket was for?"

"Hell, if I know. I'm just glad they bowed out at the last minute. You know how I feel about..."

"Monica, this is important to me. I've hired a private investigator. I think James is seeing someone."

"Well, I should hope so. You've been divorced for close to a year now and I guess he needs to get on with his life. Ain't no need for him to be sitting around waiting for you to come around. Hell, Lord knows you don't know which way is up.

Everyone knows, you're just as fickled as the world is round. When you had him you took him for granted and were always too damn busy to be bothered. Now that he's moved on you think he might just be the one for you. That's what I've been trying to tell your dumb ass, Alexis. You can't continue to treat people just any kind of way and expect for them to sit idly by."

"Thank you for those words of wisdom, mother Mary. Now tell me, if you can see fit to come down off your high horse for just a minute and tell me who James is seeing?"

"I told you I don't have any earthly idea you damn worry wart but if I had my guess I'd say nobody. I'm sittin' there tryin' to figure out how to approach you and all he wants to know is how you're doing and what you've been doin'."

"Seriously?" Alexis asked, her tone changing when she heard this. "So how did you tell him about Philip? You didn't make it seem like we were an item did you?"

"No, woman. I just told him that I'd had a little too much to drink and you'd found us in bed together and thought that I disrespected your house which I thought was my house as well since that is supposedly my room or so you had me believe."

Alexis smiled.

"It is your room. And this month's utility bill is right there on the counter waiting for you to help out in your house. Seriously though, you really should think about giving up that little rat hole of yours and movin' in. Although I don't know, you'd probably end up screwin' the damn super when he came to change the light bulb." Alexis laughed.

Monica played along but saw little humor and for the first time got a fairly good picture of how Alexis really saw her.

"Monica you know I have to apologize as well. I'm sorry I called you a 'ho. A lot of the times I see you in myself, you know. I think we both screw men. We just do it differently and for different reasons. I screw 'em but not literally and I always make sure it's beneficial. You screw them and receive no benefits with the hope that love will somehow magically appear. I hate to tell you girlfriend but that sorta shit only happens in fairy tales. That shit ain't happening out here in the real world.

Anyway, tell me more about James. Did you know the bastard took out a restraining order not allowing me to come within fifty feet of the house which I helped paid for? Did he tell you that? Now what is that if not another woman? Someone's tellin' him what to do. You know as well as I do that James doesn't have the smarts or the gumption to come up with something like that on his own."

"No he didn't tell me. But I'm sure you did something to provoke him. What did you do—pull a gun on him, too?"

"Don't be silly. I stopped to pick up some papers and offered to give him some and his ass just turned around and walked away."

"There had to be more than that," Monica said. "As much as you hate rejection, I know that you didn't just let it go at that."

"Well, I may have made a little bit of a scene in the driveway but nothing to warrant a damn restraining order."

"C'mon you're not tellin' all, 'Lexis. James is too low key to take out any kind of order unless you had turned it out. Now 'fess up. What really happened?"

Alexis was feeling good now. She had her girlfriend back in the fold. And thanks to Monica knew that she had both Philip and James eating out of her hand once again. She could call the dogs off now since she was pretty sure that James wasn't seeing anyone. And with Monica doing Philip and he thinking that she had something on him there was no need for her to even worry about stringing him along. His own guilt and the threat of being turned in was enough to keep him in check and greedy ass Monica could take over catering to his every whim on his trips to Detroit if she didn't wear his little young ass out first.

Who knows how long it had been since Monica had gotten any before that day with Philip, Alexis chuckled to herself. And Alexis couldn't ever remember anyone nearly as bright or handsome as Philip ever having crossed Monica's threshold. Probably have to go over there and drag him away from her. Talk about being tied down. Philip's gonna wish he was tied down when Monica gets through bouncin' up and down on him.

With her real estate ventures demanding all of her free time she hardly had any time left for anything else and was quite content with Philip supplying her the money to purchase parcel after parcel of prime real estate.

Since she'd come into a little pocket change, she literally hated throwing any money away and had become even more frugal than she'd been before. And Monica could help her with that as well.

Still, unconvinced that James wasn't seeing anyone and assuming that Monica would just naturally agree to go on seeing Philip she went to the computer. She would have little time to consider anyone else and though she'd had her suspicions she never really doubted Monica's friendship or her relationship with James. They'd been buddies long before she'd entered the picture and knew Monica had never had any interest in James aside from being drinking buddies in high school.

Convinced that she finally had all her ducks in a row, Alexis e-mailed Officer Davis and requested that he fax her his bill and informed him that she would no longer be needing his services.

With Monica around she could have her take James out once a week to keep her abreast of his goings-on and not have to pay a hundred dollars an hour to some private investigator who would, at some point in time, want to trade in his services for hers. No, she didn't need the hassle or the bill when she could get Monica to do it for free. Returning from the computer station Alexis stopped at the bar poured Monica a healthy drink then waited till she was half finished before saying anything.

"I need you to do me a favor, sweetie. I need you to keep an eye on James for me until I decide what I'm going to do with him. I'm still not convinced that he's not seeing anyone and I really don't have any way of telling with him not wanting to speak to me and the restraining order and all."

If Monica had been stunned when Alexis gave her what amounted to permission to see Philip, she was completely undone now and was ecstatic when she heard the request but played it off knowing that if she seemed to eager then Alexis would immediately become suspicious.

"You have got to be joking. I will not," she said adamantly. "I'm not going around spying on James. He happens to be a friend of mine. Just like I wouldn't do it if he asked me to spy on your sorry ass."

"Look Monica, I'm not sure that I know what love is but James may be the closest I've ever come and if I decide that he is what I want, I at least want to know what I'm up against and I have no way of telling from my vantage point. You are really and truly my last best hope."

"Do you know what you're asking? Don't you think that James would be a tad bit suspicious if all of a sudden I just showed up on the regular and started snooping around? Has that occurred to you?"

"Look, Monica, make me the bad guy."

"That's not hard to do." Monica laughed.

"Seriously, make me the fall guy and let him air things out. You can be his sounding board. Kind of like an out so he can get things off his chest and I in turn can learn what mistakes I made and how to be a better wife. I really want to be a better wife you know."

"Since when Alexis? You had twenty years to practice. What makes you think that if you couldn't get it right in twenty years you can get it right now? This is me remember? The only reason you want any part of that man's life is 'cause he kicked you to the curb and you can't stand rejection. *Damn! Why don't you grow the hell up and think about somebody else for a change. Let him enjoy his peace of mind. Heck, if he's seeing someone else and they can make him happy or give him what he needs why can't you leave him alone and let him enjoy his new found happiness? Boy you're a mess.* Dipping in and out of people's lives. *Geez!*"

"Ah, sweetie, don't look at it like that."

"Well, tell me. How am I supposed to look at it? No, don't even bother to answer that, Alexis. Answer this one instead?"

"Go ahead, sweetie."

"Does it ever enter your mind that I may have a life aside from you?" she asked.

"Of course it has," she answered grinning.

"Then when am I supposed to entertain, spy, whatever you want to call it on your husband and *my friend*?"

"So you'll do it then? That's my girl. I knew you wouldn't let me down."

"I didn't say I would," Monica commented.

Chapter 14

Monica left Alexis at a little after nine that evening and was ecstatic though she was still having mixed feelings about deceiving her girlfriend. Each time she did she could hear Alexis' calling her a fat ho' and was suddenly alright with her decision. Still, she didn't want to be involved in something that would come back and haunt her in the end so as soon as she walked into her apartment she picked up the phone and called Philip who sounded as though he'd been sleeping for a month.

"Hello."

"Hey, sweetie. I did just like you asked me to and it couldn't have gone better. It went so well I 'm thinkin' about movin' straight to Hollywood—you know—get me a little place across from MGM so I won't have to travel so far when they call me to take Halle Berry's part in her next movie. She thinks she's got it locked down but anybody that could've seen me tonight knows Monica Manning will be the next big name up in lights," she laughed.

"That good, huh?"

"Even better than that. I think we may be talking, Hollywood Blvd.—you know—the walk of fame where all the great actors sign their star or put their footprints," she continued.

"So give me the skinny…"

Monica gave Philip the gist of what had gone down and he seemed even more pleased than she.

"So you can have me. Well, that's mighty nice of her to just give me away. I'm really offended by the fact that she thinks so little of me but that's great at this point in time. The bigger question that concerns me though is that now that she's given me to you—will you take her up on the offer?"

Monica was glad Philip couldn't see her smiling and was flattered that he was still interested making only night together more than just a roll in the hay. After all, he was rich and handsome. He was all the things every girl dreams of and she was flattered. He was also very ambitious and aspiring for greater heights and climbing the corporate ladder just as fast as he could.

It was like the tortoise and the hare with her just plodding along at a steady pace. No, as much as he appealed to her he really was too fast for a country girl like her. She didn't know how to explain it to him but the last thing she wanted to do was hurt him anymore than he'd already been hurt. So, she did her best to dissuade him at this point in time at least.

"Philip, don't you think its best that we concentrate on the plan and sort of let this thing with Alexis play out before we think about you and I?"

"I'm not sure. I really haven't thought about it that much. Not that aspect anyway. Sounds like you're getting cold feet though. A few days ago you told me I should've just shown up and not asked you anything and we had to worry about Alexis' crazy-ass then. Now she basically gives you free reign just to keep me out of her hair and now you're renigging. What's up?"

"Oh, I don't know, Philip. The whole thing has me quaking in my boots. There are so many things going around in my head. You've got me involved in some shit I don't even know about. I don't have a clue as to what you're up to. She's handing me you on a silver platter and asking me to spy on her husband who just so happens to be one of my good friends and now you're putting pressure on me to see you."

"There's no pressure. I was under the impression that you wanted to see me."

"I do it's jus that..."

"Good then I'll see you sometime next week after I get back from Miami and I hope you're ready for the time of your life. Do you have any vacation days coming?"

"Well, yes—why do you ask?"

"I'm gonna need you to take Thursday and Friday off next week and check Alexis' agenda for me if you can and see what she has on tap."

"I'll see what I can do. But I do need to know what the plan is before I go any further."

"I'll tell you when I see you," he said before hanging up the phone.

Monica was stunned. There was no I love you or take care. No goodbye. No nothing. Monica sat back on the futon cradling the phone and smiled. Damn he was good. She suddenly felt aroused and had to admit that every time he spoke to her she got the same feeling. No wonder he and Alexis had hit it off they were by their very nature assertive. Only on him it was becoming. Monica couldn't see how any girl, not on top of her game, could handle Philip Dalton's very persuasive methods. She had spoken to him for less than twenty minutes and he had her taking two vacation days though she had no idea why, checking Alexis' agenda and   invited himself to see her and demanded—well—not exactly demanded but had her leaving the following weekend open though she had no idea what they were doing. Aside from that he had her involved in some hair brained scheme whose details she hadn't a clue. Then to top it off he'd left her with one arm cradling the phone, smiling and wondering what the hell had just transpired while her other hand was hard at work between her legs slowly stroking her coochie and fantasizing about seeing him again.

Damn that man. She'd planned on calling James and informing him of her evening with Alexis but after a glass of wine and a cigarette, she closed her eyes and went back to dreaming of the very handsome, very chic, very sophisticated, Mr. Philip Dalton before exorcising herself of any feelings she was having for him at that moment.

James was more her type. He was slow, plodding, never in a rush just happy to get there when he got there. They seemed to have everything in the world in common and Lord knows he could bury the hatchet when it came to making love. Philip, on the other hand, triggered everything in her. The mere thought of him made her hot and horny. And both times she'd seen him she'd wanted to strip him bare and just ride him. And despite their age difference she was quickly coming to realize that he was the one in control. It suddenly dawned on her that for her own welfare she'd better keep him at arm's distance and keep a close eye on him as well.

The following morning Monica called Alexis to see if it had all been a dream or had she really meant all that she'd told her the night before and found that Alexis was as chipper as ever.

"Hey girl just called to see how you were doing?" Monica said opening the door to get a sense of where Alexis was coming from.

"Couldn't be better. Did you get in touch with James?"

"Didn't have a chance. Got home and went straight to bed. I was a little tired from being screamed at and chastised."

"I am sorry for some of the things I said, Monica. I hope you will forgive me. It's just that sometimes I don't know if I'm going or coming. It used to be that whenever I felt like I was overwhelmed James would put everything in perspective for me but without him it just feels like the whole world is caving in on me. It doesn't help not having you to talk to either. But I'm glad you called. What's up?"

"Not a damn thing. I just wanted to know if you were sincere about me seeing Philip?"

"I certainly am. You know he's really a sweetie pie but I just can't get over James. And with me trying to stay on top of the department, trying to get my feet wet in real estate and the market I just don't have the time for a relationship and all the crazy shit that comes along with it, right now."

"I think you're just afraid of letting anyone really get to know you."

"You might just be right."

"Or maybe you just don't like men?"

"I think that may be closer to the reality. At least not when they want to get up close and personal," she laughed.

"Anyway, I was wondering if you knew when Philip was coming back into town. Thought maybe we could do dinner or something along those lines. Maybe you could talk to him and put in a good word for me. Maybe, stir the embers kind of rekindle the fire, if you get my drift."

"I suppose I could do that. But I'm back in Chicago this weekend so it'll have to be next weekend at the very earliest. Why don't you just invite him up for the weekend yourself—you know—spend a nice, cozy weekend at home? You could use my place if you feel more comfortable then you wouldn't have to worry about momma or Bridget dropping by and interrupting anything," she said in an attempt to make amends.

"Oh, hell no! My last two experiences haven't been ones I look upon too highly. The first time I was looking down barrel of a gun and the second time I was—I don't know how many—fat ho's," Monica laughed.

"I'm tryin' to make up for my stupidity but you're just not going to let me live it down. Are you, wench?"

"Trust me Alexis, when I look at the source I have to take it with a grain of salt."

"Oh, no you didn't!"

"Look I've got to get back to work but I may just go there to clear my head and get away from home so don't come in raisin' hell and trying to blast somebody. Okay? It's just me."

"Then why don't you fly to Chicago with me. I could use some company and we could do some shopping when I get finished with the b.s."

"No, I think I'll pass this time. I really don't know what I'm doing yet. But anyway thanks for the offer and you have a good trip."

"Don't know about all that but I'll talk to you when I get back

Sunday evening. And by the way, if you get a chance stop by my office, I have two fifty dollar gift certificates for Ruby Tuesday's if you want them. You might consider taking James to dinner and finding out who the bitch is he's seeing if you change your mind about Philip coming."

"I know you don't want to hear this, but I think you're barking up the wrong tree. Why in the hell would any man want to get into another relationship after being in bed with you for twenty years?" Monica laughed.

"You've got a point there."

"I didn't mean that as a compliment."

"Oh, go to hell." Alexis said just catching the irony. "Look, I've got to go. Talk to you when I get back, sweetie. Love ya."

Monica hung the phone up on her desk shuffled a few papers before searching the outer offices to see if anyone had been watching and then dug through her purse in search of her cell before dialing the 212 area code. Reaching Philip's office she was disappointed to hear a recording stating that he would be out of his office until Monday. Suspicious she wondered if it were a mere coincidence that both he and Alexis were out of town on the same weekend.

She had to admit that her normally suspicious nature was now bordering on the brink of paranoia and she hated being caught up in a triangle without knowing the details of what she was subscribing to. There was a cell phone number on the recording where he could be reached in case of emergency and before thinking she'd dialed that and was on the phone with Philip.

"Well, darling I just called to tell you that your little girl will be out of town this weekend."

"I know. She just called me to give me the heart rendering news about you."

"And what news is that?"

"Seems that you've been in love with me ever since you met me and she's not sure where her head is at and being that she's never been one to stand in the way of true love she felt that it was only right for her to move aside so that we could meet our fate. She'd known since day one that there was a certain vibe between us. And perhaps that's why she'd grown so angry when she found us in bed together. But now she realizes that she can't stand in love's way and what was meant to be would be so she was going to bow out gracefully. Besides after making love to me it was obvious that that's not where my heart lay. She really hated conceding so she had done everything she knew how to make me hers but after speaking to you she knew that we had something so much deeper. She invited us to dinner next weekend with the hopes that we can remain friends and she sincerely hopes that this won't affect our business relationship."

"Oh what a crock of bull. Damn, my girl is good. And you said?"

"I asked her how she could just make decisions like this for me. I explained to her that what had transpired between us was no more than a case of two people in close quarters that felt a physical attraction towards each other that was heightened by a few drinks and the out come was no more than them getting together to express how they felt about each other at that particular time. But there was really nothing more. There was nothing to build on like what she and I shared.

Then I told her that the chances I was taking I wouldn't have taken for any other woman in the world. And the only reason I did it was because I felt that we—she and I—were building a future together."

"And she said?" Monica asked laughing.

"She told me that you had expressed such a caring, deep seated devotion for my well-being when she spoke to you last night that there was no way she was going to stand in the way of her best friend who she'd known for close to thirty years. Then she spent the next half an hour telling me what a beautiful person you are."

"Well, that part is true," Monica laughed.

"She went on about all the trials and tribulations—all the heartbreak—you've experienced as the result of no-good men. And if I had any inclination of sleeping with you and then just moving on then the next time she saw me she would make sure her aim was better."

"No she didn't?"

"Oh, but she did and she claims she was doing it all for you. Then she had the nerve to laugh and tell me that this wasn't an easy decision for her to make but it was something she felt in her heart and soul that she just had to do. And that's not all. She claims that after finally getting the chance to sleep with me after waiting all this time, she really hated losing me to you but she had to admit that you were the better woman. And she knew you were the better woman because of the way I responded to her lovemaking."

"And how was that?"

"Well, in her eyes I didn't respond at all. I asked her how I could possibly respond with her having me gagged and all. And she said that when it was over I never even mentioned it which in itself let her know that my heart was with you. But hold on. Here's the kicker. And to tell the truth she'd never be able to compete with you in the bedroom because after all you were so much more experienced in that area," Philip said laughing.

"No, she didn't!" Monica had to laugh as well at that one.

"That's what she told me but wait there's more. Are you ready for this? In twenty years she's only had the occasion to sleep with one man and she never did anything but lie there flat on her back and never moved because that's what he told her to do. But now she's finding out through her reading that there is so much more to making love than just lying there helplessly like she'd been doing. But since her divorce she's had a chance to get more in touch with her inner self. She's had a chance to inquire and some of the women's journals suggested that she experiment sexually and get to know herself better. So, after giving it some really hard thought she demeaned herself by going into one of 'those places' and purchasing a woman's toy. I guess that means she bought a dildo. Anyway, after not getting any response from me she was wondering if that was the problem with James as well. Maybe she's just not knowledgeable enough in bed."

Monica was laughing hysterically.

"Philip I'm not sure I want to hear any more of this or go along with any plan you may have in the working. It's obvious," she said choking on her own laughter, "that Alexis is fuckin' crazy."

"Anyway, let me finish. She took the toy home and tried it out but she wasn't even sure if she was using it right. In any case it made her feel really uncomfortable and she wondered if other women did this or if she was in a minority of one so she took the damn thing and threw it out. But she's convinced now, more than ever before that her problem with men is her inadequacy in bed and that's why she's so afraid of a relationship. After all what does a man see when a man looks at her?"

"Is this still her talking?"

"Yes it is. Now may I please finish? A man sees a beautiful woman with a body that's just screaming out to him and then when he finally gets her into bed he finds out that she's a lousy fuck. That's her worst fear and whereas before it was just a premonition she had, now it's a reality. And she knows it's a reality because my body language told her so. After ten months of me trying to seduce her she finally gives in and when it's over she can't even illicit a response from me."

"Oh my God! Philip are you sure you know what you're doing? You may just want to walk away from this one."

"No. hold up, there's more."

"There can't be!"

"Oh, but there is! Life goes on though…"

"Is this her again?"

""Yes, c'mon now. Try to keep up," Philip laughed.

"Now, don't you start acting like her. But anyway go ahead, continue."

"So, she concludes by telling me that life goes on and she'll just have to deal with idea that life's dealt her another vicious blow and all she can now is pick herself up, dust herself off, and start all over again. But she's glad to find that two people she cares so much about are finding some happiness as the result of her sacrifice.

Still, she wonders if she'll ever be able to keep a man with her inadequacies in the bedroom. She would like to get better but she has no idea how to? Then she asked me if I thought that I could teach her. You know just go slowly and walk her through it in the same way I taught her how play the stock market and it could be our little secret since she didn't know how you would take it."

"Huh uh? Tell me she didn't say that. Philip, tell me she didn't say that," Monica said in utter disbelief.

"I would not lie to you."

"And what did you tell her?"

"I told her that she couldn't make decisions on who I saw and who I didn't see. I told her that I was crazy about her and never felt this way in my life. And I'd come too far to just let the whole thing come down to this but I would talk to her more about it later when I saw her.

To be perfectly honest the whole phone call threw me for a loop. I didn't know how to play it but I knew if I agreed with the first proposition she tossed my way she'd be suspicious so while I work it out I'd leave her thinking that nothing's changed in the way I feel about her. And she'll believe it because it flatters her ego and her ego runs her life. Anyway, you called to tell me what? That you loved me and had been rather hasty in your decision and don't know you can wait another week to see me. Correct?"

"Not exactly. I called to tell you that I may be staying at Alexis' this weekend and that she will be out of town. I believe that's what you asked me to do isn't it? And I being your little heartthrob do everything you say. Is that not true?"

"I only wish. If that were the case you'd be in New York and I'd be giving you hot oil massages instead of getting the 4-1-1 on a mad woman over the phone."

"Well, maybe that can be arranged," she said flirting and was sorry almost as soon as she said it.

"You're only saying that because you know I'm headed the other way. Anyway, see if you can find the titles to all of her real estate holdings. They may be in a safe deposit box which will be a bitch to get access to but if my suspicions are right, Alexis is not going to pay for a safe deposit box and will probably have a portable safe lying in the back of one of her closets. If you find it scan them and fax them to me a.s.a.p.

I know you're curious as to what I'm doing, but trust me its better that you not know that way should anything go wrong you won't know a thing then you can't suffer any repercussions. On the other hand, it'll give me some leverage so I can get from under her thumb and show her the error of her ways at the same time. Let me give you my fax number at home so you can send them there instead of to the office where there's a chance they could fall into the wrong hands."

"Okay, wish me luck, Philip and remember, I'm trusting you."

"Hey, Monica."

"Yes, Philip?"

"I know I shouldn't say this and I don't know how you're going to take this being that we really don't know each other that well but I really think we are going to have something really special together."

"I'm not really sure I understand what that means."

"I'm not either. It's not what I intended to say but I guess it'll have to suffice for now."

"And why is that?" she asked.

"Because they're calling for boarding passes and my flight's about to leave. Besides I'm not sure I'm in full control of my emotions right through here. The truth is I haven't been able to spend one waking moment since I met you without you clouding my thoughts. What would you call that?"

"A simple case of infatuation?"

"I can think of another word that I think would better define it, but I don't want to be caught out there alone when I say it so I'll wait 'til I see you. That gives me a little more time to reassess the situation."

"Well, it's nice to know you're human, Philip."

"Is that what it is?"

"Yeah, emotions sometimes cloud our views but trust me you'll be fine and I'll call you if I come across anything. You be safe, you hear?"

"You too, Monica. Call me, baby."

Monica spent the better part of Saturday shuffling through Alexis' personal papers and at the same time asking herself why she was doing it.

Alexis called on numerous occasions from her hotel room, obviously bored to tears over having no one to harass or make miserable. And James phoned so many times, Monica wondered if he was in a bind or in heat. Probably just bored and lonely she thought. The more he called, the more she was inclined to lean towards Philip, who didn't seem nearly so needed. Monica wondered if the stereotype about New Yorker's being faster and wiser was true. The country-assed niggers around here certainly didn't impress her, acting as though she were the fulcrum that kept everything in Detroit turning.

She liked the idea of staying at Alexis' place so she could get away and escape the drama that was quickly becoming her life, but the cell phone brought the drama with her. She swore she was going to toss the damn thing if she heard that it ring again. But no sooner had she made this decision than the annoying thing rang again. Screaming in frustration she glanced at the number and recognized Philip's cell.

"Hey, baby."

"Oh, it's baby now."

"I would like to think that," he said hesitantly. "Don't you want to be my baby? I thought it was an endearing term that might just draw you a little closer to me. You do want to be close to me, don't you?"

"Jury's still out."

"Well, I hope they return before Thursday. I just made my reservations and I should be arriving at Detroit Metro at a little after one, Thursday afternoon. I didn't know if you would be working or not so I thought I'd better check and see what was what."

"Yeah, I'm working 'til three. Didn't know you were getting in that early…"

"I wasn't but I couldn't wait to see you so I changed my flight to an earlier one so I'd have more time to spend with you."

"I thought we were going to pull back a little—you know—kind of concentrate on the task at hand before we even thought about moving forward?" Alexis asked knowing full well she was as guilty as he was.

"We did say that? Didn't we? Or better yet—you made that suggestion. I never agreed to go along with it."

"Sure you did."

"You know it's a funny thing but *you* can say virtually anything you want. You can tease and seduce me but I do the same thing and stop signs go up immediately. It's like you invite me in the yard and then you want to cut my foot off for stepping in. Why is that?"

"A woman's prerogative, I guess," Monica replied.

"We'll have to talk about that."

"And some other things to…"

"Hope they're positive."

"I bask in an aura of positivity."

"Hope there's room for me."

"I may let you share my halo. Depends on your performance. We'll see. By the way did you get a chance to see a doctor while you were home?"

"See there you go again and to answer your question I did that the day I got back. Says I'm fit as a fiddle but suggested I watch you Detroit women. Seems that was not the first case. In fact, he mentioned your name as soon as he saw the damage."

"You need to quit, Philip," Monica laughed.

"Sure did. I believe he called it the Monica Manning strain. Said it's very common in the Midwest. Gave me some antibiotics and sent me packing. Said I'd be good as new by the time I see you again."

"Hope he gave you a note to give to me. Anything else would be unacceptable."

"I knew I forgot something," he laughed.

Monica's phone beeped in her hand for what seemed like the thousandth time that day. Glancing at the caller I.D. she knew this was one call she couldn't put off any longer.

"Philip I've got another call. Let me get back to you when something turns up. If you don't hear from me today or tomorrow call me on Monday."

"Will do, if I can wait that long. Talk to you later."

Monica hit the flash button; pretty sure the other caller was history by now and was surprised to find James still on the other end.

"Hello."

"My goodness, Monica. Do you ever sit still long enough to answer the phone? I've been calling you forever."

"And how are you James? I remember trying to teach you correct phone etiquette back in high school but I see that little lesson still got by you," she said rather coldly.

"Sorry, babe it's just that I've been trying to reach you and…"

"And I'm quite aware of that but a girl cannot be readily accessible. If she is available at a man's every whim it only decreases her magnetism. C'mon, you should know that's Lesson 101 in the 'how to get a man handbook'," she laughed.

"Sounds like a page right out of Alexis', how to tease a man handbook', if you ask me."

Monica was somewhat taken back by the comment and could sense the urgency in James' tone, and didn't appreciate the reference in the least.

"Didn't know I was supposed to stand by at the ready waiting for your calls and I really don't appreciate being compared to your ex-wife. Her behavior is not something I try to emulate."

"I'm sorry, Monica. It's just that I really have been looking forward to seeing you and spending time with you. Don't know why I thought you felt the same way too. Then I don't hear from you for days. It's just a little frustrating is all. By the way, what are you doing tonight? I thought maybe we could go out a little later, maybe grab a bite."

Monica was sorry she'd come off so abruptly and appreciated his concern but after talking to Philip the conversation with James always seemed mundane, almost boring in comparison. Philip was like a shooting star, a supernova in her eyes whereas James gave the appearance of a sedentary planet moving, revolving but if someone didn't point it out one would never know. He was solid. Solid as a rock. What she claimed she'd always wanted in a man but Philip's flash, the glare and his brightness seemed to outshine everything she'd ever known and although deep down she knew that James was more right for her from the perspective of age and commonalities, it was Philip that gave her goose bumps when they spoke.

Truth is, she'd not made a commitment to either and decided that since it wasn't in her power to dissuade Philip from calling and Alexis had opened the door to her seeing both then that's exactly what she would do. Though in all honesty she didn't have a clue how to maintain two relationships with two very different, very possessive men she was damn well gonna try. For the time being though, the idea appealed to her greatly and if there was a will then she might as well have her way.

"Sorry James, I've just been very busy is all. I should have called you but I've been kind of tied up."

"Hope you mean that figuratively?" he laughed.

"Of course, silly."

"Never can tell. Alexis used to have a fetish about tying people up. I thought it might be some kind of little secret initiation ritual with you Catholic school girls or something," he said still chuckling at his own joke.

Monica was stunned and thought about Alexis tying Philip down. So this was nothing new and wondered if this tidbit of information might just help Philip in his quest to make Alexis atone for her sins and then thought better of it. That was an uncompromising situation she didn't want to put him in. Then wondered if she weren't becoming perhaps a little possessive or maybe even jealous herself.

"No. I think Alexis may have a lock on the whole dominatrix thing. That's really not me or at least I don't think that's me. I've never been in that situation."

Monica smiled. So Alexis was a freak. The thought tickled her though she hardly knew why.

"Never know until you've tried it. Oooh the things I could do to you with you bound and gagged."

"You behave and you might get the opportunity," she said teasing.

"What are you doing tonight?"

"You don't beat around the bush, do you?"

"At my age, I can't afford to," he replied still laughing. "Anyway, like I was saying, how about a late night dinner down at Bentley's. You ever been?"

"No, I haven't, but I can't tonight. I'm over here at your ex's house, as we speak, trying to catch up on some homework. I'm taking an online course and I'm way behind. My pc went down and I'm trying to get this stuff finished up before she gets back."

"You sure now? They tell me Gerald Albright's there and if I remember correctly you used to love jazz."

"Traditional," she replied still shuffling through Alexis' important papers trying to find deeds and titles and whatever the hell Philip had asked her to look for.

"I'm not sure I know the difference but dinner with some good company and a little smooth jazz in the background could really set the stage for the rest of the night, you know."

"James, if I didn't know you better I'd get the distinct impression that an evening out is just your means of eliminating the foreplay which as every man should know is the most essential part of the lovemaking process. Without the foreplay then it's reduced to nothing more than cold hard sex which is nothing more than a booty call. I hope that's not what you're suggesting."

"It is beyond me how a woman's mind works. I ask you to dinner with the hopes of spending a little quality time with you and you somehow associate that with foreplay and sex. Lord, if that's the case, then every time you eat at McDonalds you should be having sex right after. That would equate to three times a day if I follow you. No wonder you're behind on your work."

Monica was hardly listening.

"I found them!" she screamed.

"Found what? Are you even listening to me?"

"Listen, James, I've got to go. Pick me up at ten thirty at my house. Oh, and I meant to tell you, Alexis told me to take you out and find out who it is that you've been seeing. I'll talk to you tonight."

"What?"

"I'll tell you tonight, sweetie. Gotta go."

And with that Monica hung up the phone and called Philip back to tell him the good news. She was excited but only because she'd spent the better part of her day looking for papers that she wasn't sure even existed. She really hadn't expected to find anything at all but here they were, clear as day, all neat and tidy in a folder labeled simply 'real estate'. Now she had one last thing to do.

It was six-thirty now and with all the papers in front of her she wondered if she would be finished by ten-thirty. Philip had obviously turned off his phone, which quieted her excitement somewhat but she still had a task ahead of her.

Monica was finished by ten and had everything she could do to put everything back in order so that it appeared untouched and headed home. She hadn't really had a chance to look at the bevy of paperwork before her but realized that Alexis' real estate holdings were far in excess of two mil and wondered why her friend chose to teach at the university at all. It was obvious she had a certain proclivity when it came to buying and selling property and a keen eye for what was a good investment. Why she forced herself to get up at the crack of dawn and make time each morning was beyond her.

Arriving home she showered and quickly changed into the most provocative thing she could find, a shimmering, silver low-cut dress with spaghetti straps that exposed all but the nipples of her breasts and bunched them together so tightly that her bust size seemed to double. It hit her just below the knees revealing a pair of perfectly shaped dark brown calves that seemed to melt right down into the six-inch open-toed, sling backs which showed her perfectly manicured feet.

The time at Curves was finally paying off even though she had difficulty finding the time. Nevertheless she'd found the time despite her being preoccupied with Philip, James, work and school. And – well—having lost another forty pounds she was feeling particularly good about herself and how far she'd come in only the last month. Still, she wondered if it was really Curves or all the running she was doing with her new lifestyle. Didn't matter though. What mattered was that she wasn't changing any of it. Aside from Alexis and the drama she brought into everyone's lives all was good on the home front and in fact better than it had been in years.

Throwing a light touch of mascara on Monica stared into the full-length mirror just outside of the bathroom door and marveled at how far she'd come. She felt good and strong. And though she wasn't there yet the truth was she'd never been this close.

Hearing the bell ring, Monica grabbed her bag and her cigarette case and headed for the door but not before glancing in the mirror for a final check.

"Damn, baby, you do look good if I must say so myself," she said admiringly.

Monica made sure she took her sweet time answering the door

the way some women will do when they know they're looking good. She took a long, deep, breath in an attempt to play down the fact that she was feeling almost as good as she looked then sighed in an effort to encourage some negative thought that would settle her down and put her on an even keel.

Wanting to give James the impression that seeing him was no more than a favor to him Monica took her sweet time in answering the door. Not wanting to seem too anxious she wanted it to seem as if he was dragging her away from some terribly engaging activity that had her complete interest. In her eyes he was no longer the one in demand. She was.

A month ago she would have literally begged for some tall, dark and handsome gentleman to be knocking at her door. But not tonight.

Tonight she was doing her best to give off the impression that he was intruding on her precious time and should feel honored that she let him into her life at all. Well, that was the impression she wanted to give off anyway and that little pause, the minute or so before she unlocked the door enabled her to do just that.

Hell, in her own eyes she was a queen, always had been and losing a few pounds hadn't changed her one bit. If they'd only had an ounce of sense in their thick skulls they would have certainly recognized that before. Shit, and come to think of it James had been no better than the rest of those knuckleheads running around chasing some skinny bitch with no more cerebral tissue than Mr. Potato Head. That's why he'd ended up with that deceitful, street corner hustler for a wife.

It had taken him twenty years to finally come to his senses and now he wanted her to rush because he'd finally come to the realization that he'd made a mistake and wasted too many years of his life. The idea angered and served to bring her down another notch. And that's exactly where she wanted to be, grounded firmly with no hopes and dreams of tomorrow but like the AA manual overly stated, just taking one day at a time. Not wanting to appear overly eager Monica sat down on the sofa and listened as the doorbell rang again then took out her cigarettes and lit one as she checked her makeup.

Just because he stood six-foot-seven in his stocking feet and had that dark wavy hair momma used to always refer to as good hair or because he was built like one of those naked sculptures chiseled in stone that graced the Louvre was no reason why she should race to the door to let him in. Let him wait she thought, smiling to herself.

Let him wonder if perhaps she'd found something better to do with her Saturday evening than to spend it with him. And she hoped that this was no regular occurrence like Thursday night bowling with the boys or just another convenient filler for his agenda. Work Monday through Friday, spend a couple of hours each night getting the truck tuned up and ready for the track in the spring, Thursday bowling league with the fellows, Friday beer night with the boys at the pool hall, Saturday wash the car then the truck, mow the grass stop by Monica's, get your dick sucked. Go to church on Sunday morning after whorin' around all night Saturday with the girl you should have married and give a testimonial around fornication that'll have all the old women screamin' amen while the young ones line up to see who's next in line.

'No it wasn't going to be like that. In fact, I shouldn't go at all', Monica said to herself. 'I should just let him call for another two or three days and pretend I had to go out of town on business or something. Keep him guessing. Alexis was right about one thing. You can't be too easy or else you become a nonentity and as soon as that happens they don't have any more use for you.

Monica crushed the cigarette out in the ashtray. It took fifteen minutes to smoke a cigarette and that was sufficient amount of time for him to stand there gaping, wondering where in the hell she could be. In her eyes her stock had just doubled and if he had an ounce of brains he should be absolutely dying to see her by now.

Monica's hunch proved correct and James stood there with his mouth wide open as she opened the door and graced him with her presence.

"Damn woman! Please tell me how in the hell I ever let you pass me by."

"I was asking myself the same thing just now," she said smiling in appreciation as she looked up at the tall, handsome man in front of her and watched as every logical thought she'd just had crumbled into dust and debris like the remains of the World Trade. All that was left standing was the distant memory of her resolve not to seem too easy.

"You're not looking too bad yourself, Mr. LeBrandt," Monica said desperately trying to regain some of the composure that seemed to fly out the door when she opened it and saw James standing there.

"We could skip dinner."

"Not on your life," she replied hoping that he wouldn't see through her remarks and take her right there in the living room.

'Damn, the man is fine. Lord please help me to get my coat and ease the fuck out this door before he sees how badly I want to gobble his ass up. The hell with dinner, I already know there ain't nothin' on the menu that looks this damn appetizing.

But wait. I am *supposed* to be a lady. A woman in control of her emotions and desires, a woman who is supposed to have the strength and resolve to postpone gratification for the sake of the end result. And in the end if I really want this man then I can't appear starving and hungry as if he's the greatest thing to enter my house since sliced bread.

And with that thought, Monica reached up and grabbed James' neck and pulled him to her and kissed him deeply. Responding in kind he pushed her into the hallway and returned her kiss.

"James."

"Yes, baby."

"The zippers on the side."

"Baby, we're in the hallway," he said grinning.

Hearing James' remark, Monica regained her composure, looked around to see if any of the neighbors were watching then quickly gathered her resolve.

"Let me grab my coat," she said her embarrassment showing.

The evening turned out to be even better than Monica could ever have expected. And as much as she protested the new smooth jazz that everyone was listening to she had to admit that Gerald Albright was one talented brotha even if he was forced to do that smooth jazz shit to sell records.

And despite all of her previous comparisons between James and Philip, the highlight of the evening had to be the conversation— well—at least it was in the club. She'd never laughed so much in all her life and James seemed to be enjoying himself as well telling of his students and even the episode that forced him to get a restraining order on Alexis.

"Out there rubbing that thing in the driveway... Let me tell you. It got so good to her that she forgot that I was standin' there. You know she's got a bit of that exhibitionist shit in her. Anyway she forgets I'm there although she's supposing to be putting on a show to seduce me and get me to take her inside and then she gets to moanin' and screamin'. I guess she was on the verge or something. Anyway, I look up 'cause she's getting louder and louder and ol' lady Oakley, my next door neighbor who's gotta be close to ninety is standing there in the doorway staring straight into the car. So I move away from the car so ol' lady Oakley can get a clear view and see that I'm not killing this fool and Alexis won't stop even after I tell her no, emphatically and tell her the neighbors are watching. Hell. That just seemed to turn her on more. I don't know.

Now, picture this. I've got Looney Tunes Jr. sitting in the driveway masturbating like crazy and here I am the president of North Gate Village Community Watch responsible for maintaining proper decorum in the community and I can't get this crazy heifer to stop screaming and throwing herself around the damn car.

I saw ol' lady Oakley starting to walk over to get a closer look with her nosey self and so I meet her halfway between her yard and mine and tell her that Alexis is having an epileptic fit but that it should all be over in a matter of minutes. In the meantime, she's insistent on calling EMS. I've got all I can do to convince her not to but before she finally goes back inside someone already has.

I'm looking around and by this time all the doors and windows in the neighborhood are watching. People start coming out of their houses and she's still just a rubbin' away and sweatin' and moanin'

I guess she was stuck or something 'cause she got to cursing and screaming some more. Wasn't nothing I could do short of giving her some and that wasn't happenin' so I just start praying that the whole thing would be over soon 'cause I don't know what in the hell else to do.

So, anyway, I start picking up my rake and the rest of my tools lying around the front yard and said to myself maybe if I just go on in the house she'll quit acting like a goddamn fool and go away. But I think that only made matters worse 'cause the heifer got out of the car and got to cursing up a storm. Called me everything but a child of God.

And ol' lady Oakley is still standing there in her doorway watching the whole thing so I walked over to her and whispered, 'she has Tourettes too'. Well, by this time I'm totally embarrassed not to say a little angry too but does Alexis care? Hell, no! She made it plain that I was going to give her some or there would be hell to pay. I haven't been outside since; not even to get the paper.

Monica was in tears by this time.

"You certainly know how to pick 'em, James," Monica said now in tears.

"That's not funny, Monica. It took twenty-five years to establish myself as an upstanding community member and a good neighbor only to have it torn down by this spoiled brat in a matter of a few minutes because she couldn't get her way. So, I called the police but by the time they arrived she was long gone and I was left standing there while ol' lady Oakley stared at me and just kept sweepin' the same spot in her driveway and shaking her head."

Monica couldn't remember having a better time and couldn't

wait to get home. If it was the last thing she did she was going to show James just how much she appreciated him for remaining the same sweetie pie she'd always known despite her saddling him with Alexis and wasting so many years of his life. She'd make up for a good part of it tonight though and James didn't need to do anything but sit back, relax and enjoy it. Dinner may have been on him but dessert was on her.

Arriving at her apartment Monica was surprised when James kissed her at the door and turned to leave.

"You're not going to stay a little while and have a night cap with me," she asked.

"Well, I guess I could."

James walked into the apartment had a seat on the living room sofa, unbuttoned the navy blue, Versace blazer grabbed the bottle of Crown Royal and poured himself a healthy serving.

"Why were you so hesitant about coming in?" she asked.

James smiled. "You're very observant. I'm not hesitant about coming in. You don't know how badly I want to come in and stay in for that matter but I just got out of a relationship that was based on sex. I don't want you to think that that's all I want from you. I want to build upon what we have and have a full and complete relationship with you, Monica."

"Ahh, that's so sweet. But isn't that like putting the horse before the buggy. I do believe we've already crossed that line, James."

"That's true but this is the first time in I don't know how long that I've actually felt anything like this. I don't want the reason I'm with you to get misconstrued. And I'm not saying that you would do that. It's been my experience that women fall in love with love whereas men have a tendency to fall in love with sex. I'm not sure I believe that but one thing I do know Monica and that is if men do fall in love with sex it wouldn't be at all hard to fall in love with sexin' you. I have never and I'm being truthful never experienced a woman that made me feel the way you did that night in bed."

"You need to stop, James. Thank God my complexion won't

allow you to see me blush."

"I'm being serious, Monica. I don't know if it's because you were always an enigma to me or the fact that I finally had my fantasy come true or if it's the fact that this just might be the first time that I've ever made love but one thing's for damn sure, I need to know— I need to be sure that if I let my heart go this time it's for real, for the right reasons and the feeling is reciprocated."

"My goodness James, I don't know mean to make light of the way you feel but you sound more like a woman than I do when it comes to this. Might be time you threw on some boots and spurs and cowboy up. Hell, there ain't no guarantees when it comes to love and relationships. Most people go into it blind or fully knowing what to expect and years later the principles in the whole deal have changed and people just don't feel the same way they do when they started off. They grow and change and don't always move along the same paths. That's just life. I don't know what to tell you. That's just the way it goes. I don't think they enter into the situation hoping or thinking that it's going to fail.

There are no guarantees or mail in warranties that come along guaranteeing anything but a fair shot at making it work so I can't guarantee you anything. You'll never know if you don't just jump in with both feet. It's just a chance you have to take."

"I see you've got jokes. That's okay though I do recall my daddy giving me some very profound advice before I married Alexis. Something along the lines of not stepping into every hole you see. I didn't understand at the time but as funny as it seems I understand a whole lot better now."

"I don't get it James. I'm not really sure what you want me to tell you or try to assure you aside from the fact that I'm not Alexis and that you've got to do what you feel. Then work and pray at it to insure some measure of success. A relationship is like a job. It's a lot of hard work. It demands a hundred and ten percent from both parties if it's going to stand a chance of working. What else can I say?

Is it that you don't trust me? Was there ever a time that you've known me that you doubted me or the way I felt about you?"

"No, I can't say that I've ever doubted your word or your intentions but we're moving pretty fast and I'm not sure what your intentions are. And until I do I think it best that I take it kind of slow—you know—just to protect myself. I would like to think that you're open when it comes to a relationship with me but I'm not exactly sure what you're thinking. Feel free to jump in at any time."

"I don't know what you want me to say James. Are you looking for a commitment? Is that what you're asking me or are you asking me for some assurance that I won't be the one to break your heart? Do you want me to tell you that I never thought I would be the one to finally get to enjoy your company after standing in a long line of pretty women all wanting the same thing? Is that what you want me to tell you?"

"All except the last would be fine and if you added your intentions for us in the future then I could probably work with that."

"I understand what you're asking me James and even though everything feels right at this very moment I'm not sure I can or am ready to answer you at this time. Give me some time and I'm sure I can give you some of the answers you're looking for but for right now I guess friendship is the best that I can offer if you want me to be truthful about it."

"It's not the answer I was looking for but I guess it'll have to do—for now. Doesn't mean I won't keep the pressure on."

"I certainly hope you do. And to show you just how sincere I am and how much I respect your wishes I'm going to ask you to leave since I don't share your sentiments. I dressed this way with the hopes that I could entice you to make love to me the way you did the first time. But since you can't and my opinion doesn't count I think it best you leave before I just take what I want. Anyway, you're not going to sit here and tease me so there's the door, save the kiss and know that I intend to keep the pressure on as well. And

just to show you how sincere I am, I want you here at eight forty-five tomorrow morning so you can escort me to mass and make sure you bring a change of clothes. Nothing fancy. An old pair of jeans and a flannel shirt will do fine for what I have in mind. And like I said, save the kiss. A kiss has too much emotion and may lead to other things and we wouldn't want that —now would we?"

Monica all but pushed James out of the door and took a deep breath before muttering to herself. 'Now that's a good man—a damn good man'.

Chapter 15

The picnic following church on the following day was quiet, yet as wonderful in Monica's eyes as the evening before had been.

Sitting there alone on the grassy slopes of Belle Island Monica felt alive, refreshed and wondered why the Lord had sought to bless her at this juncture in her life. And although she hardly understood his workings she'd learned not to look a gift horse in the mouth—not that she looked at the Lord her Savior as a gift horse—but she thanked him nonetheless for his blessing as she had done earlier in the day.

A bottle of champagne capped off the afternoon and both she and James sipped freely without a care in the world. Still, despite a slight buzz, Monica felt a little out of sorts as James drove back to her place knowing full well that as adamant and fixed in his ways as he was, he hadn't changed his mind and the thought of their making love was probably out of the question.

Monica hardly minded with all she had to do to get ready for work on Monday but the idea that he didn't want to sleep with her was disquieting to her to say the least and left her feeling a little inadequate in her quest to get this man.

With sex, she always had that one weapon, that one lure to fall back on. Without it she wondered what else he could possibly see in her as so intriguing and the fact that he'd told her no and rejected her when it came to sleeping with her made everything just a little more difficult, a little more complex and for the first time ever she found herself having a hard time relaxing in his company.

If it was a meaningful and fruitful relationship he wanted then as much as she hated to admit it, she couldn't help but feel she would end up disappointing him. All anyone had to do was look at the guys she'd dated over the years to know that she was no novice when it came to the dating game. And yet if marriage was any barometer of a successful relationship then she'd been a complete and utter failure.

Anytime she found herself truly enamored by a guy she could always use sex as a final resort almost like a sort of backup plan to insure his being there. James, however, had taken the game to a new level eliminating her hole card forcing her to rely solely on her wits. And even though she professed a greater self-esteem nowadays she still wasn't sure her newfound confidence were little more than window dressing to cover up years of painful denials. One thing was for sure. There was nothing here to fall back on but Monica.

Pulling up to the curb in front of her building James turned to her. Monica wasn't sure if she was to lean over or lean back. Unaccustomed to her new role she gathered her things together and began to thank James for a wonderful afternoon when he interrupted.

"First time I've been to church in quite some time and first time I've ever been to a Catholic church. I'm not sure I get all the genuflecting and all the standing. Is that just ceremony or to keep the old folks awake and the middle aged ones like me in shape? I wasn't quite sure but overall I enjoyed it."

"I'm glad to hear that." Monica said not knowing how to respond. This was usually the part where the guy leaned over to kiss her, grabbed the back of her head, jammed his tongue down her throat and held on to the back of her neck while his free hand undid the buttons of her blouse, unlocked her bra and caressed and played with her nipples in a vain attempt to get her hot enough for her to invite them upstairs. It hardly ever worked but that's what she was used to. This, on the other hand, was as foreign to her as anything she'd ever known and truth be told she was just a wee bit out of sorts not having to fend off a man bent on getting upstairs, inside of her apartment and then inside her.

"Well, I'm glad you enjoyed the service. Maybe we can do it

again next week if you're not busy."

"Yeah, maybe." He said nonchalantly and gave Monica the impression that he might just be being nice and chances were he probably hadn't enjoyed it at all but was just telling her that as a way of being nice before dismissing her.

All through the afternoon she'd had the feeling that James hadn't really been there, like something was on his mind. At times, she couldn't help feel like he was just going through the motions; that something was troubling him, but like Marshall she refused to ask, sensing that whatever the problem might be it somehow involved her.

She reasoned. If it was that time again—that time when men have to summon up some type of courage to say exactly what they want to say—which usually was that they didn't want to see her anymore for this reason or that she wasn't going to help or rush them to reject her. Now, sitting in front of the house she knew as only a woman does that's been in similar situations so many times before that James was on the verge of revealing something she hardly wanted to know or deal with at this juncture. Hell, what was it about her that constantly drove them away?

"So, is that a yes, James?"

"Oh, I'm sorry. My mind was in a different world."

"Has been all day. I get the sense that there's something you want to tell me?"

"No, not really. I was just thinking about today's service and the minister's message."

"Priest's…"

"What?"

"Priest not minister. In the Catholic church they're referred to as priests not ministers." Monica said in an attempt to prolong the inevitable.

"My fault. In any case, I was thinking about the *priest's* sermon. He mentioned the fact that it's our responsibility to reach outside of ourselves and our own very limited experiences in order to grow in Christ. I guess what he was saying is that we need to have the strength to look beyond our daily rituals and take chances to better, not only ourselves, but those around us as well. I'm not sure if he was referring to the genocide going on in Darfur or the Kenyan refugees or the man next door. But being very limited I could only reach so far outside of myself and my thoughts kept going back to what you said last night. That's all."

"So you were listening. For a minute, I thought you were just biding your time and praying that the whole thing would end sooner than later. So, you really did enjoy it?"

"I did. What's not to believe? He was as eloquent as I've heard. He had no need to scream or shout or roll all around the aisles and act the fool to get his point across but like I said I took it personal, though. I'm sure those weren't his intentions when he was writing his sermon."

"And how is that?"

"Well, I thought about what you were saying last night. In fact, I've been thinking about that all day."

"I knew something was on your mind."

"Yeah, anyway you were telling me almost the same thing when you were talking about relationships. If I understood you correctly, you were trying to convey the message that with everything a risk is involved. Even something as simple as buying a television. I don't think the manufacturer sells a television with the idea that his product is going to break within a thirty day period but should it, there's always a little yellow warranty card that accompanies it."

"I said that."

"No, but you alluded to the fact that there is nothing that's one hundred percent foolproof and everything you do in life comes with a risk. Some are greater than others but none are completely risk free. After being with Alexis for twenty years and suffering the pains of a marriage on the brink most of that time it's kind of hard for me to step out of the box and take a chance as your minister—I mean priest suggested. But if I'm to grow as a person and with you

I've got to step out of the box, out of my own little comfort zone and take a chance at life instead of hiding from it."

Monica smiled. This is not what she'd expected at all and quickly realized that she was also in a little box of her own filled with rejection, compounded annually with no interest, and little or no return on her investment when it came to men. It was evident though that her conversation with James was already paying dividends that she could hardly have dreamed of at the time she was telling him.

"So what are you saying?"

"Well, I guess what I'm saying is that I can't let the mistakes I've made in the past shadow my future. It's high time I stopped looking back and move forward. I'd like to do that with you, Monica."

"Goodness! This is a lot for a girl on Sunday morning. Sure, this isn't the champagne speaking or just the fact that you went home last night and thought about the fact that I was there for you and you passed on an opportunity most men would have died for," she joked.

"I'm not gonna lie. I thought about that and I regretted that I passed on you last night but I don't regret how I felt. And right now I guess I want my cake and eat it too. I want to love you with no holds barred. I want to make love to you every waking hour. I want to spend every free moment I have with you and think of you every minute I'm not with you. I want you to cloud not only my dreams but my life."

"Definitely, too much champagne," Monica joked to mask her uneasiness. "Remind me to pick up some more first thing in the morning. Go ahead keep talking."

"Stop joking, Monica. I'm dead serious."

"Sorry baby, it's a defense mechanism. I really don't know what to say. I half expected you to tell me this was it or you were having second thoughts. Maybe even something along the lines of you thinking about working it out with Alexis. I really thought you were going to tell me something along those lines. That's what I'm used to around this point in a relationship. I have to admit I'm in a state of shock. I really am. I guess this means you'll be accompanying me to church next Sunday?"

"The next time I accompany you to church I hope I'll be accompanying you up the aisle."

"Okay, slow down. There's no need to say anymore. *You're really starting to scare me now.* Trust me. I'm getting the message. You really don't have to add any more to it. Trust me, you're in there. I just need to change the sheets first. You've got it. Passed the test with flying colors and I'm yours when you want me. I'm already lighting a cigarette for you when you finish and get ready to roll over. What can I say? These are the things I've been waiting all my life to hear and now that you've said them I really don't know how to respond."

"Say you'll have me and we can make this work, in spite of everyone and everything."

"I hear you sweetie. I'm flattered but don't you think it best that you consult me on any decision that may involve me?" Monica said relieved at the sudden turnaround in James' behavior and his admission. It was a godsend in comparison to what she'd been thinking.

"Just thought we were on the same page is all."

"We may be but you can't just go assuming."

"So what you're saying is that I extended my heart and soul to you and you still have some reservations."

"The only reservations I'm thinking about at this particular time are the one's we're going to make down in the islands that has us lying on a sandy beach sipping margueritas with you by my side. In the meantime I want you to go on being you and feel assured that I'm here for you. I just have a few things to clear up before I can really give you all of me. That's all."

"Does that include other men?"

"Nothing serious."

"So there is someone else?"

"Like I said, there's nothing to concern yourself about. After what you've just told me I really see no need for a safety net and I couldn't imagine being in better company than you."

"So who is he?"

"Just a friend."

"Did you sleep with him?"

"Don't you think that's kind of personal?"

"Yes. Now did you sleep with him?"

"Once."

"Okay. Just need to know what I'm up against."

"Nothing more than your own insecurities."

"And I'm supposed to accept that and let the matter drop?"

"That would be nice."

"Then consider it dropped."

"Just like that?"

"A new beginning, baby. Can't beat a dead horse. Relationships are built on trust and I have to trust the fact that you say he's old hat."

"Not yet but he soon will be."

"That's kind of cold."

"Doesn't bring what you bring to the table and never made me an offer like yours."

"I've been practicing."

"And I can tell."

"What else have you been practicing?"

"Not much else that I can do alone."

"You need some help rehearsing."

"Somebody with your expertise would prove invaluable."

"Do you have the time?"

"And the place. Would you like to come up for a few?"

"Don't know if a few will do."

"I missed last night, you know."

"And whose fault was that?"

"My own stupidity I guess."

"Well, if we cram I think we can get last night's lesson in."

"And today's as well?"

"I'm pretty sure we can do that and if you're lucky perhaps we can start on tomorrow's lesson as well."

"You think?"

"I think we both need to make up for lost time."

"How far are we going back?"

"Twenty years."

"That far? We'd end up spending the next twenty in bed at that rate."

"A problem?"

"Not as far as I can see. Maybe we can rewrite the Karma Sutra."

"For the new millennium?"

"An updated version?"

"No, just a revision."

"No need to remake the wheel."

"Just perfect it."

"Shall we get started?"

"Waiting on you."

"I'm already there."

"Kiss me and tell me you love me."

"After you've completed your assignment."

"Then let's get started."

James and Monica woke up in each other's arms somewhere around one a.m.

"Beautiful," he said looking at her naked flesh.

"What's that?" she said yawning and somewhat surprised to find him still there. She was sore, but not hardly as sore as the first time.

"You! You were simply beautiful."

"Are you saying that I am beautiful or that the act was beautiful?"

"Both," James said grinning like a school boy that just stolen a pack of Topps baseball cards for the bubblegum and missed the hundred thousand dollar Honus Wagner insert.

"Feel like you made up for the other night don't you?" Monica asked still half sleep.

"Sorta, why do you ask?"

Monica sat up, took a Newport from her cigarette case, lit it, turned her pillow to the cool side, took a drag and exhaled deeply, before speaking.

"I hardly thought it was—what did you say—beautiful."

James was shocked and the shock showed on his face.

"What was wrong? I don't understand."

"Oh, it was okay but from my vantage point you still need a lot of work when it comes to freeing up your emotions. Here let me show you what I'm talking about."

Monica slid down to the bottom of the bed, pulled the cover over her head and then lifted it from atop her head.

"On second thought I think that seeing me will certainly bring you more pleasure."

And with that said she took his penis into her hand, guided it into her mouth and worked at it with her warm but supple fingers while sucking the tip ever so gently. In minutes she felt his back arch and become rigid. Using her free hand she placed her hand on his rock hard abs pushing him backwards and took all of him into her mouth and throat and sucked with the force of an undertow in a Caribbean hurricane until she felt him erupt, shooting wave after wave of hot lava in her mouth. Swallowing each and every wave she continued with him screaming loud enough to not only wake the neighbors but Peoria and Chicago as well. When there was nothing left she slowed her pace some and watched as fought to free himself of her. But there was no escaping and she continued to suck until his screams became mere moans and his moans merely whispers and he was sound asleep again.

The following morning Monica awoke feeling awfully chipper for a Monday. She dreaded the idea of going back to work but dragged herself out of bed only to find James already gone. She was glad he'd left before she got up especially since she had no idea how he would see her after what she'd done. In many respects he was older than her father. And she hoped he wouldn't frown on her for wanting to please him last night. Men were funny in that regard though. Sometimes they'd grab you and hold you afterwards or turn into raving lunatics and become almost obsessed with the act.

There had been one guy that had made Fatal Attraction seem like a PG movie after she'd given him some, stalking her and the whole nine. Then there were the others who only saw her as soiled goods afterwards no more than common street trash. It was always different and she wondered how James viewed her attempts to please him. But there was no time to think about that now. She was running late as usual, and Mondays always found her desk laden with a stack of papers and files a mile high, and messages out the kazoo.

Arriving at the offices of Brooks and Dunnehey, Monica grabbed the stack of phone messages off her secretary's desk and inquired.

"Anyone looking for me?"

"No it's been surprisingly quiet for a Monday, Ms. Manning. But Mr. Dalton called several times as well as Mr. LeBrandt. I take it you had a pretty fruitful weekend?"

Monica smiled then headed to her office to find it just as she'd left it on Friday. Pouring herself a cup of Maxwell House Monica took a deep breath before having a seat behind the large oaken desk.

The fact that Philip had already called several times bothered her a little and she was forced to think about Alexis' concerns when it came to Philip. He may be good at whatever it was he did on Wall Street but he had some things to brush up on when it came to wooing a woman. Sure every woman liked to be courted but to be pestered was a horse of a different color. Half of the intrigue of the game was the chase. But there was no intrigue, no chase here at all. Philip was persistent, adamant and at times pushy in his pursuit and it was already starting to be a turn-off.

Monica wondered if it was because of the age difference but couldn't remember any guys being so persistent when she was in her twenties. Then again, she couldn't remember any guys being interested at all when she was in her twenties. But then she'd changed, matured and gotten her life together somewhat since then or at least she would like to think she had. Shuffling through the papers on her desk, Monica smiled and realized that she wasn't being fair.

The only reason that the thought of calling Philip didn't appeal to her this morning was because she'd just spent a wonderful two days with James and was feeling on top of the world. And the minute she picked up the phone and heard Philip's voice she'd probably find some negative quality about James and a reason to put him on the back burner.

The reality that she was desperately trying to hide from was that she was falling in love, if she wasn't already and had a decision to make and the thought did not particularly appeal to a woman that had spent the better part of her adult life without a man of her own. James and Philip both appealed to her. And she knew with out a shadow of a doubt that she was in love with James. And yet Philip with his drop dead good looks, quick wit, and scholarly attributes sparked something deep inside of her as well. She hardly knew him as well as she knew James but there was no doubt that she wanted to get to know him.

They were as different as day and night and each brought with them their own special qualities that made them appealing but in completely different ways. If only there were some way she could mold them into one. But since she couldn't, Monica knew that a decision would have to be made. And soon. She had just given James her word that she would cut all ties with Philip and she'd tried. She really had and that was before James told her that he loved her but she knew the minute she picked up the phone and heard Philip's voice all bets were off. Still, she had to try.

"Philip Dalton, please."

"One minute Ms. Manning, let me check and see if Philip is still in his office. I though I saw him heading down to the lounge a minute ago. This is Ms. Manning isn't it?"

"Yes, it is." Monica replied surprised that the secretary would be so forward as to assume it was she.

"I'm certainly glad you called Ms. Manning. Here it is Monday morning and this place is in its usual state of chaos and Philip's got me calling you every two minutes. I'm sorry about all the messages."

Monica smiled. The secretary's admission only served to boost her ego.

"Not a problem."

"I don't know what you've done to him but I haven't seen him this flustered in a month of Sundays. Oh, here he comes now. Hold on while I transfer you."

Monica was beaming and no sooner had he picked up the receiver and she heard his voice then she knew that she was going to have to see him one more time. There would be no sex, she assured herself but she had to see him in person and tell him that she was involved with someone else and hoped that he would understand.

"Good morning. Philip Dalton here."

"Good morning, Philip. And how are you this lovely spring morning?"

"Couldn't be better now that I hear your voice. Listen, I got your message Saturday evening but I got kind of tied up and couldn't get back to you right then and there. Tried to call you yesterday but I guess your cell was off and no one answered at the house. But I did receive the faxes."

"Do you know your friend has close to three million dollars in real estate holdings?"

"No, I didn't know. I take it that's good?"

"Good? That's phenomenal being that she's only been in the loop for a little over a year. It's not fluid or anything but it still shows a certain propensity or acumen for making money that most people lack."

"You sound impressed?"

"To the extent that she's good at what she does, yes I am. I admire that in anybody. It's just too bad that it comes as a result of cuddling up to people and using them to make a dollar. I see drug dealer's everyday that prey on people in their quest to make a dollar. They grow rich but I can't respect them for killing people for their own benefit. Sorry, I just can't see it. They do the same thing right here in my office. But anyway, it's good to know. I can't really talk now but I hadn't heard from you and you asked me to call. Is everything alright with you?"

"Couldn't be better."

"Well, that's good to hear. I'm pretty swamped here and I'm trying to do a little extra since I'll be out of the office on Thursday so if I don't get a chance to call before Thursday I'm just making sure you have my flight number and arrival time."

"I certainly do. I think you've given it to me at least three times," she laughed.

"Just kind of excited about seeing you."

"Your secretary told me."

"Oh she did, did she? I'll have to have a long talk with her about putting my business in the street," he laughed. "Do you miss me?"

"You don't know how much," Monica said doing her best to be sarcastic but knowing she couldn't pull it off.

"See you, Thursday, baby." He said before hanging up.

"Damn!" Monica shouted as she sat there listening to the dial tone.

He'd done it again. She had all intentions of talking to him and telling there was no need to get his hopes up. That there was nothing going on and their attention should be on Alexis and carrying out his little plan. Instead she'd listened to him once again, become weak and unable to tell him exactly what was on her mind. Well, that wouldn't happen Thursday. On Thursday it would be no more Mr. Nice Guy. They would be friends and that was the extent of it.

Chapter 16

The rest of the week proved uneventful for Monica. Alexis called constantly inviting her to lunch and to go shopping but more than anything to find out if Monica had gotten any further in her search to find out who the heifer was James was seeing. Seems she'd called him all weekend at home and he'd been gone all of Saturday evening and all of Sunday and hadn't returned home Sunday night. She knew this because she'd driven by the house Sunday evening on her way home from the airport and her flight hadn't arrived until a little after twelve. And James was always in bed no later than nine-thirty on a Sunday evening.

She'd been so angry she thought about sitting out there waiting until he arrived home just to see what time it'd been and was glad she hadn't since she called him again at seven o'clock Monday morning and he still wasn't there. She'd even thought about stopping by Monica's just to get some stuff off her chest but knew Monica's old tired ass went to bed even earlier than James'. So disturbed was she by the recent chain of events surrounding James and his erratic behavior that Monica agreed to meet her downtown by the university just to let Alexis vent.

"Girl, I know James. I know all of his habits and ain't no way in the world anything is going to keep him out on a Sunday evening past eight o'clock unless it's a woman.

This is the beginning of March Madness, too. James won't even leave the house during March Madness. Trust me, when the college basketball tournament comes around he ain't movin'. He'll sit there and watch four or five games in a row then jump in the bed and watch ESPN and the highlights of the games he just got finished watching. Whoever this bitch is he's seeing must be fine as hell."

Monica, who was in the midst of a chef salad almost choked to death on that last remark.

"Are you alright? Geez! For a moment I thought I was going to have o skip the Heimlich and go straight to mouth-to-mouth. It's a good thing you recovered or you may have died waiting for me to give you mouth-to-mouth," Alexis laughed.

"Go to hell. If I had choked to death then who the hell would you have gotten to do all your dirty work?"

"Hell, I ain't getting' no results from your ass anyway. I asked you close to a week ago to take this fool out and wine and dine him, I even gave you two gift certificates for a free dinner for two and what do I get for my generosity? *Nothing.* Not a damn thing."

"I don't know what you want me to do. Tail him. Set up roadblocks. Tap his phone. Set up a stake out? Who the hell do you think I am, Magnum P.I. or somebody? Look I asked the man if he was seeing someone and he said no. Now what more can I do? You want me to go into the house and check the sheets for stains and look for fingerprints?"

"No, I guess you're right but you two have always been close. I'm sure that if you really put forth a little effort then you could find out a little more than you're telling me. Hell, you used to be the Joan Rivers of the school newspaper in high school. You had the scoop on everybody."

"I was the editor of the school newspaper, Alexis. That was my job. I ain't getting paid to do this."

"You weren't getting paid then."

"I was getting grades, good grades as compensation."

"And now you're getting my friendship as compensation."

"I'll take the grades."

"Be that as it may, Monica, I'm going to find out who the hell it is that's sleeping with James and when I do…"

"And when you do—then what? Are you going to act like a goddamn fool and pull a gun on her like you did Philip and stand around and scream and yell and shout crazy ass threats at her until the police come to take you away? Face it Alexis. You're divorced and there's really nothing you can do if James decides he wants to begin seeing other people. You gave up any claims to him when you signed the divorce papers and it's high time you let it go and get on with your life."

"Sorry but that's not an option. I don't know if you remember me telling you awhile back that if I see something that I want that I intend on getting then I wouldn't let anyone or anything get in my way."

"I remember."

"Well, nothing's changed. And if I decide I want James or just want him to be celibate until I decide what I want to do with him then that's exactly what I intend to happen."

"You're not being reasonable and that's not really fair, Alexis. It's not fair to James."

"I don't give a fuck about being fair to James. I'm about being fair to Alexis right through here."

"And that's all that matters?"

"Yes. Right through here that's *all* that matters." Alexis said sipping her Long Island Iced Tea.

"I see. Well, how do I come into play?"

"Look if the tables were turned and it was your man out there seeing another woman after you'd spent twenty-two years sharing the same bed together and that was the closest you'd ever come to lovin' somebody and you asked me to help find out what was up I wouldn't have any problem at all checkin' up on the bastard."

"Alexis LeBrandt I am really starting to believe that you really don't like men."

"*Whatever, Monica.* That's really neither here nor there. What I need to know is if you'll just give it one more shot. Just try. That's all I'm asking you. Just see if he's got another woman. If he does I may just take your advice and bow out and let him grow old with the bitch."

"You would never."

"No I sure wouldn't now would I," Alexis laughed, "I'd spend the rest of my days making sure that every waking moment was pure hell for both of them."

"You probably would," Monica said shaking her head from side-to-side in a show of pity and contempt.

"Do you remember the officer that let me in the backdoor of the Radisson when Philip first came to see me?"

"Yeah, what about him?"

"Well, I had him on a retainer doing the same thing I'm asking you to do. He's the one that told me that you and James had gone out that night."

"No you didn't?"

"Oh, but I did. Paid him five hundred an hour plus expenses for him to tell me that you two went to a damn play. A waste of goddamn money."

"And here I am doing the same thing for free."

"That's what I'm trying to tell you. You don't have to. And it wouldn't take you half the time to find out what it took him two weeks to find out because James trusts you. He'll let you go places it would take Ricky years to find out simply because you're old friends. Take the money for a week, Monica. Just give me one week. That would be like doubling your salary and you could hit some of those restaurants and jazz clubs you're always talking about at the same time. Chalk that up to expenses and the whole things on me."

"Have you no shame, Alexis." Monica asked shocked that Alexis would even consider making her such an offer.

"You could do this Monica and save me a whole lot of money. After all he is your friend."

"He wouldn't be if I did some shit like what you're suggesting."

"But you're already doing it. You might as well get paid for it."

The words stuck in Monica's craw and for a moment she thought she was choking again. It was a lot of money and she could certainly use it but...

"So, you'll do it?" Alexis asked knowing that Monica was giving her proposition some hard thought.

"Deposit the money directly into my savings and don't call me until Monday. I don't want to see or hear from your corrupt ass 'til then. Then if I have some information I'll give it to you and if I don't I'll give you your money back. Look, I gotta go. You watch your back you connivin' ho," Monica said as she gathered her things, "somebody's gonna make you pay for your heathen ways sooner or later."

"But until then, I'm on top of the world," Alexis replied holding her glass up as if she were toasting someone, "I love you, honey."

Monica didn't respond and found her way to her car. She had to let James know before she did anything else but leery of Alexis watching she made sure she drove a considerable distance from the bar before flipping open her cell and calling James to inform him of Alexis latest hair brained scheme and get his reaction.

She couldn't believe Alexis would actually stoop so low but James knowing his former wife the way he did said, 'yeah, that's the way she works', and even went so far as to tell Monica to string her along for a couple of weeks, maybe a month with tidbits of information and maybe even get some pictures with him and some of his students just to shake her up.'

"Might teach her a lesson about always dabbling in somebody else's business," he joked.

What neither knew was that Philip was working along those same lines only his plan was on a much larger scale in comparison and after meeting Monica at the airport they agreed that he would only spend the Thursday and Friday with Monica. On Friday evening he would call Alexis apropos of nothing and let her know that he was on the way to her house with some earth shattering news that just couldn't wait.

"And you're still not going to tell me what you have up your sleeve?" Monica asked.

"Don't want to put you in a compromising position," Philip responded, as he leaned back to stretch his long narrow frame on the burgundy leather sofa. I do like the place though. You've got an eye for color and I really like the African artwork."

"Well, thank you. Another drink?" Monica asked.

"I'm not sure. The last time I had a drink with you I wound up with you seducing me. Then again, fill it up and let's see what happens."

"Philip Dalton. If we're going to reminisce let's at least get the story right."

"I was pretty sure that's what happened."

"Uh uh, Philip. Don't even try it. You're just trying to get on a subject you know I don't feel real comfortable talking about right now."

"I don't understand. The last time I saw you that's all you wanted to talk about."

"Things change."

"Not here. You still look good to me."

"In this old thing?"

Monica had purposely changed into the purple; flannel housedress momma had given her for Christmas. The first time Alexis and Bridgette had stopped by neither of them could stop laughing. Telling her she looked just like Barney. She'd put it on for just that reason tonight hoping to dispel any advances from Philip but it was as if he didn't see it at all. Handing him the glass of Bacardi he grabbed her hand, pulled her down on the sofa next to him and kissed her gently.

"Uh uh, sweetie," Monica said pretending to pull away without having moved an inch.

"Not tonight, Philip," she said as her tongue entered his mouth.

"You and I both know that long distance love affairs don't work," she said.

"Then we'll have to amend that little problem and if it'll put your mind at ease I've already begun working on that but I think you're right about one thing."

"And what's that?" Monica asked as she tried to put her glass on the coffee table and not move from Philip's lips who had abandoned her lips in favor of her earlobes and neck.

"You do need to get rid of that robe," he said.

"You don't like it?"

"Not at this moment."

"And why not at this moment?"

"It's in the way."

Monica caught herself as Philip tugged at her zipper.

"No, Philip. I'm sorry baby, I just can't? She said zipping up her robe.

"Why is that?" Philip asked puzzled by the sudden turnaround. "Is it something I said? Something I did?"

"No, it's nothing you've done. It really has nothing to do with you. I just can't right now that's all. Please don't try to figure it out."

"I wouldn't know where to begin."

"That's just it. I don't know where to begin either. Everything's been moving so damn fast that I don't know which way is up and until I figure some things out I think it better that we just remain friends."

"I kind of figured something like this was happening. I had a feeling when I didn't hear from you over the weekend and then when I did the phone calls were always pretty short and abbreviated. But I'll tell you what. I love you and you're not going to push me away that easily. If I have to wait on you to come around then that's what I'll do but you will come around. Believe that."

"That confident, huh?"

"No, I wouldn't say that I'm that confident but I'm a firm believer in persistence overcoming resistance and when I get finished wining and dining and serenading you, you'll beg me to be yours. Did I tell you I loved you?"

"I heard something along those lines but figured you were either jet lagged and talking out of your head or those frequent flyer miles were catching up to you."

"I'm not playing Monica."

"How can you even say something like that and this is only the third time you've been in my company?"

"Fourth time if you want to include the day you picked me up on the corner," Philip smiled. "I wasn't aware that there was a time limit that let you know when it was a person could know that their in love. As much as you try to hide from the reality you've only been in my company a short amount of time and we've already made love."

"I was drunk."

"And I'm staying in your home for three or four days."

"I must still be drunk."

"Face it. You have the same feelings for me that I have for you even though you may be afraid to admit it. I had to come to grips with the idea so I could move on and follow up. It's not hard for me to tell you that I'm in love with you Monica."

"And what was it that kept you traipsing around behind Alexis for close to a year? Was that love too?"

"Infatuation."

"With what? Her body?"

"...her mind as well. She's no slouch you know."

"This I know."

"But she doesn't bring to the table what you bring."

"And what exactly does that mean?"

"As far as a total package you are it. At least in my eyes you are."

"Okay hold up. Wait just one damn minute. Table. Total package. You might want to choose a better choice of words. Don't know if you noticed or not, but I'm a little self-conscious about my weight and these references you keep referring to have me a little shaky," Monica joked.

"Goodness, Monica do you have to joke all the time?"

It was like déjà vu and Monica had to turn and make sure it was Philip and not James sitting there.

"I'm sorry," she said.

"Anyway, you were referring to me being attracted to Alexis and I have to admit that I was very much attracted to her but for all the wrong reasons. In a way I saw a reflection of myself in her and I'm glad I did. It gave me a better perspective of where I was going. It made me take a good hard look at myself but then I met you and for lack of a better word I finally understood what my father was telling me about settling down with a woman you're totally compatible with. Now thanks to you I understand what he was saying. He wasn't referring to looks. He and my mother have been married for a little over fifty years and she's no stunner but I can honestly say I've never seen a happier couple. And do you know why?"

"No, please tell me."

"Because they're friends first."

"And?"

"And two weeks ago when you picked me up from the airport and we spent that evening together when you decided to let your hair down and be Scarlet O'Hara I knew that I had not only found a friend but that I found something else as well."

"And what was that?"

"I found a soulmate. I found a woman that embodied everything I could possibly want in a woman. You're charming, with a wonderful sense of humor and attractive and witty."

"Don't stop there we have time?" Monica joked.

"See that's exactly what I'm talking about. And then when Alexis pulled the shit she did I saw another side that was both bright yet very practical and I knew before I got off the plane back in New York that I was in love with you; that I had to have you."

"And how do you propose doing that?"

"You wait. You'll see. Take your time. You can wear a chastity belt if you like but you'll be mine when this is all over."

"Think so, huh? You think you're that good, do you, Mr.

Dalton?"

"That good."

"Well, let's see. Let's start with some basics since you have my life planned out for me and consider me your soul mate. Let's just see how compatible we are? Let's just pretend I'm a prospective employer and you're looking for a position as my spouse or better half. Let me just give you a quick interview to see if you're right for the position. Are you ready?"

"As I'll ever be, go ahead," shoot Philip said smiling and sipping the Bacardi.

"Do you like children?"

"Love 'em."

"So you want children?"

"After they're fully grown, have left home and on their own," Philip said smiling.

"Philip. I need you to be serious," Monica said laughing.

"So you love children but don't want any. Is that how I should interpret that?"

"That is correct but I enjoy practicing."

"Practicing what?"

"Practicing to have children," he replied taking another sip.

"Oh I can see this is going nowhere. How am I come to understand how you've come to see us as soulmates if you won't be serious?"

"I was doing my best Monica Manning impression."

"Touché, now, may I continue?"

"Sure go right ahead. I'm all ears."

"Okay since you're so preoccupied with sex. Tell me what your favorite position is?"

"I would have to say that that would be any position that would allow me to be with you. How am I doing so far?"

"Oh, you're impossible," Monica laughed. "I give up. Look, make yourself comfortable. There's a refrigerator full of food if you're hungry. I've got to throw some clothes on. I've got a friend holding some movies down at Blockbuster that I need to pick up before eight. You can ride with me if you like or shower and unwind if you're not up to it. I should be back in about a half an hour."

"Not a chance of you leaving me here, woman. I plan to smother you and enjoy every second of every minute of every hour that I have in your company. Remember I'm on a mission to win you over baby and that means doing all I can in the limited time I have."

"Well come on then." Monica said as if she were talking to one of her nieces or nephews who were always underfoot and always trying to tag along behind auntie.

'Once in the car though it was a different Philip that she saw and the jokes and laughter were displaced by a grim seriousness etched on his face that let her know that fun time was over.

"Monica, I'm going to have Alexis invite you over for dinner on Saturday evening. Tell her how much I would enjoy seeing you while I'm in town and I'm going to need you to do something for me?"

"So, what else is new?"

Phillip ignored the remark and continued.

"Okay you wanted to know my plan for evening the score with Alexis."

"I did and I do."

"Well, I'll tell you this much. I'm trying to sell Alexis on the idea that the stock market is about to go belly up over the next few months and that she needs to pull her money out and invest in a housing development some friends of mine are setting up right outside of Atlanta's perimeter. She's a sucker for real estate investments from what you've sent me and I have everything set up where she could stand to make a bundle on paper."

"On paper?"

"Don't read more into it than what it is, Monica. Just follow the script for now and trust me on this one. In any case I need you to find out what she's doing next weekend at which time I hope and pray she's busy. One of the properties she's supposed to invest in is supposed to open next weekend. It's a strip mall and I'm hoping that she's going to attend the grand opening. Anyway, what I need for you to do is ooh and ahh and make a big to do over the whole idea as I sell it and when she can't get away to see it I need you to step right up to the plate and volunteer to go in her stead."

"Like, doesn't anyone ask me if I have any plans anymore?" Monica said doing her best impersonation of a Valley girl.

"Once she buys the idea then that's it but I need you to really be there for me. I'm going to bust in with news that just can't wait. What I need for you to do is to step in and sort of curtail my enthusiasm. Tell me or have me wait 'til after dinner 'til I spring my idea on her. I need you to get a couple of bottles of wine since you say she's not a wine drinker. And hopefully that'll dull her senses enough that she's not concentrating on every minute little detail of the project. Right now all I to do is give her an appetizer, get her mouth wet, tease her—you know—just whet her appetite. That's all I want to do at this point. I want her to think about the possibilities. I don't want to sell her any more than the idea at this point.

Then next weekend when you get back you can go on and on about how spectacular the whole area is and how you were thinking about cashing in your IRA's and 401 to invest. Tell her you're even thinking about moving south just to be closer to such an exciting new venture.

As far as you're concerned it's a win-win situation with little or no downside as far as you can see. Then I'll hit her later on in the week with how I'm doing the same. But at no time will I ask her to invest. Anyway, that's where we are for now."

"Do you think you can pull it off.?"

Monica laughed. "Did you see my Scarlet O'Hara?"

"Yeah, that's what I'm afraid of," Philip said grinning. "Anyway, the first thing I do when I get there is bubble over with excitement to show her how great the news is without revealing any specific details. I'll probably take a shower and ask her if it's alright if you join us for dinner because I have some great news and I'm looking for investors. And of course she'll say yes since she's trying to push me off on you. And like I said, you ask me to hold off until after dinner and until we're quite sure she's tipsy before springing it on her. Of course, I have to be charmed by every thing she does and will continue to follow her around like the puppy dog I once was. Anything else would give her the idea that I have no interest in her and even though she has no use for me other than what I can do for her I can guarantee that if she doesn't get the attention from me or I turn it solely to you she'll be upset to no end."

"You may even end up tied to the bedposts again," Monica laughed.

"God forbid."

With Monica keeping Philip at arm's distance the days leading up to the big dinner served as nothing more than a friendly get-together between two friends that seemed as if they'd known each other their entire lives. At night the two made the trip to Blockbuster then came back sat around the fireplace and cuddled. He holding her in his arms nibbling on her ears and her neck, telling her how it was just a matter of time before she would be his and his alone and they would be sitting together somewhere in the tropics with not a care in the world and if there would be no babies then there would certainly be lots of dress rehearsals.

In the evenings, Monica arranged the dining room table in just the manner she'd seen B. Smith do it on countless occasions and a candlelight dinner would ensue.

On the second night she even let him share her bed after he promised to be good and stay on his side. And he had—well—for the most part he had. After several denials he settled for a kiss and fell fast asleep. Both had to admit that they hadn't enjoyed another person's company in who knew how long and Monica didn't think about James or the promise or his proposal once in the entire two days Philip was there.

Monica had to admit, though she refused to tell Philip, that she thoroughly enjoyed every minute of the time they'd spent together but she didn't want to lead him on and so she had refrained. He hadn't made her choice any easier but at least she'd given herself enough breathing room to allow herself to make a rationale decision. Still, she wanted to be sure.

And when Philip decided to tell 'Lexis he was catching a Saturday afternoon flight instead of his customary Sunday frequent flyer so he could spend his last day with her she never; not for a minute, gave it a second thought.

Philip had enjoyed himself as well letting it be known on more than one occasion during his rather abbreviated stay. As he was about to leave he noticed a marked change in her whole attitude. When he approached her around her sudden mood swing he found her to be sullen and unresponsive at first but after prodding her to talk to him he was able to ascertain the root of the problem.

"What's wrong, baby?"

"Nothing, Philip." Monica answered as she hoped to fold his clothes.

"Something's wrong. The whole time I've been here you've been beautiful. There's obviously something wrong."

"I just hate the fact that you're going over to that woman's house and spending the night. You ask me to trust you but this is a bit much. Turn the situation around and ask yourself how you would feel if you were in my shoes?"

Philip thought for a minute then smiled.

"And I thought you didn't care. Thought we were only friends?"

"Oh, I hate you."

"Doesn't sound like it, right now. If anything I think I detect a note of jealousy."

"Fuck you, Philip!"

"Whew! Those are strong words coming from you. Would it be better if I told her I had reservations at a hotel and come back here? I'd much prefer that."

"No. You go ahead and do what you have to do in keeping

with your little plan. I understand. I don't have to like it but I understand."

"Weren't you the one that told me that a person can only do as much as you allow them to do?"

"I said that but Alexis is a horse of a different color. She's already raped you and *from what you tell me* you didn't particularly allow that. *Or did you?"*

"You are jealous aren't you? So why all the pretense and attempts to hide your feelings these last two days?"

"First of all, I'm not jealous and second of all, I was not trying to hide my feelings. I allowed you to stay in my house and for that matter you slept in the bed next to me."

"So, if that's the case why wouldn't you allow me to touch you?"

"That's not the point, Philip. Because I wouldn't let you sleep with me doesn't mean that I want you spending the night at another woman's house."

"Do you trust me?"

"It has nothing to do with trusting you, Philip. It has more to do with trusting her? It's just the whole idea. And what am I supposed to do while you're there."

"Know that I love you and would never compromise the possibilities with you not even for someone as fine as Alexis' ass is," he joked."

"See you think this shit is funny. Put yourself in my place and tell me you'd be laughing. I doubt if you'd even give me a second thought if I did some shit like that."

"This is really bothering you, isn't it?"

"I'll be alright."

"I told you I could tell her I'd made reservations at the Radisson—well—maybe not the Radisson."

"No, you go right ahead. I guess a relationship is nothing without trust."

"Oh, so we do have a relationship?" Philip asked glad for this admission on her part.

"Of course, we have a relationship. We're friends."

"And that's it?"

"For now. And if it were or had the possibility of being more, I don't think this would be the time to ask about it. That's for damn sure."

"You're really upset about this."

"You're starting to become redundant."

The ride to Alexis was quiet though not exactly what one might call peaceful. There was an uncomfortable silence that Philip hadn't encountered since meeting Monica.

Every now and then he'd glance over in her direction, to find a tear streaming down the soft brown cheeks he'd come to love so much. If he could only make her see, only make her understand that she was the one that made his heart bang like a thousand drums in a college band, that she had become his reason for living and that he hardly felt complete anymore unless he was in her presence. If he could only make her see, that this was something he felt compelled to do and when he finished there would be plenty of time for them. She just had to trust him and be patient.

Philip hummed the Luther Vandross remake of Forever, For Always, For Love, and fidgeted with his briefcase so as not to look at the tears and the pain he was causing. He had to admit that as much as he hated to see Alexis, he was grateful to leave the thick aura of insecurity so prevalent on the ride over.

As he grabbed his overnight bag and briefcase he turned to Monica who seemed to have regained her composure and asked, "You will be there for me won't you?"

Not bothering to look in his direction she replied, "Yes Philip, I'll be there," then drove off without so much as glancing in his direction.

Relieved that that was over, Philip took a deep breath before entering the lobby and collecting himself enough he headed for the apartment and prayed that he would catch her with someone so he could leave.

But as usual Alexis was there alone, and dressed to the tee. Philip wondered if there was a time that Alexis ever let her hair down and relaxed then shook his head when he considered what an absurd thought that was. No, she was always on top of her game. Always looking for an angle, studying something or another that would put her one up on the next guy and keep her from ever being caught with her pants down.

Seeing Philip at her door she seemed genuinely surprised and more than a little happy to see him. If this was an act then she had to be the best actress he'd seen since Hepburn in The African Queen. No, it was obvious that Alexis was genuinely glad to see Philip for whatever the reason and the hug and kiss she bestowed on him let him know just that. Somewhat caught off guard by the reception Philip took a step back before moving forward to gather his bearings.

"Come in! Come in! Oh, Philip what a pleasant surprise! And what prompted you to just drop in from out of the blue?" she asked but before she continued. *"Was this supposed to be our weekend together? Oh, it doesn't matter. It is now. Come on in. Here, let me take your coat. Did I apologize for the way I acted the last time you were here? Oh, it doesn't matter. Nothing matters now that you're here."*

Philip, more than a little stunned by the warm reception, grinned at the woman standing in front of him, making all this fuss and wondered what kind of ill-trip she was on this weekend then thought about what Monica said about being careful and her being dangerous. The words hit home a little harder now.

Regaining his poise, Philip realized that Alexis was no novice at the game and could turn the charm off and on at the drop of a hat. There was no need, therefore, to look at her happiness as anything more than another one of her games. Only problem was, he didn't know what type of mad scheme she was up to now. Be that as it may he needed to take it slow, keep it as cordial as possible with the overtones of business and continue to follow the script regardless of her antics.

Philip hugged her then glanced around the apartment to see if anyone else was there. Seeing that they were alone he relaxed.

"Come in and have a seat. I'm sorry I didn't haven't had a chance to call you but with mid-terms and all it's been kind of hectic."

"I understand."

"My phone does receive calls though. What's your excuse?"

"The same; work and something new I have going on. That's why I'm here. I was supposed to be here next weekend but what I 'm so excited I couldn't wait."

"Hope its good news," Alexis said "you've got me worried now. For you to fly all the way out here without calling or anything then something must be wrong. Okay tell me what's happened."

"You leave me in charge and you expect for something to go wrong?" Philip joked as he loosened his necktie.

"Well then, what's the news? Must be something good?" she asked nervously.

"Not good, *fabulous!*" Philip replied.

"Oh, really? Well, if it's that good then spit it out. When you get to be my age you don't have a lot of time for playing, 'guess what happened next', she chuckled.

"A drink?" she asked.

"Chivas and milk if you have it," he replied.

"Oooh, top shelf... *Things must be good! What are we celebrating?"*

He had her now. He'd peaked her curiosity. So, this is what got Alexis off. Well, something had to and up 'til this point he had no clue as to what it was that made her cup runneth over. Feeling her enthusiasm, he paused then coolly changed the subject. So, how's work?"

"Philip, you're changing the subject. Tell me what brings you this way. This is not like you to just show up out of the blue. It's not like you live right down the block. So, tell me already."

"I will but right now I'd like to get out of these clothes, maybe take a shower if that's alright with you. I left New York, had an unexpected call, had to fly to Atlanta, missed my return flight and was on standby when I decided to let you know the good news in person. But the sight of you makes my news pales in comparison to you. The sight of you has taken everything out of me," he grinned.

"You're playing with me, Philip and you know how I hate when you do that."

"No different than the last time I was here and you decided you wanted to play games with me," he said laughing. "Course now that I'm all better maybe we could switch roles."

"Oh so you are all better and what about Monica? Is this gonna be a three-some this time."

"Don't do threesomes but you might wanna call her. She mentioned wanting to invest if something came along that I felt was a sure-shot. I don't know how she's fixed for cash but she might wanna get in on this. That is if it's alright with you?"

"Oh, so that's what this is all about. You just wanna see Monica again. Is that it?"

Philip wondered if maybe he'd come on a little too fast or maybe a little too strong and knowing how perceptive Alexis was decided to pull back some.

"I must admit that she makes a nice supporting actor but I like the stars baby, not the second runner ups."

There that should do it. He was playing to her ego now, flattering her and she was at once taken back. What Monica had said was true. She didn't necessarily want him but he couldn't just walk away on his own. She had to dismiss him but there was no way in the world he was going to dismiss her, especially for someone like Monica who wasn't even in her league.

"Oh, for a minute I thought you were brushing me off and putting me in the already completed file," she laughed knowing full well that she had the boy's nose wide open and that he was hers, hook, line and sinker.

"That is what you told me to do though."

"What's that?"

"You suggested that Monica was feelin' me above and beyond and well that I should think about seeing her."

"I said that?"

"You did."

"Now that you mention it," she smiled, "I do remember vaguely suggesting that. And you gave it some thought," she asked the smiling now leaving.

"I did."

"Consider it—I mean—seeing Monica?" Alexis asked her concern growing.

"I certainly did," he said watching her anger grow before grabbing her in his arms. "Thought about the possibility for all of half-a-heartbeat."

"And what did you come up with?" she asked.

"Came up with the fact that I've invested too much time and energy in you, Ms. LeBrandt to even consider having you push me away now. You know I'm crazy about you Alexis and I had to ask myself where in the hell you come up with such hair-brained schemes as throwing in the towel and fixing me up with Monica."

Philip pulled her towards him and kissed her full and hard. He felt her go limp in his arms and wondered if Alexis LeBrandt might have a weakness after all. Releasing he turned and grabbed his suitcase and headed for the shower.

"Philip."

"Yeah, babe."

"I'm going to call Monica but do me a favor."

"Anything. You name it."

"Well she's a bit overwrought with not being able to get a man and I think she really has her sights set on you. I told her that I'd do everything I could on her behalf to let you know how she felt so if you don't mind let's keep the intimacy on the down low. I don't want her to think that I've gone back on my word or anything like that. Might even want to flirt with her a little. Give her the idea that there's still a window of opportunity, if you get my drift."

Philip listened from the hallway before heading to the bathroom and turning on the water. As he stepped into the shower he was still having a hard time grasping what she'd just told him.

The warm water felt good and he wondered how long it would take him to wash away the memory of Alexis when this was all over.

A week or so ago she hadn't given him the time of day other than to push him off on Monica and request that he throw a little sex her way when he was in town as well. Now he was certain that the reality of losing him caused her to change her mind. Or perhaps it was the possibility of something new and grand being in the works and she wanted to keep him closer than ever. Whatever it was he was sure it had nothing to do with him. As usual it was all about Alexis. He and Monica were nothing but pawns in one big chess game.

As he stepped out of the shower into the sauna like bathroom Alexis poked her head in the door and grinned. Grabbing a towel in a vain attempt to cover himself he wondered what could be so damn important that she couldn't wait 'til he finished.

"I can't wait 'til this is over so I can have some of that she said, staring at his naked body.

"Most people knock?" he said angrily before catching himself.

"*Sorry!* What? Too many horror pictures," she said sarcastically. "Just wanted you to know that I called your girl and she said she had to make a stop but she was on her way. Oh, and by the way, Philip, I don't mean to beat a dead horse and I'm not sure if I told you or not but Monica is working for me now so please try not to be too affectionate right through here or at least while she's here. She's really had a hard time with men and I don't want her to get the impression that I'm stealing her newest heartthrob away from her."

"Not a problem," he said only half hearing her.

Philip didn't know why he let Alexis rattle him so but for some reason she grated on his last nerve and he wondered if her rejection of him had something to do with it. She had never had any attention of doing anything but using him and he knew that or at least after awhile he'd come to that conclusion and ever since then he simply detested her…

Philip stopped, hesitated for a brief moment before her words registered. 'Working for her? How was that possible and when had all this started? In what capacity? Monica hadn't mentioned anything of the sort. He couldn't call or even speak and tonight was out of the question. Alexis could never know they'd been in contact with each other or it would blow the whole thing. But working for her… Perhaps that would explain the sudden turnaround in Monica's behavior. Until he knew more, he would not only have to be conscious of Alexis, but Monica as well.'

Philip dressed rapidly throwing on a navy blue, cardigan and blazer to match, his favorite charcoal gray pants and the black penny loafers with the tassels dangling. He looked ready for the cover of GQ.

"Philip, Monica's here are you dressed?"

"Be right out," he said noticing that despite her advice, Alexis was already starting the charade. Now Monica would be wondering why he was undressed. Splashing on a little of the Red cologne he was so fond of he stepped into the living room and approached Monica as if he hadn't seen her in years.

"Okay, you two that's enough hugging. You two get any closer and you'll wind up back in the bed again," Alexis laughed.

"That's not a bad thought," Phillip replied and then was sorry he had.

Neither Philip nor Monica appreciated the comment and it showed. Monica sat down on the living room couch next to Philip and he eyed her wearily. She was dressed better than he'd ever seen her with a beige pants suit, cream colored blouse that contrasted nicely and a pair of beige flats with the back out. Her hair was pinned up in the back in a bun and though it resembled his fourth grade school teacher Ms. Divacchio he had to admit that Ms. Divacchio had never looked quite that good.

"I take it we're all drinking?" Alexis asked as she headed for the bar.

Alexis stood with her back towards them and Philip arched his eyebrows in fond appreciation of her outfit and was surprised when a large bulge began to grow in the front of his trousers. Monica smiled as she noticed the tent that now raised the crotch of Philip's pants then leaned over and patted it gently and whispered, smiling, "down boy, now's not the time, there's work to be done."

Philip, more than a little embarrassed, grinned as well.

"Philip just dropped in Monica. Says he has some earth-shattering news that just couldn't wait and refused to breathe a word of it to me until you got here. I don't know what you've done to him but I wish you would give him the thumbs up. I'm just dying to know what it is. But first I'd like to apologize for the way I acted the last time I was in your company."

"Apology accepted," they said in unison.

Alexis handed them their glasses then held hers up to propose a toast.

"Here's to good friends, profitable business ventures and long and fruitful lives."

"Here, here," said Monica a little more reserved than usual.

"And to new partnerships," Philip added.

"So is that what this is all about?" Alexis asked.

"Quite possibly," Philip replied. "Shall I begin?"

That was Monica's cue and she was right on time and Philip had to smile at her adeptness.

"Let's hold all the business and talk of partnerships until after dinner. I just got off work and my head is spinning. Can we just relax for a few before we get into anything serious?"

"Damn, girl. I've been sitting here twiddling my thumbs on the edge of my chair waiting for you to get here so I can hear the news that had Philip fly all the way out here and you want to wait 'til after dinner? I know he's anxious as well if he flew here instead of calling. I've known him for close to forever and if it's one thing I know is that there's not a lot that shakes him up. Whatever it is that made him get us together, it's gotta be big. Now, can he please tell us before I have a heart attack and die?" Alexis pleaded.

"Maybe Monica's right. Yeah, I'm excited but then I just left Atlanta and I guess that's why but maybe we should grab a bite to eat first. In my hurry to get here I didn't even think about dinner but now that you mention it, I'm famished." Philip added.

"See what you've gone and done now, Monica." Alexis said playfully.

"Do you two always bicker and fight," Philip asked jokingly.

"Ever since I've known her she's been under the impression that she's my mother," Monica quipped.

"You needed someone to look after you so you didn't wind up hurting yourself," Alexis replied.

"And how was I so fortunate as to get you as foster mom of the year?" Monica asked smiling contemptuously.

"No one else would take the job and I just felt sorry for you," Alexis quipped.

"Oh, God why have you forsaken me?" Monica replied her eyes searching the heavens, "and left me with this evil ogre. Dear Lord I ask you."

"Evil ogre?" Alexis laughed. "Let me tell you Philip. You will never anyone—and I mean anyone—in all your born days moodier than this child here. Her sister and I used to hide from her on certain days when we were little and went away to summer camp because she was so damn evil."

"You need to stop, Alexis. Philip doesn't know me that well and you're giving him a bad impression of me already," Monica commented seemingly embarrassed by the truth of Alexis' statement.

"If he knew what I knew he wouldn't have invited you here at all. I have to ask why I bother myself sometimes." Alexis laughed.

"She seems sweet to me," Philip added.

"That's because you don't really know her. They just did that kid's movie based on Monica's life. What was the name of it?" Alexis asked knowing full well what the punch line was. "Oh, yeah. Shrek. That's her. She's always walking around with her head down, evil, ready to snap somebody's head off with that tongue of hers at the drop of a hat. She's just being nice cause you're here."

"Thanks for putting in a good word, Alexis." Monica said laughing.

"Do I seem like that to you, Philip?" Monica asked.

"Well, now that you mention it..."

"Oh, go to hell, both of you. What is this? Gang up on Monica night? You're just jealous 'cause I'm looking so damn good tonight," she said standing and twirling around once for both to see.

"I have to admit, you do look rather nice Monica. *I'm lovin' that suit.*" Alexis said walking to the bar for a refill.

"*Jones of New York, baby. You like? Nothin' but the best. I got that from you 'Lexis.*" Monica said. *Had to stop on the way over here to grab something to wear. Nothing else fits.*"

"You're going to fade away to nothin' soon, if you keep going the way you're going.

"Another sixteen pounds, baby and I'll be satisfied." Monica yelled.

"You go girl! You sure you ain't bulimic or some shit?"

"No, just Curves baby girl and a lot of hard work." Monica replied as she sat back down.

"Been doing them two party push ups again, huh?" Alexis teased.

"I'm tired of telling you to go to hell. Next thing you say smart, I'm gonna jump up the way Henry Lucious used to do and spank that ass for runnin' off at the mouth in front of Philip here."

Philip's head popped up. He'd been sitting there quietly, quite content and trying not to get involved in their ongoing rivalry and was surprised to hear his name come up.

"And who's Henry Lucious?" he asked so as not to appear to be ignoring the two women.

"That's her daddy. Henry Lucious used to walk 'Lexis to and from school from pre-school when I met her straight through to high school. We used to all feel sorry for her ass back then. Alexis couldn't do shit. If 'Lexis even thought about looking at a boy Henry Luscious would be in that ass. Pick up a rock or a stone. Henry Lucious would be in that ass. I'm telling you Henry Lucious did not play. Me and a bunch of the other kids would follow 'Lexis and her daddy home from school. We used to walk right behind them. I mean not more than two steps behind her and call her names and pick at her until she was ready to fight and she was always ready to fight somebody over something. Over anything... Do you hear me? Anything. That's why Henry Lucious use to have to walk her to and from school because she had this wicked ass temper. Oh, but then I guess you've seen that side of her. You see, that's why I remained so calm. I've seen that shit countless times. The funny thing is, she couldn't beat nobody but she always wanted to fight. Anyway, we'd walk behind her and pick at her 'til she couldn't take it anymore and then as soon as she'd turn around to say something, Henry Lucious would say, *WHOOP* and slap her upside that big head of hers and we'd fall down in the street and roll." Monica screamed.

"How'd he do it?" Philip asked the tears rolling down his face as well.

"He said, *WHOOP*. Just like that," Monica repeated showing Philip against an imaginary head, as she and Philip doubled over n the couch.

"Everyday it was the same thing. Everyday we'd pick at her dumb ass and everyday she'd turn around to say something back and everyday Henry Lucious would say, *WHOOP* upside her big head and everyday we'd roll out into the street and just cry watching her big head flop over to the side," Monica said the tears rolling down her face as she thought of Alexis' head jerking to the side.

"Go to hell, you witch!" Alexis screamed.

"Come here, sweetie," Monica said beckoning to Alexis, "does your head still hurt, sweetie?

I really truly believe that all those whoopins really did something to this child though and when I tell Mr. Henry now we both agree that the girl ain't been right since."

"Monica Manning you are the absolute worst." Alexis said laughing.

"Enough of the walk down memory lane though. I've got to agree with Philip, right through here," Alexis said, "I am a little on the hungry side myself. Anybody feel like Italian. I was thinking about maybe ordering in."

"Sounds good to me," Philip said.

"That's fine," Monica agreed still laughing.

"Well I can call Bella Villa. They deliver and the food's absolutely scrumptious unless you know of someplace better," she said looking at Monica.

"No this is your side of town. You know it far better than I do," Monica replied.

"Okay, well let me take your orders before I call. You know how Negroes do. Get on phone and start changing the order three or four times after they hear the nigga in front of them order somethin' better and I just ain't got the time for that shit wit' y'all trying to make me look stupid."

"Listen to her trying to sound like she's from the 'hood. Did you hear that, Philip?" Monica asked.

"Better not Henry Lucious hear that," Philip said.

*"No, siree! Be like, **WHOOP!**"* Monica said doubling over again.

"Are you two going to order or not?" Alexis said smiling good naturedly.

Philip wiped his eyes and placed his order. "I guess I'll have the chicken cacciatore," he said still grinning.

"And I'm going to have the veal scaloppini, as usual and Monica I guess you'll have the, *'WHEW! Don't I look good Curves salad*

369

with no dressing. Okay let met call that in?" she giggled as she pirouetted in the middle of the living room floor the way Monica had done showing off her new outfit only moments before.

"That's alright, 'Lexis," Monica smiled as Alexis placed the orders.

Dinner had been better than excellent and along with the two bottles of Chianti which the women consumed there was nothing left to do other than sit back and relax.

Philip served coffee after dinner but refrained from giving Alexis more than a half a cup so as not to negate the affect of the wine and began his presentation.

"Recently I received a tip from a rather reliable source that the bottom is about to fall out of the market." He said.

Alexis who had replaced Philip on the couch sat straight up.

"What? I thought you were here to give us some good news," she screamed the panic evident in her eyes.

"Would you be still and let the man finish," Monica chided.

"Be still. Girl, you don't know what I have invested!"

"Don't you think that if there was some bad news, Philip would have told you before now? *Stop being so damn impulsive. Goodness.* Go ahead Philip. I apologize for her rudeness," Monica said cheerfully obviously feeling the effects of the Chianti.

"In any case over the next four or five months we're going to see a big turn around and I'm afraid it's not going to be good. However, there are alternatives. With both the interest rates and mortgage rates at an all-time low there couldn't be a better time to invest in real estate. The only problem is, is that because of the economy most people can't afford to invest in real estate or anything else at this point. If however, there are some that can invest then there's no better time than now.

Alexis was listening intently, hanging on each and every word. She knew Philip was absolutely right about the real estate market. She could personally attest to the growth potential but he still hadn't said anything that was of real value so she waited, wondering what he had in store for her this time and wished the hell he'd hurry and get to the point. She was sure he was going slow on Monica's account and really wished her fat ass hadn't been there at all. That and the fact that she had had too much wine. Sitting through a whole bunch of mumbo jumbo irritated her but she remained quiet and hoped that he would get on with it.

"Since I've been back from London I've been studying the trends and met a group of financiers who are and have been taking groups of people, conglomerates and giving them the opportunity to invest in certain real estate ventures which have proved quite beneficial on a short-term basis and I believe that's what we're interested in. An investment with a high yield and a quick turnaround. That means we see our profits quickly as opposed to a safer investment with a lower yield over a longer period of time. The only difference is the size of the investment. With a short term investment it always—well—in most instances it requires a sizeable investment."

"And what do you mean when you say sizeable?" Alexis asked. He was talking her language now. Dollars and dividends.

"Well right now we're looking at somewhere in the neighborhood of one point five to three mil," Philip said before pausing to take as sip of his drink and let the numbers settle in.

Monica sat back and pretended to slap herself upside the head and said, "*WHOOP*, that certainly takes me out of the running," and laughed before sitting all the way back on the couch.

Alexis, was on the other hand, in deep thought and you could almost see the wheels turning as she calculated as best she could with the Chianti fighting every step of the way.

"And what's the return on an investment like that," she asked.

"Well, we're looking in the neighborhood of somewhere between six point five and seven million on a three million dollar investment," he said calmly.

"My goodness. You don't play do you Philip?" Monica said.

Alexis wished Monica would shut the hell up. She was small potatoes and wondered why Philip had even bothered to invite her.

She certainly didn't have that kind of money. Hell, Alexis wasn't even sure if she could raise that kind of capital herself but if it was all Philip said it was and the returns were that great she knew that if it had to happen then she'd find someway to make it come to fruition. But then there was Monica running her mouth again.

"Philip darling, you guys are playing high stakes poker here with chips that I can't even dream of so let me ask you something?"

"Go right ahead, Monica."

"Why in the hell are you telling me this?" she asked sitting up on the edge of the sofa.

Alexis laughed, "I feel you girl."

Philip paused, looked at both women and then continued.

"I'm not sure anyone in this room has three million to invest on a whim but I've just been down to Atlanta to see the site and the plans and although we may not have the money individually if we pool our resources and perhaps even go as far as to borrow against our assets then we may just be able to pull this thing off. As you probably are well aware of, Atlanta is the fastest growing city for Blacks and a whole new development is being built on Atlanta's perimeter. One hundred thousand homes are being built as we speak. In the center of it all is a prime piece of real estate on which will be built Atlanta's newest mall. It will be comprised of stores that are unique to the southern landscape but stores that are proven draws. I'm talking Macy's, Gimbels, Sak's Fifth Avenue, and Bloomingdales just to name a few that are already committed. Stores like Old Navy and lesser known stores have put in bids but have already been turned down.

What we're looking at is an upscale mall with some large department stores such as the one's I've named as well as your designer shops like Prada, Versace and Gucci all of whom will cater to the nouveau rich, the so-called Black bourgeoisie. This is only the third mall of this type in the country and like the other two will be Black owned, run and operated. The brothers that are putting this thing together along with my help are only offering this to me because I had the foresight to back them when they first got started.

I put them in contact with the right people so they could accrue what was needed to assume a small businessman's loan. Believe me, they are no longer small business men. I have for you Hoover's online financial stat sheet which you can obtain free on any home pc that gives you the breakdown of their holdings as well as their growth and other essential items needed before making an investment of this type. Now I will go as far as to say that I have a little over one point two million at the ready and am looking for an additional one point eight to do business. That's not to say that I expect for either of you ladies to beg, borrow and steal to get the difference. What I am merely offering you is an opportunity to fly down and take a look before either of you decide if you have the slightest interest. That's also not to say that the price may not go up substantially as building materials and other things arise. But the top should not exceed another half million at most.

It's a helluva of an investment opportunity if you ask me with a tremendous upside. I guess that's why I'm so excited. That and the fact that I just saw the site and met with the architects. Everything's state of the art but that's not the kicker. The best part of the whole thing is the turnaround. The mall is scheduled to open its doors in 2011. That's three years. The day the doors open is the day you will see your money compounded. That's three years ladies."

Both women sat up. To say they were stunned would be an understatement.

"I understand why you are so successful at what you do," Monica said smiling. "I felt like I was in the boardroom. Very professional, Mr. Dalton."

"Oh, Lord you've got her swooning again, Philip. Has she swooned for you yet?"

"Is that the Scarlet O'Hara impression?"

"Oh, God then she has swooned for you. I bet if you checked them bloomers she's got on she's probably soaking wet." Alexis laughed.

"Alexis stop. You're embarrassing me." Monica said.

"But really how in the hell do you think I could possibly afford to take part when you're talking those kinds of numbers?" Monica asked.

"It's funny people ask me that same question each and every day. And this is what I tell them. Money is not about paper. Money is an idea. For instance you have a 401K, probably some IRA's, maybe even a few small investments tucked away. You don't want to touch those. What you want to do is borrow against them. I'll give you an example. I hope you don't mind me using you as an example, Alexis."

"You're among family—even if that is the Black sheep you're talking to at this moment—anyway go ahead..."

"Like I was saying, Alexis is buying this condo or perhaps it's paid for..."

"Hah, that's a joke," Alexis shouted. "Sorry. Proceed."

"Alexis, please. I'm trying to learn something." Monica said.

"Then you're definitely in the wrong place. The short bus stops on the corner though. It'll take you where you need to go." Alexis commented.

""In any case, Alexis is purchasing this condo and if she's been extended the credit to purchase then the bank looks at her as a fairly secure risk and will allow her to purchase other properties based solely on the fact that she has holdings that are in good standing and as long as she remains in good standing she can continue to borrow and the more she borrows the greater her credibility is and the more she can borrow. Do you understand?"

"It's called collateral Einstein," Alexis added.

"So, you see the notion of money as most people know is not really what it appears to be at all."

"So what you're telling me is that I can use my so-called holdings to go into this thing?"

"Precisely." Philip responded.

"But even with that, I still don't have—what did you say—one point eight million?" Monica replied.

"You don't have to. I'm just throwing the package out to you. You invest what you feel comfortable with and your return will reflect that. But at twice your initial investment I thought I'd give you the opportunity to come in with me before I take it back to the boys on the block and let them have a piece of the pie. I've got a couple of friends, two White guys in the office who have been begging to invest but I've got 'em on hold presently.

They went down last week to view the property and are chomping at the bit but they don't need it. And the whole thing is that we're hoping to keep it a Black thing in the main so I thought I'd give you a crack at it and then if I fall a little short of what I need then—hey— they're in. What can I say? I hate to do it but I can't risk losing out on this. Opportunities like this come once in a lifetime and I'd be all but a fool to pass on this one.

In any case, I'd like for you two to at least go take a look next weekend. Talk to the brothers. Get your feet wet. See if it appeals to you and get back to me. Then next Monday, I'm going to put my bid in and let the chips fall where they may."

Philip took a deep breath, went to the bar and poured himself a drink. There, that was it. It was on Monica now and so far she'd been exemplary.

"Damn, Alexis you're quiet. Let me hear from you. I don't know anything about real estate or investing and much as I hate to say it if you think it's a good idea then I'd like to take a stab at it."

"I don't know what to say, Monica. This isn't something that you just jump into. Philip's talking an awful lot of money. More money than I've ever imagined investing in any one single venture. Usually I like to keep the little assets that I have sort of spread out. That way if something doesn't work over here I always have something else to fall back on. This would mean me liquidating everything or taking out an astronomical loan on all my holdings— everything I own—and not to doubt Philip but if for some reason this doesn't matriculate—well then—who knows. So I don't know what to tell you."

"Well, I guess that's fair enough," Monica replied.

"Like I said this is not a decision that you rush into and I'm sorry that I just came to you with it being that everything needs to be consummated by the Monday after next but it's something that I was excited about and I thought I should share it. If you do or don't take the opportunity I understand fully but whatever you do, don't make a hasty decision when it comes to something of this magnitude especially if it's going to have such a profound effect on your future. Give it some time, mull it over and get back to me. Don't feel bad if you have to decline. Like I said, there are a few people chomping at the bit and may be a 'lil more fluid when it comes to a project of this magnitude. I just thought I'd give you the first crack at it is all. Anybody want a drink?"

"No, I believe I've had quite enough," Alexis mumbled.

"I'm good for now," Monica said.

"Feel like I took all the life out of the party," Philip said smiling. "Why's everyone look so down and depressed? I thought I was bringing you good news."

"I'm not depressed but I do have a question and it's rather of a personal nature, if you don't mind?" Monica said.

"No he will not marry you because you have a big butt and a new suit on. Now hush so I can think," Alexis chirped. "Now Philip what did you say the overall cost was?"

"Close to three million."

"And the return would be?"

"Between four point five and six million but that's a conservative estimate. It could be quite a bit more but no less," he replied.

Alexis went to the dining room, poured herself another glass of Chianti and returned to the Queen Anne chair, kicked off her shoes and curled up in it.

"Now may I ask my question, your highness?" Monica said smiling at her girlfriend.

"As I said Philip, this may be a little personal..."

"Would you go ahead and ask the damn question already?" Alexis shouted.

"I was just wondering before I was so rudely interrupted what your net worth was?" Monica asked.

Philip who had been pouring over some paperwork, and sipping his drink at the same time sprayed alcohol all over the place in disbelief. He couldn't believe Monica had gone there.

"Excuse me?" he asked grinning.

"Girl ain't got no more tact than a wet dishrag," Alexis chided. "You know, Monica, I really and truly wonder what's wrong with you sometimes. You don't ask people how much their worth."

"You do if you want to know," Monica replied, "See I ain't all highfalutin like you. To me it's all a matter of common sense. A man comes in here that I hardly know and asks me to invest my life savings in a venture I know little or nothing about. I want to know everything about that man before I drop a penny into anything. Now, if you'll excuse me I believe I asked Philip, not Alexis what his net worth was."

Philip eyed Monica wearily. This was not in the plan and he had no idea where she was going with it but decided to go along.

"Well, if you're talking about how much money I could put my hands on today then I don't truthfully know." Philip answered still puzzled.

"No what I'm asking is on the day that you place the bid how much money will you be able to raise on your behalf?" Monica asked.

"I believe I answered that earlier. The best that I can do is somewhere around one point two million."

"There she goes trying to get married again," Alexis interjected.

"One point two million dollars is a lot of money Philip and how much of that one point two million dollars is yours?" Monica asked.

"Every penny," Philip replied.

"And is that money raised as a result of stocks, holdings and other investments you have?" Monica asked.

"Damn Monica if you can't do it then you can't do it. Ain't no reason to put the man on trial. You sound like the damn IRS or some fuckin' body trying to hang him up on income tax evasion or some shit."

"Go ahead Monica. I'm curious to see where you're going with all of this." Philip replied smiling knowing exactly where Monica was going now. It was a shrewd ploy that couldn't have been pulled off any other way than at the spur of the moment in order for it to have any authenticity.

"I'm just curious to know what percentage of what you own in stocks and bonds and other holdings you are contributing to this little venture of yours is all."

"One hundred percent," Philip replied.

"So, on Tuesday when you go to work what will you be left with?"

"The fact that I have my job and the idea that I will receive a paycheck on Friday?"

"And in two years since you've been there how much have you earned in commissions?"

"Oh, I'd say somewhere in the neighborhood of a million. And how much is your annual salary?" Monica asked.

Alexis was on the edge of her seat now.

"A little less than a hundred thousand a year," he replied.

"So what you're telling me is that the majority of the money you make is from investing for other people?"

"Precisely."

"So what the hell are they making if you've earned a million in two years," Monica asked.

"I hate to even think about it but that's why I'm branching out on my own now. I'm a little tired of putting money in other people's pockets while I get the drippings." Philip added.

"I'd hardly call a million drippings but answer my question."

"Which was?"

"How much have you made for them?" she asked.

"Oh, I'd have to venture and say somewhere in the neighborhood of a hundred million give or take."

"And you are considered to be one of the top stockbrokers on Wall Street?"

"Depends on who you ask but I would like to think so."

"You're much too modest, Philip. I read an article about you in the Wall Street Journal, not more than a week ago that's says, and this is according to a poll taken by your peers, who are predominantly White that you're the hottest young prospect on the Wall Street scene today. And that's among primarily middle and older aged conservative White men. I think there's a lot be said for that."

Alexis was listening intently and could hardly believe what she was hearing.

"You reading the Wall Street Journal or Philip being in the Wall Street Journal. I don't know which one is the bigger surprise," she added, "Why didn't you say something, Philip?"

"What is there to say? It was just a small article," he replied quite embarrassed with all the hoopla.

"Alexis do you mind if I finish grilling Philip so I can get a sense of what I need to do? Tell me something Philip have you made any particularly bad investments since you've been with the brokerage?" Monica asked.

"Of course, I'm human. Besides, that's just all part of the game. You have to be cognizant of that when you begin. With market fluctuations and the like it's difficult to be one hundred per cent sure about every hunch and move you make. But sure, I've made a couple of bad calls. In fact, I've made one huge mistake this year already."

"Bad investment?" Alexis asked.

"You could say that. In fact I would say it was probably the worst one I've made yet," he replied.

"Did you lose a bundle?" Alexis asked.

"It's not always about the money, Alexis. I lost someone I really and truly had faith in *over* money and that's a lot worse and hurts a whole hell of a lot deeper than losing a few dollars. You can always make money but good friends, like you and Monica are a rarity," he said to answer her question.

Monica smiled knowing exactly what Philip was alluding to. Alexis though hanging on Philip's every syllable seemed to miss the irony altogether.

Chapter 17

It was close to one o'clock when Monica finished giving Philip the once over and all three were tired beyond belief. Philip had thrown a lot at them and Monica had performed wonderfully well in Philip's eye. The questions she threw at him in the end were both poignant and resonated something Philip knew without having to be told.

Monica was astute in a way that both he and Alexis lacked. She understood people and the way they thought. That was her gift. She knew that although Philip's proposal probably worked well with the Wall Street crowd that were there solely to invest it was quite a different story for two women who had at no time in their life could attest to having an extra dollar to just throw around.

Alexis despite having made a small fortune thanks to Philip, was hardly a high stakes player. In fact, the more she accrued the fewer chances she was bound to take. And if he had had the power to invest one point eight on Alexis' behalf without her knowing it and called to celebrate a windfall that would have been one thing. Taking every last dime and delving into a completely different venture was something else altogether and would take a bit of convincing. And this Philip was not ready for.

Still, Monica knew that Alexis had always been in awe of high stakes players. Monica also knew that the idea that Philip had a net worth of more than a million dollars elevated him in Alexis' eyes. The idea that he was the top man in his field and was willing to invest every dime that he'd ever made on his own behalf and in his own future was also a feather in his cap.

Not only that, but the idea that this Black man had been entrusted with millions of dollars to invest by White men in a White only venue and made close to a hundred million for them spoke volumes as well. The Wall Street Journal's pronouncement and the confirmation by his peers didn't hurt either. No these were all closing arguments presented to sway the jury of one who sat there second guessing this young Black man's every word.

But if Monica was an astute judge of character—and she was—and if she knew her girlfriend— and she did—then she knew that these were things Alexis respected above and beyond the principles involved. If there was a turning point—a way in which to close the deal and bring her into the fold then Monica knew these would be the key arguments.

Walking Monica to the car that evening when she insisted on going home and Alexis had not opposed Philip was unusually calm and reserved although he praised her constantly on her late inning ploy.

"Beautiful, save babe. Simply beautiful. I could feel myself losing her until you jumped in and saved me from myself," he said although his usual smile was nowhere to be found on this cold and windy evening.

"Well thank you, Mr. Dalton. You weren't too bad yourself."

"That's something I do every day but not with same panache that I saw when you took over the floor. It's almost as if you were meant to sell and I'm going to be honest with you, Monica. There is nothing harder in the world to sell than an idea. You walk into a department store and see something and all five senses come to the forefront. First you see it, then you smell it, feel it, taste it and finally after you do all that the salesperson let's you know all about the product you've just experienced. I guess what I'm trying to say is that it's tangible. An idea, a concept is not. You have to almost conjure up an image that has people doing those same things in their mind and that's no easy task but you pulled it off with a flair that would make any broker proud. Ever think about real estate. That would be a breeze for someone of your ilk."

"I'm not sure I would agree, Philip. This was not a case of selling a dream or an idea. This was more along the lines of finding a persons' aspirations, as well as their foibles and exploiting them. Knowing Alexis as long as I have gave me some insight into key points that you were overlooking. You see I think the most important thing in selling something and you can probably attest to this better than I since this is your field of expertise but I think that most important aspect of selling would be knowing the buyer or in your case knowing your client. Most of the time the seller doesn't get that opportunity but in a situation like this it's easy because I know her so well.

You see, chances are I probably couldn't sell water in the desert to anyone else but I know Alexis. I know she's always wanted to be wealthy and therefore is captivated by anyone with money and it's not just the money. It's the fame and the notoriety that she believes accompanies the money. But what she really desires more than anything else is to have the confirmation and respect of her peers. And I hate to say this but if they're White then that really gives her credibility. It's really sad but the land and the promise of a mall run and operated by Black folks really has no affect on her whatsoever. She has no positive self-concept, no self-awareness, no pride in herself, so she can't possibly have any pride in her Blackness. You could have saved the sales pitch aside from the profit margin. All that matters to her are the numbers. Nothing else really matters to her at this juncture in her life."

"Well, thank you Ms. Manning for putting all of that into perspective." Philip replied.

"Not a problem. But speaking of problems, I don't know if you're aware of it or not but she's going to take you to task tonight and tomorrow. That little so-called dismissal she gave you a week ago is no longer valid. You've sparked her interest once again. The idea of her making that kind of money is going to drive her into an absolute frenzy. Trust me Philip she's going to be all over you tonight. Just the idea that you have that kind of money makes you tantamount to Jesus in her eyes and little ol' Monica will just have to find her own man after tonight."

"That bad, huh?"

"Worse. Trust me. She's going to be all over you like a cheap suit. Pardon the cliché. That's why I really didn't want to get involved with you on a sexual basis and kept suggesting that we keep it platonic," Monica lied making Alexis the fall guy once again.

"And what does Alexis have to do with you and I?" Philip asked trying to understand Monica's reasoning.

"Are you that naive? With the proposal you just threw out and the type of money you're looking to have her invest you've basically reduced yourself to being a retainer. She's going to endear herself to you in every way she can. You've rekindled any embers that might've been smoldering. All she sees me as is interference now. Believe it or not this is worse than finding us in bed together. She all but told me that I can have you in any way I deem necessary but stay out of her business matters with you.

You see she didn't want anything to do with you until she caught us in bed together. It sparked her interest. You were hers and I was going somewhere she hadn't been and she couldn't have that. She figured that maybe there was something there that she hadn't come across. With your proposal tonight you've stimulated every nerve in her body. I don't know if you know it or not but you've elevated yourself right to the top tier of the thing she most covets. And of course the one thing she covets more than anything else is the dollar bill.

She's going to do everything that she can to suck the very marrow from your bones if there's any possibility of her getting rich. Funny thing, she kept mentioning marriage when I was grilling you on your finances but the truth of the matter is she would gladly accept your proposal if you went in there right now and proposed." Monica said.

"I think you're carrying it a bit far, now sweetheart," Philip laughed.

"Laugh if you want to, but you don't know what you're dealing with," Monica replied lighting a cigarette. "You know I really don't know what you're up to. And my gut feeling tells me at this point that I don't want to know anymore than I already do. I will say this much though. If you really think that Alexis is going to invest in you then you have to know that you're going to have to sleep with her to insure it working. I know this and you may be unaware of this but that's the reason I suggested we remain as friends."

"And if I refuse?"

"You'll scare up some doubts in her mind and you'll have an extremely hard time convincing her that you're in this for her and because you're in love with her," Monica said rather matter-of-factly.

"She has to be in control. She needs to know that everything you do is because you're weak for her and can't bear to live without her. Throw her a curve and refuse to sleep with her and she'll have to wonder why the hell you want to be with her to begin with. You see Alexis' lure is that men desire her for her body. She doesn't have the self-confidence that she exudes or pretends to have. She just uses her body as a means of procuring anything she wants. You tell her that that doesn't interest you and she's lost, dumbfounded and apt to be suspicious. That's the only way men tend to approach her and even though she detests men she realizes that this is her best asset and puts up a pretty good facade to get what she wants."

"You know her, don't you?"

"Like a book. Anyway, like I said, I thought I wanted to know the plan but you were right about one thing. I didn't need to know because if my suspicions are correct then you're playing a very dangerous game," Monica said as she hit the alarm on her car. "And then again, I wish I had slept with you one more time for old time's sake."

"So what do I do?"

"I really can't answer that Philip although I do believe that you were being honest when you told me that you loved me. I just don't know how much you love me. I have this gnawing feeling that you and your girl both have this overwhelming need to win at any cost. I'd also be willing to bet that you don't handle defeat very well. You could very well walk away from this thing and chalk it all up to experience. You don't need the money. That's for sure. But you can't let it go. Both of you have a penchant for vengeance and can't see the brighter side of life for trying to make someone pay who ultimately wronged you and that's sad."

"Monica..."

"Don't say it, Philip? I know you want to tell me that if anything occurs or she puts you in a compromising position that you'll call me or grab a cab because you don't want to jeopardize our relationship but save all that. You're not going to be happy with my suggestion and if you don't come to a decision that you're happy with then this is going to gnaw at you for the rest of your days so go ahead and handle your business."

"You see, I wasn't going to say that at all."

"Oh, perhaps that's what I was hoping you'd say."

"Maybe I should agree with you but I've come too far to turn back now and maybe you're right but this is something I have to do. And I guess I'll see you tomorrow afternoon," he said.

"Don't come with the idea that my feelings are changed. Your staying here has made it clear that we can't be anymore than friends. Is that understood, Philip?"

"I hear you. Doesn't mean I won't try," he said grinning, "but before you go, let me ask you something."

"Yes?"

"Alexis mentioned that you were working for her."

Monica explained the situation with James and was sorry she had almost as soon as she finished telling him. It did no more than add fuel to the fire and he hated to think of Alexis cuddling up to him while still trying to pull her ex back into the realm of possibilities. The fact that she would even consider soliciting Monica who happened to be Monica's friend to do the surveillance only went to show that she had no ethics or scruples.

He'd looked surprised when Monica first told him that she she'd accepted Alexis' offer. But after explaining that she had no intention of doing any more than taking Alexis' money Philip felt a little better.

Of course she'd take Alexis' money as sort of a backhand slap in the face but she had no intention of following her friend James anywhere. Philip fell out laughing when she told him that the only thing she did for the five hundred dollars a week was to make sure she ate out more than once a week or twice a week to have something to put on her expense account. The only other effort she put forth to collect her pay was to switch cars with her sister for the week just in case Alexis came snooping around to see if she was on the job. Philip died laughing and Monica truly hoped that that in itself would be enough revenge and though he found the whole situation humorous Philip hardly seemed satisfied.

Philip promised her he'd see her the following day and Monica even went so far as to promise him she'd cater to his every wish if he'd get in the car now and forget about the revenge factor. When he refused she knew that she'd done all she could, kissed him on the cheek and headed home.

Back upstairs, Alexis had changed into a red see through night gown and a pair of red mules with fir that made her look like she'd stepped straight out of a Victoria Secrets catalog. The sight of her shook Philip and he had to remind himself that he was a man first and foremost and wasn't immune to beauty.

Philip quickly reminded himself that he was on a mission and had a job to do. This was the telling point. It was clearly evident that Alexis was trying to bring him back into the fold; reducing him to being no more than as Monica referred to him—her retainer.

What bothered him was that everything Monica told him up to this point had been on point and as he looked at Alexis something else rang out clear and true and he hated the fact that she had been so right. Alexis had every intention of making love. No, that was a misconception. There would be no love making.

Instead, Alexis would smother him with her seal of approval and in the morning he would wake up and be rendered helpless once again—perhaps even more helpless than before. He would do her bidding for her, make the safe investment with the high yield and pray that James would finally go away so that she could be his and his alone. Or he could play the role, he had assigned himself right up until the bitter end. But the fact that Monica would not be there ate at him. He thought about grabbing his bag and heading for the door but Alexis was there and the mere sight of this woman thinking she could manipulate him ate at him.

"Wanna join me for a nightcap before we call it a night or should I just bring the bottle in with us?"

'With us?' So, Monica had been right again. Confused and weary, Philip took a shot at Monica's theory. If there was any truth in her theory about Alexis' deep seated hatred of men then she should have no problem with not wanting to cater to him in bed.

"We have a lifetime for that 'Lexis. Right now I'm bushed all I want to do is get some shut-eye. I've got an early flight tomorrow," Philip said yawning.

"I like the way you said that, Philip."

"What's that?" He replied hoping she was referring to the part about his flight and being bushed.

"The part about us having a lifetime together. Oh, you alluded to it before but you've never come right out and said it. Do you think there's a possibility of that happening?"

"I don't know Alexis. I guess we'll just have to wait and see," he replied.

"And in the meantime, can I try and convince you. I don't know if Monica is clouding your memory or what. I know you spent an awful long time downstairs with her," Alexis said fishing.

Philip perked up when he heard the mere mention of Monica. "Oh, I think, matter-of-fact I'm almost sure she's going to invest in my proposal. She wanted to know the ins and outs of divesting her

IRA's and 401K so I gave her the skinny with the clause attached that I wasn't expecting or recommending that she drop her all in it just because I was doing so. I think that was the fact that pushed her over the edge."

"You're really that confident?" Alexis asked.

"Never been so sure of anything in all my life," he replied.

"And you're investing everything you have in it?" she asked trying to get a feel for his state of mind.

"Even borrowing a little from mom and dad to round off the numbers," he said cheerfully.

"And you'll be left with what?"

"Lunch money, well at least for a day or two," he chuckled.

"You know I never have any ready cash," she said waiting for Philip to give her the push to continue but he said nothing letting her know that he was finished with the conversation for the night. His dismissal of the subject only aroused her interest more as he hoped it would.

"But I could make up the difference you need if I were to borrow against my real estate holdings," she said.

This had been his plan all along and he felt a warm sensation glowing inside him that made him want to jump for joy but he remained calm.

"There's really no need for that Alexis. I don't know if I mentioned it but there are a couple of fellows at work that I kind of promised..."

Before he could finish she cut him off.

"I didn't want to say anything to arouse any jealousy with Monica being here knowing that she really isn't in the ballpark with the kind of money you're talking but like I said if I borrow against my properties I could probably come up with the cash by then and still let my stocks ride until you feel that it's a good time to pull out of the market," she said hoping that he would be glad to hear this bit of news but instead she was surprised to find that he was somehow cold and indifferent after having been so warm and excited only a few hours earlier.

"Why aren't you saying anything Philip? It's almost as if you don't want me as a part of this. Or was it Monica that this whole thing was intended for?"

"Come on sweetheart. You're starting to sound like you're jealous. And as fine as you are how could you ever be jealous of Monica? Perhaps you haven't noticed but there's light years difference between you two."

"Must not be a whole lot of difference. You slept with her."

"I slept with her because you gave me the impression that all I was to you was your broker and she pretty much confirmed that when she told me what a difficult time you were having getting over James."

"No, she didn't!" Alexis yelled.

"Don't get mad at her, baby. It's the same thing you were telling me at the time and after all I am a man and did you ever think that besides my obvious physical needs which you continually dismissed that I might have slept with her just to spite you and because I was tired of hearing about James?"

Alexis laughed.

"What are laughing at?" Philip asked.

"I'm laughing because that sounds exactly like some ol' off the wall shit that I probably would have pulled. And poor Monica paid the price again. I swear that girl is forever coming in for a raw deal."

"That's why I want her to invest so badly," Philip said, "I'm really trying to make up for the way that I used to her. You can't just go through life using people and I guess I feel a wee bit guilty about the whole thing," Philip said his head dropping.

"So how much does she have?"

"Well, looking at her IRA's and 401k combined I think we're looking at about two hundred grand."

"And when the deal is done she should have ten times that according to you?"

"Hell, that's a lot of cheddar and a lot of guilt for one roll in the hay with you. Shit, fuck the guilt. That shit is nothing new to Monica. A few drinks is usually all she gets and you're giving her in excess of two million. Must have been some damn good pussy." Alexis laughed.

"I should be filthy rich then with the money I'm putting up. Let you fuck me and make you feel guilty and Lord knows Robin Leach may have me on 'Lifestyles of the Rich and Famous'. Goodness gracious, Philip, at those rates why the hell am I sitting out here making small talk. C'mon and see how many times you can fuck me in the next three years 'til the dividend check comes rollin' in. Hell, by then, I could make Oprah look like small potatoes," Alexis said doubling over in laughter.

"That's not funny in the least, Alexis." Philip replied angrily. He was mad that he could see what he could not before as exposed her true colors."

"C'mon Philip can't you see what Monica is doing. You're thinking you're fucking her and you got fucked. I just happened to walk in and catch you. As soon as she found out you were a stockbroker and made a few dollars she tried to throw the pussy at you. That first night she was here and she claimed she didn't have any heat she was doing nothing more than sizing you up. You had to know she was trying to give it to you to wrap you up. She didn't bite her tongue. Even when I told her to stop she continued trying to toss it your way. And I wouldn't be surprised if she's calling you now at work and trying to get you to stop by her apartment. Trust me I know the girl. I've known her for thirty something years and bad as I hate to admit she's a whore who will fuck any man out there for a ring on her finger. And that she will readily admit. Now here you are trying to pull her in and make a few dollars because you feel guilty about using her for one night when men use her ass everyday for free."

"I didn't know," Philip said because there was no other way to respond and allow himself to still call himself a man when it was over.

"Look Philip, I'll put up her share and mine and all I ask is that you leave her alone. I pay her a rather healthy sum in addition to what she makes at work. Trust me the girl's not suffering."

"Well, I just thought that with all of your holdings and your ability to make money that this would benefit her more since she really is struggling and has no idea how to turn a dollar."

"Most of the world is ignorant and I ain't trying to teach 'em at this point in my life." Alexis commented.

"I hear you," Philip responded. He was tired and drained and wanted nothing more than to sleep for ten or twelve hours but Alexis had something else in mind and he knew it.

In bed he lay there with her snuggled up, her head in the crook of his arm. Lifting her head up, she laid it on his chest, looked up into his eyes and said, "Philip, I want to apologize for being so crass a few minutes ago but I want you to just stop for a moment and think about how long it took for us to get to know each other before I decided that my feelings were strong enough for me to sleep with you. How could I possibly call myself a lady and look myself in the eye if the second time I met you I was willing to sleep with you. How would you have looked at me? Anyway, I don't really want you to answer that. I just want her out of our lives because I know that Monica is in love with you. She hides it for my sake but I know. I just know and I won't have anything or anyone jeopardize our relationship. Do you hear me Philip?"

"I hear you, Alexis," Philip replied.

"Philip?"

"Yes, Alexis."

"I want you to know that I've fallen in love with you."

This was too much. Philip wondered if Monica had written the script and had to admit that as good as Monica was she couldn't hold a candle to this award winning actor when it came to putting on a performance. Unable to go on with the charade he looked for his suitcase and his pants but before he could come to grips with his decision she stopped him.

"Philip?"

"Yes, Alexis."

"You're awfully quiet. Are you trying to go to sleep on me or are you thinking about your dumb ol' proposal again?"

"A little of both I suppose."

"Well, I'll tell you what? I'll have Monica go down to Atlanta on Monday, in my stead, since I have mid-terms this week and can't get away and if she brings her fat ass back here gushing all over herself then I'll have the check in your hand by Tuesday morning but there are stipulations."

Philip pretended not to hear and was elated by the news though he feigned being half asleep.

"Are you really sure that's what you want to do? God I don't know what I'm gonna tell those guys back at the office."

"You're always worried about other people and what they think. If it's one thing I'm going to teach you before I grow old and weary it's to learn to say the hell with the other guy."

"You just tell them that it's a done deal that's all and I'll do the same with Monica. I sure won't have a problem telling her she's out. I'll tell her just as soon as she gets back from Atlanta and right after I drop a check in her hand for a couple of grand. *Two million my ass.* That can go right in my own pocket," Alexis laughed.

"Anyway, I'll have the money to you by Tuesday morning at the latest but like I said there are stipulations."

"And what are those?" Philip mumbled still pretending to be half asleep.

"Well first and foremost I want a commitment from you."

"Haven't I told you that I love you countless times?"

"You have, but I want more than that. Hell, Philip for close to two million dollars…"

"I told you I don't need your money, Alexis," he said sitting up on his elbows and causing her head to fall to the bed.

"Oh, no you won't. You take my money and invest it in these

393

little penny ante companies and I get chump change as a return but when the really big deals come along you want to cut me out altogether. *Oh, hell no, Philip Dalton. I'm in. Do you hear me? I said I'm in as a partner."*

Philip had to laugh.

"Stop trippin'. I was just teasin'. You think I'd take those two white guys and your fat friend before I'd take you? Now stop trippin' and stop making stipulations like you're in control of something because you're not. In fact, you should be lucky I let you in at all. The last time I was in this room you tried to shoot me," he laughed.

"Guess you're never going to let me live that one down, huh?"

"Not in this lifetime." Philip replied.

"In any case, I still have stipulations and you will adhere to them. Is that understood?"

"Don't know. Depends. But anyway, I'm listening."

"Philip Dalton, I want you to marry me and I want you to marry me soon—say—within the next month. I'm forty-two years old and that doesn't allow me a whole lot of time to be wooed and seduced and courted and all that other shit. Besides we've been together for a year and I feel like I know you well enough and what I do know about you I like."

Alexis paused then sat up to see the expression on Philip's face.

To say he was shocked would be an understatement but what shocked him were not her words but Monica's words that forecasted this whole scenario not more than an hour or so earlier.

"Well say something, Philip darling."

"What can I say, I'm shocked. Only last week I was ready to give up all hope when you told me you were too busy and tried to pass me off to your girlfriend. Just last week you told me that all you really needed me for was to tutor you in bed. This week you want to marry me."

"I'm sure you're aware of something called a woman's prerogative."

"Is that what this is?"

"Yep, that's exactly what this is although I still may need a little remedial help in the bedroom. But I'm not finished."

"There can't possibly be more."

"Well, there is."

"I'm listening."

"I don't want you to wear a condom when we make love tonight. Like I told you, I'm forty-two years old and I might have a year or two left but I want to have a child—your child before it's too late. Hell, Philip, I can do it right this time. I don't have to work. I can stay home with my baby and love him and nurture him and spoil him and do all of the things I couldn't do with my others. Philip, are you listening?"

"Yes, Alexis I'm listening," he said.

"Then respond, Philip. Tell me what you think, about my proposal. I told you what I thought of yours," she said staring at him and Philip truly wished he were clairvoyant just so he could figure out what went on in this woman's twisted mind.

"Well, what do you think?"

"Does this answer your question," Philip asked pushing the sheet down below his waist and taking the condom off she'd managed to slip on when they'd first gotten into bed. He now wondered if the whole condom thing was just for effects too. She certainly hadn't worn one the first time. Was he supposed to really believe that she was sincere now and in love enough to suddenly want to have his child?

Chapter 18

Monica couldn't remember the last time she'd had such a hard time sleeping. In only two days she'd grown accustomed to Philip's arm being wrapped around her waist and his warm breath on her neck as she slept. And now as far as she knew someone else was sharing that comfort.

And as much as she kept telling herself that they could never be more than friends she hated to admit that she had feelings for him that went far beyond friendship. It was five a.m. She wanted to call him and leave a message on his voice mail telling him to get out of there but she knew the damage had already been done by now or at least she suspected.

Alexis would never leave him alone after hearing an offer with such a lucrative potential as he'd just put on the table and the idea that he was running in such circles only assured her that she was going to offer him some. She wanted to call, wanted to tell him, wanted to beg him not to take it but she knew that Philip's first priority was to make Alexis pay for all the pain and suffering she'd caused him over the past year. Monica knew in her heart that Philip loved her. And to call him and offer him an ultimatum was not an option but a mandate that she felt fully within her right to decree. If he wanted any parts of her life then regardless of what had already happened she wanted him up and out of there now. She should have done it last night. The hell with his plan. Nothing good ever came out of being vengeful anyway. Nothing that is but more pain and heartache and it never succeeded in leaving anyone feel any better.

If she'd been thinking she would have realized that Philip was no better than anyone else. Sure, he had an aptitude for making money but he also had his shortcomings and pride was one of them. Now pride had him lowering himself to this woman's level. She hated the fact that she'd gone along with the madness and not had the gumption to stake her claim on him and pull his ass out of there.

Monica picked up the phone that had been sitting idle since Tuesday. Since she and Philip had been talking her wireless minutes had all but doubled and since she rarely called anyone outside of the area she had never considered getting a long distance plan.

Her last bill had been astronomical so she'd turned it off and left it sitting. This was really the first time she'd picked it up in almost a week. It was Saturday morning now and as she glanced at the face of the tiny Nokia she couldn't help but notice the number of messages. There were thirty thirty-seven, mostly from momma and Bridgette but the remaining twenty were all from James and she at once felt a pang of guilt sweep over her body as she thought about the fact that she'd again been so swept up in all the crazy theatrics that Philip brought to the table that she'd forgotten to call James and see how he was doing.

He, who was always so calm and consistent in everything he did not only deserved her attention but her time as well. With James there were no mysteries or intrigue or drama just a heartfelt warmth and a peaceful calm and yet, time and time again she found herself putting him on the backburner for the hectic roller coaster ride that both Philip and Alexis brought to her otherwise peaceful existence. She couldn't understand it but felt too ashamed to call him now. All she did was apologize to him for being inconsiderate and she hardly felt like apologizing now. Besides if she called he'd most certainly want to see her and she just had too much going on this weekend to be entertaining James.

Seeing his number flash before her made her put the phone down. How could she possibly tell Philip what he was doing was wrong, that it was destroying her on the inside when she was basically doing the same thing. Putting the phone down she leaned back on her bed, fished around in her bag until she found her cigarette case, took out a Newport, lit it and inhaled deeply before letting out the smoke.

Her thoughts returned to Philip and Alexis and she wondered what it was they were doing at the moment. She could just imagine Alexis, prancing around in some little two piece thong with her ass hanging out, bending over to pick up this and that just to give Philip a better view and he sitting there trying to be resilient, talking about his plan when all he'd been wanting to do since he met her was to get between those little nasty thighs anyway. She was sure that in reality that was all he had on his agenda when he first started talking to her.

And although he was smooth enough not to come right out and say that that's exactly what he wanted he might have been better off than playing the role and pretending that he wanted to get to know her as a human being. At least if he'd spoken up at the outset he wouldn't have felt so bad when Alexis dismissed him eleven months later without so much as even letting her sleep in the same bed with her.

That, after all, was the real reason why he was angry and felt wronged and Alexis was no more wrong than he was. He didn't ask and although she knew what it was he was trailing behind her for. She didn't offer and when he'd come to an impasse and considered her taking his kindness for weakness he'd become adamant and obsessed with making her pay. Now they were at the crossroads although Alexis had no idea how dearly she was going to pay. But he hadn't commented as Monica hoped he would when she told him that he was going to have to pay. In fact, he ignored her as if he had already figured that one out and was more than willing to screw the bitches' brains out for having made him wait this long.

It was she who had been slow to figure things out this time. So enamored in the pomp and circumstance that accompanied the big time city boy, Monica was the last to know and had only been along for the ride. Of course he loved her but it was business first and until he handled this piece of agonizing failure, until he had exhumed the skeletons and dealt with the ghost of his own failure he could not love her or move on. It was all about winning. And win he must even if it meant losing her.

Monica looked at the cigarette that had burned down to the words Newport and then smoked them too before putting it out. Philip had to win. She remembered the conversation she and Alexis had had some months ago at Starbucks and remembered Alexis telling her that a man's goal in life were consumed with the idea of conquest and victory. Anything less would not suffice. When it came to women the battles were hard fought but a loss was out of the question. There was a chance even if it was remote at best of him losing her. Still, he felt obligated to risk it just so he could exact some revenge on a woman hardly worth his time. And if that meant him sleeping with her then he'd do that too.

Monica pulled the covers over her head as if blocking out the sunlight from that broken blind could also block out her feelings but they shone through as brightly as the sun on that March morning. She'd promised herself that she would play the field. She'd make sure this time that she'd make the right decision. That had been weeks ago when this whole ugly charade had seemed somehow beautiful, almost a godsend but she was no closer to playing the field than she had been then and found herself in the unfamiliar position of having two men tell her that they loved her.

Problem was that up until now she'd not even entertained the idea of how she felt. But this morning with the messages from James looming larger than ever and the thought of Philip sleeping with 'Lexis she had a hard time evading the fact that she'd been duped by her own ploy to stay somehow aloof when in truth she'd fallen in love with not just James but with both of them and with no way out.

She could remember sitting with one of her college professors' one night, a very dapper, middle-aged gentleman whom she was very fond of for the simple reason that he had no ulterior motives, wasn't trying to knock her boots and had more women than he could shake a stick at. When she asked him if he ever got tired of dating and why he needed such a surplus of women when one would suffice she was surprised when he told her that one woman could not fulfill his needs.

At first she thought he was speaking only of his sexual appetite but on listening further, he explained how each one brought something unique and different to the table and each had their place in completing the whole. She had to stop and wonder now if the absence of men in her life was the reason she felt the need to keep both on board at first or was she like her friend the professor that saw each of them as an integral part of the whole. They were, after all, as different as night and day and each had qualities that she loved in a man but she was not offering either of them anything but a disservice if she couldn't fulfill their needs. And James was if nothing else, needy. His life was simple and afforded him too much time whereas Philip had to make the time.

And though James was the logical choice, there was something about Philip that made her feel alive and she liked that. Now, here she sat worried about him and how all she wanted to do was see him and take him back into the fold. Oh, how she wished she had made love to him despite the fact that she knew he would be with Alexis the following night. It didn't matter now and if he walked through that door this very minute with the smell of Alexis' expensive perfume saturating his clothes and the taste of Alexis on his body and enveloping his mind she would ignore the obvious and gobble him up right then and there so badly did she want him at that very moment.

But there was no knock and she knew she couldn't call. There was nothing she could do at all but wait. And she had to wonder, as she lay there agonizing, if this is what they were speaking about when they spoke about the joy of love.

There was no agonizing anywhere within the condo located on the corner of Jefferson and Main. Although, Philip did his best to rip her insides out with each thrust and Alexis screamed as if he were killing her the simple truth of the matter was that she enjoyed every minute of it.

Sure, he'd been rough but he was nowhere as big as James and she accommodated him well. When she noticed that he seemed to work harder and dig deeper each time she yelled she tried to let the whole world. At first she couldn't understand it. Was he intentionally trying to hurt her? Or was this just one of those freakish things that turned men on?

. She'd read about how some men like to be domineering in bed and how subservience in lovemaking could be the ultimate aphrodisiac. She'd responded well to the idea of having a man be a man, well, at least in the bedroom. She did her best to let him know he was in control doing exactly as she was commanded to do. And then she gathered all the knowledge of lovemaking she had, which amounted to what she'd read in the latest issue of Essence and a Zane novel and with this rather limited bit of knowledge Alexis said in the sexiest, most seductive voice she could muster, *"Oh, Philip stop! You're hurting me."* Every woman he'd ever slept with used the same line. Every single woman and there had been few. They all used it and he had to wonder what handbook that came out of.

.   Unaware of how common her ploy was she hardly seem to care. All she knew was that the minute she said it Philip Dalton did everything he could possibly do to make sure that he tried to drive himself straight through her. What he didn't know that the more he tried to penetrate the more she would scream because she wanted him to do just that. Loving every thrust Philip had to wonder if this was the way Alexis gained her release. Was this the way she chastised herself for all the evil she'd done? He wondered. He'd read about women who wanted to be spanked in the bedroom and how psychologists or psychiatrist or some type of so-called professional drew a correlation to their wanting to have their feelings of guilt addressed and somehow chastised subconsciously. It was all a bunch of mumbo-jumbo to him but if that was the case with Alexis then he was going t chastise the hell out of her.

.   When he grew tired of berating her and her screaming he turned over on his side, only to have her shake him before he could doze off.

She was staring at some magazine and pointing to some pictures he could only half see and he wondered what the hell she could possibly want now.

"Philip darling."

"Yes, sweetie," he answered.

"Do you know that I came seven times in a row? I've never come more than three times in a row in my entire life. You are truly amazing. It's like you woke up feelings in me that I never had. God, you're good. I feel like I'm blessed to have you around. You know the first time we had sex I really couldn't tell how you were with you being tied down and all. Plus, it had been so long and I was really trying to do anything other than trying to relieve myself of all that back up build up. I guess I was being selfish but tonight—oh my God! I couldn't believe your energy and your stamina and..." Before she could finish, Philip interrupted.

"Alexis, lovemaking ain't like watching ESPN baby. It's not something you do then sit back and watch the highlights while you breakdown different facets of the game. I really don't need the color commentary or the play-by-play." Philip said before closing his eyes.

"I'm sorry baby. I just got a little excited that's all. You have to remember that it's been awhile and—well—after all this really is our first time and I've never been with anyone other than..."

"I know. You've never been with anyone besides James and you need me to teach you and you're really excited to learn new things and you like the fact that I'm being so patient with you and..." this time Alexis cut him off.

"And since you're being such a wonderful teacher and broadening my horizons then perhaps we can try this," Alexis said pointing to one of the diagrams in the magazine.

Philip glanced at the magazine, couldn't believe the diagram Alexis was showing him recognized the position immediately then turned to Alexis who sat there grinning.

"You can't be serious. I don't know a woman in the world that would request something like that," he commented smiling.

"I'm not your average woman," she replied.

"I don't think you know what you're asking for," he said the thought appealing to him so much so that he felt himself get hard again though he was quite exhausted from trying to kill it the first time. "If you think I was hurting you earlier believe me you don't know what pain is. That's painful," Philip said pointing to the picture in the book.

"Oh, please you weren't hurting me at all. I just said that because I know it turns men on and I wanted you to fuck me the way I need to be fucked instead of pretending to treat me like a fragile little school girl and that was the best way I knew to get you to stop playing around outside of coming right out and telling you that I wanted you to pound the shit out of me. Gets the same results and its s'pozed to be lady like."

Again Philip was shocked. So he hadn't caused her any pain. He couldn't even win in the bedroom. She was still manipulating him, still had him eating out of her hand and he was still too naïve to recognize it. Here he was, expending all of his energy, drenched in sweat trying to make her as sore and raw as she'd left him on their last encounter and here she was dismissing his attempts at bringing her pain as suitable and begging to up the level. Well, if he hadn't brought it then he would certainly bring it now. She certainly didn't know what she was asking for and he'd be the last to tell her. This time when she said, 'Stop, Philip you're hurting me her words would not be full of the lies and contempt she'd heard previously but would be filled with and agonizing truth she would remember long after he was gone.

"Turn over baby," he whispered kissing her neck gently as he turned her over on her stomach and pulled her butt up off the bed and towards him. With her head on the pillow and ass arched skyward Philip had to smile and had to admit if nothing else that Alexis was one fine specimen of a woman perfectly proportioned in every sense of the word. She was the kind of woman his father used to refer to as a 'hammer'. Philip had never understood the connotation but that's exactly what he had plans on doing now. Hammer her sweet ass.

Philip got up slowly and moved around behind Alexis and wondered if the tiny woman in front of him was aware of what she was asking for. Philip moved behind her placed both hands on her hips and moved her up into a position where he could easily enter her.

"Philip?"

"Yes, sweetheart?"

"Don't you think you need to get a lubricant or something before you go there? I have some KY jelly in my top drawer."

"No I'm fine," he replied. No need for her to worry about him and he certainly wasn't worried about her. One thing was for sure, he certainly didn't want to do anything to help her ass enjoy it.

"I'm worried about you tearing yourself up again. That's all. Not trying to be a nag or anything," she replied.

Philip thought for a moment then took the jelly an d rubbed a little on the tiny hole before applying a healthy dab to himself. Looking down at her he couldn't understand why this would ever appeal to her as small as she was but there she was, her ass bare and ready and waiting.

"Is there something wrong, sweetie," Alexis asked making her cheeks bounce in unison like some damn peacock mating call. She reminded him one of those strippers he'd seen in the clubs down on the lower Eastside that his co-workers were so fond of. He'd made more deals in those sleazy little rat holes than he'd ever made in the office but he hated them.

He hated the way the women came across as if a jiggle of the boobs and a wiggle of her ass was going to make him leave any parts of his salary with them. No matter how they cuddled up next to him and whispered things to him about what they could do for him—never—not once did he leave anything more than a smile and a promise of 'maybe next time with them.' Not a goddamn dime and yet here he was with Alexis, her ass up in the air jiggling like some goddamn porno star expecting him to do the same thing.

Philip lined up behind her like a quarterback behind his center ready to blast straight up the middle and when she called his name again to see what the problem was and why the sudden delay he did just that with all the anger and remembrances he could muster of their time together only this time when she yelled, 'Philip you're hurting me', there was a different ring to it, a different tone altogether than he'd heard earlier and it awoke something in him that hardly made him feel good about himself. Still, he continued.

She was moving now, moving every which way she could to get away from the sudden pounding she requested and each time she moved he moved in unison. He watched as her freshly manicured nails grabbed the sheets and tried to move from under his two hundred pound frame and just as she had gotten most of the hurt out of her he would relax his body so that all his weight was once again on her and he was fully inside of her again. And of all the things she'd told him this was the one thing he could believe. She'd never done this before. At times he thought her scream for him to stop was genuine but it mattered little now. At other times it almost sounded like she was egging him on. He couldn't be sure but of what thing he was sure and that was that she'd think twice before screwing someone else.

Feeling himself about to come, Philip grabbed her wrists and held them at her sides to make sure that she couldn't pull away while he waited for the feeling to subside enough so that he could begin again. By this time, she'd stopped screaming and crying and chattering or whatever the hell she'd been doing. Philip looked at her face still face down in the pillow and noticed the tearstains. Seeing them he felt himself go limp inside of her and cursed himself for being soft or compassionate or whatever the hell it was that let her up and off the hook and made him take him take her in his arms and kiss her tears away.

Only two weeks ago the roles had been reversed. All she had greeted him with when it was all over was a rather unfelt halfhearted

I'm sorry. If anyone was sorry it was he. No matter how angry he was this was not the way to exact justice. Feeling guilt like he'd never known before he watched as she moved out of his arms, to the other side of the bed, turned off the night light and pulled the covers up before closing her eyes.

Two hours later, Philip still lay there thinking, as he stared up at the ceiling in the dark room asking himself what it was he'd become. Had this woman who only a few short months ago clouded his every thought reduced him to this? It was true. He had never in his life felt like he'd ever loved or hated someone or something as much as he hated Alexis LeBrandt but then there had been a time he had loved her almost as deeply. If she had only reciprocated things could have been so different. Now the only feelings he could seem to arouse were pity and sorrow for her transgressions. Transgressions that he could not simply let go without paying for.

He knew that that last episode was totally out of character but then everything he'd done in regard to her over the last several weeks had been out of character. And he was for the first time in his life not liking what he saw in the mirror. He reminded himself of what he had tried so hard to avoid for so long. He saw it every day. And despised the cold, hard calloused way those surrounding him went about their livelihoods. Though he wasn't sure if it was the line of work or the company he'd recently been keeping he saw it more and more in himself each day. He'd told himself when he reached that point, when he'd become that bitter then it was time to get out and lying there staring at the ceiling that night with Alexis next to him he knew one thing. This would be the last week and the last time he would feel the way he did at that very moment.

No sooner had he come to this proclamation then Alexis turned to him. It was obvious she'd been awake the whole time.

"Philip?"

"Yes, love?"

""Philip would you do me a favor?"

He wanted to apologize but the anger ran to deep and he could not bring himself to tell her that he was sorry not for her but because he'd allowed for her to take him so far from his true nature. He was truly ashamed that such anger and bitterness would have him lose sight of the man he'd worked so hard to become. Oh, how he wished he'd taken Monica's advice. Since he couldn't bring himself to say how he really felt, deep down in his gut, in his soul, he said nothing.

"Philip, I asked you if you would do me a favor."

"Sure, sweetheart. Anything," was the best he could manage.

"Would you take me again? Only this time, make love to me," she asked turning now to face him.

Philip said nothing. He was glad for the reprieve and as much as he hated going through the motions with someone he didn't want to be with when he could have been with Monica, the woman he loved he turned and put his leg across her only to have her push him away.

"Not like that Philip. I want it the same way; from the back again. And this time, please finish."

Chapter 19

Philip awoke late the next afternoon. It was the day before Easter and the skies were cloudy and overcast. He had expected to feel like a new man. He expected to feel rejuvenated.. Instead he felt betrayed, angry and unfulfilled. He'd wanted nothing more than retribution and he'd found nothing that gave him a sense of satisfaction. There was only the sense that he'd done nothing more than demean himself. He was in a deep dark cavernous abyss the type, which he had never known. And the more he tried to free himself from the twisted turmoil, the more he sought to wriggle free from whatever it was that was holding him, the deeper he sank. It reminded him of quicksand or at least the stories of those who had been caught in the quagmire, those who had with every ounce of strength they could muster tried to wriggle free and found themselves only sinking further until all light finally gone they disappeared never to be heard from again.

That's how he felt that cold, blustery, Saturday afternoon, one day before Easter as he arrived at Monica's. As he knocked on her door, he hoped and prayed that she would see his obvious pain, welcome him with open arms bringing some solace to whatever it was that ailed him. He wondered if she'd been right about vengeance being the Lord's and knew she was. Exacting revenge—well—the little he tried to exact had only made him feel worse somehow. And despite the fact that they were both aware of what he'd done on the night previous, she opened the doors to her heart welcoming his torn, tattered body and wrapped him in a warm cloak of quiet comfort.

He'd broken down that afternoon. He'd broken down in tears for the first time since he was nine and learned of his twin sister's leukemia. It had only been the two of them. And when she passed a year later he wondered why it couldn't have been him. He'd spent the rest of his years trying not only to make his parents proud but also tried to make tem forget. But who could forget?

He'd been bitter at first but over time he came to realize that the bitterness and anger only held him back from being all he could be so he'd made a pact with himself that he would let go and move on and that he did exceeding everyone's dreams and beliefs and leaving her memory, her legacy for someone else to shoulder. There was no time, he conceded to be angry, to place blame and seek retribution. There was simply no time.

Over time he came to realize that there would be no forgetting her memory. He simply used her death as motivation to push himself. Why he couldn't do that with Alexis LeBrandt, someone he'd not known nearly as long as he'd known Megan, his own flesh and blood, was beyond him. Minutes later he found himself weeping gently his mind a collage of scrambled thoughts in front of a woman he hardly knew. Warm and caring Monica wrapped her arms around him and held him before whispering in his ear.

"Do you want to talk, Philip?" she asked hoping to free some of the demons he now harbored.

Philip shook his head but the stout woman ignored this and poured him a stiff drink before returning to the sofa where she took his hands in hers and ignored his unresponsiveness.

"You feel worse for having gone?" she asked more in an attempt to bring solace to herself than as a reaffirmation of her advice.

Philip shook his head, and then added, "I don't know, Monica. I just don't understand, is all."

"Funny thing about this thing called life. I hate to bring up something as insignificant in your eyes as age but there is something to be said for age and wisdom."

"And that is?" he said turning to face her, the tears still flowing freely.

"Well, with age a person often grows tired. But in the fatigue they know they can't just run and jump and frolic like they used to be able to do a few years earlier. Sometimes they can't understand why they can't and it bothers them but over time they just come to the realization that they can't. Doesn't mean that they don't have the desire to they just can't. So, they pick the times they can," she answered hoping he would understand her inference.

"And? I'm not sure I understand."

"I'm trying to find the adage but it has something to do with picking your fights. Do you remember the Kenny Roger's song from, 'The Gambler'?"

"Can't say that I do," Philip replied, having no idea where she was going.

"There's a lyric in it that says, something to the effect that, you gotta know when to hold up, know when to fold up, know when to walk away and know when to run. You've got to count your blessings...' and so on and so forth. But the most important part for you at this juncture is, 'You've got to know when to run.' Seems to me you're having an especially difficult time with that concept."

"I suppose I am," he acknowledged, "but I'm angry. I hate the fact that this woman walks around with this pompous attitude..."

"Philip, stop right there. We know Alexis, know what type of person she is and hardly approve of the way she treats anyone who gets close to her or in her way. That's a given but if you believe in the Lord Jesus Christ then you have to have faith in him and believe that he will handle Alexis and those like Alexis in a way befitting her actions. You have to believe that and let this thing rest."

"I can't do that Monica."

"And you can't do that why?"

"I just can't that's all," he replied.

"And why can't you? You're really starting to disappoint me Philip. I admired you because of your maturity, your logic and your foresight. But you're not using any of those God-given attributes here. Alexis is nothing more than a test. Can't you see that? Something the Lord has put in front of you to see just what type of man you've become. He wants to know if he can humble you to the point that you ask Him for His help in a situation that you find beyond your control.

He may even be asking you as he puts Alexis and myself in front of you to test your vanity. After all, she is an extremely attractive woman. She's like the apple in the Garden of Eden. Come on Philip? When you're in a situation that asks for you to extend yourself beyond your human capabilities where do you turn for help, Philip?" Monica asked pulling all the stops out to make Philip think.

"I agree with you in the fact that I believe that the Lord puts some obstacles in our way as we travel down this path but I don't believe he expects us to turn to him for help on every occasion,"

"That's exactly what he expects us to do, Philip. He expects for us to seek Him, and ask him for guidance so that we can get through the rough times with some insight so that we can make the right choices when it comes times to make other tough decisions. What you're doing right through here is turning your back on him and letting him know that you don't need his help, that you're bigger than he is, that you can handle anything that he throws your way and as you can see you can't. Keep letting your ego tell Him that you don't need Him and he'll keep making the cross you've to bear a little heavier than it was the day before until it eventually breaks you.

Humility is putting ego aside and allowing yourself to succumb to His wishes. That's what I was trying to convey to you about age. With age comes wisdom—the wisdom to know that there are a host of things out here that are bigger than we are. Things that can make you and break you in a matter of seconds, minutes, hours…But there is nothing that can ever break me—not a human at any rate because when the cross gets too heavy to bear I simply turn to Him and ask Him for his guidance before I think about taking another step in any direction."

"Monica Manning, I believe your calling has been missed," Philip said smiling.

"Don't joke Philip."

"I'm serious. In any matter other than this I would heed your advice in a heartbeat but this is something I just feel too strongly about,"

"That's the devil working right there," Monica stated.

"Yeah, and her name is Alexis LeBrandt," Philip laughed.

"And if you know that then why the hell can't you leave that alone. All she is a test. Can't you see that?

Right now, at this point in time, Alexis has brought you nothing but pain and misery, nothing but heartache. She's turning you into someone you don't want to be. She's making you, molding you more and more in her image. You're doing things that are wrong and you know this. You're lowering yourself to get down in the dirt and duke it out with her. And you and I both know that when you get down in the dirt and start mudslinging you can't help but get up a little dirtier and little more beat up than you were.

Let me just say this, Philip. It's hard to get dirty standing up and walking tall in His image, baby. Remember that. That's all I 'm going to say about it. You're a grown man and the decision is yours but don't come crying when she whips your ass again. You're the one that went looking for a rematch 'cause your ego won't allow you to accept the fact that you can't beat her."

Monica hoped that last remark wasn't fueling the fire. That hadn't been her intention when she said it but he needed to know and she'd never been one to mince words. He couldn't beat Alexis. Everyone involved knew it. Monica knew it. Alexis knew it and Monica only hoped that if Philip didn't know it he would come to the realization as well. No longer was it a question of how Alexis had wronged him. It was more than that now. Now it was a matter of ego's and wills.

One thing was obvious. In the day or so since she'd last seen him, Philip had changed from the happy go-lucky, Wall Street businessman to become a bitter and morose stranger, a hollowed out version of his old self. Now, he reminded her of an old boxer and friend of her father's that used to come around the house when she was growing up. When she met him he was well past his prime and retired from the ring. He owned an old filling station that had two pumps with no gas that had been rendered obsolete by the evolution of time and the emergence of the convenience store.

Eddie George was his name. At least to the best of her recollection that was his name. Anyway, any time old Eddie would come around he'd be shadowboxing, painting a jab here and a left hook there. And she guessed the fact that she was big only enticed him to throw a couple in her direction every now and then. And that really didn't bother her that much—well—that was, until he connected. But even then she had weathered the storm. But what really bothered her about Eddie George was that everything, his entire life was centered on his winning the middleweight championship that he did.

He lost his next fight and first title defense and though he continued to fight another ten or fifteen years he never regained that middleweight belt. And that didn't bother her. What really bothered her was the way he spent the next thirty years or so still sitting around, talking about getting in shape and how if he just trained for a few months he could get his title back right then and there. He had to be close to sixty then.

Everyone used to listen and shake their heads like, 'yeah Eddie just a little trainin' and you'll be right back on top', or 'there ain't a middle weight out there that could hold a candle to you Eddie boy—not the Eddie I seen take the title from Jersey Joe Walcott back in '54'. Anyway that's what everyone would tell him to make him feel good and I guess because even at sixty he still had a pretty fair jab everyone agreed so he wouldn't have to show 'em that he still had it. But somehow after that championship 'bout ol' Eddie somehow forgot to move on and a lot of people that knew him thought that his winning the title might not have been the best thing to happen to him but the worst thing to have ever happened to him since that one day back in '54 when he won the title belt never allowed him to move on with his life. He forgot everything else in life except getting that belt back. Nothing else in life was important.

The same thing was happening to Philip who now seemed obsessed with making Alexis pay for her indiscretions. And if Monica hadn't given her word that she would see this thing through she would have bailed out that afternoon. Well, if not for that and the fact that she was in love with him.

Sitting there on the futon in the den, Monica watched as Philip shuffled though some paperwork and sipped. She'd never seen him drink, quite so profusely and though it hardly frightened her it did deepen her concern. He seemed tense, overwhelmed and somewhat on edge and hardly muttered two words the entire afternoon. Seeing this side of him she recognized his need for space but by the six o'clock rolled around he needed to realize that she had needs as well and so after taking a quick shower and lighting some scented candles Monica lay caution to the wind and slid into bed next to Philip and massaged his back gently until he feeling the warm soft hands turned, and took her into his arms and into his life.

She could never remember making love that many times in a single night and except for a cold slice of pizza shared between the two there had been no interruptions—well—except for Alexis calling to see if she was willing to fly down to Atlanta on Tuesday to check out Philip's claims.

Monica, so preoccupied with the thought of climbing back into bed and picking up where she and Philip left off, quickly agreed and it only dawned on her that Alexis must have accepted Philip's proposal or at the very least must be seriously considering it.

She was surprised to find herself smiling and quickly felt nauseous at her taking some measure of happiness in someone else's pain. She still didn't know the details of Philip's plans or even want to know but she knew his motives and that was enough to let her know that she didn't want any parts of it. But here she was smack dab in the middle of whatever was about to go down. Again she wished she hadn't given Philip her word and then made up her mind that that was no excuse at all and she was finished with whatever it was. And no sooner than she'd hung up the receiver she let him know. He smiled, acknowledging her requests and empathized with the pain she must be feeling at the same time. He was, he admitted, only sorry he had ever involved her in the first place and would be more than grateful when next Monday arrived and he could put the whole thing behind him as well.

And then they had made love. Each time they made love, Monica thought of how Alexis must have felt only a few short hours ago as she felt his warm tender body caressing her. Had it been love Monica wondered or some deep-seated obsession coupled with revenge on Philip's part?

She could never have done anything like that except for love. She wondered as she lay there with Philip by her side how people could be so nonchalant when it came to giving of themselves with no heart or soul involved, guiding them. She couldn't understand but as Philip mustered the forced to bring her to another screaming climax there was thing she could certainly understand. And that was Alexis suddenly seeming so receptive to his proposal; a deal that would ultimately net one of them millions.

Philip may not necessarily have known the inner workings that make women such complex entities but if he fathomed one thing when it came to women it was the idea of a woman being multi-orgasmic. It was something Monica had only come to know recently. Philip held the key to Pandora's Box and she was all too willing to let him keep turning unlocking her deepest inhibitions as he made his way in and out all through that evening and the night to follow. Hell, if he had asked her to sell her soul to the devil in the middle of one of those orgasmic splurges she may have considered that too.

Monica screamed as she rose up in the bed dripping sweat and digging her nails deep into Philip's shoulders. She was holding on and praying he would last the round through and he had, even as she had wrapped her thick thighs around his buttocks in an attempt to keep him deep inside of her so she could feel every single inch of him.

He made no effort to pull back but only sought to change

direction leaving him not just in her but grinding against her clitoris and tapping every inch of the bottom of her vagina. She'd never felt anything like this before and wondered if the IRA's and 401K's were enough to keep him locked in this position forever. She wondered what else she could give him and even wondered how opposed he would be to her being his mistress and slave. Anything would be okay if he'd continue to love her in this fashion until they were both old and gray. Monica smiled then giggled at her own thoughts. Call her a nympho, even a freak if you liked but if it felt this good then she could live with that.

She felt herself rising now, and wondered if he was coming as well. She certainly hoped so because she had no more to offer and didn't want to leave him unfulfilled and yearning. After this there would be no more. She knew herself. She'd spent after the last go round. But he'd somehow managed to arouse her again with his playful nibbling around her sweet spot. Monica bit down deeply on her bottom lip and the pain did as it was supposed to making her forget that she was on the verge of another orgasm. When the feeling left her midsection in favor of the salty taste of blood in her mouth Monica relaxed though briefly and eased back from his shaft though it was no easy task and allowed him to return to his long easy thrusts. She would wait and he would come with her this time as a grand finale. She was sorry she hadn't had a chance to love him the way she had intended to pulling out all the stops but she was both sore and tired by this time and he seemed to be content enough with just burying himself in her time after time after time until Monica began to wonder if he would ever relax and have something left for the next time they would be together.

Realizing that Philip was on a mission and had no intentions of letting her sleep and compose herself Monica whispered into his ear with the hopes of bringing him to a finale.

"Philip. I want you to come for me baby. What do you need me to do baby?"

There was no need for a response and she planned on doing

nothing more than she was doing right then but she wanted to place the possibilities, the idea that there was more, so much more than what he was feeling now. Not waiting for a response she continued with all the little dirty nuances she could muster and waited between each to see if he was growing harder and more rigid and was on the verge so she would know when to hush and meet him at the pass so they could ride in together. And then when it seemed that he was right there hanging on by the edge she laughed as she had learned to do in past experiences of just this type. A laugh so loud and bizarre that it made her lover stop and wonder what the hell was wrong. A laugh that made them swallow their ego's and wonder if she was laughing at their lovemaking. Then and only when she felt them start to die off as they always did and start to go limp inside of her she'd reach down into their overly inflated egos and tell them to fuck her like a man. It never failed and after wondering what the hell they had been doing they'd reach back and summon something from deep within that said ,'I'm gonna fuck the shit out of this bitch and ride her like there was no tomorrow.'

Philip she knew was no different and when she whispered in his ear to, 'stop bullshittin' and fuck me, goddamit', she found Philip quite receptive. Then to make sure that he would remember this as the fuck of his life she began yellin'.

"Yeah, Philip. That's it baby! Yes, baby! Stop! Right there. Oh, yeah stay there baby. That's the spot. Yes. Right there! C'mon Philip! Fuck me baby. C'mon! You've got to grind in my pussy, baby. C'mon, Philip. Don't be afraid of the pussy baby! C'mon Philip. Is that the best you have sweetheart? Fuck my pussy like it's never been fucked before baby. Oh yeah! There you go! That's my baby. That's it. It's yours baby. Make it yours baby. Put your name on it baby. It's your pussy baby."

And the more he drove himself deep down into her chasm in attempt to give it his name, the more Monica screamed until alas she could no longer speak and simply clenched her teeth together letting a slight giggle escape and a sound somewhat reminiscent of a snake slithering in a grassy field as she let her breath and orgasm escape her body at the same time.

"Sssssssssssssssssssssss," she moaned relaxing and feeling the orgasm sweep over her now.

"Damn!" before rolling over and clutching her pillow in both hands while the tiny ripples she liked to call aftershocks moved in waves through her body.

"Damn, you're good Philip!" she said not bothering to turn and even look in his direction.

So many thoughts crossed Monica's mind as she drifted off to sleep. Of course, she thought of Philip but she also thought of James and promised herself that she would call him just as soon as she woke up. And then she thought of Alexis. As hard nosed as Alexis was, there was no way her little narrow ass could have endured such an onslaught as Philip had just bestowed on her—and reckoned that if she had—then no wonder she'd called here agreeing to anything Philip drew up.

Maybe Philip hadn't liked the idea of sexing Alexis. Maybe it had gone against his every principle. Maybe he knew all along that that would be the closing argument for his presentation—a sort of addendum to the deal which said—'and when the dividends rolled in you're also allowed one charity fuck a month in celebration of our most recent success.

Maybe Philip *was* aware of what it would take to break Alexis down. Maybe she'd been the one that was naïve. Maybe Alexis was right and she was a ho'. After all, she'd allowed him to sleep with her without a second thought after just having made love to her best friend. Monica wasn't sure what the story was or what to think anymore when it came to any of these things but found herself smiling at the thought of how Philip must have certainly whipped the pussy into a frenzy for 'Lexis tight ass to agree to giving up to close to two million dollars.

Monica always wondered about her own sexual tendencies. Wasn't like she could ask someone if the fact that she liked oral and anal sex was normal or the fact that it really aroused her when men talked dirty to her during sex. Oh, sure she could have asked the ladies down at the Women's Center who'd been in her sexual therapy class but half of them were so confused she ended up mentoring them.

Although she'd been invited to take part in a three-some on more than one occasion she wasn't feelin' that shit at all. Still, she would have given her right arm to have been a fly on the wall last night to see Philip lay the pipe and force Alexis' hand in signing the papers. If he had even given her a tenth of what he'd just shown her, then Alexis had already signed the papers and handed over the cashier's check. And if his motives had been correct then chances are he could have signed her up to do some missionary work on behalf of the Catholic Church on the Gaza Strip. That she would have really liked to see. And with that thought, Monica closed her eyes and fell into a much-needed sleep.

It seemed like no sooner than Monica had drifted off than she heard the doorbell. In reality, it had been more like six hours and glancing over at the clock she noticed that it was a little after eight-thirty. It was Easter Sunday and she wondered if this is what it felt like when Jesus arose from the dead. She felt somehow replenished, reborn and could go on now, knowing that Philip was there and hers to be had if she so chose.

Whoever was at the door, however, was certainly persistent. Monica was pleasantly surprised to find Philip already up and preparing coffee as she headed to the front door. He had on her purple Barney robe she wore around the house and she had to laugh at the idea that it looked better on him than it did on her. Grabbing the sheer see-through negligee she'd worn to bed last night Monica went to the door expecting to find Bridgette standing there waiting to head to the market as she did every third Sunday of the month and was shocked to find James standing there instead. A bouquet of red Poinsettias in his hand he handed them to her and was mildly surprised when she stood there staring.

"Did you forget that I was ordered to be here this morning to escort you to church?" he asked not even mentioning the fact that he'd left more than a dozen messages, none of which she'd bothered to return.

Monica, still speechless did not move.

"Well are you going to invite me in?" Unsure of what to do, Monica took the flowers from his hand.

"Have you changed your mind about church or is this little outfit supposed to entice me to forgetting my religion altogether? Lord knows I might just have to do that and hit a later mass," he laughed.

"What do you want in your coffee, sweetheart. Cream and sugar good?" Philip shouted from the kitchen.

"That's fine," Monica replied turning to the kitchen.

Hearing the gruff voice, James already in the foyer turned to look at Monica, who dropped her head. She wanted to tell him that it wasn't what he thought but how could she? It was exactly what he thought and as he gazed at her again in utter disbelief James turned but not before letting a small package drop from his hand and headed out the door.

.

Chapter 20

Monica didn't know how many times she called James that week. By the end of the week it seemed like she was calling on the average of every hour on the hour. Yet, he hadn't returned a message. Distraught she drove past the house and even attempted to knock at one point but when that ol' nosey woman from next door came to see who it was that wouldn't stop knockin' she'd turned, embarrassed and left.

As the week dragged on she realized that she hadn't heard from Philip either. In fact, the only person she did hear from was Alexis who wanted to know how Atlanta was. When she replied that it was everything that Philip had said and more she felt relieved that her part in the whole charade was over. Convinced that the last six months or so had been no more than a dream suddenly transformed into a nightmare, Monica returned to the spa, and her book club with a newfound zest.

She resigned herself to the fact that she probably would not see or hear from Philip or James again and chastised herself, but briefly, for choosing the wrong man once again. She'd gotten caught up in the emotion of the moment and given of herself too freely but she had to admit she was glad for the moments she shared with both.

That weekend she spent her Saturday as she had so many times before snuggled up with a bowlful of Orville Redenbacher's new, kettle corn and a copy of Kill Bill 1 and 2 from Blockbuster and was content to watch Lucy Liu do her thing. She thought about calling James on several occasions but declined. And although she wasn't exactly bored she had too much time to think and welcomed her return to work on Monday morning.

Late as usual, she was surprised to find a rather large parcel on her desk. Taking the letter opener to her left she made haste in opening the parcel which had been sealed tighter than a witch's tit. Despite the size of the box, Monica found nothing more than a small envelope inside with a letter which simply read, 'Gracias! Couldn't have done it without you. Will be returning to London within the month and hope that you will join me there shortly, thereafter. It's funny but I feel no better than I did before. Guess you were right after all. Have picked out a rather quaint old English estate for us on the outskirt of London in an area known as Hampstead Gardens Suburbs, which I feel you will adore. I'm also considering an old farmhouse in southern France. You've never been there but I'm sure you'll adore it.

Wish you could be here to help pick this one out. Oh, and as far as that conversation about children I must apologize. I'm sorry, for being somewhat nosey the last time I was there but I needed some rather pertinent info that I was pretty sure you wouldn't have given me so I took the liberty while you were showering to access your checking and savings accounts so I could do a transfer of funds. I have also set up a Swiss account for you. A representative will be contacting you soon around the account and the distribution of funds.

At this point, please go to your computer and access you accounts but whatever you do, do not call me at this time concerning these matters as it is too risky. I will be leaving sometime around the latter part of this week or early next week. All I ask is that you trust me as you have done in the past and know that I am madly in love with you. Oh, and by the way did I tell you that I love you. Hoping to see you soon Scarlet. Love you, Clark Gable.'

Monica smiled glad that he had at least had the decency to stay in touch after getting what he wanted out of her. That was at least the gentlemanly thing to do even if he had no real plans for a future and all the little trimmings and bric-a-brac about her visiting was a nice touch too. He certainly did things in a big way. He did but Monica knew, deep down in her heart that whatever Philip had done he was doing to cover his own tracks. He knew that Alexis was no play toy—nothing to joke around with and if he had done anything to scam her then she would track him to the ends of the earth to get him.

He was obviously worried about her being the weak link and that's why he'd only shared a minute bit of the plan. Now he was covering his tracks. And though she'd been curious in the beginning she was glad she knew nothing now. Still, she found herself more than a little peeved that he had taken the liberty to access her bank accounts and gone so far as to put a grand or two in there to pay her to keep her mouth shut. He should have known she wouldn't talk and if for some reason she did she really didn't know anything anyway. He'd made sure of that. So what was the big deal?

Monica not only grew angry at Philip but at herself as well for having fallen once more for some sheisty underhanded dealings that had only served to pull her in to be used once again in the name of love. She recalled him telling her how much he loved her and she wondered why she hadn't stuck to her resolve to take care of Monica for Monica's sake as she'd first set out to do. Maybe Alexis was right after all. Maybe they were another species intent on conquest at any price. And then as if by the habit of design Monica picked up the phone and called Alexis.

"Hello Alexis," she said hearing her girlfriend's voice and was at once sorry she'd called.

"Don't say nothin' honey," Alexis yelled, I know. He got you too didn't he? Took every last dime I had. But this shit ain't over yet. I'm just sorry I got you involved. I told you time and time again that men ain't shit and to top it off I'm pretty sure I'm pregnant by the bastard. But don't worry baby. Like I said I apologize. Look, I'll be out of town for the remainder of the week but I can almost guarantee you that you'll have your money back if I have to pull it out my ass, baby. Creditors still don't know that I don't have a penny to my name but I've got a little over a week 'til the first and I intend to have every dime back by then or the Security and Exchange

Commission will learn of every insider trader tip he every gave me. That's securities fraud no matter how you look at it and I've got the records to boot. I just e-mailed him and let him know exactly what was about to transpire if I didn't receive compensation. Hold on, honey I've got a message. Oh, no he didn't. This motherfucker has lost his mind," Alexis yelled.

"What happened?" Monica asked.

"One of those automatic responses. Says he's out of the office indefinitely or something to that effect. Listen girl, I don't know what type of game he's playing but I certainly intend to find out. When I do I'll call you. Right now I've got to get out of here before I lose my mind.

First, I wake up throwing up and then Dr. Philbin tells me that it's nothing more than morning sickness. I can't believe this shit and now this. Picture me walking around here at forty-two walking around here with this bastard's baby and and... Hold on there's another message. Oh, that's from the bank talking about insufficient funds. Lord have mercy. Monica, I think that bastard's cleaned out my accounts as well. Have you checked yours?"

"No, I certainly haven't."

"You might want to girlfriend," Alexis suggested on the verge of panic now. "Call me back on my cell when you do I've got to get the hell out of here before I lose it completely. Hold on here's another message. No, there's three two from banks saying insufficient funds and oh, here this fool is now. I hope he has a reasonable explanation for this fuck up," Alexis screamed.

"What does it say?" Monica inquired as she tried desperately to pull up her accounts at First City and prayed that the same thing hadn't happened to her. But there was no response.

Monica repeated the question. "What does it say? Is it from Philip? Tell me it's all a mistake?" she said not knowing what else to say and sorry she'd called. But still there was no reply.

"What does it say?" Monica repeated.

"Would you shut the hell up, Monica? I'm trying to understand.

All it asks is if I believe in the Law of Karma—whatever the hell that's supposed to mean. What the hell is that Monica?"

"What?" Monica asked smiling now.

"The Law of Karma? What the hell is that?" Alexis asked, pondering the e-mail in front of her.

"The Law of Karma simply states that what goes around comes around."

"Well if that's his idea of a joke or if there's some underlying meaning that escapes me I'm damn sure going to have him break it down for me. Either that or the SEC and the Wall Street Journal will break it down. I'll have that bastard's name plastered on every tabloid in New York. I'll make his shit look worse than the Enron scandal and I guaran 'fuckin' tee that Philip Dalton will never sell another stock in his life. Monica! Are you still there? Baby, don't worry I'll handle it. Trust me I'll handle it. I'm on my way to the car as I speak and believe me whatever he took you will receive back ten fold.

Believe you me; my carrying this bastard's baby is not by accident. Let me tell you, I handcuffed him two weeks ago and took it then just in case he was gay or believed in that marriage before procreation shit and I *made* him give it to me just this weekend before I sent his ass home. That was after you made him disclose his net worth. I told myself then that this bastard's gonna pay dearly for wanting for wanting to run with the big dogs when he should've never left the porch. Now he's gonna pay child support, palimony and everything else I can think of. I told you a long time ago that these motherfucker's weren't shit and when you found out his net worth I made sure that he was going to be bound to me for life so don't worry I've got an insurance clause second to none. What's wrong Monica? Talk to me baby. Oh, Lord he must have gotten you too. Are you into your bank account?"

"Yes," was the best Monica could muster so shocked was she by what she saw.

"Don't worry baby. When I get back you'll be fine. Just hang on. I'll call you when I get back in town. I love you, sweetie." And with that the receiver went dead. Still, Monica held it to her ear sitting transfixed in her the large leather swivel chair unable to move her hand still cradling the mouse as she stared into the twenty-inch monitor counting the zeroes behind the two and the five. There were a total of five giving her a net worth of two point five million dollars and that was only in her savings. A few minutes later, a similar amount emerged in her checking and she hadn't even thought to access the Swiss account. Sitting there a grin fixed on her face that could have engulfed the Atlantic, Monica scrolled and clicked on where it said you've got mail and read the short e-mail. Took nothing for myself. Don't need the money. Have something better than money. I have you. After a while, I intend on giving her the money back. Only used the money as a sort of short-term loan. Really was an investment opportunity in Atlanta only the return was quicker and higher. It was a high yield and very risky but I guess the gods were with us this time. But I'm afraid you were right about vengeance being the Lord's. I hardly feel any better and have decided to give her an even million over the top of her investment. She deserves quite a bit more but I don't feel that repentant. Lol. Anyway, I'm closing things out here and you can give her everything back as or when you see fit. Her account is set up in a First City Bank deposit box. The key is in the back of your kitchen drawer, to the rear. Never had any intentions of destroying her. Just wanted her to see the error of her ways. See you soon. Philip.

Monica couldn't have been more ecstatic. So he was actually all he appeared. And she was a millionaire, which meant that she could take the rest of the day off if she was so inclined to do so. She'd wanted to call Philip and thank him and warn him at the same time of the impending danger but he had made it clear that she wasn't to contact him even by e-mail and she knew that he was a big boy. He'd shown her that and he could certainly diffuse Alexis. Besides, there was really nothing to the whole charade. It was just a matter of teaching her a lesson. A lesson that needed to be taught. Monica

Manning sat back in her office and prayed and thanked God and called momma, then Bridgette and invited them all over for dinner that Sunday as a sort of a going away gesture and gave them all a nice little envelope as a going away present to ease some of the everyday pain of life and wanted for nothing. Well, that is nothing except to hear from James whose memory still ate away at her. And it was at that moment, somewhere during dinner, right after the blessing was said and the mashed potatoes were passed amongst the three women that she decided to stop by the house on her way out of town and at least apologize for the hurt she'd caused him and to ask for his forgiveness. It had been almost a week or so since the whole she-bang had taken place and though there had been no word from Alexis or Philip she was out of there. London was fine and if it meant her staying there alone until he decided it was time for her to come she wouldn't have wasted a minute and would already be there when he summoned her. God how she missed him.

On Friday evening, Monica stopped at her local post office and picked up her passport. She would be leaving the following Tuesday but there was no need to be rushing and trying to get everything accomplished at the last minute. It was enough trying to have a yard sale with no yard and trying to clean out the remainder of her stuff. Momma kept claiming she didn't have enough room to store twenty years worth of junk and it had made Monica so angry after all she'd done that she went out and bought momma a new house. Then Bridgette tol' her if she needed anything else stored she would make sure that she didn't have enough room either in case she needed a reason to buy her house as well and she had.

And everything was going pretty much as expected and Bridgette decided to handle anything else left up in he air so she could concentrate on getting spruced up to see Philip when a knock was heard at the door.

Bridgette never let Monica answer anymore and was constantly telling her she needed a bodyguard. Monica would only laugh and ask why. Then Bridgette would go off about rich people being kidnapped and Monica would just laugh and tell Bridgette that if she would keep her big mouth shut no one would ever know she was rich.

Yet, whoever was knocking at the door was having a chilling effect on everyone inside and Monica always perceptive felt the sudden change as she made her way down the hallway. She was shocked to see James standing there. As she approached the smile widening across her face she noticed stain of dried tears on James' face and tried to imagine what could be so horrendous as to make this mountain of a man shed a tear.

Approaching him, he held out his hand. In it was a copy of the Wall Street Journal whose headlines read.

Investor Shoots and Kills Top Wall Street Broker then Turns and Kills Herself and Unborn Baby in a Triple Homicide.

Detectives have no motive.

The End

Printed in the United States
210885BV00001B/89/P